Vanished

Center Point
Large Print

Also by Irene Hannon and available from
Center Point Large Print:

Deadly Pursuit
Lethal Legacy

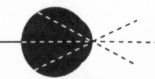

**This Large Print Book carries the
Seal of Approval of N.A.V.H.**

—Private Justice #1—

Vanished

IRENE HANNON

CENTER POINT LARGE PRINT
THORNDIKE, MAINE

This Center Point Large Print edition is published
in the year 2013 by arrangement with Revell,
a division of Baker Publishing Group.

This book is a work of fiction. Names, characters, and
incidents are the product of the author's imagination or
are used fictitiously. Any resemblance to actual events,
or persons, living or dead, is coincidental.

The text of this Large Print edition is unabridged.
In other aspects, this book may
vary from the original edition.
Printed in the United States of America
on permanent paper.
Set in 16-point Times New Roman type.

ISBN: 978-1-61173-635-9

Library of Congress Cataloging-in-Publication Data

Hannon, Irene.
Vanished : a private justice novel / Irene Hannon.
pages ; cm.
ISBN 978-1-61173-635-9 (library binding : alk. paper)
1. Women journalists—Fiction. 2. Private investigators—Fiction.
   3. Missing persons—Investigation—Fiction. 4. Large type books.
   I. Title.
PS3558.A4793V36 2013b
813'.54—dc23
                                          2012036012

To my nieces,
Catherine and Maureen Hannon,
who listened to this tale in its
very early stages as we sat in front of a
crackling fire on Thanksgiving.

Thank you for loving my stories—
and for all your ideas.

❖ 1 ❖

What a lousy night to get lost.

Moira Harrison peered through the April rain slashing across her windshield. Even at full speed, the wipers were no match for the torrential onslaught. The faint line bisecting the narrow strip of pavement—the only thing keeping her on the road and out of the ditch filled with churning runoff immediately to her right—faded in and out with alarming frequency.

Tightening her grip on the wheel with one hand, she cranked up the defroster with the other. Fogged-up windows were the last thing she needed. As it was, the high-intensity xenon headlights of her trusty Camry were barely denting the dense darkness of the woods-rimmed rural Missouri road. Nor were they penetrating the shrouding downpour.

So much for the premium she'd paid to upgrade from standard halogen.

She spared a quick look left and right. No light from house or farm broke the desolate blackness. Nor were there any road signs to indicate her location. Maybe a St. Louis–area native would be better able to wend his or her way back to civilization than a newcomer like her, but she doubted it. Dark, winding rural routes were confusing. Period. Especially in the rain.

With a sigh, Moira refocused on the road. If she'd known Highway 94 was prone to flooding and subject to sudden closure, she'd never have risked subjecting herself to this poorly marked detour by lingering for dinner in Augusta after she finished her interview.

Instead, she'd have headed straight back to the rented condo she now called home and spent her Friday evening safe and warm, cuddled up with a mug of soothing peppermint tea, organizing her notes. She might even have started on a first draft of the feature article. It wouldn't hurt to impress her new boss with an early turn-in.

A bolt of lightning sliced through the sky, and she cringed as a bone-jarring boom of thunder rolled through the car.

That had been close.

Too close.

She had to get away from all these trees.

Increasing her pressure on the gas pedal, she kept her attention fixed on the road as she groped on the passenger seat for her purse. Maybe her distance glasses were crammed into a corner and she'd missed them the first time she'd checked.

Five seconds later, hopes dashed, she gave up the search. The glasses must still be in the purse she'd taken to the movie theater last weekend. That was about the only time she ever used

8

them—except behind the wheel on rainy nights.

It figured.

The zipper on her purse snagged as she tried to close it, and Moira snuck a quick glance at the passenger seat. Too dark to see. She'd have to deal with it later.

Releasing the purse, she lifted her gaze—and sucked in a sharp breath.

Front and center, caught in the beam of her headlights, was a frantically waving person.

Directly in the path of the car.

Less than fifty feet away.

Lungs locking, Moira squeezed the wheel and jammed the brake to the floor.

Screeching in protest, the car fishtailed as it slid toward the figure with no noticeable reduction in speed.

Stop! Please stop!

Moira screamed the silent plea in her head as she yanked the wheel hard to the left.

Instead of changing direction, however, the car began to skid sideways on the slick pavement.

But in the instant before the beams of the headlights swung away from the road—and away from the figure standing in her path—one image seared itself across her brain.

Glazed, terror-filled eyes.

Then the person was gone, vanished in the darkness, as the vehicle spun out of control.

Moira braced herself.

And prayed.

But when she felt a solid thump against the side of the car, she knew her prayers hadn't been answered.

She'd hit the terrified person who'd been trying to flag her down.

The bottom fell out of her stomach as the car continued to career across the road. Onto the shoulder. Into the woods. One bone-jarring bounce after another.

It didn't stop until the side smashed into a tree, slamming her temple against the window of the door to the accompaniment of crumpling metal.

Then everything went silent.

For a full thirty seconds, Moira remained motionless, hands locked on the wheel, every muscle taut, heart hammering. Her head pounded in rhythm to the beat of rain against the metal roof, and she drew a shuddering breath. Blinked. The car had stopped spinning, but the world around her hadn't.

She closed her eyes. Continued to breathe. In. Out. In. Out.

When she at last risked another peek, the scene had steadied.

Better.

Peeling her fingers off the wheel, she took a quick inventory. Her arms and legs moved, and nothing except her head hurt. As far as she could tell, she hadn't sustained any serious injuries.

But she knew the person she'd hit hadn't been as lucky—a person who might very well be lying in the middle of the road right now.

In the path of an oncoming car.

Her pulse stuttered, and she fought against a crescendo of panic as she tried to kick-start her brain. To think through the fuzziness.

Okay. First priority—call 911. After that, she'd see what she could do to help the person she'd hit while she waited for the pros to arrive.

Plan in place, she groped for her purse. But the seat beside her was empty. Hadn't her purse been there moments before?

With a herculean effort, she coerced the left side of her brain to engage.

The floor.

Her purse must have fallen to the floor while the car was spinning.

Hands shaking, she fumbled with the clasp on her seat belt. It took three jabs at the button before it released. Once free of the constraint, she leaned sideways and reached toward the floor—just as the driver-side door creaked open.

With a gasp, she jerked upright. A black-shrouded figure stood in the shadows, out of range of her dome light.

Her heart began to bang against her rib cage again as a cold mist seeped into the car.

"I saw the accident. Are you all right, miss?"

The voice was deep. Male. And the only clue to his gender. The monk-like hood of his slicker kept most of his features in shadows.

But she didn't care who he was. Help had arrived.

Thank you, God!

"Yes. I . . . I think so. I banged my head against the window, and I'm a little dizzy. But . . . I hit someone on the road. I need to call 911. And I need to help the other person."

The man leaned a bit closer, and she glimpsed the outline of a square jaw. "You've got a nasty bump on your temple. Moving around isn't a good idea until the paramedics check you out. I'll help the person you hit." He tipped his head and looked across her. "Is that blood on the passenger seat?"

As Moira shifted sideways to look, she felt a jab in her thigh. "Ow!"

"Watch the broken glass. Lean a little to the right." The man restrained her with one hand on her upper arm as she complied. "Hold on a second while I brush off the seat."

He was silent for a moment, and she shivered as the wind shifted and the rain began to pummel her through the open door, soaking through her sweater.

"Okay. I think I got most of it."

He released her, and she collapsed back against the seat. As he retracted his hand, she caught a

12

quick glimpse of his gold Claddagh wedding ring. The same kind her dad wore.

Somehow that comforted her.

"Stay put." He melted back into the shadows, beyond the range of the dome light. "I'll call 911 and check on the other person. Give me a few minutes."

With that, he closed the door.

Alone again in the dark car, Moira tried to keep him in sight. But within seconds he disappeared into the rain.

As the minutes ticked by and the full impact of what had happened began to register, her shivering intensified and her stomach churned.

She could have been killed.

And she might have killed or seriously injured someone else.

Wrapping her arms around herself, Moira closed her eyes as a wave of dizziness swept over her.

At least help had arrived.

With that thought to sustain her, she let the darkness close in.

Why was she so cold?

Why did her head hurt?

Where was she?

Moira struggled to lift her eyelids, then blinked into the darkness.

What was she doing in her car?

Clenching her fingers around the wheel in front of her, she nudged her brain into action until, bit by bit, the mind-numbing grogginess dissipated. She'd hit someone on the rain-slicked pavement. Her car had spun out of control. She'd slammed into a tree—and banged her head against the window.

But someone had stopped. A man. He'd said he would check on the victim and call 911.

Moira frowned and looked around.

There was no sign of any emergency equipment. Nor of her Good Samaritan.

Lifting her arm, she tried to read the time on her watch. Too dark. She fumbled for the dome light. Flipped it on. Squinted. The hands were fuzzy, but it looked like . . . 9:30?

She'd been out cold for more than an hour?

No way.

She checked her watch again, angling it a different direction.

9:30.

How could that be? Unless her eyes were lying to her, the police should be here by now. An hour was plenty of time for help to arrive. Even in the rain. Even on a deserted road in no-man's-land.

Despite the lingering sluggishness in her brain, she came to the only possible conclusion—and the jolting truth shut down her lungs.

The man had never called 911.

14

He'd simply left.

But . . . why stop at an accident scene if you didn't intend to help?

And what about the person she'd hit? Was he or she still lying in the road? Or in a ditch on the side? Perhaps gravely injured?

A surge of adrenaline shot through her, tripping her pulse into double time.

Breathe, Moira! Stay calm.

Forcing herself to keep inhaling and exhaling, she snagged her purse from the passenger side floor and dug for her phone. Once she had it in hand, she opened the glove compartment, silently thanking her father for drilling into her the importance of keeping a working flashlight in the car for emergencies.

Tonight certainly qualified.

As she shoved her door open with her shoulder, she punched in 911. At least the rain had slowed to a steady drizzle.

She lurched to her feet while the phone rang, clinging to the door when the ground tilted beneath her feet.

"911. What is your emergency?"

The question registered, but she was too busy trying to stay upright to answer.

"911. Please state the nature of your emergency."

She tightened her grip on the door and focused on forming the words. "Car accident."

"Are there injuries?"

"Yes." Moira leaned against the door, trying to orient herself.

"I'm dispatching an ambulance and the police as we speak."

"I-I don't know where I am."

"We have your location from the GPS in your phone, ma'am."

"Oh. Right." She knew that.

"How many vehicles are involved?"

"One." And it was on the wrong side of the road, she realized. Facing the direction from which she'd come.

"Can you describe the nature of—"

She didn't wait for the rest. Now that she'd placed the emergency call, she needed to find the person she'd hit.

Pushing off from the car, she scrambled up the small embankment toward the road. Her flashlight picked up the skid marks at once, and she worked her way back to the spot where she'd begun to slide, all the while looking for signs of the victim.

But no one was lying in the road.

No one was lying in the ditch.

No one responded when she called out.

She stopped in the middle of the road, flummoxed. This didn't make sense. The person had to be here somewhere.

Retracing her steps, she continued to search

until she heard the distant, welcome wail of a siren. Finally. Help was on the way.

She staggered to the side of the road, above her car. Maybe a police officer whose head wasn't pounding and whose vision wasn't going in and out of focus would have more success locating the person she'd hit.

The patrol car slowed as it approached and pulled onto the shoulder. Leaving on the headlights and the flashing light bars in the front and rear windows, a youngish cop slid out. With a glance at the bashed-in back fender of her car, he crossed to her.

"I'm Deputy Davis, ma'am." After giving her a quick sweep that lingered on her temple, he took her arm and started to guide her toward his vehicle. "Why don't you sit down? An ambulance is on the way."

She held back. "No. We need to keep looking."

"Ma'am?" He paused, clearly puzzled.

She moistened her lips, trying to think coherently despite the throbbing in her head. "I hit someone."

Twin furrows appeared on his brow as he scanned the wooded area. "We don't get too many pedestrians around here, ma'am. This road isn't even used a whole lot by *drivers*. Are you sure it wasn't an animal? A deer, maybe? We have a lot of those."

"I know what a deer looks like, Deputy." She

jerked her arm free of his and took a step back. If he wasn't going to help her search, she'd continue alone. "It was a person."

"Okay." He held up his hands, palms toward her, in a placating gesture. "Man or woman?"

"Woman. I think."

He tilted his head. "You think?"

Moira caught her lower lip between her teeth. "It was dark. I only got a glimpse of her in my headlights, and she was wet. But from the build, and her eyes . . . yes, I'd say it was a woman."

"All right." He gestured toward his car again. "Why don't you sit and I'll take a look?"

From his tone, she could tell he was humoring her.

And she didn't like it.

But as long as he was willing to continue the search, she'd go along with him. Because she needed to sit. Fast.

Fortunately, she reached the patrol car at the same moment her legs buckled.

He made a grab for her and eased her down on the passenger side. "The ambulance will be here any minute. In the meantime, stay put. I'll be right back."

"That's what the other guy said too."

He cocked his head. "What guy?"

Oh yeah. She'd forgotten to mention that.

"A man stopped after the accident. He said he'd check on the woman I hit and call 911. I must have blacked out after that. When I came to, he was gone."

"Was it another motorist?"

"I don't know. He just appeared out of nowhere."

Deputy Davis's headlights were behind him, leaving his features shadowed, but Moira had no trouble reading the skepticism on his face.

"Look, I'm not making this up." She glared at him. "There was a man here."

"Okay. We'll talk more in a minute."

He closed her door, and she watched through the rain-spattered window as he examined the skid marks with his flashlight. Checked the embankment on her side of the narrow road and the ditch on the other. Planted his free hand on his hip and stared into the empty darkness.

The throbbing in her head intensified.

He'd come up as empty as she had.

But how could that be? She hadn't imagined the woman on the road. Her unsuccessful evasive maneuver was what had sent her skidding into a tree.

Based on the deputy's expression when he rejoined her, however, he wasn't buying her story.

Pulling open her door, he shrugged. "I don't see anything, ma'am." As another distant siren floated through the air, he gestured to her temple. "Head injuries can do strange things to the memory. And visibility was poor. Was this . . . person . . . running across the road?"

"No. I glanced away for a second to zip my purse after I felt around for my glasses, and when I looked up again, she was standing in the middle of the road, waving her arms."

His eyebrows rose a notch. "You have glasses you weren't wearing?"

Uh-oh. Big mistake. That admission would make her story even less credible.

She shifted in the seat. Time for damage control. "I have a pair for distance that I wear on occasion. As it turns out, I left them at home. But I can see well without them. They just enhance my night vision a little."

Though he didn't comment, his silence communicated a lot.

A gust of wind blew a spray of chilly drizzle through the door, adding another layer of cold damp-ness to her already-wet clothes. Moira shivered and wrapped her arms around herself. A real hug would be better, but this would have to do. Hugs had vanished from her life as surely as the figure in her headlights. The romantic kind, anyway.

"Where is home?" The officer shifted sideways to block some of the rain.

"St. Louis. Brentwood." Her teeth started to chatter. "It's a s-suburb."

"I'm familiar with it." The siren was close now, and he angled toward the approaching vehicle. "We'll have some help for you in a minute. What brought you out here tonight?"

"I was in Augusta."

"Pretty spot. Visiting the wineries?"

She heard the inference under the casual question. And resented it.

"I wasn't drinking, Officer. I was w-working. The road was closed when I tried to leave, and I got turned around on the detour."

"I'll say. You weren't even close." He watched the ambulance pull into view and slow to a stop behind his car. "Let's have the paramedics check you out. Then we'll talk some more."

He joined the technicians, who were climbing out of the vehicle. After exchanging a few words she couldn't hear, all three walked her direction.

The technicians circled around toward her. The deputy slid into his own seat and began to fiddle with the computer. Running a license check, no doubt. Trying to determine if she was some nutcase.

But as she answered the paramedic's questions and looked straight ahead while he flashed a light in each pupil, she knew Deputy Davis would find no explanation in her DMV file for her behavior tonight—nor anywhere else. She'd never gotten so much as a parking ticket. As he would discover, she was a normal, law-abiding citizen.

Unfortunately, in the absence of any supporting evidence, she doubted her clean record was going to convince him her story was true. He'd file a report citing her head injury and the lack of evidence to substantiate her claim, move on to the next call, and forget about tonight's incident.

Truth be told, she couldn't blame him. The whole scenario was bizarre. In his shoes, she might do the same.

In her shoes, however, the perspective was different.

She knew she'd hit someone with her car. A desperate woman who'd been seeking help.

And she knew something else too.

She wasn't going to be able to file away this night and forget about it as easily as the responding cop would.

Because that woman's terrified eyes weren't going to let her.

⋙ 2 ⋘

Moira parallel parked with two quick twists of her wrist, set the brake on her rental car, and eyed the discreet sign beside the storefront office on the Kirkwood side street.

Phoenix Inc.

This was the place.

And she must be nuts.

What sane person would set herself up for more humiliation?

Tapping a finger against the steering wheel, she frowned. So far, everyone had dismissed her tale about Friday night. That cop, the paramedics, the hospital personnel. On the plus side, no one had checked her for drugs. Or asked her to submit to a Breathalyzer test. They'd all agreed a deer was the likely cause of her wild spin across the road and had attributed her confusion to the mild concussion she'd sustained—no matter how vehemently she'd stuck to her story about the two people who had vanished.

And in her muddled state, she'd almost let them convince her.

But she wasn't muddled anymore. After four days, the pounding in her head had subsided to a dull ache. And she was more certain than ever no deer had caused her accident.

Still . . . why waste her lunch hour on a beautiful day like this to hole up with some private investigator who in all likelihood would come to the same conclusion as everyone else?

Yet as she watched a young mother, toddler in hand, window-shop on the quaint street, she knew the answer.

That woman's eyes were haunting her. Day and night.

Despite the warmth of the sun coming through the windshield, a shiver swept through her. No matter how hard she tried, she couldn't banish the chill from her heart or eradicate the lingering feeling of terror that woman had transmitted in a few fleeting seconds.

She had to do something. And with the police

out of the picture, a PI was her only option. Otherwise, she'd never have mentioned the distressing incident to a co-worker—even if said co-worker happened to be one of her best friends from their college roommate days. But Linda's crime beat gave her access to cops, and Moira wasn't going to settle for anything less than a cop-recommended PI.

Ex-detective Cal Burke at Phoenix Inc. was the name that had come back.

And she had an appointment with him in—she checked her watch—five minutes.

Okay. Decision time.

Flee or forge ahead?

Capitulating with a sigh, she grabbed her purse and slid out of the car. As long as she was here, she might as well go in. If nothing else, this free consultation might provide some fodder for small talk at social events.

Like there were so many of those.

But that was a dilemma for another day.

As she crossed the street, she checked out the picture window to the right of Phoenix's front door, hoping for a glimpse of the interior. No luck. The glass was tinted. And the door itself was a sturdy number. Solid wood—and locked. Only after she tried the knob did she notice the intercom and a small sign to the side, instructing visitors to press the button for entry.

It all seemed a bit cloak-and-daggerish, but

what did she know? Most PIs handled a lot of messy divorce cases; maybe the Phoenix crew had had a few nasty encounters with irate spouses who didn't appreciate being put under surveillance by their better—or worse—half.

She depressed the button, and a moment later a woman's voice greeted her.

"How may I help you?"

"Moira Harrison. I have an appointment with Mr. Burke."

"Yes. He's expecting you. Please come in."

A click sounded near the door, and Moira braced herself as she pushed through. From everything she'd heard, most private investigators operated on the cheap and at the fringes of the law. They might have glitzy websites, but a lot of them worked out of their cars.

Based on the reception area, however, Phoenix Inc. was several steps above that stereotype. A spotless, nubby Berber carpet covered the floor. Three chairs upholstered in a neutral, patterned fabric were clustered around a glass-topped coffee table off to one side. Colorful, artsy photos of landscapes and close-up still-life scenes covered the walls.

Classy.

Most of all, she liked the prominent rectangular wooden plaque with the brass lettering, which mirrored the wording on the Phoenix website: Justice First.

But there was one jarring element.

Moira tried not to stare at the twenty-something receptionist seated behind a cherry desk, but it was difficult not to with her triple-pierced ears, unicorn-tattooed forearm, and spiky platinum-blonde hair sporting a long swath of bright purple in the front. A necklace of shells lay against the modest neckline of her purple knit tunic—the hue an exact match for that swatch of hair. When she stood to circle the desk, her wide, studded belt came into view. As did black leggings and silver platform sandals. Iridescent plum toenail polish was the final touch.

Oh, brother.

Despite the impressive law-enforcement credentials listed for the three PIs on the Phoenix website, Moira was not getting positive vibes.

Tightening her grip on the strap of her shoulder purse, she took the hand the woman extended.

"Nikki Waters." As the receptionist gave her a firm shake, some subtle change in her features told Moira that Nikki knew she'd been assessed and had come up lacking. Maybe it was the slight tapering of her eyes. Or the speculation in their depths.

But what did that slight twitch of amusement at her lips mean?

"Please have a seat." Nikki gestured to the upholstered chairs. "I'll let Cal know you're here. Would you like some coffee or a soft drink?"

"No, thank you."

The woman turned to go back to her desk.

Moira hesitated.

Stay or leave?

She cast another glance at the receptionist, who'd retaken her seat and picked up her phone. All the while watching her as if expecting she might bolt like a frightened rabbit.

Moira straightened her shoulders. Not happening. As long as she was here, she'd see this meeting through.

Calling the woman's bluff, she chose a chair and planted herself.

But if Cal Burke came out with a mohawk or a shaved head or sporting an oversized medallion on a heavy gold chain, she was out of here.

Grin tugging at his lips, Cal dropped the receiver back into the cradle and stood. Once again, Nikki's creative cue system had come in handy. Moira Harrison wasn't just here. She was "waiting" to see him.

Translation: she was guarded and nervous and might not wait a whole lot longer.

He slipped his arms into the sport jacket he kept handy for initial meetings with wary clients. Time to pull out the stops to make a good first impression.

Settling the jacket with a flex of his shoulders,

he exited his office and started down the short hall toward the reception area.

"Hey! You going to lunch?"

At Jim Devlin's query, he paused in the doorway of his colleague's office and surveyed the piles of paper on the desk and the mound of manila folders beside the filing cabinet.

"A little behind in our filing, are we?"

Dev narrowed his eyes. "I've been working round the clock on that workers' comp case—as you well know. And since someone gave Nikki three weeks off for her honeymoon"—he arched an eyebrow at Cal—"who was I supposed to get to help me organize this stuff? The file fairy?"

"Now that's an interesting picture." Cal propped a shoulder against the door frame and slid his hands in the pockets of his slacks. "But look on the bright side. Maybe you'll appreciate Nikki more now."

"I appreciated her before."

"Tell her that once in a while."

"I watched her kid brother while she was in Hawaii on her honeymoon, didn't I?"

Okay. He got points for that.

"So what about lunch?" Dev added another file to the towering stack on his desk. "I'm starving."

"Can't. I've got a consult with a new client. Bring me back a burger, okay? And fries."

"I'll consider it." He leaned back in his chair and swiveled toward the window to survey the blue sky, fingers linked behind his head. "Nice day. I think I'll try out that new sidewalk café down the street. Soak up some sun. Why let Connor get all the rays?" He swung back toward Cal. "Tell me again why he got the executive security gig in Bermuda and I got the workers' comp case?"

"Sorry, buddy. When the client saw Connor's Secret Service background, it was a done deal."

"So an ex–undercover ATF agent is chopped liver?"

"He didn't want an ex–homicide detective, either. At least *you* have time to stop for lunch." Cal pushed off from the door frame and started toward the reception area.

A chuckle followed him down the hall. "I'll think of you while I laze around in the sun. Have fun!"

Fat chance. Wary clients had to be handled with kid gloves. And they weren't usually a load of laughs.

On the plus side, though, Phoenix was in the enviable position of being able to be selective. If he didn't get positive vibes, this meeting would be over fast. In which case he might be able to join Dev for lunch after all.

He smiled. A nice, juicy burger at a sidewalk café on a fine spring day. It didn't get much better than that.

But when he opened the door to the reception

area and Moira Harrison rose from her perch on the edge of her chair, all thoughts of the burger and the weather and the sidewalk café fled.

His potential client was a knockout.

Maintaining a neutral but pleasant expression, Cal took a quick inventory as he approached her. Early thirties. Slightly frizzy strawberry blonde hair that skimmed her shoulders. Green eyes. Height five-six, five-seven, using his own six-foot-two frame as a gauge. Her black slacks and subtly patterned black and gray jacket showed off her trim figure, and she was clenching the strap of her shoulder purse in a tight fist. Her posture was stiff. Her ring finger was bare.

She also sported a sizeable bruise on her temple that her soft, wispy bangs and a heavy application of makeup hadn't quite been able to conceal.

While Cal did his rapid appraisal, she reciprocated. After eight years as a cop and four years in this business, he was used to being sized up. It went with the territory.

When her grip on the purse strap loosened and the taut line of her shoulders relaxed a fraction, he knew he'd passed.

And for some weird reason, her tacit approval pleased him.

"Cal Burke." He smiled and extended his hand. She took it, her slender fingers firm in his. "I hope you didn't have any trouble finding us." He released his grip and gestured toward the door that led to the hall, falling in behind her as she walked toward it.

"No. I used MapQuest. There weren't any directions on your website."

"On the left." He pulled the door open, then motioned down the hall, ignoring Dev's stretched neck and thumbs-up as he passed the other man's door. "Most of our clients are referrals, and Nikki is always glad to provide directions. Please . . . make yourself comfortable." He indicated a chair at the small round conference table in one corner as they entered his office.

While she settled in, he took his time retrieving a pen and a tablet of yellow lined paper from his desk. Cautious, uncertain clients needed a few moments to get comfortable. To build their confidence level. The law enforcement citations and commendations and diplomas on his wall did the trick in most cases—the very reason they were there.

Out of the corner of his eye, he watched her give his office a discreet perusal. If she was like many of his clients, she thought PIs belonged to one of two extremes: glitzy, Ferrari-driving investigators like Magnum PI, or sleazeballs on the shady side of the law who dug up dirt in messy divorce cases.

Truth be told, Magnum was off the scale completely. Nobody could do a tail in a red sports car and not get made.

On the other hand, there were a lot of sleaze-balls out there.

As she'd soon discover, however, Phoenix took the higher road. The sign in the lobby said it all.

He joined her at the table, checking out her clasped hands. Good. Her fingers had relaxed.

"I understand from your initial conversation with Nikki that one of my former detective colleagues at St. Louis County recommended us."

"Yes. Cole Taylor, I believe. I asked a friend at the *Post-Dispatch* who covers the crime beat to check with her contacts. I didn't want to take a chance by picking a firm at random."

"And end up with a seedy investigator who works out of some dingy office, operates on the edge of the law, and spends his time digging up dirt on unfaithful spouses."

A pink stain crept over her cheeks. To her credit, though, she didn't try to deny he'd nailed her concerns.

"Something like that. I assumed the police wouldn't recommend a firm they didn't respect, and the ex–law enforcement credentials for the PIs on your website are impressive. So was the tagline about justice."

"It's more than a tagline. We live that motto." Cal leaned back, keeping his posture open. Candid. "A lot of PIs will work for anyone who's willing to pay the bill. We don't. Because of the credentials you mentioned, we have more business than we can handle. Also, since the firm was established four years ago, we've solved a couple of police cold cases at the request of the families involved. That's put us in the enviable position of attracting other interesting cases in addition to a lot of corporate, insurance, and protection work. Thanks to the demand for our services, we have the luxury of taking on only cases we think have merit."

She exhaled. "I hope you'll think mine falls into that category."

"A great segue." He smiled and uncapped his pen. "Why don't you tell me what brought you here?"

A flicker of distress darted through her eyes, and she tightened her linked fingers. "I have to warn you, the whole thing is kind of weird. And I also have to be honest about my financial resources. I may not be able to afford you. I didn't budget for this."

"We can get to the fee schedule later. Why don't you tell me your story, and we'll go from there?"

"Okay." She swallowed and moistened her lips. "It all started Friday night when I went to Augusta to do an interview for a feature story. I work for the *Post* too."

Cal listened as she recounted the details of the night, jotting some notes on the tablet, asking a few questions, tuning in to visual cues, assessing the veracity of her tale, weighing probabilities.

By the time she finished, he was intrigued—but cautious. And not overly optimistic Phoenix could turn up any more than the sheriff's department had.

"I tried to get a copy of the police report yesterday, but they told me it hadn't been filed yet. Otherwise, I would have brought it with me." She finished her account and took a deep breath.

"We can get it. Probably faster than you can. Let me ask you a few other questions. Augusta is in the heart of the Missouri wine country. Did you have anything to drink with your dinner?"

The firm line of her mouth told him she didn't like that question. Or perhaps it had been asked once too often already. "No. I don't drink. I showed the deputy my dinner tab to prove that, and gave him the name of my waitress if he wanted to verify my claim."

"How fast were you driving?"

"I'm not sure. Not that fast. The rain was bad. But I did speed up a little right before the accident. I was in a wooded area, and I wanted to get away from the trees because of the lightning."

He checked his notes. "You said you were dazed but conscious when the so-called Good Samaritan appeared. Yet you lost consciousness after that. For an hour. That's a long time to be unconscious from a slight concussion. What did the ER staff say about that?"

She wrinkled her brow. "I don't know that we

discussed it very much. At that point, my head was pounding, and my memory starts to get blurry."

"All right. Let's back up. You said you think the person you hit was a woman. Can you describe her?"

Regret pooled in her eyes. "I wish I could. It all happened so fast, and I only got a quick glimpse. Plus, she was wet. I do know she had short dark hair, and she was wearing a tan raincoat. I had the impression she was thin." Moira closed her eyes, as if trying to extract more specifics from the image in her mind. "I think she was on the short side. And young. Under thirty."

"Okay. What about the man?"

"His face was hidden by the hood. I couldn't make out any distinguishing features. But he wore a Claddagh wedding ring."

He tapped his pen on the table and studied her. His instincts told him she wasn't a woman given to fancies—or to seeing things that weren't there. She was a reporter, trained to be observant, to notice details. She had clear memories of the events of the evening before and after the accident, up until her arrival in the ER. If she said she'd seen a woman in her headlights, he was inclined to believe her.

Proving that, however, could be extremely difficult.

Besides, what was the point?

"Ms. Harrison, I'm confused about one thing."

"Just one?"

At her wry inflection, his lips quirked up. The lady had a sense of humor. Nice.

"Why are you bothering to investigate this? Assuming there was a woman there, she's (a) a stranger, and (b) long gone."

She leaned forward, posture intent, no hesitation in her response. "Because it's the right thing to do. I saw that woman's eyes. She needed help. Maybe she still does. I can't walk away from that. If I don't try to get to the bottom of this, who will?"

A woman who believed in doing the right thing—despite the inconvenience to herself and unfavorable odds. Impressive. And her ethics meshed with the principles on which Phoenix had been founded.

He tipped his head toward the simple gold cross that hung on a slender chain around her neck. "I take it that's more than a piece of jewelry."

"Yes."

At the quiet conviction in her voice, Cal's heart skipped a beat. Lindsey would have said the same thing—and in the exact same tone. The strength of his wife's moral compass and her certitude and passion about the causes she believed in and supported had always blown him away.

Even after five years, the reality of his loss was like a punch in the gut.

Clearing his throat, he stood and crossed to his desk. "I'll tell you what. Why don't I take a look at the police report and have a chat with the responding deputy? Then we can talk again." He opened a drawer, pulled out a client contact form. "In the meantime, it would be helpful if you filled this out for our file." He returned to the table and set it in front of her, along with a pen. "We always do a topline background check on new clients to ensure our services aren't being used for some illegal end."

She examined the sheet. "I suppose that makes sense." She flipped it over to the blank side, as if searching for something more. "What about the fee schedule? And don't you want a retainer?"

"Usually. But we waive it in some cases. And it's a bit premature to discuss fees. Talking to the deputy and reviewing the police report won't take long, and that may be as far as we get."

The corners of her eyes crinkled in distress. "I hope not. I can't stop thinking about that woman. There have to be answers somewhere."

"We'll dig for them if we find even the slightest lead to investigate."

"Do you charge by the hour?"

She was back to the money. Obviously, it was an issue.

"Yes." He hesitated, then quoted her their standard rate.

Her eyes widened. "Wow." She breathed, rather

than spoke, the word. "I think I'm in the wrong business. My budget isn't going to buy more than a few hours of your time."

He retook his seat at the table. "Let's not worry about that yet. You know those cold cases I mentioned earlier? We did those pro bono because we didn't think justice had been served and we believed they deserved a second look. The side benefit was that they ended up bolstering our credibility and bringing in a lot of new business that more than made up for the fees we didn't receive. This case could do the same."

Her chin rose a fraction. "I'm not looking for charity. You deserve to be paid for your work."

"And if the woman you saw was truly in trouble, she deserves justice. For now, let's just say we're both doing a good deed."

She hesitated. Her gaze flicked down to the gold band on the third finger of his left hand, with its pattern of etched crosses. "I'm impressed."

"Why don't you reserve that comment until we see what I can find?"

"The fact that you're willing to try despite the apparent lack of evidence says a lot."

She picked up the pen and tackled the form, saving him from having to formulate a reply.

Just as well. Compliments—even implied ones —always made him uncomfortable.

After collecting his notebook and pen, he returned to his desk. He had plenty to do while she worked on the form. A report to complete for the child custody case he'd finished yesterday. Some addresses to track down for a defense attorney whose "justice first" philosophy meshed with Phoenix's. A skip trace to run on a deadbeat dad.

But he couldn't concentrate on any of them—thanks to the potential client sitting a few feet away.

He stole a glance at her. She was bent over the form, faint creases on her brow, lower lip caught between her teeth. An intriguing woman with an intriguing story—who also happened to be very appealing. He liked her principles. Her sincerity. Her subtle sense of humor.

And he liked how she looked.

A lot.

His pulse kicked up a notch, and he frowned. Not appropriate. Moira Harrison had come here to seek his professional services—and he didn't mix business and pleasure. Ever. None of the Phoenix PIs did. It was a bad practice that could compromise objectivity.

So why did he have a feeling he might have difficulty maintaining a professional distance with this client?

And why did that make him feel guilty?

But he knew the answer to the second question.

Cal swiveled away from Moira, toward the framed photograph of a tropical seascape that had once graced the pages of a national travel magazine. Lindsey had had the ability to take ordinary scenes and imbue them with depth and magic and possibilities, her touch transforming them into more than they'd been before.

Just as she'd transformed him.

And in the five years she'd been gone, his love for her hadn't diminished one iota. He doubted it ever would. She'd captured his heart with her vivacious smile that long-ago day he'd pulled her over for a traffic stop and she'd charmed him out of writing a ticket. It had been hers ever since.

End of story.

Compressing his lips into a firm line, Cal turned back to his computer and began typing his report. And he didn't look up—didn't let himself look up—until Moira spoke ten minutes later.

"I'm finished." She rose, crossed to his desk, and handed him the form.

A quick scan told him she'd left some lines blank. Social Security number. Date of birth. License number. Didn't she realize he could get all that information in minutes?

As if reading his mind, she spoke. "I don't like to give out a lot of personal data. But I suppose it won't be hard for you to track it down."

"No." Why lie?

Despite his candor, she didn't offer to provide the missing information. Maybe she hoped he wouldn't bother checking it out.

Not a chance. The gaps on the sheet left him more intrigued than ever.

"Why don't I contact the deputy, get the report, and give you a call in a day or two?" He double-checked the form to verify she'd included her address and cell phone number.

"That works." She retrieved her purse, settled it on her shoulder, and held out her hand. "Thank you for your time today—and for treating my story more seriously than anyone did on Friday night. I'm not crazy, Mr. Burke. I know what I saw."

He returned her steady clasp, fighting a disquieting urge to hold on longer than necessary. "I have no reason to doubt you, especially with your journalism background. What kind of writing do you do?"

"For now, I'm filling in wherever they need help until an investigative slot opens. That was my specialty in Springfield, before I moved here a few weeks ago."

"Promotion?"

She flashed him a quick smile. "Yes."

"Congratulations. From what I hear, journalism's a tough business these days. You must be good." She didn't respond as he fished a card out of his pocket and handed it to her. "My cell number is on there too. Feel free to call at any time if you think of additional information that might be helpful."

"I doubt I will. I've been over the events in my

mind dozens of times already." Nevertheless, she tucked the card into a pocket in her purse.

"Let me show you out." He indicated the door.

She exited, and he followed her down the hall.

The reception area was deserted when they passed through and said their good-byes. No surprise there. Nikki hadn't wasted any time getting back to her Pilates regime after she returned to work from her honeymoon yesterday. Fitness was high on her lunch-hour priority list. Far higher than the mess in Dev's office.

But his partner's pile of files would have to wait another day, anyway.

Because he had a research assignment for Nikki this afternoon that he hoped might help clear up a mess far greater than Dev's.

❧ 3 ❦

"Okay. What's the scoop on the babe?" Dev strolled into Cal's office and plopped a white restaurant bag on his desk.

Cal swiveled away from his computer and reached for the food. "The *babe* is a potential client. Moira Harrison. Did you get some ketchup? And what took you so long, anyway? You've been gone two hours."

"I'm glad you missed me." Dev smirked at him. "Ketchup's in the bottom. And I had an errand to run." He dropped into the chair across from Cal's desk, shoved his hands in the pockets of his khaki slacks, and stretched his legs out in front of him. "So what's her problem?"

"Take a look." Cal nodded toward the hot-off-the-fax police report on his desk and unwrapped the burger. He managed to get in three large bites while Dev gave the document a quick read.

His partner summed up his reaction with the same word Moira had used. "Weird."

"Yeah, I know." Cal fished around for any stray fries in the sack. "I also talked to the responding deputy. He didn't have anything new to add, except to confirm she'd been treated for a concussion."

"So what does she want us to do?"

"Find out what happened to the woman she saw."

"The woman she *claims* she saw." Dev set the report back on the desk, his expression skeptical. "What's your take?"

Cal wiped his mouth with a paper napkin. "My gut tells me she's legit. I'm having Nikki run some background on her, but I don't think she'll find anything odd."

"People who've been hit by a car don't typically walk away. And what about the so-called Good Samaritan who also disappeared?"

"I have no idea." He took another bite of the burger.

"The deputy noted on his report that she wasn't wearing her glasses."

"I saw that. It's not a restriction on her license —I already checked. But I'm surprised she didn't mention it when she was here. I've got it on a follow-up list of questions."

"Does that mean you're going to take this on?"

He swirled a fry in the ketchup. "I haven't decided yet. Besides, I'll need you and Connor to weigh in if I do. Our fees blew her away. This would have to be mostly pro bono."

"You haven't proposed a freebie for a couple of years. I doubt Connor will object."

Cal didn't think he would, either. But he intended to abide by the rule they'd agreed to: all voted yea, or the case was turned down. It was the only fair way to operate, since pro bono work put more pressure on the other two partners to make up the difference in revenue.

"If I decide this is worth taking on, I'll call him." He finished off his burger and snagged the final two fries.

A knock sounded at the open door, and Dev looked over his shoulder. "Nikki! My favorite person!"

She snorted and breezed past him toward Cal's desk. "Don't try to sweet-talk me. I'll get to your mountain of files when I have less important things to do. Besides, would it have killed you to put a few away while I was gone?"

"And mess up your impeccable filing system?"

"Nice try, buddy." She rolled her eyes at him and set a file folder on Cal's desk. "At least some people appreciate my more advanced skills."

"Hey, I appreciate them."

"Right." She perused the remains of Cal's high-carb lunch with a disapproving sniff but confined her comment to three words. "It's your heart." Then she slid the folder toward him. "Your new client is clean as a whistle, based on a preliminary background check, but I did find one thing of note."

"Have a seat." He gestured to the chair beside Dev and rubbed the incriminating salt and grease off his fingers with the napkin.

She sat and crossed her legs.

Dev gave her toenails a slow perusal. "Nice polish. Does it glow in the dark?"

"Ha-ha. And for your information, Steve likes it."

"Speaking of the new groom—how is he adjusting to married life?"

She gave him a smug smile. "Ask him some-time."

"I think I'll wait until the honeymoon glow wears off." He settled back in his chair.

She folded her arms. "You know . . . it's a lucky thing I'm not the sensitive type."

"You wouldn't last a day around here if you were." Cal grinned at her.

"Too true." She shook her head. "You guys all need to find a good woman and settle down. That would mellow you out—and maybe teach you to keep your offices clean." She shot a pointed look toward Dev, which he ignored.

But she was right, Cal conceded. A good woman could have a profound effect on a man's life.

Tamping down that melancholy thought, he opened the file folder. "Let's see what you found." He examined the data Nikki had compiled. All the blanks on the background sheet had been filled in, including Moira Harrison's age. Thirty-three. Two years younger than him. Nikki had also clipped several printouts to the back of it. "Nice work. Fast too."

"I try. I printed out a few of her articles from the *Springfield News-Leader* and attached them. She's a real crusader. Take a look at the first sheet behind the questionnaire."

Cal flipped over the form. It was an article dated a year ago, not by Moira but about her. His eyebrows rose at the headline.

NEWS-LEADER REPORTER NOMINATED FOR PULITZER PRIZE

He scanned the article. She'd been nominated in the Investigative Reporting category for a series that exposed two city council members for taking bribes, shaking down companies for political contributions, and creating ghost jobs for friends, family, and political cronies. Both had been indicted and were awaiting trial.

No wonder she'd gotten an offer from a bigger paper.

He turned the clipping around for Dev to see.

His partner gave a soft whistle. "The lady's no slouch, that's for sure. And that lends a bit more weight to her story."

No kidding.

"This is very helpful, Nikki. Thanks." Cal set the clipped papers on his desk.

"Well, back to the salt mines." Dev stood and gestured for Nikki to precede him. "Will you work on my files if I say pretty please?"

"I might be able to squeeze it in later this afternoon."

"I'll throw in a latte from Starbucks tomorrow."

"Sold. And make it soy, no whip."

As the two of them disappeared down the hall, Cal leaned back in his chair, rested his elbows on the arms, and steepled his fingers.

A Pulitzer prize–nominated investigative reporter had serious credibility. If Moira Harrison said she'd seen a person—or two—on the road Friday night, he was more inclined than ever to believe her. Even if she hadn't been wearing her glasses.

But believing her wasn't enough to get to the bottom of this mystery. And unless he came up with more than he had now, there wasn't a whole lot he could do to help her.

Much as he wanted to.

"Sorry. I burned the pork chops and had to start over. Thank goodness I married a patient man."

As Linda huffed out her apology, Moira shifted sideways on the bench to watch her friend approach. Some things never changed. Linda had been perennially late in J-school too. But she always showed five or ten minutes after the appointed time for their twice-a-week walk. Moira gave her watch a discreet glance as she rose. Today it was five.

"No problem. Who could complain about waiting in a place like this?" She gestured to the ducks on the lake and the bed of tulips in front of the pavilion. "Thanks for telling me about it."

"Tilles Park is a gem." Linda did a sweep of the picturesque setting. "And best of all, it's almost in our backyards. So how did the meeting with the PI go?" She struck off toward the circular road that wound through the park.

"Okay, I guess." Moira fell in beside her. "The firm seemed more reputable than I expected."

"My guy at County gave it high marks. Cal Burke in particular. I got the impression they worked together on a few cases until Burke retired."

Moira sent her a questioning look. "He's too young to be retired."

"Don't be too sure. A lot of public servants can kiss off their jobs after twenty or twenty-five years."

"Unless he's very well preserved, Cal Burke hasn't hit forty yet."

"Really?" Linda swept her long black hair into a scrunchy band. "I just assumed he was older. Most law enforcement types who become PIs are retired. I'll have to get the scoop from my contact about why he left. What's he look like?"

"Tall. Dark-haired. Brown eyes. Solid."

Linda wrinkled her nose. "Solid as in one too many doughnuts?"

"No. As in stalwart. Honorable. Someone you could count on."

Linda turned her head without breaking stride. "I see he made quite an impression. Is he good-looking?"

"Yeah." Very.

"Woohoo." Her friend beamed at her. "This whole experience may have some side benefits you never dreamed of."

"Forget it. He's married." She picked up her pace.

"How do you know?"

"He has a very distinctive wedding ring."

"Too bad." Linda's face fell. "But one of these days you'll meet a handsome, stalwart man who isn't. And you need to be open to that. You can't discount all men because of one bad experience. It's time to write off Jack and move on."

"Trust me. I've written him off."

"Sorry. Not buying. You guys broke up a year ago. If you'd moved on, you'd be dating again."

"I've had more important things to do."

"Like what?"

"Work, for one."

"You can't work twenty-four hours a day." Linda cocked her head. "Or maybe you can. Maybe that's what it takes to be nominated for a Pulitzer prize. Which eliminates me from the running. I'm not that dedicated."

"Not true. You work hard."

"But Scott comes first."

Moira couldn't argue with that. Since Linda and Scott had married two years ago, her friend's priorities had shifted. Her own might have too, if things had worked out with Jack. But hard as the breakup had been, what if she hadn't discovered his true character until after she'd married him?

Now that was a scary thought.

Moira suppressed a shudder.

Her phone began to trill, and she pulled it out of her pocket to check caller ID, grateful for the distraction. "I need to take this. It's the garage with the estimate for my car."

"No problem. I'll make a few circuits of the playground. That'll keep the blood moving."

Linda gestured to a loop path that branched away from the main road and set off.

Pressing the talk button, Moira greeted the technician, who got down to business at once.

"We'll, she's fixable. That's the good news. The bad news is it won't be cheap."

The man rattled off a list of things that needed to be replaced, including the back fender, bumper, trunk lid, and taillights on one side. Her head was spinning by the time he finished.

And when he gave her the total, the bottom fell out of her stomach.

Why, oh why, had she opted for a high deductible and lower premiums when she'd renewed her car insurance three months ago? Yes, she'd been accident-free. Yes, the odds had been in her favor that her record would continue. But what was that old saying about being penny wise, pound foolish?

"That about wraps it up, ma'am. You want us to go ahead and get started?"

What choice did she have?

"Yes, fix everything." Visions of a menu featuring macaroni and cheese for the foreseeable future danced in her head.

"I'll have her ready for you by the end of next week."

"Perfect." She started to say good-bye, then frowned. "Wait a second . . . what about the broken window?"

She heard the sound of rustling paper. "I don't see any notation about that. I checked your car out myself before I turned her over to one of the boys, and I didn't see any broken windows."

"But the man at the accident scene said there was glass on the seat."

"I'll take another gander, but I don't think we missed anything. The only broken glass we saw was the taillight. Did you have a ceramic mug or a hand mirror in the car?"

"No."

"Hmph. Well, I'll give it another going-over, but if you don't hear back from me within the hour, assume I didn't find anything."

"All right. Thanks."

Slowly Moira slid the phone back into her pocket. She was beginning to feel like Alice in Wonderland, where nothing was as it seemed.

"What's the bad news?" Linda strode over and lifted her arm to swipe her forehead on the sleeve of her T-shirt.

"Dollar-wise, or in terms of mental health?"

"What's that supposed to mean?"

"The repair guy says there was no broken glass in the car."

"That's a bad thing?"

"More weird than bad. The guy who stopped to help me at the accident said there was glass on the seat. And I felt it. It was sharp. He had me move aside so he could brush it off."

"That *is* strange."

"So what else is new?" Moira blew out a breath. "First I imagine a woman. Next I imagine a man. Now I imagine glass. If I didn't have a bruise on my temple and a mind-numbing repair bill staring me in the face, I'd start to think I imagined the whole thing."

"Maybe the PI will find some evidence that supports your story."

Moira moved forward again. "I'm not holding my breath. All he has to go on is my version of what happened and the police report, and I know what the deputy thought. I have a sinking feeling this is going to be a dead end."

"It's not like you didn't try."

"I know. But something bad happened Friday night, Linda. That woman was terrified. If I don't try to figure it out, no one will."

"What else can you do, if there aren't any clues to go on?"

Not much.

But letting this thing die didn't sit well.

As they moved on to more innocuous topics, Moira tried to focus on the soft evening sunlight, the sweet smell of lilacs, and the soft pink petals of the dogwoods ruffling in the gentle breeze. But the placid setting did nothing to calm her churning stomach. She was used to digging deep for stories. To searching for truth even if that meant disturbing the status quo, no matter the

53

risk. And she'd do it again in a heartbeat. Giving up had never been her style.

Except this time she didn't know where to dig.

Cal Burke was her last hope.

And if an ex-detective couldn't help her solve this puzzle, Linda was right.

She might be at a dead end.

"I think we're at a dead end, buddy."

"Yeah." Cal propped his fists on his hips and surveyed the accident scene, which had turned out to be closer to Defiance than Augusta. Then he followed Dev back to the gray Taurus. "Thanks for coming out with me."

"I didn't have anything better to do on a Tuesday night. Especially in a white utility van. Not that I don't appreciate we all drive company cars, you understand, but my vehicle-of-the-month is putting a serious crimp in my social life. It is not, shall we say, a date dazzler. I'm counting the days until I get the Explorer from Connor in May."

"He won't be back until Saturday. Use it until then."

"I might. On Friday night, at least."

"Hot date?"

"Maybe."

Flashing him a quick grin, Cal squinted into the setting sun and did a final three-sixty sweep. They'd walked every inch of the road near the skid marks—and well past. Ventured into the woods on both sides. Checked out the drainage ditch. Did a thorough search of the area around the tree with the freshly ripped-off bark where Moira's car had come to rest.

And they'd come up with zilch. Zip. Nada.

If anyone else had been around the night of the accident, they'd left no footprints, tire marks, hubcaps, or personal belongings of any kind, including pocket change, shoes, or glasses.

"Assuming there was anything here to find, the torrential rain could have washed it away." Dev gave the scene one last survey too.

"I know."

It was time to go. The sun was setting, and they had a thirty-five-mile drive home.

"Ready to call it a day?" Dev started toward the passenger door.

Cal hesitated. Caught his partner's arm. "Wait. Let's do one more pass. Moira said the woman was standing about fifty feet away when she slammed on her brakes. Why don't we mark that spot from the beginning of the skid tracks, assume she was thrown, and do a search in a tighter radius?"

Dev didn't object, though Cal wouldn't have blamed him if he had. They'd gone over the whole area thoroughly already, and daylight was fading.

His partner did have a comment, though. "She got under your skin, didn't she?"

Cal opened the passenger door and leaned down to retrieve a flashlight from the glove compartment, willing the flush on his neck to stay below his collar. "Her story did. I'm convinced she saw more than a deer in her headlights. And I don't think she imagined the guy who stopped, either."

"If she didn't, we have a real mystery on our hands."

"One that won't get solved if we give up."

"Okay. Gauntlet accepted. Hand me a flashlight too."

Cal passed the second one over, and Dev gestured to the pavement. "You take the right side of the stripe, I'll take the left. You want to go out twelve feet from the center point?"

"Sounds reasonable. She wasn't driving at a high speed. I doubt a person would have been thrown farther than that."

Cal flipped on his flashlight, aimed the beam at the pavement, and began a second, meticulous search, dodging a curious motorist who happened by.

Ten minutes later, as he was about to complete his circuit and call it a day, the beam of his light landed on a small white object wedged between two broken pieces of asphalt at the side of the road. It looked a lot like a rock, but the shape made him pause.

Dropping down to the balls of his feet, he kept the light focused on it. Leaned closer.

"Find something?" Dev joined him.

"I don't know. What does that look like to you?" He pointed to the peanut-sized object.

Dev inspected it. "A rock?"

"I think it's a tooth."

His colleague bent down. "That's possible. Let me get a magnifying glass and some tweezers."

"Bring the camera too. And an evidence envelope."

Two minutes later, Dev was back. Cal laid a nickel beside the object and moved back as Dev took a close-up shot.

After removing one of the pieces of asphalt, Cal gently worked the object out with the tweezers and held it up.

It was a tooth.

"Wow. I can't believe you spotted that."

"Twenty-twenty comes in handy on occasion. You want to fill out the envelope?"

"Yeah." Dev fished a pen out of his pocket and noted the case number, date, time, location, and a description on the front. After initialing it, he flexed it open.

Cal dropped the tooth inside, sealed the manila flap, and added his initials to Dev's.

"This may not mean anything except that someone lost a tooth in this area." Dev stood. "Could be from a kid who fell off a bike. Or even an animal."

"I know. But it won't hurt to tuck this away in our evidence closet."

"It's not enough to take on this case, Cal."

At his partner's quiet comment, Cal led the way back toward the car. "I know that too." Much as he'd like to help Moira Harrison, there simply weren't any tangible leads to track down.

They slid into their seats in silence. Cal buckled up, started the engine, and aimed the car toward St. Louis.

And as they began the long drive home in the dusk, he found himself dreading tomorrow, when he'd have to call and give a lovely lady some bad news.

Why wasn't there any broken glass in her car?

Still wrestling with that question, Moira slid the key into the lock on the front door of her condo, twisted the handle, and stepped inside. The loud beep of the security alarm reminded her to punch in her code, and she did so on autopilot. Lucky thing she and Linda were such good friends, considering how she'd zoned out for the remainder of their walk.

She tossed her keys on the table in her tiny foyer and headed straight for the shower. It might only be April, but the day had been very warm, and her tank top was clinging to her.

Moira lingered under the cool spray, wishing

she could wash away the memory of Friday night and all its repercussions as easily as the water washed away the grime of the day.

On second thought . . . maybe she wouldn't want to wash away everything that had happened. Meeting Cal Burke had been pleasant, despite the circumstances—and his marital status. If he was as ethical and honorable as he seemed, his wife was a lucky woman.

A little niggle of envy surprised her, and Moira did her best to subdue it as she reached for a towel. Just because she'd picked a loser didn't mean she begrudged Cal's wife her good fortune. Nor Linda hers.

But why couldn't she get lucky in the romance department?

Before her melancholy degenerated into a pity party, she shut off the water, gave herself a vigorous rub with the towel, and tucked it around her sarong style. She had a nice life. A tad lonely once in a while, true, but there were other compensations.

Like Pulitzer prize nominations.

As she leaned down to retrieve her blow-dryer from under the vanity, a greenish spot on her left thigh caught her eye in the mirror. She shifted sideways to check it out.

Was that a bruise? Right where she'd felt the glass on Friday night?

Brow furrowed, she swiped a hand towel over

the mirror to clear away the lingering steam and edged closer.

The skin wasn't broken, but yes, there was a round, quarter-sized bruise.

She did a quick body check. Other than the purple-hued bump on her temple, that was the only other mar on her skin.

But if broken glass wasn't the culprit, what had caused it?

Moira didn't have a clue.

All she knew was that it added one more piece to an ever-growing puzzle.

⇒· 4 ·⇐

Moira slid onto a stool at the pass-through island in her tiny kitchenette, picked up her fork—and wrinkled her nose. She liked macaroni and cheese just fine, but every other night since she'd gotten her car-repair estimate more than two weeks ago? Overkill.

It was, however, easy on a budget that had just taken a big ding.

She poked at the noodles, rested her elbow on the counter, and settled her chin in her palm. For some reason, the silence in her condo felt oppressive tonight. Maybe because it was Friday and, as usual, she had no social plans.

It was going to be a long evening.

As she reached over and flipped on the small television at the end of the counter, a muffled rendition of "Für Elise" drifted her way.

Leaving her dinner behind, she jogged into the living room to retrieve her cell before voice mail kicked in. After a quick glance at caller ID, she pushed the talk button.

"Hi, Dad."

"How's my favorite daughter?"

She smiled. Their phone conversations always followed the same opening script—one of the few things in her life that had been predictable of late.

"Your only daughter is fine."

"Just wanted to check in and make sure you got your wheels back."

"This afternoon. Almost good as new."

"And you're feeling okay? No side effects from the concussion?"

She dropped into her favorite reading chair and propped her feet on the footstool. "No. I'm almost good as new too."

"I'm glad that's behind you. An accident was the last thing you needed while learning the ropes on your new job."

And that wasn't the half of it. But her father didn't need to know about the vanishing people. That would only worry him.

Besides, it was over. Once Cal Burke had called her the day after her visit to his office, she'd been forced to concede defeat. If a pro like him couldn't find anything to investigate, there must not be anything to find. She had to let it go.

Even if she couldn't shake the feeling that she'd failed the terrified woman in her head-lights.

"That's how life works, I guess." She pulled off her pumps and wiggled her toes to restore circulation. If she hadn't had to attend that luncheon today and interview the celebrity keynote speaker, she'd never have subjected her feet to such torture. "And speaking of the new job, it's going well."

"Good to know. Steven said the same when he called a couple of days ago."

"Where is he, again?" It was hard to keep up with her globe-trotting engineer brother.

"Finishing up that job in Dubai. Must be quite a place. He told me a great story about a trip he took out to the desert. Rode a camel, ate dinner in a bedouin tent, watched a belly dancer perform, tried all kinds of exotic food and—"

". . . a great honor." A voice from the television grabbed her attention, and she tuned out her father to listen.

"And I thank God for the opportunity to do such worthwhile work with the talents he gave me."

Her heart stopped.

Stuttered.

Raced on.

That sounded like the voice of her disappearing Good Samaritan.

She scrambled to her feet and raced back to the kitchen. The man was finished speaking, but she caught a quick glimpse of him before the shot switched back to the anchor at the news desk. Mid-fiftyish and distinguished-looking, with a touch of gray at his temples. There was nothing familiar about him—except his voice.

"That's very inspiring." The female anchor spoke to the reporter who'd covered the story and was now seated beside her.

"Yes, it is. Dr. Blaine started Let the Children Come with his own seed money and a dream, and thousands of children have benefitted. As the governor said this afternoon, it would be hard to think of someone more deserving of the state's humanitarian of the year award."

"Thanks, Brett."

The anchors moved on to the next story, but Moira continued to stare at the screen.

"Moira? Moira, are you still there?"

From a distance, her father's question registered, and she forced herself to switch gears.

"Yeah, I'm here." Even as she responded, she was pulling out her laptop. "Look, can I call you later? Or tomorrow? I need to follow up on some information I just received."

"Sure, honey. But don't work all weekend, okay? You need some downtime too. Remember what Euripides said: 'The best and safest thing is to keep a balance in your life.' "

Despite her distraction, Moira had to smile. Leave it to Dad to view—and dispense—parental advice through the lens of ancient Greece. He'd been studying and teaching classical philosophy for so long, the words of the earliest sages were as much a part of him as his lifelong passion for tying trout flies and attending Shakespearean plays.

"I'll file that away, Professor. Talk to you soon."

After pushing the end button, Moira set the phone on the dinette table and booted up her laptop, drumming her fingers on the polished oak as she waited for the computer to wake up. This would probably be a dead end too. A physician who'd won a humanitarian of the year award would never leave injured people at an accident scene.

But the similarity in voices was too striking to ignore.

The computer finished its start-up gyrations, and she opened her browser, then typed in "Dr. Blaine Let the Children Come."

There were plenty of hits.

She started with the first one and worked her way down the screen.

The more she read, the more she was convinced she was on the wrong track.

Dr. Kenneth Blaine, age fifty-six, was a

respected pediatric surgeon in St. Louis. Twelve years ago, after visiting rural Guatemala with a group of doctors on a humanitarian mission, he'd been so moved by the plight of the children that he'd founded Let the Children Come. The 501c3 organization was dedicated to raising funds for a free children's clinic that provided medical care, nutritional assistance, and prenatal counseling in that country. Dr. Blaine continued to take a team of volunteer doctors to the clinic for two weeks every year. He'd won national recognition for his work, including a commendation from the president, and was active in his church.

There was more. Much more.

Disheartened, Moira sat back.

What were the odds a man like that—pillar of the community, great humanitarian, benefactor to the most needy, stellar role model—would be her missing Good Samaritan?

Smaller than winning the lottery.

Yet the doctor's voice seemed so familiar.

She needed to listen to it again.

Searching the local station's website, she found the segment from the news program and watched the whole thing, beginning with the governor presenting a plaque to Dr. Blaine, followed by the brief clip from his acceptance speech.

She replayed it, closing her eyes to concentrate on the voice alone. Her Good Samaritan's voice had been a bit gruffer . . . but the tonal quality was very similar. Still, three weeks had passed, and a voice was one of the hardest things to retain in memory. Even the voice of a loved one. Plus, many people had similar voices.

This was a real stretch.

Frowning, she rose and wandered back to the kitchen. Her macaroni and cheese was cold now, congealed into a hard glob on her plate. She considered nuking it, but why bother? Her appetite had vanished—just like the two people on that rainy night.

Fork in hand, she jabbed at the unappetizing mess. Maybe she should call Cal Burke. He'd been kind when he'd contacted her to break the news that there was nothing to go on. Apologetic, almost. As if he believed her story and wished he could help her. Why else would he have told her to call him if there were any new developments or if she remembered anything else that might be helpful?

Did this qualify?

Maybe.

But she needed to be more certain before she bothered him again. "Sketchy" was a more-than-generous way to describe this lead.

Moira pulled some plastic wrap out of a drawer, sealed up her dinner for another night, and mulled over an idea.

Why not ask her boss if she could interview Dr.

Blaine for a feature story as a follow-up to his award? That would give her a chance to observe him up close, in person. And something he said or did might put her mind at rest. Reassure her he had no connection to her nightmare.

She slid the macaroni and cheese into the refrigerator and grabbed a container of yogurt, balancing it in her hand as she pondered that plan. As far as she could see, it had no downside.

And when it led nowhere, as it surely would, perhaps she'd at last be able to move on, knowing she'd done all she could to help the terrified woman who'd reached out to her for that one brief moment in the glare of her headlights.

"Who's Moira Harrison?"

At Connor's question, Cal swiveled away from his computer to find the third member of the Phoenix PI team eyeballing the file folder on his desk. The one he should have relegated to his dead case file two weeks ago.

The one he hadn't been able to bring himself to put away.

"A case I'm not taking." He slid the file closer to him and set his Connemara marble paperweight on top of it.

"Getting a little proprietary, aren't we?" Connor's teasing tone morphed into a wince as he eased into the chair across the desk.

"Getting a little old, aren't we?" Cal leaned back

in his chair and tapped his pen against the palm of his hand.

"Don't rub it in. And the next time a protection job in an exotic locale requires participation in sports, I intend to read the fine print. Especially if the sport involves water."

"He asked up front if you were certified to dive."

"But he neglected to mention the diving would be done in submerged caves and narrow passageways not designed to accommodate a six-foot-three body. I felt like a contortionist. Then he topped that off with kayaking and parasailing. Whatever happened to golf?"

Cal chuckled. "Did the guy ever work?"

"He made an occasional appearance to rev up the troops. But hey, he owns the company. Who's going to call him on it if he plays while the minions have their meetings?" He gestured toward the file. "That must be the Pulitzer prize nominee with the vanishing people."

So much for his diversionary tactics. "Yeah. Did Dev tell you about it?"

"Who else? Is she as hot as he claims?"

Cal compressed his lips. Usually he found Dev's appreciation for pretty ladies amusing. Today it rankled him.

"It's a moot point. We're not taking the case."

"Then why is the folder still on your desk?"

Sometimes it was a pain working with dogged

ex–law enforcement types. Even if they were college buddies—and shared an Irish heritage.

On the other hand, they came in handy in dicey situations.

"I haven't gotten around to putting it away yet."

Connor inspected his neat, everything-in-its-place desk. Didn't say a word.

Didn't have to.

When his partner rose, his grunt of pain didn't elicit one iota of sympathy.

At the door, Connor turned. "By the way, Dev told me to give you a hard time. Mission accomplished." With a mock salute, he disappeared down the hall.

Shaking his head, Cal hefted the paperweight and weighed it in his hand. Dev's hair might be dark auburn now, but he'd been a carrot top as a child, with a mischievous streak to rival Dennis the Menace. Or so his mother had confided one Christmas in college when Dev had invited Cal home because his dad had been on an overseas assignment and he had nowhere to go for the holiday. Much to Dev's embarrassment, his mother had dragged out the old family album one snowy Minnesota afternoon and regaled Cal with tale after tale of her son's escapades.

Cal smiled. The stories were great ammunition. And he still had a few of the most humiliating ones tucked away.

He pursed his lips and rocked back in his

chair. Siccing Connor on him about Moira Harrison might merit pulling one out.

On the other hand, that might be a tactical error. It could suggest his buddies had gotten under his skin. That *she'd* gotten under his skin. Better to let it rest. Save his ammo for another day.

He set the paperweight back on his desk and ran a finger along the edge of the slender file. Better to let this sit too. If he reacted, put it away as a result of their ribbing, they could come to the same conclusion.

So he'd leave it there for another day or two. Solely as damage control.

At least that's what he told himself.

Moira finished paging through a lone copy of *Business Week* for the second time, then scanned the other choices on the table beside her. *American Baby, FamilyFun, Parenting*. No *Wall Street Journal*. No *Newsweek*. No *Economist*.

Then again, it *was* the office of a pediatric surgeon.

Setting the magazine aside, she checked her watch. Whatever emergency had required Dr. Blaine's presence at the hospital was lasting far longer than the woman behind the smoked-glass window had implied. One by one the other patients had rescheduled and left. Only one mother remained, cuddling a sleeping toddler whose arm was in a cast.

The woman looked her way and offered a tentative smile. "I guess we're the last holdouts."

"Seems like it. But I'm thinking about bailing too. I was supposed to be his last appointment of the day, but"—she tapped her watch—"the day's almost over."

"I know." The little boy in her arms let out a sigh, and she brushed the fine hair back from his face with a gentle touch. "But I'm going to stick it out unless they tell me he's not coming back at all."

"Looks like your little one has had a tough time."

The woman nodded. "My husband's car was broadsided by an SUV two weeks ago. He's down with a dislocated shoulder, but Tommy took the brunt of it." Her voice choked, and she swiped her fingers over her eyes. "Sorry. It's been rough."

"I'm sure it has. Seeing any child hurting is hard, but when it's your own son or daughter . . . I can't even imagine." Moira sent her an empathetic look. "Is his arm broken?"

The young mother swallowed, took a deep breath, and stroked her fingers over the boy's forehead. "Yes. Plus he had a ruptured spleen. I don't think I'd have made it through without Dr. Blaine. He even gave me his personal cell number when I fell apart one night in the hospital. Told me to call him anytime I got

71

scared or needed answers. Now there's a man who practices the Hippocratic Oath."

At the glowing endorsement, Moira shifted in her seat. The accolades for Blaine kept piling up. In all her research, she hadn't found a single negative comment about this paragon of pediatrics.

He couldn't be her man.

Meaning all she was going to get out of this visit was a nice interview. The mystery woman would forever remain a mystery.

At least she'd tried.

"May I ask why you're here? You don't seem to have a child in tow."

At the woman's question, she managed a smile. "I'm a reporter with the *Post*. Dr. Blaine won the governor's humanitarian of the year award recently, and we're going to do a feature story on him."

"I heard about that. And I'm glad he won. A doctor who goes above and beyond for his patients deserves to be recognized. Plus all the work he does for the children in Guatemala . . ." She shook her head. "He's an amazing man."

The door leading to the examining rooms opened and a woman in a scrub top stepped through. "Sorry about the delay, ladies. Dr. Blaine just returned. I can show you both back now."

Moira joined her while the other woman stood carefully, keeping a firm grip on her son. Then they both followed her back.

"This is the doctor's office." The nurse paused beside a door and motioned Moira inside. "Make yourself comfortable. He'll be with you as soon as he's finished with Tommy." She smiled at the sleeping toddler.

The nurse continued down the hall, and Moira touched the young mother's arm as she passed. "Good luck with your son."

She smiled. "Thank you, but he's in great hands. I have every confidence in Dr. Blaine."

As the small group moved away, Moira turned toward the office, trying to muster up some enthusiasm for the interview. It wasn't as if she'd expected Blaine to be her man, anyway. All her research had painted him as a person of sterling character. This patient's rave review simply reinforced the accolades.

Settling into the chair across from the burled walnut desk, Moira opened her notebook and took her usual inventory of the setting. You could learn a lot about people from the things they chose to display in their personal space—hobbies, family, passions.

In Dr. Blaine's case, his passion was obvious. His walls were covered with framed photos from the clinic in Guatemala funded by his nonprofit corporation. Some featured only the children. Others included him. Several focused on the volunteer pediatric team from the United States that visited the clinic annually, showing them at work both inside the facility and outside the adobe structure. Blaine's medical credentials were displayed as well, but the clinic shots dominated.

Moira inspected the desk, bookcase, filing cabinet. All were meticulously neat and uncluttered, the few folders on the desk lined up with military precision. There wasn't a single personal item in the room. No knickknacks. No coffee mug. No family photos. Were it not for the clinic photos and a couple of cascading pathos plants, the room would have zero personality—or warmth.

Not what she imagined after talking with the young mother in the waiting room.

The woman in the scrub top stuck her head in the door and smiled. "May I offer you a soft drink or some water?"

"No, thank you."

"Dr. Blaine should be with you in less than five minutes. Follow-up visits tend to be quick, but you never know with him. He takes as much time as patients—or parents—need." She hesitated. "Sure I can't get you a beverage in case the wait is longer than you expect?"

"I'm fine."

With a nod, the woman closed the door halfway and continued down the hall.

Moira looked at her notebook and reviewed the questions she'd prepared in case her subject was reticent. But she hoped he wasn't; free-flow interviews produced far more interesting material.

She added a note about the doctor's willingness to give out his cell number to distraught parents, then checked her phone messages and started returning calls.

Several minutes later, while she was setting up an interview for Friday, the door behind her opened.

Shooting an apologetic glance over her shoulder toward the doctor, she held up one finger and turned back to complete the call.

"Thursday at 1:00 sounds fine. Your office in the Ridgeway Center. Is there a room number?"

As the woman on the other end of the phone gave her further directions and she scribbled in her notebook, the doctor entered the room and took his seat behind the desk.

"Okay. Sounds great. I'll look forward to meeting you." After pressing the end button, Moira directed her attention to the surgeon. "Sorry."

"I'm the one who should apologize. I kept you waiting far too long." He smiled and leaned forward, extending his hand. "Moira Harrison, I presume."

Once again, the uncanny similarity of his voice to her Good Samaritan's unnerved her. It was downright weird.

Forcing up the corners of her mouth, she

reached across his desk and took his hand. "Yes." The strength of his grip surprised her, and she tried not to flinch.

He must have caught some nuance in her expression, however, because he loosened the pressure at once.

"I appreciate the *Post*'s interest in my work. Feel free to fire away with your questions and I'll do my best to answer them. Or at least make something up." He shot her an engaging grin.

She opened her notebook, trying to focus. Wishing she could check out his left hand to verify he wasn't wearing a Claddagh ring.

Unfortunately, his hands were folded in his lap, hidden from her view. But she'd get a look at them before the interview was over. Not that she needed the absence of a ring to prove he wasn't her man. Whoever had stopped on that rainy Friday night would be able to recognize her even if she couldn't recognize him. And if it was Blaine, surely having her show up on his door-step would unsettle him. Yet her presence didn't seem to faze him. He was relaxed. Personable. Pleasant.

So much for her tenuous theory.

Moira gave him another forced smile. "Before we talk about your charitable work, could you tell me how you became interested in pediatric surgery?"

"Of course. I always knew I wanted to follow in

my father's footsteps and go into medicine. He was a brain and spine surgeon. A remarkable man. Incredibly intelligent and brave. Anyway, in my early years of medical school, I planned to specialize in brain and spine surgery as well. Then I did a pediatric rotation and discovered I had a knack for working with children. They loved me and I loved them. You might say it was a mutual admiration society."

"Did I read somewhere—perhaps another article—that you also have a special interest in geriatrics?" Moira checked her notes.

He didn't respond at once, and she looked over at him.

This time his smile didn't reach his eyes. "I've always had an affinity for older people too. And I do make nursing home visits through a program my church sponsors. Motivated by charity rather than medicine. But for a career, the younger set won, hands down. There's nothing more gratifying than helping a young child heal and go on to fulfill his or her potential."

Scribbling in her notebook as he spoke, Moira finished capturing his quote before moving on to the next question. "Do you have children of your own, doctor?" As she looked up, she caught a flash of sadness in his eyes.

"No. My wife and I weren't blessed in that way. But I've always believed God has his reasons for everything. If we'd had our own family, I might not have had the time or energy to start Let the Children Come."

The perfect segue to talk about his work in Guatemala.

"Tell me how that came about."

His face grew more animated—and intent—as he described his first trip to a Guatemala clinic in the rugged western highlands.

"My pastor hooked me up with a volunteer medical mission. It was, to use a cliché, eye-opening. I'd never seen such destitution and incredible need. Especially among the children. Seventy percent are malnourished. Eighty-three percent live in poverty. Spina bifida is rampant, in large part due to dietary issues and poor pre-natal care. It was appalling. I came home knowing I had to find a way to help on a more ongoing basis."

He leaned forward, his passion about his cause almost palpable as he knitted his fingers together and placed his hands on his desk.

But as he continued to speak, Moira didn't hear a word he said.

All she could do was stare at the gold Claddagh ring on the fourth finger of his left hand.

❯❯ 5 ❮❮

Chomping down on a carrot stick, Cal reached for the vibrating BlackBerry on his belt without taking his gaze off the employee exit of the upscale hospice. Once he had it in hand, he flicked a quick glance at caller ID.

Not a familiar number.

He hesitated. This wasn't the moment to lose focus, not with his subject scheduled to come through the door any minute. But the guy's car was at the end of the lot. He should have plenty of time to alert Dev and Connor even if he took the call.

Swallowing the mouthful of carrots, he pushed the talk button. "Burke."

"Mr. Burke . . . it's Moira Harrison."

Now he was distracted.

He took a breath to steady the sudden leap in his pulse. "What can I do for you?"

"There's been a new development. I'm sorry to bother you on your cell after hours, but I didn't want to wait until tomorrow to talk about this."

"You're not bothering me. And there's no such thing as after-hours for a PI. What's up?"

"A couple of things have happened in the past few days. They don't prove anything, but the coincidences are unsettling."

The door of the hospice opened, and Cal shifted his attention back to the task at hand as their thirty-six-year-old male Caucasian subject exited.

"Hold for a minute, okay?" He didn't wait for a response. After setting the phone on the seat beside him, he grabbed the walkie-talkie and pushed the talk button. "Our guy's on the move. Stand by."

He watched through the dark-tinted windshield of the van as the man slid behind the wheel of his SUV. Waited until he started the engine and drove toward the street. Pressed the talk button as he exited.

"He's heading west on Lamping. Over."

"Copy." Dev's voice crackled over the walkie-talkie, followed by silence for thirty seconds. "Okay. I've got the eye. Connor, you with me?"

"One block back. You're in sight."

"It's all yours, guys. Good luck. Over." Cal set the walkie-talkie back on the seat and picked up his phone. "Are you still there, Ms. Harrison?"

"Yes. But it sounds like you're busy—and with a far more important job than mine. Look, I'm probably overreacting, so—"

Cal cut her off as he watched a few more employees exit. "You don't strike me as the over-reacting type. Where are you now?"

She hesitated. "In my car. I'm just leaving an interview with a doctor at Mercy Hospital."

"I'm in West County too." The proximity was

too close to ignore. "Do you know the Starbucks at Mason and Clayton?"

"No. But I know those streets."

"Why don't I meet you there? I could use a cup of coffee, and it's always better to talk in person." That was a stretch. Phone calls were often more efficient—especially in a tenuous case that was also pro bono.

Moira's hesitation told him she'd come to the same conclusion. "Are you sure? I've already taken up a lot of your time, and you haven't charged me a dime."

"This is off the clock. I'd be stopping for coffee with or without your company." That was true—although the stop would more likely be at a QuikTrip rather than Starbucks.

No matter. It worked.

"Okay. I'm leaving the parking lot now. I think I can be there in less than ten minutes."

"I'm even closer. I'll grab a table. See you soon."

He tossed the phone onto the seat beside him, made the final entry of the day in his surveillance log, and exited the lot.

Maybe it was a good thing her file was still on his desk after all.

Twelve minutes later, he spotted her through the window as she came up the steps to the Starbucks entrance.

Dev was right.

Moira Harrison was hot.

The setting sun caught the red in her hair, turning it to copper, and her fashionably short slim black skirt and dress heels showed off a pair of killer legs. The fitted, short-sleeved green-and-black plaid jacket that hinted at her appealing curves wasn't too shabby, either.

His adrenaline spiked, and he took a sip of coffee. *Steady, Burke. Remember, she's a client—and you're not in the market.*

When she pushed through the door, he stood.

She spotted him at once, eyeing his disposable cup with dismay as she wove through the tables to join him in the far corner.

"I was going to get your coffee."

The very reason he'd bought it before she arrived.

"I needed a caffeine boost after surveillance duty." He thought about offering to buy her drink too, but before he could decide whether that was smart or not, she headed to the counter, tossing a comment over her shoulder.

"Give me a sec."

He sat again as she placed her order, his back-to-the-wall seat giving him an excellent view of those amazing legs—and the interior of the coffee shop. An unnecessary precaution today, but old detective habits died hard. Especially ones that had saved his hide on more than one occasion.

When she turned to rejoin him, she was juggling both a disposable cup and a plate.

He rose as she approached to pull out her chair, and the courtesy seemed to surprise her.

"Thanks." She slid into the seat, placing her drink and plate on the table. "I don't run into such polished manners very often. Your mother must have raised you well."

"She did. And my older sister finished the job after Mom died."

"Were you young when you lost her?"

"Young enough. Fourteen."

Her features softened in sympathy. "I'm sorry. That had to be tough."

"It was. But I had good memories. That helped."

"There's a lot to be said for good memories." She broke the scone in half. "Have you had dinner?"

"Not yet, but I've been munching on carrot sticks."

She wrinkled her nose. "Healthy, but not very filling."

"Better than chips for surveillance, though. High-carb stuff makes me sleepy, and nodding off is a no-no."

"Makes sense." She slid the plate his direction, placing half of the scone on a napkin in front of her. "It's not much, but it might tide you over until you can get a more substantial meal."

"I can't take your food."

"Yes, you can. After all the macaroni and cheese I've been subsisting on since I got my car repair bill, I don't need a whole scone. Too many calories."

Given her trim figure, he doubted she had to worry. But when his stomach rumbled in anticipation, he capitulated.

"Thanks." He picked up the scone and took a big bite. "Much better than carrot sticks."

"I'm sorry again for interrupting. It sounded like things were hopping when I called."

"Yeah. All three of us are working the case, but I'm off the hook for the evening. Dev and Connor got night duty."

"Three PIs on one case." She broke off another piece of her scone. "Is that typical?"

"No. But the organization that hired us wants to deal with this problem quickly and without publicity."

"Must be a messy situation."

"Very." His mouth settled into a grim line. An employee suspected of watering down codeine and selling the good stuff on the black market could badly tarnish the hospice's reputation. They wanted the guy nailed. Fast. As did Phoenix. Anyone who would deprive suffering people of pain medication should be locked away.

"Why don't they call the police?"

Cal forced his lips to relax. "We're much more discreet and under the radar than cops. Also faster. Law enforcement doesn't have the man-power to devote to an investigation like this. Once we have the evidence, we'll turn it over to them for the cleanup." He took a sip of coffee to wash down the last of his scone and got the conversation back on track. "Now tell me about your coincidences."

She pressed her fingertip against the crumbs on the table, transferring them to a neat little pile in the center of her napkin. "This is almost as strange as my disappearing people story. Brace yourself."

As she recounted the latest development, Cal gave her his full attention. But the more she revealed about Dr. Blaine, the more he was inclined to believe the voice similarity was, indeed, a coincidence.

Until she dropped her bombshell about the ring.

That put a different spin on things.

"So what do you think?"

At her query, he drummed his fingers on the table. "You're right. It's weird."

"You don't think the ring and the voice are just a coincidence?"

"Maybe. Coincidences do happen—a lot more often than people realize. But two with the same person?" He shook his head. "That's pushing it. Did you mention anything to him about that Friday night?"

"There was no opportunity. Besides, once I

saw the ring, I was barely able to form a coherent sentence for the rest of the interview." She leaned forward, intent. "Plus, whoever that guy was on Friday would recognize me. Blaine didn't give any indication he'd ever seen me before. So if it was him, he doesn't intend to admit it. And why would a man like him stop and offer to help, then disappear, anyway?" She blew out a frustrated breath and combed her fingers through her hair. "None of this makes sense."

No, it didn't.

But he wasn't sure he could offer her much help. The man wasn't accused of anything. Just the opposite. He was being lauded—by the governor, no less. Nor would the police be of help. Without evidence of wrongdoing, they wouldn't touch this.

"You think it's hopeless, don't you?" The taut line of Moira's shoulders suggested aggravation more than defeat.

"I wouldn't go that far, but it is a challenge." Cal took another sip of coffee. "However, you're a crack investigative reporter or you wouldn't have been nominated for a Pulitzer prize." At her startled look, he raised his cup in salute. "We did our homework. Congratulations. In any case, with those kinds of credentials, you must have sound instincts. What do they tell you about this situation?"

She gripped her half-empty cup, her gaze never

wavering from his. "That something's out of whack. Big time."

Her fervent response was convincing.

As Cal considered his options, several students from the nearby college hurried past to claim the oversized rectangular table in the center, intent on their destination. One of the girls caught the strap of Moira's tote in her own dangling purse, pulling it off the back of the chair. Moira made a grab for it, her arm shooting out.

That's when he saw the jagged scar. Three inches long on the outside of her upper arm, it looked to be a couple of years old.

She caught him staring as she straightened up and her sleeve settled back into place, masking the gash.

He wasn't going to pretend he hadn't seen it.

"Accident?"

"Mugging."

His heart skipped a beat. "When?"

"Two years ago. Except it wasn't a mugging."

"What do you mean?"

She shrugged. "I was doing an investigative piece on gang-related drug problems. Asking questions the leaders didn't like. One night, I was supposed to meet a contact who'd promised me information. Instead, I ended up cornered in a dark alley by knife-wielding gang members who suggested that wandering in places I didn't belong could be dangerous. They took my purse to make it look like a robbery, but it turned up a few days later in a dumpster with all my cards intact. And they left me with this souvenir." She flipped her hand toward her arm as if the wound didn't matter.

But it did to him.

Cold anger, his standard reaction to senseless violence, churned in his gut.

Moira had been attacked with a knife.

She could have been killed.

"Hey." She started to reach out to him, her eyes wide. Then drew her hand back. "It's okay. I'm fine. I got the story, and several gang leaders got indicted."

He wasn't certain what she'd seen in his face, but he did his best to slip a neutral mask back on. "I didn't realize journalism was that dangerous."

"That was an aberration. Most of the stories I do aren't risky."

"But you don't shy away from the ones that are."

She didn't blink. "No. And I'm not going to shy away from this, either. I need to get to the bottom of it. For my own peace of mind, if nothing else."

And she'd do it with or without Phoenix's help. He'd make book on that. Any woman who had the guts and tenacity to stand up to gang members wasn't going to back down from a pediatric surgeon.

Cal tapped his finger on the table. "I'll tell you what. Let me talk to my partners. Get their take on this. Can I call you tomorrow?"

"Yes. And thank you for meeting me before going home." She stood. "Please give my apologies to your wife."

He stuck her cup in his and picked up her plate as he rose. "No apologies needed. My wife died five years ago." For once his throat didn't close down as he said the words. Odd.

Moira's lips formed a small O and her eyes widened. "I'm so sorry."

"Yeah. Me too." This time, his voice rasped.

He crossed to the trash can, deposited their cups, set the empty plate on the barista's counter, and took a deep breath, buying himself a few seconds to regain control.

By the time he rejoined her and gestured toward the front door, he had his emotions in check. "I'll walk you to your car."

"That's not necessary."

He managed to summon up the hint of a smile. "My mom would disagree—and I wouldn't want to disappoint her."

With no further argument, she preceded him to the door. As they stepped outside, she indicated a silver Camry. "That's it."

"Convenient. I'm parked next to you."

She surveyed the Mercedes to the right of her car. "Nice."

"Try the other side."

Her brow wrinkled as she sized up the van on the left. "That's a carpet cleaning business."

"Or a surveying firm, or an electrical company, or a half dozen other businesses. Depends on which magnetic sign I put up." He took her arm as they descended the steps. "You don't think I always dress like this, do you?"

She gave his uniform-like dark green slacks and beige shirt a quick sweep. "Cover for surveillance?"

"Bingo." He opened her door, and she slid inside. "I'll be back in touch before noon tomorrow. Your cell okay?"

"Yes. Thank you again."

"Nothing to thank me for yet. Drive safe."

He closed the door and circled around to the driver's side of the van. While he fished out his keys and climbed behind the wheel, she backed out and accelerated toward the exit.

As he watched her disappear, a sudden impulse swept over him to take off after her, wave her over, and invite her to dinner. He was tired of eating alone, and she sounded fed up with macaroni and cheese.

But that was crazy. He'd never been the impetuous type.

Gripping the wheel, he quashed the renegade urge. His memories of Lindsey were enough to sustain him.

Besides, it seemed Moira Harrison might become a client after all. And the unwritten rule was that Phoenix PIs didn't date clients.

Not even hot ones.

• • •

"You with us, Connor?" Cal positioned the speaker phone on the conference room table and took a seat beside Dev.

A yawn came over the line as a U2 song played in the background. "Yeah, I'm here. But I'd rather be in bed."

"I'll be back to relieve you at noon," Dev reminded him.

"Promises, promises."

"You guys got some nice shots last night when you followed our subject to the mall parking lot. We ought to be able to wrap this up soon." Cal turned a pen end-to-end on the yellow tablet in front of him.

"I can't believe he did the handoff out in the open like that, even if it was dark. The guy's a real amateur." Dev shook his head.

"Not to mention a scumbag." Connor's voice was laced with disgust.

"Go ahead, Connor, tell us how you really feel." One side of Cal's mouth quirked up.

"Hey. I don't have to be PC anymore. That's one of the beauties of this job. I can call it like I see it without pussyfooting around or worrying about department protocols. And what that guy's doing is unconscionable."

"I agree." Dev's face hardened. "We do our job, not even the best defense attorney will get him off."

"Hopefully we caught him in the act with one of the motion-activated cameras you planted when you went to fix that 'electrical problem' last week at the hospice." Cal checked out his partner's blue work shirt, jeans, and tool belt. "Are you retrieving today?"

"Why else would I be dressed like this?"

"Because you have a secret wish to be Tim the Tool Man?"

"Cute."

"I thought it was." Cal uncapped his pen and switched gears. "Okay. Let's move on to the reason I asked for this meeting so we can all get back to work."

"Moira Harrison." Dev grinned at him.

Cal shot him a disgruntled look. "How did you know that?"

Smirk still in place, Dev lifted one shoulder. "Call it intuition. Or it could be the fact that I just happened to notice her file is now front and center on your desk when I just happened to wander into your office to borrow your stapler before this meeting."

"So you were trespassing?"

"Nah. We're all friends here."

"Don't push your luck, buddy."

"While this exchange is highly entertaining, could we get to the point? My talk radio show is about to start." Connor's last word ended on a yawn.

"Eat some of those pistachios you carry around or you're going to fall asleep." Cal played with the cap on his pen. "Okay, Dev's right. This is about Moira Harrison. There's been a new development."

He could only see Dev's body language as he spoke, but Cal suspected Connor was having the same reaction. Dev folded his arms over his chest. Cocked his head. Raised an eyebrow.

Translation? Curious but skeptical.

As he finished, Dev leaned forward. "This guy sounds like a boy scout. What do you propose?"

"We could dig a little into his background. There might be something that would help us get a handle on what's going on. And Connor, just to be clear, this would have to be a pro bono case." Moira's macaroni and cheese reference last night flashed through his mind. Journalism might be a noble profession, but from everything he'd heard, it didn't pay squat—even for Pulitzer prize nominees. "She doesn't have the resources to fund a full investigation."

"The hospice job is paying well. So did my gig in Bermuda. I don't see a problem with pro bono unless this gets a lot more complicated than we expect. I'm okay with some preliminary digging."

Cal looked at Dev.

The other man shrugged. "I'm in."

"All right. I'll work with Nikki on this. She loves projects."

"Unless they involve filing," Dev groused.

"Mountains of filing," Cal corrected. "Besides, she got you squared away, didn't she?"

"Yeah, but it took a Starbucks latte three days in a row."

"Well worth the price." Cal recapped his pen. "I'll keep you guys in the loop as we . . ." His BlackBerry began to vibrate, and he pulled it off his belt. The number registered at once.

Moira's cell.

Odd.

She knew he'd been planning to call her later this morning.

"This is her now. Hang tight for a second." He pushed the talk button. "Burke."

"Good morning. This is Moira Harrison. Am I interrupting anything?"

"No. As a matter of fact, I was in the middle of discussing your situation with my colleagues."

"Well, there's been another development."

"Do you mind if I put you on speaker? No sense me repeating everything after we hang up."

"Sure."

He pushed the speaker button and positioned the phone so Connor could pick up the conversation. "Moira, Jim Devlin and Connor Sullivan are also on the line. Go ahead."

"I know you were going to call me later this morning, but I just checked my voice mail and discovered Dr. Blaine left a message for me late last night. He invited me to shadow him for a day as background for my article. I'm inclined to accept, although it's not necessary for my story. But I wanted to get your read. I've done lots of personality pieces in my career, and this kind of offer is unusual."

Cal exchanged a look with Dev. The other man nodded.

"Connor?" Cal directed the query toward the speaker phone.

"I don't think it's a bad idea."

"Moira, there isn't much downside to this. It will give you a chance to do some more observing, and maybe—if he is your man—he'll slip and say something that gives us more to go on."

"But if it is him, why would he want to take the risk of having me hang around? Wouldn't he be afraid of making a mistake?"

The lady asked astute questions.

Dev supplied the answer to this one. "He might be worried about how much you know or suspect." His partner rested his elbows on the table and steepled his fingers. "This could be an attempt on his part to pick your brain too."

"I guess I can see that. Is there anything specific I should dig for?"

"No." Cal jumped back in. "Unless you can somehow bring up that Friday night. It would be interesting to see his reaction—and what he offers about his own activities. When would you do this?"

"He suggested tomorrow."

"Can you work it into your schedule?"

"Yes."

"Then do it. And touch base as soon as you finish. In the meantime, we're going to do some digging into the good doctor's background."

"I already did a lot of searching on the net."

Cal exchanged a smile with Dev. "We have other sources, including proprietary databases."

"So you're willing to work with me on this? Even though I can't afford to pay much?"

"That's not a problem. We've already discussed it, and the case interests us."

Him more than the others, perhaps. But at least his colleagues had gone along with him. And Dev did seem intrigued.

Or was he just thinking of their hot new client?

He narrowed his eyes at the other man.

"All right." Moira's voice interrupted his dark thoughts. "Thanks a lot, all of you. Cal, I'll call as soon as I finish tomorrow."

"Talk to you then." He tapped the end button on his BlackBerry.

"Cal? Moira? When did you two transition to first names?" Dev waggled his eyebrows.

Ignoring him, Cal rose. "I'll keep you guys in the loop."

Dev's chuckle followed him out the door, sending a rush of heat to his neck.

One of these days, if his partner didn't knock off the ribbing, he might have to pull out one of those old embarrassing stories he'd been saving. Maybe the one about Dev's humiliating faux pas at his senior prom.

Cal dropped his tablet on his desk and smiled.

Now that would be sweet revenge.

⇒• 6 •⇐

Adjusting her surgical mask, Moira shifted into a more comfortable position as she watched the delicate procedure from a stool off to the side in the operating room. Three nurses and an anesthesiologist hovered around the newborn baby, all poised to respond instantly to Kenneth Blaine's clipped instructions.

"Come in there. Shadow in. Really engage. Good. Cut it."

Silence, broken only by the beep, beep, beep of the heart monitor.

"Touch the nerve. In between there. Bring it over to your side as far as you can."

She'd been listening to the man for hours, ever since her 6:00 a.m. arrival at the hospital. And the more she heard him speak, the more the voice of her Good Samaritan faded into the recesses of her memory.

"Saline in . . . okay. No bubbles. Get suction."

Beep . . . beep . . . beep.

"Tim, give us a little downward pressure on the NG tube."

The problem was, she was losing her ability to distinguish between the two voices. It wasn't as if she had a recording of her Good Samaritan's voice, after all. She was only relying on her concussion-clouded memory.

Besides, the man in the green scrubs and magnifying headgear was totally impressive. Incisive, authoritative, and meticulous with his surgical team; empathetic and reassuring with the worried parents he'd talked with after his first surgery of the day, a repair on the cleft palate of an eight-month-old.

"Right angle. Take your Bovie. We're going to have to be up more."

This surgery seemed more complicated. She double-checked her notes for the problem he was correcting. Esophageal atresia. The baby's esophagus ended in a blind pouch rather than connecting to the stomach. Blaine had given her a matter-of-fact briefing, tossing out terms like cyanotic, aspiration of fluid into the trachea, and respiratory distress as they'd chugged down a quick cup of coffee before heading into the operating room.

"More forward thrust on the NG."

Beep . . . beep . . . beep.

"Irrigate out and then we'll bring our chest tube in . . . right up here."

Cool. Confident. Competent. That described the pediatric surgeon to a T. How could he possibly be her Good Samaritan?

"Let me have that Blake drain as well. One on your side."

But the ring was still a sticking point. No matter how hard she tried to dismiss it as coincidence, her investigative training refused to let her.

When the surgery at last wound down, Blaine motioned for her to follow him out.

As they exited, he stripped off his latex gloves, tossed them in the contaminated waste bin, and removed the magnifying headgear. "I hope that wasn't too intense for you."

"No. It was very interesting."

"Glad you found it worthwhile. Let's talk to the parents."

She followed him out. Watched as he reassured the distraught mom and dad. Tagged along as he did his rounds. And learned nothing to suggest that her tenuous theory about his identity had any basis in fact.

This whole thing was turning out to be a bust. Six hours into her shadowing, she'd had no chance to have a real conversation with the man. He'd been on the go every single minute. If he'd wanted to impress her with his work ethic, he'd succeeded. But she hadn't accepted his invitation to be impressed.

She wanted answers.

"Hungry?"

He tossed the question over his shoulder as they left the final patient's room.

Her interest perked up. This might be her chance to probe a little. Perhaps her only one. "Yes."

"Me too." He waited until she drew alongside him before continuing down the hall. "Believe it or not, the hospital food isn't half bad, and it's convenient." He checked his watch. "I start seeing office patients in an hour. Do you mind if we eat here?"

"Not at all."

"Any questions about the day so far?" He punched the elevator button, and the door opened immediately. "That's a first. There's usually a wait." He stepped aside to let her precede him.

Moira squeezed in among a man holding a squalling baby, a patient in a wheelchair manned by an aide, and assorted medical staff and visitors. No chance for conversation here.

But she intended to take full advantage of their quick lunch. All she had to do was find an innocuous way to broach the subject of that fateful Friday night.

Ten minutes later, after they'd gone through the line and claimed a table in the quietest corner of the cafeteria, he caught her off guard by providing the perfect opening.

"That looks like the remnants of a nasty bruise." He unloaded a dish of fresh fruit from his tray and gestured toward her forehead. "I noticed it in the office on Tuesday. Accident?"

Her heart began to hammer as she removed her plate of baked cod.

Stay cool, Moira. Don't blow this.

"Yes. My car ran off the road and into a tree three weeks ago in that bad rainstorm we had on a Friday night. You might remember it. I've never seen such incessant lightning." She slid into her chair, watching him.

He took her tray, stacked it on top of his, and placed them at the far end of the table before settling into the chair across from her.

"I remember it well." He picked up his fork and scooped up some chicken stir-fry. "I was at an Opera Theatre fund-raising dinner that night. My next-door neighbor is on the board, and he hit me up for a ticket. I'm not a big opera fan, but what can you do?" He lifted one shoulder.

Moira's spirits took a dive.

He had an alibi.

She was back to square one.

If the doctor noticed her sudden deflation, he gave no indication. "I remember dashing from the car to the restaurant and spending the next three hours in a damp tuxedo. It was not an auspicious evening—and I'm sure yours wasn't, either. Any injuries besides the bruise?" He slid another forkful of stir-fry into his mouth.

Moira broke off a piece of fish she didn't want. "A mild concussion. I was lucky."

"Very. Head injuries of any kind are nothing to treat lightly. Did you have family around to call on while you recovered?"

"No." She moved her rice around the plate. Took a deep breath. *Let it go, Moira. You were wrong. It's over. Switch gears.* "My dad lives a couple of hours away, though. In Columbia. I can always count on him in a pinch, but I didn't need to bother him with this. It wasn't that bad."

"Is he affiliated with Mizzou?"

"Yes. He's a professor. Classic philosophy."

The doctor was making short work of his lunch, and she'd barely put a dent in hers. She forced herself to take another bite of fish. The man had patients to see; she needed to pick up the pace. No sense prolonging this.

"An interesting occupation." Blaine started on his fruit. "Do you see him often?"

"As often as I can."

"I take it you're close."

"Yes. Even closer in recent years, since my mom died. My brother's job takes him overseas a lot, so mostly it's just me and my dad."

He stopped eating. "A relationship with a father can be a very special thing." There was a subtle

102

undertone in his voice of—melancholy, perhaps? —and his eyes grew distant.

"Is your father still living?"

He blinked, gave her a strained smile, and finished off his last spoon of fruit. "No. He died many years ago, unfortunately. Far too young. But my memories of him are very clear. Count your blessings that you still have your own father." Setting down his spoon, he examined her plate. "You're not making much headway."

"I guess I wasn't as hungry as I thought. I'm ready whenever you are."

"I can return a couple of calls if you'd like to eat a little more. It'll be a long, full afternoon." He checked his watch. "We don't have to leave for about ten minutes."

She considered her half-eaten lunch. Might as well take another stab at it. She wouldn't be eating again for hours, and tonight's menu was macaroni and cheese. Again.

"Thanks. I'll do that." She picked up her fork, and he moved off to the side.

The distance between them, along with the muted hum of conversation in the cafeteria, masked his voice. Just as well. At this point, any sense of familiarity could be due to the simple fact that she'd been listening to him speak all day rather than to any similarity to the mystery man.

Besides, everything she'd observed and learned today—combined with what she already knew about Blaine—reinforced the doctor's stellar reputation. She ought to write this off. And she would, in a heartbeat.

Except for the ring.

"Watch this." Connor leaned forward in his chair, intent on the screen in the conference room. "That sprinkler-head camera Dev planted caught it all."

Cal sat on the edge of the table, his gaze fixed on the monitor.

Key in hand, their suspect entered the locked storage medication room, holding a bottle of water. The key was no surprise. Picking the lock was possible but too time consuming in a public place, except for experts. Their guy had probably made a wax impression of one of the nurse supervisors' masters and filed down a blank to match. Or taken a rubbing of the key and done the same thing.

The man moved to a cabinet. Reached to the back and retrieved what appeared to be an empty water bottle. Filled it one-third full with codeine. Then he watered down the remainder in the original bottle, returned it to its shelf, stashed the now-empty water bottle he'd brought in with him at the back of a shelf, and left the room. The whole procedure took less than four minutes.

This guy had the routine down.

Connor hit the remote, and the screen went

black. "Time to turn this over to the narc unit, don't you think?"

"Yeah." Cal stood.

"I'll coordinate with the director of the center. Make sure it's handled low key."

"That's why he's paying us the big bucks. But the sooner the better." A muscle flexed in Cal's cheek, and he inclined his head toward the blank screen. "I'd like to see that guy busted ASAP."

"Agreed." Standing, Connor stretched. "You hear from our Pulitzer prize nominee yet?"

"No. She thought it might be a long day."

Connor twisted his wrist to see his watch. "Speaking of long days—it's 6:00. I'm calling it quits. See you tomorrow."

They parted in the hall, Connor stopping only long enough to grab his keys off his desk before heading for the rear door. Cal continued to his office. He ought to go home too. No reason to hang around waiting for Moira's call. She had his cell number.

On the other hand, he hadn't yet plowed through all the stuff Nikki had unearthed on Ken Blaine. Might as well hang around a little longer. There was nothing to entice him home, anyway. No savory smells wafting from the kitchen. No new photos arrayed on the dining room table awaiting his appreciative scan. No laughter or music or stolen kisses.

No Lindsey.

As he circled his desk, his throat constricted. Would the empty ache ever go away?

Before his sudden melancholy could take hold, however, his BlackBerry began to vibrate.

Moira?

The familiar number on the LED display confirmed his guess. He pressed the talk button, dispensing with the greeting. "I've been expecting your call."

"Sorry it's so late." She sounded weary—and dejected.

"Long day?"

"Very."

"Productive?"

"I guess you could say that. He has an alibi for that Friday night."

Not what he'd expected.

"I know you have great investigative reporting skills, but how did you discreetly manage to introduce that subject?"

"I didn't. He brought it up indirectly by mentioning the bruise on my forehead. I told him about the accident, and he countered with a story of his own adventure that night, at a fund-raiser for Opera Theatre. His next-door neighbor talked him into buying a ticket."

Meaning there were witnesses to his alibi.

Still . . . something didn't feel right. He couldn't put his finger on it, but he'd learned long ago to listen to any niggle of doubt, no matter how vague.

The distinctive high-pitched beep of car power locks opening sounded in the background as Moira continued. "I guess it's a dead end after all, despite the Claddagh ring."

Cal regarded the file Nikki had compiled. "Let's not give up yet. Where are you?"

"Just leaving his office at Mercy. He puts in twelve-hour days. And I thought *I* worked long hours."

"Do you have all your notes with you from the interview on Tuesday?"

"Yes."

"Why don't we put our heads together and take one more look at everything?"

A couple of beats of silence ticked by. "Are you sure? There doesn't seem to be anywhere else to go with this, and it's obviously been a long day for you too."

"I don't have any plans for the evening."

When that admission was met with more silence, a sudden thought blindsided him. Maybe *she* had plans. Maybe there was a boyfriend waiting for her somewhere. A woman like Moira would only lack for male companionship by choice.

For whatever reason, that notion didn't sit well with him. But it was a definite possibility. So he tacked on a caveat—and held his breath. "Unless you do."

"No."

The tautness in his shoulders eased. He didn't stop to analyze why. "I'm still at the office. We were wrapping up a case. Do you want to swing by here?"

"Sure. I should be able to get there in fifteen minutes or so. No . . . wait. Make it half an hour, if you don't mind. I have to run a quick errand first."

"No problem. That will give me a chance to go through the rest of the material on Blaine before you arrive. See you then."

As he slid the phone back onto his belt, the whisper of a smile tickled the corners of his lips.

Perhaps the evening ahead wouldn't be quiet and empty after all.

Balancing her notes on top of the large supreme pizza box, Moira reached up to ring the bell at the Phoenix front door. It took two tries. The white bag containing the cans of soft drinks and napkins kept getting in the way.

As she waited for Cal to greet her over the intercom and release the lock, she bit her lip. Maybe he'd already grabbed a quick bite at one of the nearby neighborhood restaurants while he waited for her. She should have let him in on her impromptu dinner idea.

Oh well. Too late now. Worst case, she'd have leftover pizza for breakfast for the next week. Or two.

The handle of the door rattled, and she retreated a few inches. He must have come to the front to greet her rather than simply press a switch to open the door.

That earned him another gold star for good manners.

An instant later he pulled the door wide. As he homed in on the pizza box, the gleam of appreciation—or was that hunger?—in his eyes reassured her she'd made a sound call.

"I come bearing food. Since you won't let me pay, the least I can do is feed you."

He relieved her of the pizza box and the bag, then ushered her in. "I'd say you shouldn't have, but I'm starving."

"Join the crowd." She edged past him, close enough to get a whiff of a subtle, rugged, masculine aftershave even the aroma of pepperoni couldn't disguise.

Nice.

She had to fight the temptation to tarry.

He shut the door behind her and motioned her toward the hall. "We can eat—and talk—in the conference room. I was going to order out for us, but you beat me to it." He held an access card over a pad beside the door that led to the offices.

She wrinkled her brow. Why hadn't she noticed that on her first visit?

As if reading her mind, he snagged the door and pulled it open for her. "During the day,

Nikki controls the release from her desk. There's a con-cealed button on the floor."

She was treated to another whiff of that appealing scent as she moved past him. "I didn't realize a PI firm would need such aggressive security measures."

"Second door on your right. Not all firms do, but we've dealt with some sensitive cases. Plus, all three of us have potentially dangerous enemies from our past law enforcement lives." He followed her in and set the pizza and bag on the table.

"That sounds a little scary."

He shrugged and looked into the bag. "That's one of the risks of a law enforcement job. You learn to deal with it."

"Have you ever had anyone actually come after you?"

A muscle in his jaw clenched. "All three of us have our war stories." He pulled out four aluminum cans and the napkins. "I could have provided the drinks."

The answer to her question was yes. But he didn't want to talk about it.

Message received.

"When I bring dinner, I also bring drinks. I didn't know what you preferred, though, so I brought a selection. No time to pick up dessert, however."

"The pizza's plenty. Thanks for doing this. And any of the drinks is fine with me. Take your pick while I grab a notepad and Blaine's file from my office."

As he disappeared out the door, she opened the lid on the pizza box, selected a diet Sprite, and pulled out her own notes.

Once he returned, he gestured to the chair at the end of the table and took the one at a right angle to it after she sat.

"I got a loaded pizza. I figured we could pick off any toppings we didn't like." She helped herself to a slice.

"I like them all." He chose the lemonade from the remaining cans of beverages, picked up a piece of pizza, and took a large bite.

"Me too."

Cal demolished his first piece without much conversation, but after snagging a second slice and depositing it on his napkin, he pulled his notepad closer. "I know Blaine told you he has an alibi for that Friday night, but before we close this case, let's take one more careful look at the situation. I do have a question for you first, though. I noticed on the police report of the incident that you mentioned you were distracted for a moment when you reached for your glasses. Any reason you weren't wearing them?"

She wiped her mouth with a napkin. "I left them at home, in a different purse. I guess I should have mentioned them in our first meeting. They help me to a small degree with distance vision, especially at night, but they're not a restriction on my license."

"I know. I checked."

That didn't surprise her.

She glanced around the room, focusing on the corner at the far end of the rectangular table. "There's a vase of silk flowers on that cabinet. Rather exotic. Orchids, birds of paradise, anthurium. They're in a tall, clear glass vase with a fluted edge. The front of the vase is etched with a fleur-de-lis design, and there's Lucite in the bottom to simulate water."

One side of his mouth hitched up. "Very convincing." He picked up his pen. "Okay, why don't you read through your interview notes from Tuesday while you eat? If you come to anything that reminds you of an impression you had, stop and tell me. No editing. Let's not decide yet what's important and what's not."

"Okay." She popped a stray piece of pepperoni into her mouth and opened her notebook.

They continued to eat in silence as she perused her notes.

"Here's something. During my prep for the interview, I'd read somewhere he was interested in the elderly. But when I asked him about that, he passed over it quickly. All he said was that he visited nursing homes through a program with his church, but not in a professional capacity. I got the feeling he didn't want to talk about it.

The subject seemed to make him uncomfortable."

Cal jotted on his tablet but remained silent as she read through the rest of her notes and finally shook her head.

"There wasn't anything else that gave me pause. Besides, once I saw the ring, my powers of observation were compromised, to say the least."

"All right. What about his office?"

"It was very sterile. Other than the framed photos of his clinic in Guatemala, there was no personality to the space. Not even a picture of his wife."

"Interesting." Cal took a swig of lemonade and jotted another note on his pad. "Let's move on to today. Walk me through it and focus on anything that struck you as odd or curious."

"I didn't have all that much personal interaction with him except at lunch. Professionally, I think he's highly skilled and very respected by his peers and his patients."

"Then let's concentrate on your experience during lunch."

She frowned and stared at the blank wall across from her, reconstructing the conversation in her mind. "He took me off guard by bringing up the bruise immediately. It's faded a lot, so I was surprised he noticed it. We talked a bit about our families too. I got the feeling in the interview Tuesday that he and his father—also a doctor— were close. I could see a lingering sadness in his eyes when he mentioned today that his dad had been dead for many years, and that he died too young. There may have been some hero worship going on there." She picked up a stray piece of mushroom and added it to the slice of pizza on her napkin. "Not much to go on, is it?"

"I don't know." He wiped off his fingers, wadded up the paper napkin, and tossed it onto the table as he ticked off the notes he'd taken. "Discomfort at your question about his interest in the elderly. No pictures of his wife in his office. Hero worship of a father who died young. Each of those could suggest interesting scenarios. But I'm most intrigued by the fact that not only did he invite you to shadow him, he made it a point during your limited conversation to volunteer an alibi for that Friday night."

Moira swallowed the last bite of her third piece of pizza. "You think he could be trying to deflect suspicion?"

"That's one theory. If he is your man, he might have wanted to head you off at the pass by impressing you with his professional standing and making certain you knew he could prove his whereabouts on that Friday night."

"But if he can prove where he was, he isn't my man."

" 'If' being the operative word. Maybe he hopes an alibi will discourage you from further investigation."

"Well, it's working." Moira picked up a napkin and swiped at the beads of condensation on her soda can. "The truth is, after listening to him speak all day, I can't distinguish between his voice and my Good Samaritan's anymore."

"That could also be part of his strategy."

"And I thought *I* was paranoid."

"There's a difference between paranoia and healthy suspicion."

"Are we crossing the line here?"

"You tell me." He linked his fingers on the table and leaned closer, eyes steady and intent. As if he was looking into, rather than at, her. "Trust your instincts, like you do on a story. What are they telling you to do?"

Keeping her gaze locked on his, she thought about how she'd felt the first time she'd heard Blaine's voice, on the news program. About her stunned reaction when she saw his ring during the interview. About the highlights Cal had just distilled. About the terrified woman in her headlights.

"They tell me to keep digging."

"Then that's what we'll do." He continued to look at her for another couple of seconds with those intense brown eyes. Finally he leaned back and picked up the file he'd brought in with him.

Moira released the breath she hadn't realized she was holding and wove her fingers together on the table.

"I had Nikki run some preliminary background for me. Nothing unusual turned up. Now that we've talked, though, I'm going to have her dig deeper on a few things while I check out his alibi."

Nikki, the punk rocker with the purple hair and seashell necklace, assisted with research?

"Um, does she do a lot of that kind of thing for you?"

Cal's lips twitched. "Don't let the externals fool you. She's a whiz with online databases and has a degree in computer forensics. We brought her on board when we opened our doors, and at this point I don't know what we'd do without her."

Computer forensics. Iridescent toenail polish.

Major disconnect.

"You're surprised, aren't you?"

A flame flickered to life on her cheeks and she fiddled with her can. Was she that easy to read? "A little."

"She runs into that a lot, but she's learned to be amused rather than offended." His expression sobered. "Nikki's had a tough life. She ran away from an abusive home at fifteen and became a street kid. But she had ambition. She got her GED and a full-time job, then applied for college. She also managed to get custody of her younger brother after the family finally splintered. He still lives with her. She got married a few weeks ago to a great guy." He shook his head.

"She's a real tribute to the power of perseverance."

Boy, had she read the receptionist wrong. You'd think after her experience with Jack she'd have learned that appearances could be deceiving—in either direction.

"Are you finished?" Cal indicated the pizza box, where two pieces remained.

"Yes."

He closed the lid. Checked his watch. Hesitated. Some odd—but pleasant—vibes wafted her way, sending a tiny trill down her spine.

"Since you brought the dinner, can I treat you to dessert? There's a great ice cream place by the old train station. It's only a short walk." He rose and began gathering up the trash, avoiding her eyes. As if he was embarrassed by his suggestion. "But given your early start, I understand if you want to call it a day."

Was he having second thoughts about the invitation already? Trying to talk her out of accepting?

She waffled. Having ice cream with the handsome PI who was doing pro bono work for her probably wasn't wise. Theirs was a business relationship, nothing more.

But then she remembered the sound advice Cal had given her earlier.

Trust your instincts.

So she did.

"Thanks. I'd like that."

Trash in hand, he sent her a tentative smile. "Okay. Let me get rid of this stuff."

A moment later he disappeared out the door.

Leaving her to wonder why a man who came across as decisive in every other way seemed uncertain about an impromptu little outing like this.

⇒ 7 ⇐

Cal slipped his wallet back in his pocket and gestured to a bench a dozen yards down the street from the ice cream stand. "We're lucky. This place is usually packed."

Moira led the way, and he followed—still unsure if he should have extended the evening. She'd given him enough information to take the investigation to the next level. It might have been wiser to call it a night and go home.

Yet as he watched her tip her head to get a better angle on her double scoop of mint chocolate chip ice cream, he couldn't conjure up one iota of regret. Sharing dessert with a beautiful, intelligent woman was far better than spending yet another evening alone.

"This is great stuff." She sat carefully, balancing her cone as the bench shifted under their weight. "However, I'm not certain I should thank you for introducing me to temptation. I see many more trips here in my future, and my hips will pay the price."

He gave her trim figure a discreet scan. "Hard to believe."

"Hold that thought. So do you live close by?"

Her casual question brought to mind far less casual subjects.

"Glendale." He took a bite of his rocky road ice cream. When would he ever manage to get through just one day without being reminded of things he'd rather forget? "Not quite walking distance, but I could jog it on a good day."

"You jog?"

He latched on to the new topic. "Three times a week. How about you?"

"No. Nothing that ambitious." She paused to wipe an errant chocolate flake off the corner of her mouth. "I do walk with a friend two or three times a week, though. So do you have one of those century houses that are all over this area?"

His cone cracked as he involuntarily tightened his grip. He grabbed for the top with his free hand, supporting it as it collapsed.

"Whoops! Let me get you a paper cup. Hang on."

Before he could respond, Moira jumped to her feet and took off for the stand with her long-legged stride, smiling and offering some comment he couldn't hear as she bypassed the line that had formed. She was back in less than a minute, brandishing the cup.

He dumped his ice cream into it. She stuck a spoon in the top, then handed him some napkins she'd tucked into her pocket.

"Close call." She retook her seat and examined her own waffle cone as he wiped the sticky residue from the melting ice cream off his fingers. "They must not be making these as sturdy as they used to. Okay, where were we? Oh . . . I'd asked about your house."

So much for any hope that the ice cream incident might have distracted her.

He finished cleaning off his fingers, wadded up the napkins, and picked up his spoon. "It's a small older home, but not in the century category. Most of those are in Webster and Kirkwood."

"Have you lived there long?"

His throat constricted, and he swallowed. "Seven years. My wife and I bought it when we got married."

"Oh."

Her sudden lapse into silence told him his attempt at a conversational tone had failed. As he was fast learning, Moira had a keen aptitude for picking up nuances.

"You know, there's one thing I forgot to mention in this whole weird story about vanishing people."

Her change of subject was telling as well. The lady also had a well-developed sense of empathy —and consideration.

"What's that?" He took a bite of his salvaged ice cream cone.

"The Good Samaritan guy said there was broken glass on my seat. And I felt it digging into my thigh. Now here's the weird part. Other than the taillight, the repair shop didn't find any broken glass. But I had a bruise in the exact spot where I felt something sharp."

If she was trying to take his mind off their previous topic, she'd succeeded.

"Any other bruises?"

"No. Except for my forehead. Mainly I had sore muscles. And the bruise wasn't big. Quarter size, at most."

He took another spoon of ice cream as he mulled that over. "How much glass was there?"

"I don't know. The man who stopped thought he saw blood on the passenger seat, and I twisted sideways to check it out. That's when I felt the glass. I think I said ow, and he had me hold still while he brushed it off the seat. Except . . . there wasn't any glass."

"And not long after that you lost consciousness. For an hour. From a mild concussion."

She let a beat of silence pass. "What are you suggesting?"

"Maybe he injected you with some kind of knockout drug."

Her eyes widened. "And I thought the ring connection was a stretch."

He leaned forward, the explanation feeling more credible by the second. "It never did make sense to me that you'd be unconscious for so long. But if you were drugged? Absolutely. And getting you out of the picture could let him finish whatever you stumbled across."

Her fingers clenched around her napkin. "You're thinking he wasn't a passing motorist at all. That he was with the woman I saw."

"Were there many other cars on that road?"

"I only saw one. It wasn't the kind of night people would be out driving unless they had no choice." A glob of melted ice cream snaked down her cone, onto her hand. She didn't seem to notice.

He reached over and wiped it away.

She didn't seem to notice that, either.

"And who better to have access to a powerful knockout drug than a medical professional—like a doctor. But why would he have had such a thing with him?" She blinked and blew out a breath. "Are we grabbing at straws here?"

"A thorough investigator looks at every possibility. However remote."

She caught her lower lip between her teeth. "Maybe it's a good thing you're going to check his alibi."

"First thing tomorrow."

She crunched into the bottom of her cone, holding her other hand underneath. The pieces that splintered off left a mess in her palm.

"My turn to come to the rescue." This time he handed her the napkin rather than take care of the problem himself. He didn't want another blood pressure spike when their fingers brushed.

"Thanks." She cleaned herself up, then leaned back against the bench while he finished off the last of his ice cream, her expression pensive. She didn't appear to be in any hurry to leave.

Neither was he, but he couldn't come up with a legitimate excuse to prolong their outing. And if he lingered over his ice cream, it would soon melt anyway.

"So do you come here often?"

At her question, he scraped up the last bite of his collapsed cone with the plastic spoon. "More now than when . . . than in the past. I like ice cream." He didn't mention that Lindsey hadn't, but Moira nevertheless seemed to follow the direction of his thoughts.

She shifted toward him on the bench, her eyes soft with sympathy. "You know, you took me off guard in the coffee shop that day when you told me you'd lost your wife, and I don't think I responded adequately. But I want you to know I'm very, very sorry. Was it . . . an illness?"

He almost wished it had been. That might have been easier to accept.

"No. She was killed by a hit-and-run driver while she was taking her daily walk, two years after we got married. She was twenty-eight."

Shock parted Moira's lips. "Oh, Cal. I'm so sorry. Was the driver caught?"

"No." But he knew who'd arranged it. Had always known.

That, however, was a story for another night. Maybe.

"It's a terrible thing to lose someone you love."

At her soft words, tinged with sadness, he looked over at her—just in time to catch a quick flash of pain in her green irises. Curious. Their preliminary background check on her hadn't revealed a spouse or ex-spouse. And in light of her comments about her faith at their first meeting, he doubted she'd have been involved in a live-in relationship.

But he sniffed a failed romance here.

That was none of his business, of course. If he didn't want her venturing into his private territory, how could he expect her to welcome probing queries from him?

Yet he was curious enough to make a cautious foray.

"You sound as if you're speaking from personal experience." He left it at that. If she blew him off, he wouldn't push.

Silence stretched between them, broken only by a mournful whistle in the distance, along with a faint rumble from the nearby tracks that signaled the approach of a train.

She wasn't going to respond.

But as he searched for some other topic to introduce, she suddenly moistened her lips and focused on scrubbing a smear of chocolate off the back of her hand.

"I am. No one died, but I did lose a fiancé to another woman. A year ago." She gave a small, mirthless laugh. "Isn't it funny how someone can be smart and intuitive on the job yet wear blinders in her personal life?"

Instead of answering what he assumed was a rhetorical question, he posed a question of his own. "What happened—if you don't mind me asking?"

She shrugged. "It was the classic story. He was cheating right under my nose. I might not have found out until too late if I hadn't returned early from a visit with my dad and decided to surprise him. When I showed up at his apartment with Chinese takeout and fortune cookies, his neighbor answered. Based on what she was wearing—or I should say, not wearing—it was obvious she wasn't there to borrow a cup of sugar. At least not in the literal sense." Her mouth flexed into a mirthless smile. "Guess what my fortune cookie said? 'Beware of false hope.' Here's the irony. Her name was Hope."

As the rumble of the train grew louder, Cal had just one thought.

What kind of idiot would cheat on a woman like Moira and risk losing her?

"I'm sorry." He had to stifle an impulse to twine his fingers with hers. "Were you together long?"

"Two years. He was the assistant youth director at my church, and the congregation loved him. Everyone considered him a fine role model for the teens. No one ever suspected the values he professed were a sham—including me. In hindsight, I don't even know why he proposed, unless he figured marriage would give him an added aura of respectability. Maybe position him for the director job, since his boss was getting ready to retire."

The train appeared in the distance, and she watched it approach. "I suppose my experience with him is one of the reasons I'm not yet convinced Blaine isn't my man. People aren't always what they seem. Including your receptionist."

"True." He raised his voice slightly to be heard above the growing rumble. "And if it's any consolation, time does take the edge off loss."

The train thundered by, and she shot him an assessing look. As if she wasn't sure whether to believe his reassurance.

Truth be told, he wasn't certain, either. Thinking about Lindsey still left an acute ache in his heart. Or it had, until recently. For whatever reason, the pain had been diminishing in tiny increments since Moira had walked into his life.

Perhaps it wasn't time that was the great consoler, after all.

Pushing that disconcerting thought aside, he gathered up their trash and walked to the litter receptacle to deposit it while the freight train continued past the station. Only when the caboose at last clickety-clacked into the distance and quiet once more descended did he turn toward Moira to speak.

But she beat him to it.

"For the record, I'm over Jack." She regarded him, her gaze steady, letting that statement sink in before she continued. "I'll admit he left me a little gun-shy about romance, but once the hurt and humiliation faded, I was more angry than anything else. At this point, I'm just grateful I didn't end up married to him."

Was that a subtle hint? An invitation? An "I'm available" message? Or simply a wrap-up statement? An "I'm okay, everything's copasetic, don't worry about me" assurance?

He had no idea. He'd been out of the dating game so long his signal-reading skills were rusty. Nor did he have a clue how to respond.

When he remained silent, she broke eye contact and glanced at her watch. "Should we start back? It's almost 8:00."

Was it? He checked his own watch. Where had the past couple of hours gone?

"I guess it is getting late. Shall we?" He gestured down the street.

She fell in beside him as they strolled back

toward his office, confining her comments to the weather and the spring flowers.

The trek was much too short to suit him.

When they stopped beside her car in front of his office, she fished her keys out of her purse and hit the power locks. "Thanks for the ice cream—and for continuing to pursue a case that still has a high chance of going nowhere."

As she stood before him, the soft glow of the setting sun bathing her face in golden light, Cal's heart skipped a beat. Dev was right; Moira was hot. But that term didn't come close to capturing her true beauty, nor her depth.

"What's wrong?" She gave him an uncertain look.

He shoved his hands in his pockets and coaxed up the corners of his lips. "I think I'm fighting a sugar rush from all that ice cream."

"Oh. Well, as far as I'm concerned, it was worth it." She hesitated, one hand resting on the top of the door, the other gripping the strap of her purse. "I had a nice time tonight."

"I did too." Better than he should have, based on the niggle of guilt in his conscience. What would Lindsey think?

She gave him a melancholy smile, as if she'd sensed—and understood—his conflict. "It was just an ice cream, Cal. No harm done." She tossed her purse onto the passenger seat. "I hope my candor won't embarrass you—but your wife was a lucky woman."

He shook his head. "No. I was the lucky one." His voice roughened on the last word, and he cleared his throat.

She didn't respond in words. Instead, she reached out to him, her fingers gentle on his arm, the warmth of her hand seeping through the cotton of his shirt—and into his heart.

Then, still silent, she slipped into her car. He shut the door and retreated to the sidewalk. Only after her taillights disappeared did he slowly circle the building toward the back parking lot.

So much for a simple, innocent little outing to the ice cream stand. After his cautious query, Moira had shared far more than he'd expected about her painful past, baring her heart and trusting him with her secrets.

Could he do the same with her? Could he dig deep and tell her about what had happened to Lindsey? Acknowledge his culpability? Hope she could forgive him as he'd never been able to forgive himself?

Funny. He'd never wanted to talk about his past with anyone. Sure, Dev and Connor knew the basics. They also knew his suspicions, and had worked as hard as he had to prove them. All to no avail.

Not that it mattered anymore. The responsible party was gone. It was time to move on personally, as he had professionally—if only he could get past the guilt and sorrow and pain that plagued his soul and was known but to him and God.

He slid behind the wheel of the van and fitted his key in the ignition. Maybe talking with Moira would help. He had a feeling she'd be sympathetic, if not empathetic. And putting his doubts and remorse into words might help diminish them.

He'd have to give that some serious thought soon.

But first, he had an alibi to check.

His hands were shaking.

Ken Blaine stared at his trembling fingers, always so steady and sure in the operating room. At least he was still able to focus while working. To put his problems out of his mind. But he didn't know how much longer he could maintain that kind of control.

All because of her.

He crossed to the wet bar in his den and examined the display of liquor in crystal decanters. Any of them would do. Scotch. Gin. Vodka. Brandy. He hardly knew one from the other, anyway. He left it to his guests to help themselves at parties. Drink had never been his vice. Surgery and alcohol didn't mix, as his father had often said.

And his father had always been right.

After working the top off the decanter of brandy, he reached for a Waterford tumbler from the shelf above, poured a generous serving, and swirled the reddish-brown liquid in the glass.

It was the color of dried blood.

Perhaps brandy hadn't been the best choice after all.

"Ken?"

At his wife's summons from behind, his hand jerked. The brandy sloshed, and he grasped the glass with both hands. The last thing he needed was a bloodlike stain on the off-white carpet. The blemish might fade, but they'd never be able to remove it completely.

When he turned, he found Ellen on the threshold. Her gaze shifted from the glass in his hand to the open decanter on the bar, surprise flickering in her irises.

He clamped his lips together and tightened his grip on the glass. "Did you need something?"

She blinked, and her usual expressionless mask slipped into place. "Your exchange called. They couldn't reach you on your cell."

Frowning, he pulled his phone off his belt. No wonder. The battery was dead.

That was a first.

And yet one more example of his growing distraction.

"Did you get a number?"

She held out a slip of paper but remained on the threshold.

He moved toward her and took it from her fingers. "Thanks."

As he read the name and number, the silence was broken by the rattle of the ice in his glass.

His hand was still shaking.

Ellen's expression didn't change, but she slanted another look at his drink.

Heat surged on his cheeks, and he shot her an annoyed glance. "Did you need anything else?"

She stood there for a long moment. Her features remained impassive, but some indefinable emotion in the depths of her eyes registered at the fringe of his awareness. He'd seen it before, on the few occasions he'd paid any attention to her in the past couple of years. Was it . . . longing? Sadness? Disappointment?

But who had time for riddles? He had more important things to worry about than his wife's enigmatic emotions.

She turned away. "No. I don't need anything else."

As she walked down the hall, he shut the door and forgot about her.

Cradling his drink, he circled his desk and set the glass on the blotter that protected the mahogany surface. Then he sank into his chair.

What a day.

For twelve hours, he'd watched Moira Harrison watch him. He'd dazzled her with his surgical skill. Impressed her with his empathy for patients.

Fed her the information he wanted her to have. He'd done everything possible to eradicate her suspicion.

But as they'd parted, he'd still seen questions in her eyes.

Thanks to a stupid ring he should have taken off before the interview.

A ring that no longer meant anything, anyway.

He took a long swallow of the brandy, grimacing as it burned a path down his throat.

What was he supposed to do now?

In the corner, the steady tick-tock of the grandfather clock picked at his frayed nerves. Why had he never noticed that annoying background noise before?

He took another drink. This one went down easier.

Leaning back in his chair, he forced himself to analyze the situation logically, as his father had taught him.

The nosy reporter might have her suspicions, but what could she prove? He'd been careful. Covered his tracks. Everything had gone smoothly, except for that one glitch.

He sighed and took another sip, letting the warmth spread through his chest. Who could have known mild-mannered Olivia would go ballistic?

But he'd taken care of that too, despite the inopportune appearance of Moira Harrison. So why do anything? Why not wait and see? No way would the police pay any attention to the reporter, on the remote chance she'd take her suspicions to them. The eminent Dr. Blaine, humanitarian of the year, deserting an injured woman on an obscure country road when he could prove he'd been at a civic fund-raiser that night? They might even laugh at her.

He swallowed the last of his drink, letting the alcohol chase away the vestiges of tension in his shoulders as a smile played at the corners of his mouth. The situation might not be as bad as he'd feared. All of this could blow over.

After a few more minutes, he rose and braced himself on the edge of the desk, giving the room a chance to settle. Then he crossed the plush carpet to deposit his glass on the bar. Natalie would take care of it when she came to clean the house tomorrow.

Once more he settled behind his desk and picked up the slip of paper Ellen had handed him. The Owens baby had gone home yesterday, but the mother was a basket case. No doubt she simply needed some hand-holding, which he was happy to provide. That's what doctors did. Comfort, cure, relieve suffering. His father's mantra had become his own.

As he tapped in the number, he took a deep breath and straightened his shoulders. He was Dr. Kenneth Blaine, respected surgeon, benefactor to the children of Guatemala, and a shining example of Christian charity in action.

And he would let no one—especially a concussed woman lost on a country road—undermine the legacy he'd created.

⇒· 8 ·⇐

"You want the goods on his wife, his father, and his charitable organization. Check. I'll get right on it." As Nikki rose from her seat across Cal's desk, Dev swerved into the office.

"Ah, Nikki, me darlin' lass. Would ye have a wee bit o' time to do a little more filing today?"

She rolled her eyes. "Don't try that blarney on me, James Devlin. Keep it for those airheads you date. Maybe *they'll* fall for it. I have more important things to do." She gestured toward her tablet.

He shot her a look of feigned indignation. "Are you impugning the intelligence of the women with whom I choose to socialize?"

"You mean like that nuclear physicist you brought to the company Christmas party? The one who thought computer forensics was some kind of new video game?"

"Very funny. But the filing still needs to be done."

"I'll do it later today. Or Monday."

"Yeah, yeah. I'll believe it when I see it."

He disappeared down the hall, toward the small kitchenette in the back.

Cal leaned forward. "Look, Nikki, this is pro bono stuff. If you need to get to Dev's filing, I can handle some of the background work."

She waved his comment aside. "I'll take care of Dev sometime today, but I'd rather start with your case. It's a lot more interesting."

With that, she retreated to the hall and went the opposite direction Dev had taken.

Half a minute later, Connor poked his head in the door. "I just read your email. Since when do you have an interest in opera?"

"I don't. But I need to get my hands on—"

"Hey . . . what's this all about?" Dev shouldered past Connor and invaded his office, pizza box in hand. "Did we miss a party?"

Cal stifled a groan. He'd meant to toss the incriminating evidence into the dumpster out back before he left last night. And he would have, if he hadn't been distracted by a certain reporter.

"No party. A working session. Moira stopped by to brief me on her day with the doctor. That's why I asked you about contact information for Opera Theatre." He directed the latter comment to Connor. "Are you still on friendly terms with that woman you dated who volunteered with the group?"

"Yeah. I heard she's engaged now, but I have her number."

"Any chance she could get me a guest list and a seating chart for a fund-raiser?"

"I can ask. Why?"

"Dr. Blaine claims he was at an Opera Theatre event the Friday night Moira had the accident. I need to check it out. If you guys have a few minutes, I can brief you on the latest."

"I'm in." Connor dropped into one of the chairs across from Cal's desk.

"Me too." Dev claimed the other. Still holding the pizza box he'd found on the counter.

Cal gave them a condensed version of last night's discussion.

"Your theory about her being drugged is . . . creative." Connor sent him a skeptical look.

"How else would you explain the nonexistent glass, the bruise, and her lengthy stretch of unconsciousness?"

"I kind of like that premise." Dev seemed to have forgotten about the pizza box. Good. "I wonder what he would have used? Morphine, maybe. It would take a few minutes to start working, which fits with her story. And an intramuscular injection would hurt, which also fits."

Cal considered him. "Is that your undercover ATF experience speaking?"

"Yeah. I learned a few things." A shadow crossed

his eyes. "More than I wanted to know, actually."

So his partner had secrets too. No surprise there. Cal suspected they all did. Despite their solid friendship, they didn't share everything—and they respected each other's boundaries.

"I think you're both grasping at straws, but I'll call my contact and see if I can get what you need." Connor rose.

Dev stood too, and tapped the pizza box. "There were two perfectly good pieces inside, you know."

"Yeah. I forgot to put them in the refrigerator."

"Preoccupied?" Dev sent a pointed glance toward Moira's case file.

Cal ignored that comment and spoke to Connor. "If your source doesn't work out, let me know and I'll come up with another angle."

"You got it."

As Connor exited, Cal steered Dev's train of thought in a different direction. "By the way, Nikki told me she should be able to get to your filing later today."

His face lit up. "No kidding? That's encouraging. Stuff's starting to spill onto the floor again."

"You could always tackle it yourself."

"Nah." He juggled the box in his hand as he exited but stopped in the hall to throw one final comment over his shoulder. "Invite me to the party next time, okay?"

Cal watched his partner disappear, then swung

toward his computer. Invite a guy who thought Moira was hot?

Not a chance.

"That was fast." Cal looked over the faxed list of Opera Theatre gala guests, grouped by tables, that Connor handed him.

"Here's a bonus. The agenda for the evening." Connor set another sheet of paper on his desk.

"You and your ex must have parted on good terms."

"It was all very friendly. We just discovered we had nothing in common."

"Verdi and Puccini versus U2?" Cal's lips flexed. "Yeah, I can see how that might be an obstacle to romance." He lifted the sheets of paper. "I owe you."

"Not a problem. Keep me in the loop. I'm beginning to get curious about this one myself. The doctor's there, by the way. Table 16."

Cal checked it out. Sure enough, Blaine's name was on the list.

But had he actually shown?

"I'll dig a little deeper."

"I figured you would." With a lift of his hand, Connor disappeared out the door.

Cal was already focused on the eight people at Table 16. Three couples, the doctor, and a woman. Were any of the doctor's tablemates the neighbor he'd referenced?

He did a quick search of the online phone directory, typing in the last names for the three couples. One number was unlisted. The other two didn't live on the doctor's street. Perfect. He didn't want the neighbor mentioning his call and possibly arousing suspicion. If the doctor had something to hide, his antennas would be up.

Choosing one of the two couples at random, he picked up his phone, pushed *67 to bypass caller ID, then tapped in the number and settled back in his chair. If he was lucky, someone would answer at one of the numbers. He needed a live person, not voice mail.

He hit pay dirt with the second number.

"Mrs. Williams?"

"Yes."

"Sorry to bother you at home." Sincere, apologetic, friendly. Just the right tone. "This is Bill Colbert. I'm trying to track down the owner of a Montblanc pen that was found near Table 16 at the Opera Theatre gala on April 15. We thought someone would eventually call and claim it, but no one has. I wondered if you or your husband might have dropped it?"

"No. Neither of us used a pen that evening."

"Perhaps someone else at your table did?" He looked again at the seating list. "I believe the Russells were seated with you, and a Dr. Blaine?"

"I don't recall Genevieve or Ed doing any

writing at the table, and I'm afraid I didn't see much of the doctor. We'd no more than said hello when he excused himself to take a call, just as the salads were being served. He never did return, poor man. A doctor's life isn't his own, is it? You have to be so dedicated to pursue that profession. It's possible he jotted some notes down during the call. You might want to check with him."

Blaine had disappeared early in the evening. No later than—Cal skimmed the agenda—7:05 or 7:10, if dinner had started on schedule at 7:00.

He set the agenda aside. "I'll do that. You've been very helpful."

"Well, I do hope you find the owner. And please tell your people the gala was lovely. I'm so looking forward to the season opening."

"I hope you enjoy it. Thank you for your support."

He set the phone back in its cradle, rocked back in his chair, and rolled his pen between his fingers.

Assuming Blaine had left the gala at the mid-county restaurant by 7:15 and jumped on the highway, he could easily have made it to Moira's location in time to be her vanishing Good Samaritan, despite the rainstorm. He would even have had time to make a small detour.

So much for his alibi.

Dev tapped on his office door. "Don't forget Mitchell is coming in this morning."

Right. The defense attorney wanted to discuss some witnesses he needed them to locate so subpoenas could be served. The meeting was on his calendar—which he hadn't bothered to check when he'd come in.

"Thanks for the reminder. By the way, Blaine's alibi just went south."

"Yeah?" Dev propped a shoulder against the door. "So what's next?"

"I'll see what Nikki turns up on the wife, the father, and the doctor's charitable organization. I'm also considering a trash cover."

Dev grimaced. "Messy job."

"But often productive. You interested in pitching in?"

"When?"

"I'll let you know after I find out the pickup schedule for his neighborhood."

"Going through people's trash isn't my favorite part of being a PI."

"I might be able to get Moira to help me sort through it if you help me collect it." Not a bad idea, actually. He'd much rather spend time with her than Dev. "She's got an investigative eye. I doubt she'd miss anything."

"Excellent plan, but don't expect it to win you any points with the lady. Count me in for the retrieval." He checked his watch. "See you in the conference room in ten."

As Dev exited, Cal swiveled back to his

computer to answer a few emails before the meeting. And by the time it was over, maybe Nikki would have some more information for him on Blaine.

"So how goes it with the case of the vanishing duo?" Linda paused beside Moira's desk in the newsroom, juggling a soda in one hand and a bulging file in the other. "I've been meaning to check in with you since I had to cancel out on our last walk, but things have been nuts."

"Hot story?"

"Yeah." She hefted the file. "Cole Taylor, the St. Louis County detective who gave me your PI's name, and his partner just busted a cold case that's been baffling the bureau for a year and a half. I've been printing out a bunch of the earlier articles and gathering police reports. Those two guys are amazing." She settled a hip on the edge of the desk. "And speaking of amazing guys . . . I only have five minutes, but give me the low-down on what your stalwart PI turned up."

"Nothing new to report. Blaine offered an alibi yesterday for the night of my accident, and Cal's checking it out as we speak."

Linda arched an eyebrow. "It's Cal now, is it?"

"We've been talking a lot. No one's formal these days." Moira picked up her can of soda and took a swig, hoping the chilly liquid would cool her cheeks.

"How informal have you two gotten?"

She set the can down, suddenly regretting she'd told Linda that Cal was a widower. "He's not interested in romance. His wife might be gone, but he's still in love with her."

"How do you know?"

Because he was completely unreceptive to my not-so-subtle overtures.

And what had that been all about, anyway? That wasn't her usual style.

Moira shrugged. "I can see it in his eyes when he talks about her."

"I don't know." Linda studied her. "You might be wrong on this one. It could be he just doesn't mix business and pleasure."

An ember of hope ignited—but she quashed it at once. She wasn't going to let herself get carried away. She'd already embarrassed herself with him once.

"I don't think so. Besides, I'd rather focus on getting this mystery solved before I dive back into romance."

"Hmm." Linda stood and shifted the folder in her arms. "You want my advice? Sometimes men need a little prodding. Don't be afraid to let him know you're interested."

"How do you know I am?"

Linda lifted her own can of soda in salute, and parroted her own words back to her. "I can see it in your eyes when you talk about him. I'll check in soon for another update."

As her friend walked away, Moira propped her elbow on her desk and planted her chin in her palm. If her interest was that obvious, she needed to tone it down. Especially around Cal. In the future, she'd be polite, pleasant, grateful, and businesslike. Nothing more.

And after this was all over, she'd walk away and leave the next move to him.

With a wish and a prayer that there *was* a next move.

When Cal returned to his desk after the meeting with the defense attorney, three file folders labeled Ellen Blaine, Dr. Alan Blaine, and Let the Children Come, Inc., were waiting for him.

One day soon he'd have to talk with the guys about another raise for Nikki. Speed, accuracy, and dependability were qualities worth rewarding.

He started with Ellen's file, the thinnest of the group. It contained only a cover fact sheet and some attached clippings. He did a quick scan. Age fifty-four. Born Ellen Montgomery in Indianapolis. Married Kenneth Blaine in her hometown twenty-eight years ago. St. Louis resident since her marriage, at two different addresses. Active in the St. Louis Herb Society and a volunteer at the Missouri Botanical Garden.

The attached backup material indicated Nikki had done a search of several local papers' archives and run Ellen through the tracersinfo website. There was nothing in the woman's background to arouse suspicions. Not even a traffic citation.

He moved on to the doctor's father. Alan Blaine's cover sheet was a bit longer. All the same basic information, plus a list of awards and honors. He'd died at age fifty-six of complications from amyotrophic lateral sclerosis. Lou Gehrig's disease.

Not a pretty way to go.

Nikki had found some old clippings about him too, and done a propriety database search as well. There was nothing to raise eyebrows in any of that material, either.

The file on Let the Children Come was thicker, and as he flipped it open Nikki stuck her head in the door.

"The trash pickups in the doctor's neighborhood are on Monday and Thursday. Sorry I couldn't come up with more on the wife and father." She inclined her head toward the files in front of him. "They seem squeaky clean."

"There might not be any more to come up with." Cal indicated the Let the Children Come folder. "Anything stand out in here?"

"I didn't have a chance to read through it. Dev corralled me about the files—and sweetened the deal with the promise of another latte."

The corner of Cal's mouth ticked up. "Isn't bribery illegal?"

"Maybe. But it worked. Seriously, if you need me to do any more digging, yell. I wouldn't mind being rescued from that disaster area he calls an office."

"I'll keep that in mind."

As she disappeared, he focused on the file. Two pages in, he opened his pencil drawer and pulled out his highlighter.

This one was a lot more interesting.

Ellen Blaine paused at the door to the bedroom she'd once shared with her husband. As usual, it was fastidiously uncluttered. And, as usual, Ken had made the bed, the comforter and pillows arranged with military precision—even though Natalie would have to unmake it again to change the sheets.

She looked away from the bed as she walked toward the closet, stifling a vague sense of regret . . . all that remained of the aching despair that had consumed her five years ago as Ken began slipping away. Her marriage was what it was, and nothing was going to change. The days were long gone when he'd spent more time tangling up the sheets than straightening them. When love had taken precedence over other obligations. When the problems of patients had been important but kept in perspective and left at the office. When children in a far-off country hadn't consumed every last drop of her husband's energy and attention.

A twinge of guilt tweaked her conscience as that last thought flashed through her mind. How selfish was that? Those poor children in Guatemala needed all the help they could get. She should be lauding Ken for doing such commendable work, just as the governor had.

But he got plenty of attention already from people who mattered. Who told him how important he was and praised his benevolence and fed his ego. He didn't need her accolades.

Or her love.

She'd finally accepted that a year ago.

Stepping into the closet, she looked around. As usual, Ken had lined up his dirty shirts at one end, on hangers. She shook her head. Nobody hung up dirty shirts—including Ken, until two years ago. He'd introduced the odd practice about the time she'd begun sleeping in the guest room.

The hangers rattled in a discordant jangle as she began pulling off the shirts. The first night she'd slept alone, she'd given some lame excuse she'd long ago forgotten, hoping the gesture would send a wake-up call.

It hadn't worked.

One night had stretched to two. Then three. Then a week. A month.

She'd never returned.

Nor had he asked her to.

Last shirt in hand, she bunched them into a wad in her arms. Natalie would take care of this chore if she asked, but gathering up his shirts each week had been a ritual for all twenty-eight years of their marriage. It was hard to break long-entrenched habits.

Harder still to walk away from a comfortable life that met all her material needs, if not her emotional ones.

As she turned, one of the shirts slipped from her grasp and she bent to pick it up. The gleam of black patent leather caught her eye, and she leaned farther down. Why was one of Ken's tuxedo shoes on the floor, in the back, rather than on its usual shelf beside its mate?

Bundling the shirts into the crook of her left arm, she dropped to one knee, reached back for the shoe, and pulled it into the light.

What in the world . . . ?

Long, deep scratches marred the shiny leather on one side, and bits of dried mud were wedged into the area where the upper joined the sole.

She stared at the damaged shoe. When had he last worn it? The Opera Theatre gala, perhaps? The one he'd committed to at the last minute and attended alone? It had been raining that night, which might account for the mud. But the scratches?

"Mrs. Blaine? I am here."

As the housekeeper's voice floated up from the first floor, she stood, shoe in hand.

"I'll be with you in a minute, Natalie."

Weighing the dress shoe in her hand, she debated what to do with it. Ken had to know it was damaged. So why hadn't he had it repaired or replaced, in his usual fix-the-problem-immediately style?

Then again, perhaps he had his reasons for doing nothing. Who knew these days? She'd long ago stopped trying to read him. Better to leave the shoe in a place where he could see it and be reminded, in case he'd forgotten about the damage.

She set the shoe in a visible spot on the floor of the closet, closed the door, and left the bedroom without a backward look.

Her feature story for next weekend's edition wasn't coming together.

Moira huffed out a breath and rewrote the first sentence—again. Moved a quote near the end closer to the beginning. Fiddled with the wording in the conclusion.

It shouldn't be this hard to write an upbeat, feel-good article about a community garden.

Unless you weren't feeling all that upbeat—and it happened to be Friday the thirteenth. Not that she was superstitious.

But the piece was due by 5:00. Less than two hours away.

She had to focus.

Thirty seconds later, as the strains of "Für Elise"

wafted from her purse, she dug around for her cell and pressed the talk button without glancing at the digital display. The last thing she needed with a recalcitrant story and an impending deadline was interruptions. "Harrison."

"Moira? It's Cal."

All thoughts of her deadline fled. "Hi."

"Did I catch you at a bad time?"

Never.

"No, not at all."

"I've got some news. Blaine's alibi fell apart."

Her heart stuttered.

Fingers gripped around the phone, she listened as he gave her a briefing on his phone call to the gala guest, processing the information as he spoke. "So he had time to get to my location by 8:30, which is about when the man appeared."

"That's my conclusion. I also had Nikki run some background on his wife and father. Nothing of special interest, except the data did verify his father died young, of Lou Gehrig's disease. But I want to follow up on a few things with his 501c3 organization. Dev and I are also going to raid Blaine's trash on Monday night, and I'm planning to go through it Tuesday after work. It's amazing how much you can learn about people from what they throw away."

She wrinkled her nose. "Not a very appealing job, though. And you're not even getting paid for this."

"Believe me, I've done messier things."

She didn't doubt that, given his background. But doing a dirty chore like this gratis didn't seem right.

Frowning, she played with her mouse, watching the cursor bounce around her computer screen as she toyed with an idea. "Look, since I can't pay you, and this case has already taken up a lot of your time . . . could you use an extra pair of hands with the trash?"

A chuckle came over the line. "Believe it or not, I was going to ask if you'd be interested in helping. With your background, I doubt you'd miss anything important, and two sets of eyes will speed up the job. I didn't expect you to volunteer, though."

"I've done my share of messy stuff too."

"Yeah, I know." All levity vanished from his voice.

He was thinking about the scar on her arm. She was certain of it. But she'd put that incident behind her, and she didn't want to dwell on it again. Nor did she want him dwelling on it.

"If I pencil you in for Tuesday night, will you provide the rubber gloves and nose plugs?" She lightened her tone, hoping to tease away his serious mood.

It worked. She could hear a hint of laughter in his voice when he responded. "Count on the gloves. And wear old clothes. We'll do this in my garage. If you have a pen handy, I'll give you the address."

"Got one." She leaned across her desk and snagged it, then jotted the information as he recited it.

"If I learn anything more between now and then on Blaine's organization, I'll give you a call. Otherwise, see you Tuesday."

"I'll be there."

As Moira depressed the off button and dropped the phone back into her purse, she suddenly felt a whole lot more cheerful—despite her looming deadline. In three days she'd see Cal again. Amazing how that thought brightened her world.

Shaking her head, Moira repositioned herself in front of the computer screen. Better not to share that reaction with Linda, who'd already decided she was smitten.

Because looking forward to going through someone's trash just to spend time with a guy was about as smitten as you could get.

9

Cal adjusted his tie, picked up his small portfolio, and slid out of the Explorer he'd borrowed from Dev. As he hit the auto locks, he studied the brick structure before him. Faith Community Christian Church was just as it looked on its website—

modest in size, older but well maintained, tucked at the end of a small business district in a tree-lined residential suburb that was quiet on this Monday afternoon.

It was also the official address of Let the Children Come, as he'd discovered from the organization's most recent annual registration report on file with the Missouri Secretary of State's office. That document had included other interesting information too. The vice president of Let the Children Come—and one of its three board members—was the pastor of this church, Reverend Dennis Anderson. Blaine was both president and a board member. The organization's secretary—and final board member —was Marge Lewis, who happened to be Faith Community Christian's secretary as well, according to the church's website.

She was the reason for his visit.

Cal bypassed the main door of the church and crossed to the small annex with the discreet "church offices" sign beside the door. Hand on the knob, he checked the street in front. A white utility van sporting a carpet cleaning sign on the side was approaching the parking lot, Dev at the wheel.

Right on schedule.

As Cal opened the door and stepped inside, a woman with cropped gray hair looked up from her desk. "Good morning."

Adopting a confused expression, Cal gave her a puzzled smile. "I'm sorry to bother you, but I was looking for Let the Children Come. Did I copy the address on the website wrong?"

She smiled. "No. This is the mailing address. It's a very small organization. I'm actually the secretary, Marge Lewis. How can I help you?"

He shut the door behind him. "I saw the news coverage about Dr. Blaine's recent award and was very impressed with him and the work of his organization. I'm considering making a sizable donation, but I always check out an organization's finances before contributing. So many charities these days devote far too large a percentage of donations to fund-raising."

"Isn't that the truth? But I can assure you we spend virtually nothing on fund-raising. Dr. Blaine would rather the money go to the children."

"An admirable attitude."

"I agree. Dr. Blaine himself makes frequent and substantial contributions. In fact, up until about five years ago, he alone supported the clinic. Such a generous man." She sighed and shook her head. "But the needs grew, and the clinic grew, and now we do look for other donors. Most of them find us because of the publicity Dr. Blaine generates for the organization."

"Like me." He gave her his most winning smile.

She smiled back. "Yes. So what can I do to help convince you to contribute? Pastor Anderson is the vice president of the organization, and he'd vouch for it too. But he's not in today."

Cal already knew that, thanks to Nikki's earlier call to the office, when she'd asked for the man. And Connor's follow-up visit, on the pretense of needing directions to a nearby café, had confirmed that Marge was the sole occupant of the small office. Great teamwork like that reminded him yet again why he was glad he hadn't decided to go it alone as a PI.

He rested his portfolio on the edge of her desk. "I'd like to see a copy of your annual financial report for the past three years. I checked the website, but they weren't posted there."

"No. Our site is very simple, in keeping with our operating philosophy. Dr. Blaine funnels all the money to the clinic rather than to glitzy graphics—or fancy annual reports, like big companies have. But I'd be happy to make you copies of our IRS 990 form. It's public record anyway. Would that be sufficient?"

"Perfect."

She pushed her chair back, crossed to the file cabinet against the far wall, and riffled through the middle drawer.

"Our fiscal year ended April 30, so this is very up-to-the-minute. It's not due for weeks yet, but Dr. Blaine always likes to take care of everything immediately, and he keeps excellent records. I'll copy the three most recent reports for you. It won't take long. They're less than a dozen pages each."

As she moved to the copy machine, Cal set his portfolio on the floor beside him and pulled out his BlackBerry. "I hope I'm not taking you away from your work." While he pressed speed dial for Dev's phone, he made a pretense of checking messages.

"Not at all. Pastor Anderson won't mind a bit. The church supports the clinic financially too—with a very modest contribution, I'm afraid. We're not a wealthy congregation." She put the first report in the feeder, pushed a button, and the machine started up.

As the copies fed through, a knock sounded on the outside door.

Marge looked over her shoulder with a frown. "I don't know why people don't just come in." She bustled over to the door and opened it. "Yes?"

"I'm sorry to bother you, ma'am." Dev's deferential voice carried into the office. "But does that white Impala in the parking lot happen to be your car?"

"Yes."

Cal resisted the urge to smile. Of course it was. He'd tooled by the lot earlier and run the registrations for the two cars parked there at the time.

"Well, I was turning around in the lot and I may have clipped your bumper. I checked, and

I don't see any damage, but I'd feel better if you'd take a look."

"Oh, dear." Marge angled back to Cal. "Would you excuse me for a moment?"

"No problem. I have plenty of messages to return." Cal held up his BlackBerry.

The woman stepped out, and Dev winked at him over her head.

The instant the door shut behind them, Cal pulled a notebook out of his pocket, rose, and strode to the copy machine. As he'd suspected, Marge had set aside the Schedule B paperwork, which listed the names and addresses of major contributors. Organizations weren't obliged to share that form for donor confidentiality reasons, but the information could be helpful, depending on the direction this investigation took.

There were only three major donors for the most recent fiscal year—the doctor himself for a fifty thousand dollar contribution, an Edward Mason for three hundred and fifty thousand, and a Clara Volk for four hundred thousand.

For the prior year, there were also three benefactors—the doctor again and two others, totaling eight hundred and fifty thousand.

The same was true for the year prior to that.

He took a quick look at the total contributions line on the 990 forms. For all three years, it was just under nine hundred thousand.

Meaning the organization had essentially relied

on three major benefactors for the past three years.

And not the same ones each year, except for the doctor.

Interesting.

Cal jotted down the names and addresses of the donors, returned to his seat, and once more speed dialed Dev.

Four minutes later, Marge pushed back through the door. "Sorry about that."

"Is your car okay?" Cal sent her a solicitous glance as she moved back to the copy machine.

"Not a scratch. But I give that young man high marks for being conscientious. A lot of people would drive away even if they did do damage."

She finished running the 990s through the copy machine, stapled them together, and handed them over.

"I appreciate this." He tucked them in his portfolio and stood. "So why is the organization headquartered here, anyway?" Cal kept his inflection casual. He already knew the answer, based on the item about Blaine's recent award in the "Congregation News" part of the church's website, but her reply would give him the opening to ask a few more questions.

"Dr. Blaine is a longtime member of the church. Never misses a Sunday service, unless he's on one of his trips down to the clinic. And he's very involved in church activities too."

"Didn't I read somewhere that he participates in your outreach program for the elderly?"

"That's right. For the past five years he's made it a point to visit our nursing-home-bound members at least once a week. Sometimes more often. Not that he talks about it. The man is modesty incarnate. We could all learn from his example."

"True." Cal fished his keys from his pocket, keeping his tone casual. "Is his wife active in the church too?"

Faint furrows appeared on the woman's brow. "No. We haven't seen Ellen in quite some time. I believe she attends a different church now. Nice woman, but very private."

Marge was a font of information.

"Well, God calls us through many different doors." Cal gestured toward his portfolio. "I'll be back in touch after I review these documents."

"I hope you'll find everything satisfactory. Large contributions are our mainstay. Dr. Blaine donates a substantial sum each year, and we always seem to have another couple of generous donors. Without them, we'd be in serious trouble. The ten- and twenty-dollar gifts are appreciated, of course, but they don't buy X-ray machines or high-priced medicines."

"That's true." He extended his hand. "Thank you again for your help."

"My pleasure, Mr. . . . ?"

"Harris. Frank Harris." He gave her fingers a squeeze and released them.

"We'll look forward to hearing from you."

With a smile and a nod, Cal exited.

Knowing a lot more than when he'd entered.

Marge had confirmed Moira's research that the doctor visited the elderly, but that he kept those visits low-key. And if Blaine and his wife were no longer compatible on the faith front, perhaps they were incompatible on other fronts as well.

There were a lot of new questions, though.

Who were the large donors from the previous three years?

How were they affiliated with the doctor?

What had prompted their very large contributions?

Why had none contributed two years in a row?

As he opened his car, tossed his portfolio onto the passenger seat, and slid behind the wheel, getting those answers jumped to the top of his priority list.

Ken twisted the knob on his closet door, walked inside, and unbuttoned his shirt, stifling a yawn. It had been a long Monday. Too bad Verna Hafer had been in such a talkative mood.

But he felt for her. It was terrible to be old and alone and reliant on others to feed you and wash you and fetch you bedpans—sometimes not fast enough. The indignities were unspeakable. Offering her an understanding ear and a comforting squeeze of the hand once or twice a week was the least he could do. And she was grateful.

Tonight, she'd told him just how grateful.

As he bent down to untie his shoes, a smile curved his lips. There was no immediate need, but . . .

His smile evaporated.

Why was his scuffed tuxedo shoe barely concealed beneath the neat row of pants lined up on their hangers?

That wasn't where he'd left it.

He distinctly remembered shoving it far back, against the wall, to be dealt with when time permitted.

Had Natalie moved it while she was vacuuming on Friday?

He picked up the shoe and examined the deep scratches. There wasn't much chance it could be salvaged. It would be better to pitch the pair and buy new ones. There'd be fewer questions that way too.

As he reached for its mate on the shelf, he heard the closet door swing all the way open behind him, and he turned.

Ellen stood on the threshold. She inspected the shoe in his hands, regarding him with the same expression she'd had the night she'd found him with a drink in his study. The night he'd needed one, after letting that nosy reporter follow him around all day.

An expression that said she thought he was acting out of character.

That wasn't good.

But as long as she was the only one who thought that, it didn't matter.

Because she didn't matter. Not anymore.

Only the work mattered.

He knew Ellen resented his shift in priorities —but that was her problem. He'd created something important. Something that mattered. Something that helped other people and made the world a better, more pain-free place. The alienation of her affections was a small price to pay in the big scheme of things.

When she didn't speak, his irritation spiked. "What?"

She lifted her gaze to his eyes. "Rose called. They're having a cocktail party Friday night, and we're invited. I said I'd check with you."

He cringed. Cocktail parties were a complete waste of time, filled with too much liquor and too little meaningful conversation. But he couldn't be rude to Ted. Not after the man's kindness to him through the years. Even if that meant suffering through the inane chatter of a party or attending an Opera Theatre benefit.

"What time?"

"6:30. I told them if we came, you'd be late."

No kidding. Even if he rushed home from the office, he wouldn't get there until 7:00. Affairs like this were the biggest benefit of having Ellen around. She ran interference for him socially and was willing to join him at higher-profile events, where appearing as a couple added an extra touch of luster to his reputation.

And why shouldn't she? As long as he indulged her penchant for designer clothes, fancy restaurants, and semi-annual trips to that high-end spa in Arizona she liked, a few social engagements weren't too much to ask in exchange.

"You can go over ahead of me."

"That was my plan."

With one more glance at the shoe in his hand, she exited.

Ken blew out an annoyed breath. He should have disposed of the ruined shoe immediately, as he'd disposed of everything else. But he couldn't have come home barefoot—and he hadn't brought any backup shoes. The boots were supposed to be the only extra footwear he needed.

Running his thumb over the marred patent leather, he looked back at the closet door where Ellen had stood. It was unfortunate she'd seen it, but a scratched shoe wasn't incriminating. Never-theless, the sooner he got rid of it, the better. It was a loose end.

And he didn't like loose ends.

· · ·

Stifling a yawn, Cal sank into the chair in his office and checked his watch. In ninety minutes, Moira was scheduled to arrive at his house, and before he left he wanted to do some research on the donor names he'd copied down yesterday during his visit to Let the Children Come headquarters.

"You're still here."

At Connor's comment, he swiveled toward the door. "Yeah. Barely." He yawned again.

"Dev cut out half an hour ago. I figured you'd do the same. He said you had him up till the wee hours doing a trash cover at the doctor's house."

"Seemed like a good idea at the time. But now I have a garage filled with garbage."

The other man chuckled and leaned a shoulder against the door frame. "Been there, done that. I hear you're going to have prettier company going through it than you had collecting it, though."

Cal scowled. "Dev has a big mouth."

"No arguments on that." One side of Connor's mouth rose. "I'm heading out, too. I didn't plan to spend the whole day running all over the city tracking down a runaway teen."

"Neither did I. At least it was a quick find." He yawned again.

"Yeah. Makes you wonder how kids think, doesn't it? Putting a bus ticket on Mom and Dad's credit card wasn't the smartest move."

"Unless he wanted to be picked up, and that was his version of a distress signal."

"Possible. The parents did seem like the fast-track, job-comes-first career types. Maybe this will be a wake-up call. Convince them time and attention are more important than a new iPod or the latest app for their son's cell phone."

"We can hope." Cal massaged his neck.

"So when are you leaving?"

"In a little while. I want to check out a few of the names I got yesterday at the church."

"Okay. See you tomorrow."

As Connor left, Cal swung back to his computer. He needed to be out of here in an hour, max, but it shouldn't take long to do some quick research on six names—especially since he was trolling. Looking for who knew what? A commonality, perhaps. Some piece of information that would give him a clue as to why they had made such large, one-time donations. An aberration that would jump out at him and suggest a further avenue of investigation—or possibly a link to that suspicious Friday night.

All of which was a long shot.

Still, it was worth the effort. Worst case, he'd be no closer to answers than he'd been when he started.

Stifling yet another yawn, he got to work.

In the quiet office, without any of the usual daytime interruptions, he covered the ground a lot faster than he'd expected. In less than the hour he'd allotted, he was ready to call it a day.

Because he'd found far more than he expected.

He shut down his computer for the night, leaned back in his chair, and flexed his stiff shoulders —the price he always paid when he grew too intent on his screen and hunched forward.

Wait until Moira heard this.

≫· 10 ·≪

Moira slowed to a stop in front of a small story-and-a-half clapboard home and set her brake.

So this was where Cal had lived with his wife.

Where he still lived . . . with his memories.

Fighting back a wave of melancholy, she slid out of the car and locked it. No self-pity allowed. She had a different kind of garbage to deal with tonight.

She edged past the white van in the driveway and approached the front porch, passing between two empty stone urns that flanked the three steps. Based on the dried-up dirt, cobwebs, and rotted leaves inside, it didn't appear as if they'd hosted anything living for a long while.

Maybe for five years.

Moira ascended the steps and rang the bell.

Fifteen seconds ticked by.

She tried again.

Nothing.

"Moira!"

At the summons, she angled back toward the front of the house.

Cal waved to her from the driveway and called out, "I heard the bell from the garage."

She retraced her steps to the driveway, giving him a quick perusal en route.

Gone were the pressed slacks, crisp dress shirt, tie, and jacket he seemed to favor at the office. Today he wore decrepit jeans perforated with a few holes and a paint-splattered T-shirt sporting an Ernie's Carwash logo.

And he looked just as appealing as he did in the more polished attire.

"Into grunge today, are we?" Her attempt at a tease came out a bit breathless.

The corners of his lips lifted. "I dressed for the job." He eyed her own jeans and soft knit top. "I can see you've never done this before."

"These are the rattiest clothes I have."

"They'll be a lot rattier after we're finished." He gestured around the side of the attached garage. "Let's use the door in the back. I don't typically open the front garage door when I'm doing a trash sort."

Sixty seconds later, after she followed him around the side and entered the two-car structure, she understood why.

The floor was covered with plastic sheeting and strewn with garbage.

It didn't smell too great, either.

If Cal noticed the odor, he gave no indication as he skirted the edge of the sheeting.

"Dev and I got their regular trash and their recycle bin. I pulled out the loose paper and put it over there." He gestured to a small pile off to one side. "That mound is everything else—aluminum, glass, plastic, miscellaneous. I got rid of some of the messier items before you arrived."

Hard to believe, given the yucky stuff spread in front of her.

Hands on hips, she inspected the mini disaster area. "Where do we start?"

"My guess is the paper will yield the best information. We should be able to go through the rest quickly. Why don't we get that out of the way first?"

"You're the boss."

"Can I get you a soda before we plunge in?"

"Sure."

As he disappeared into the house, she wrinkled her nose and gave the piles of trash another scan. Good thing she liked Cal. That was the only thing palatable about this job.

The door from the house opened and he reentered, diet Sprite in hand. He'd remembered her selection from the night they'd shared a pizza at his office.

Nice.

After pulling the tab, he handed it to her. What a contrast to Jack. Not only had her ex-fiancé neglected to open her sodas, he'd also never managed to remember she preferred her lattes skim, no whip, and with a shot of caramel. Even after two years.

"Before we tackle this stuff, I do have some news."

She took a sip of her soda and gave Cal her full attention. "That sounds promising."

"It is."

As he recounted his visit to the Let the Children Come office—including the playacting he and the other Phoenix partners had done—she tipped her head and studied him.

"What?" Cal gave her one of his probing looks.

She shifted her weight and shrugged. "I know pretexting is a common PI technique—but does the . . . dishonesty . . . ever bother you?"

He leaned back against a workbench on the wall of the garage and folded his arms, his gaze steady. "Undercover law enforcement operatives use it all the time. Do you have an issue with them?"

"No. I've had occasion to talk to undercover detectives in my investigative work, and I've been totally impressed. They take a lot of personal risk in the name of justice. But this is a civilian operation."

"Also focused on justice."

Justice First.

The Phoenix motto echoed in her mind.

When she didn't respond at once, a muscle contracted in Cal's cheek. "We don't do anything illegal, Moira. We're all well-versed in the boundaries of the law. But we do use every technique available within those boundaries to get the job done and bring the bad guys to justice. When we use a pretext, we're playing a part, just like an undercover operative is—and we're doing it for an honorable purpose, just as they are. Our ploy paid off yesterday, by the way."

His voice had cooled a few degrees, and a twinge of guilt nipped at Moira's conscience even as he piqued her interest with his final comment. She hadn't intended to question the integrity of the Phoenix operation, not after Cal's willingness to take the case pro bono purely in the interest of seeking justice for the woman with the terrified eyes.

"I didn't mean to suggest you were doing anything underhanded, and I trust that you respect the law. It's more a moral than a legal issue, I guess." She smiled to mitigate any implied criticism. "I grew up with a philosophy-professor father who passed on any number of sayings from the sages. Some of them stuck. Like, 'Truth is the beginning of every good thing.' Plato."

"I have another one for you. 'Each morning

dispense justice, rescue the oppressed from the hand of the oppressor.' Jeremiah. Or I could offer this from Proverbs. 'On the way of duty I walk, along the paths of justice.' "

Her gaze flicked down to his cross-etched wedding band.

It was clearly more than jewelry.

"I'm impressed. But there are a lot of Bible verses about truth too."

He let out a slow breath, crossed his legs at the ankles, and shoved his hands into his pockets. "I've thought long and hard about the moral issue you raise, Moira. And I dealt with it long ago, during my first year as a beat cop. When you've seen the stuff I've seen, it's a lot easier to justify pushing ethics to the limit in the interest of justice." His jaw hardened. "Even then, the bad guys sometimes win."

A flash of pain ricocheted through his eyes, and Moira knew instinctively it wasn't caused by generic disgust at man's inhumanity to man, but by something a lot more personal.

He turned away to retrieve some latex gloves from the bench, the gesture sending a clear message. He didn't intend to share whatever story had prompted that reaction. And she couldn't blame him. Not after her implied criticism.

Time to make amends.

"For the record, I agree with everything you said. I just think it's an interesting moral question. I'm sorry if I came across as judgmental."

When he shifted back toward her and handed over a pair of gloves, the anguish in his features had disappeared. "I'm sorry too. I tend to get defensive about my work. Credible, competent, principled PIs have to overcome a lot of stereotypes—some of which are warranted. Like the ones that made you cautious on your first visit to our office." One side of his mouth curved up, and he held out his hand. "Truce?"

"Truce."

His brown eyes locked with hers as he gave her fingers a firm squeeze—and held her hand longer than necessary.

Or was that only wishful thinking?

She cleared her throat when he released her fingers, lowering her head to tug on the gloves. "So how did the visit yesterday pay off?"

"According to the tax filing for Let the Children Come, the organization is primarily funded by a couple of donors each year, plus Blaine. I did some checking on those other big donors for the past three years and I found an interesting coincidence." He snapped on one of his gloves. "They're all dead."

Moira stared at him, trying to make sense of that. "How did you find that out? And . . . how could they donate if they were dead?"

"People with the means to donate those kinds of amounts—we're talking several hundred thousand dollars here—aren't nobodies, so I googled the name of the first person, looking for news articles or other mentions in the press. I found an obit from the year of the donation. That prompted me to check the obit archives to see if the others were there. They were. As for how they made the donations, I'm assuming they were bequests through wills."

She wove her fingers together and frowned. "That's weird."

"There's more. The last address for all of them was a nursing home. All different ones."

Her stomach clenched. "Like the kind Blaine visits as part of his church outreach?"

"Yeah."

"Were they members of his congregation?"

"Based on what the secretary said yesterday about the church being very modest in size and wealth, my guess is no. But I plan to check that out."

She rubbed her temple as she processed this new information. "Okay. So . . . maybe he befriended other people when he was visiting members of his own congregation in the nursing homes? Maybe they were impressed with his work and decided to leave a lot of their money to his organization? He's a very charismatic man."

"That's possible. But why two a year? Doesn't that regular infusion of capital seem a little too convenient?"

A shiver snaked through her at the sinister implication of his questions. "This is creeping me out."

Cal gestured at the mess on his garage floor. "Not too creeped out to tackle this, I hope."

"No. It actually gives me more of an incentive."

He snapped on his other glove. "Why don't you start on one side and I'll start on the other? We'll work toward each other."

"What exactly are we looking for?" She followed him over to the jumbled pile.

"Anything that gives us useful insight into the doctor's life or raises a red flag of any kind."

"Okay." She took a swig of her soda, set it on a nearby shelf beside a half-empty bag of birdseed, and dived in.

They worked in silence for several minutes, until she extracted an empty bottle of brandy.

"Is this relevant?"

Cal looked over. "Find any other evidence of alcohol?"

"No."

"Me neither. Liquor doesn't appear to be one of their vices. Probably not that important."

They went back to work, exchanging occasional comments as they sorted through the mess.

"This is interesting." Cal sat back on his heels.

Moira checked out the badly scratched patent-leather shoe he'd extracted from a grocery bag. The kind guys wore with tuxes.

Her pulse quickened. "That's suspicious."

"No kidding." Cal pulled its mate out of the bag. That one was in perfect condition. "I doubt this kind of damage was done at the Opera Theatre benefit."

"Maybe he wore it again after that, and damaged it then. I mean, why would he wait this long to throw it away if he scratched it at the Opera Theatre event? That was a month ago." Moira straightened up, rubbing her lower back. "And what does all this have to do with the woman I saw on the road?"

"I don't know. Maybe we'll find some answers in the paper stuff." He riffled through the few remaining items on the ground between them, gathered them up, and tossed them into a trash can. "Let me set up a folding table and some lawn chairs. That will be easier on our backs."

Another thoughtful gesture. And more proof of the man's keen observation skills.

Five minutes later, a pile of paper between them, they took seats across from each other and plunged into the jumble that included junk mail, scribbled notes, statements, and receipts, many of the documents stained and ripped.

This time Moira grabbed the golden ring.

"I think I've got something." She held up several cash register receipts that had been torn in half. "There are a bunch of these, all credit-card purchases. Blaine must do what I do —collect them, match them against the monthly statement, and then pitch them."

"That could be a gold mine. Let's piece them together and see what we have."

He stood, picked up his chair, and circled the table to sit next to her. Close enough for their shoulders to touch whenever he leaned over to shuffle through the pile of receipts to search for a match to the half in his hand.

Focus, Moira!

"Look at this." Cal laid a receipt on the table and smoothed it out.

She peered at the hard-to-read type, some of it obscured with a brown, coffee-like stain. Super Clean, Inc.

"Is that a dry cleaner?"

"Nope. They do car detailing. And from the amount, I'd say Blaine went the whole nine yards. Check out the date."

She scanned it again.

April 16.

On the day after the Opera Theatre benefit, Blaine had paid a hefty sum to have his car cleaned to the nth degree. As if he'd driven through mud somewhere.

Like out in the country.

"This is looking more and more suspicious, isn't it?" She glanced at Cal.

"Very. Let's match up the rest of these."

She made the next find as she pieced together a receipt from Home Depot.

"I've got a purchase of some kind of boots, coveralls, and work gloves—three days before the benefit."

Cal scanned the receipt. "The doctor doesn't strike me as the type who would normally do physical labor." He put that receipt on top of the one for the car detailing.

Ten minutes later, as Moira fitted together the last receipt, nothing else overtly suspicious had emerged. But they'd already found more than she'd expected.

"What about this pattern of receipts from a place called the Woman's Exchange?" She indicated the three she'd set aside.

"I found one of those too." Cal went through his pile and extracted it. "It's one of those genteel places for ladies who lunch."

They lined up the four receipts on the table in front of them.

Moira scrutinized the information on the slips. "Same time every Friday. Must be the wife. And she must be meeting a close friend if they do this every week."

Cal leaned back, his expression speculative. "It would be interesting to hear what they talk about, don't you think?"

She considered that, then lifted her shoulder. "I

don't know. How much could they say in a public place?"

"A lot more than you might expect. It's amazing what people will discuss under the cover of conversation buzz in a roomful of people. They seem to think it gives them privacy." He aimed a deliberate look her way. "I couldn't go to a place like that without drawing way too much attention."

She knew what he was hinting. *She* could go without drawing any attention. And who knew what she might learn?

Funny. Before they'd discussed the whole pretext thing earlier in the evening, she might have balked. But he'd convinced her that serving justice trumped minor ethical dilemmas. Eavesdropping on a conversation at a restaurant wouldn't hurt anyone—and it might very well supply a critical clue in this rapidly deepening mystery.

"Okay. I'll go."

"You're sure you're comfortable with this?"

She didn't blink. "Yes."

Several seconds ticked by as he regarded her. Then, with a dip of his head, he examined the four slips again. "She pays the bill about 12:45, give or take a few minutes."

"I'll have to get there early and think of some excuse to hang around so I can get seated right after she does—and as close as possible."

"Not a problem. There's a small consignment

179

shop there. I read an article about it a few months ago. You can browse until she arrives."

"How will I know her?"

"I'll email you a link to a picture Nikki found when she was doing her initial background search. Since you'll be dining alone, you can take a small notebook and jot down any info you hear. People will think you're making a shopping list or planning a party."

"It sounds easy enough." She picked up her can of soda, but it was empty.

"Would you like another one?"

She glanced around the garage. "I think we're finished, aren't we?"

He surveyed the empty sheeting on the garage floor and the bulging trash bags. "Yeah. I guess we are." He rose and began gathering up the scraps of paper that hadn't yielded any usable information. "But after I stow all this stuff, why don't we sit on the deck for a few minutes? It's a nice night, and it's not quite 9:00 yet. Then again, I don't have to drive home. And you might have an early day tomorrow."

An invitation, with a clear out. So did he want her to stay or not?

Sometimes the man was impossible to read.

Moira stood and began folding up the chairs and table as he disposed of the paper and plastic. Maybe she was overanalyzing. He'd invited her to stay, hadn't he? Why not go with the flow? It wasn't like a date or anything. It was a soda, simple and straightforward. She was the one with romance on the mind, not him. Still . . . why pass up the opportunity to enjoy a few more minutes of his company?

She snapped the second chair shut and leaned it against the wall, next to a dusty basketball and a garden sign on a spike that said "Bloom where you are planted."

"Another soda sounds nice, thanks. As long as you let me wash my hands first."

He paused for half a heartbeat as he picked up a bulging plastic garbage bag, biceps bulging below the sleeves of his T-shirt. "That can be arranged. As long as you promise not to comment on my housekeeping."

"Trust me. I'm not one to point fingers, considering the proliferation of dust bunnies at my own place. They seem to multiply as fast as the real thing." She tore her gaze away from his muscled arms.

He hefted the bag into a large plastic garbage can, locked the lid in place, and led the way to the door on the side of the garage. After pushing it open, he stepped aside to let her enter, then joined her in the small mudroom.

"The guest bath is through the kitchen, straight down the hall on your right. I'll clean up in the utility sink in the basement and meet you by the back door."

"Sounds like a plan."

Crossing the kitchen, which was painted an interesting shade of ochre, she took a quick inventory. There were no dishes in the sink and only a mug and small plate in the dish drain. A towel hung neatly on a bar beside the sink. There wasn't an empty pizza box or fast-food container in sight. Nor did she see any evidence of dust.

She ought to invite him over to clean up her place.

As she passed the living and dining rooms, she had no more than a fleeting impression of bright spaces and clean lines and colorful prints on the walls. All uncluttered. All looking as if the space was hardly lived in.

Why?

Was Cal a better housekeeper than he'd let on? Were the demands of his job so intense that he spent little time here? Or did he choose to stay away as much as possible because the memories these walls held were too painful to endure except in small doses—but too sweet to walk away from?

Moira closed the bathroom door behind her, soaped up her hands and arms, and rinsed away the grime. Perhaps Cal would offer a few of those answers tonight.

And if not . . . she'd enjoy their conversation and then focus on her Friday trip to the Woman's Exchange—her initiation into the world of covert surveillance.

That should be an interesting experience.

As for how productive it would be . . . who knew? Worst case, she'd have a nice lunch.

But best case, she'd learn some new information that might bring them one step closer to solving the puzzle of the vanishing woman.

⇒ 11 ⇐

Cal heard the water shut off in the bathroom and took a long chug of his soda as he waited for Moira in the kitchen.

He shouldn't have asked her to stay and socialize.

Not here.

Not in the house he'd shared with Lindsey.

Not in a place where his wife was everywhere.

He scanned the space around him, so filled with her spirit.

She was in the ceramic *Family Circus* cartoon plaque, rescued from the dollar table at a flea market, that now hung on the wall beside the sink: *Yesterday's the past, tomorrow's the future, but today is a gift. That's why it's called the present.*

She was in the lopsided, handwoven potholders hanging on their usual hooks beside the stove, bought at a craft sale featuring products made by adults with Down syndrome.

She was in the ugly, squat cactus on the windowsill, the last unsold item at a garden center clearance sale, adopted after the owner assured her it would bloom soon.

He touched one of the prickly spines that kept friends and foes alike at arm's length, tempted yet again to toss it in the trash. But the comment Lindsey had always made whenever he'd suggested that echoed in his mind.

Let's give it one more chance, Cal. It will bloom when the time is right. I know it.

Six years later, Cal was still waiting for the promised profusion of color on the barren plant.

The bathroom door opened, and he took another gulp of soda, trying to wash away the lump that had formed in his throat.

"Did I hold you up?"

Pasting on a smile, he popped the tab on the second can of soda and handed it to Moira.

He needed to get her out of the house.

Fast.

"No. I just pulled these out of the fridge." He moved toward the door. "If we're lucky, the mosquitoes will lay low for once."

Releasing the security bolt with his foot, he twisted the lock, pushed open the slider . . . and tried to ignore the fresh fragrance that wafted toward him when she slipped past.

As he shut the door behind them, she strolled over to the railing, eyeing the lights over the door and at the corners of the deck that kept shadows —and troublemakers—away.

"So much for ambiance, huh?" She smiled at him, squinting in the glare as she tipped her soda can against her lips.

"I'd rather have security." He glanced around. It *was* pretty bright out here. Not the best atmosphere for relaxation. "Let me kill a couple of these."

Before she could respond, he reentered the house and flipped the switch that controlled the corner lights.

When he returned, she'd claimed one of the white plastic chairs at the round, glass-topped table in the far corner of the deck. The one that used to be protected from the sun by a colorful, striped umbrella that was stored in the basement somewhere. He hadn't spent enough time on the deck since Lindsey died to warrant searching for it.

He settled into the chair beside her.

"Better. Thank you." She smiled at him.

"No problem." He took a swig of soda and exhaled slowly. Maybe this hadn't been such a bad idea after all. The deck held fewer memories of Lindsey, and chilling for fifteen minutes with some light and easy chitchat was a nice wrap-up for a long day that had begun with a midnight trash run.

He searched for an innocuous topic. "So your dad's a philosophy professor."

"Yeah. At Mizzou."

"Is he one of those head-in-the-clouds stereotypes?" He grinned at her.

Her mouth curved, softening her lips. "Only once in a while. My brother and I still kid him about the time he went to a mall in St. Louis and forgot where he parked his car. The security people had to help him find it."

Laughter bubbled up inside him as he took another swig of soda. "You don't seem to have inherited the absentminded gene."

"Neither did my brother. He's an engineer, currently communing with the camels in Dubai. What about your family? You mentioned a sister. Any other siblings?"

"No. She's married to an attorney with the State Department in Washington. They have two children. My dad is still active-duty Air Force, stationed in Germany."

"So no family close by."

His throat constricted, and though he tried to maintain an informal tone, his response came out strained. "Not anymore."

Silence descended, except for the buzz of the cicadas.

So much for light and easy.

Cal set his soda on the dusty table. Watched a drop of condensation roll down the side. Tried without success to think of some glib remark that would brighten the suddenly heavy mood.

To his relief, Moira came to the rescue.

"This is a pleasant spot. Very peaceful. The only outdoor space I have at the condo I'm renting is a tiny patio, and the few evenings I've sat out there I've had to listen to my neighbor's twangy country western music. I much prefer the cadence of your cicadas."

The tension in his shoulders dissipated. "I hear you. One of my partners is into U2, and much as I like everything Irish, a little bit of their music goes a long way. You must have a Celtic heritage too, with a name like Moira and that reddish hair."

"Not to mention freckles, which I'm happy to report faded as I aged." She smiled and lifted her can in salute. "To everything Irish . . . in moderation."

He smiled back and clinked his can with hers.

After taking a long swallow, she set her can on the table. "Thanks again for turning out the extra lights. This is much nicer."

"I agree. The deck is like a stage when they're all on, and I haven't been comfortable in the spotlight since I tripped on my shepherd's robe in the third-grade Christmas play and lost my beard, much to the amusement of the audience."

He meant the comment as a joke.

She took it more seriously.

"I suppose that's a prudent attitude even without your theatrical mishap, based on what you said once about you and your partners having enemies from your law enforcement days." She shifted toward him. "Is that the real reason for all the security lighting?"

Not a subject he wanted to discuss.

"Partly." He picked up his can and finished off the last of the soda. "But it's always smart to take precautions. Bad things can happen when you don't."

Like Lindsey dying.

The sweet, lingering aftertaste of the cola turned bitter on his tongue, and he crushed the empty can in his fist, the metallic crumpling sound violating the gentle stillness of the night.

When he set the mangled aluminum back on the table, Moira studied it. Lifted her gaze to his.

He could read the questions in her eyes . . . and the empathy. It chipped away at the wall around his heart that allowed him to keep his feelings of loss and guilt and loneliness at bay, nudging him to share the mistakes he'd admitted to no one— not family, not friends, not his partners—with this woman he'd known less than a month.

His pulse accelerated, and he gripped the arms of his chair, tottering on the edge of a darkness even his security lighting couldn't dispel. It had taken him months to claw his way out of that abyss after Lindsey's death. How could he even consider going back to that terrible place?

"Any bad thing in particular?"

At Moira's soft question, Cal stiffened—and stalled. "Why do you ask that?"

She lifted one shoulder and traced a trail of grimy condensation to the edge of the table, where it plummeted into the shadowy void below.

"Intuition, I guess. And that." She gestured to the crushed can. "I'm picking up a lot of tension— and anger. I'm guessing there's some incident in your past that still bothers you. But I didn't mean to pry, and I certainly understand if there are things you'd rather not share. We all have our secrets." She gave him a tiny smile, then checked her watch. "It's getting late. I better head out." She reached for her empty can.

Giving in to his instincts, he grabbed her fingers. "Wait."

She froze, and their gazes locked.

Seconds ticked by, but she didn't break eye contact. Didn't change her expression. Didn't say a word.

She just waited as he struggled with his dilemma.

And it was a big one.

Should he take a risk and open his heart to this woman—or play it safe and let her walk away?

As he waffled, she suddenly cinched his decision with a gentle, encouraging, everything-will-be-all-right-because-I'm-here squeeze of his hand.

And all at once it was.

For in that instant, he knew this woman would honor his confidences . . . and listen with her heart as well as her head.

"Are you in a hurry to get home?" His question came out hoarse, and he cleared his throat.

"No."

He stroked his thumb over the back of her hand, released her fingers, and stood to walk over to the railing.

For a few seconds, he focused on the murky darkness beyond the range of the single, low-voltage light over the back door. Gathering up his courage.

Finally he turned back to her, fingers clenched around the wooden rail behind him.

"You were right. A very bad thing did happen." He swallowed and verbalized the truth that had haunted him for five long years. "Lindsey died because I didn't take adequate precautions. And because I was selfish."

Surprise widened her eyes, but it was quickly replaced with puzzlement. "I thought you said it was a hit-and-run accident?"

"It wasn't an accident." The words came out hard. Flat. Cold. The way his heart had felt since her death.

She stared at him. "Are you saying . . . someone killed her?"

"Yes."

"Why?"

"Because of a murder case I worked on that put a drug kingpin behind bars. We never found the driver, but I know Bernie Levine was calling the shots from his cell in Potosi."

Moira held on to the arms of her chair and leaned forward, her posture taut. "How can you be sure?"

Cal swallowed past the bile that rose in his throat. "The day after Lindsey died, I got an unsigned sympathy card in the mail. The postmark was Potosi. It had been mailed the day before she was killed."

He heard her gasp across the small space that separated them and steeled himself against the pain and rage and desolation that churned in his gut as he relived the moment when the implications of that message had registered.

"We worked the case hard, but we couldn't find a tangible link between Levine and her death. A few months later I left County to form Phoenix, and Dev and I picked up the investigation again. Connor pitched in too when he joined the firm later that year. But we came up just as empty. The man knew how to cover his tracks, and he didn't make many slips. It had taken us months to gather sufficient evidence to nail him on the charge that put him behind bars in the first place, and even then it was touch and go." His jaw tightened. "In the end, it didn't much matter. He died two years ago in prison of a cerebral hemorrhage."

Several beats of silence ticked by as Moira furrowed her brow. "You said all this could have been avoided if you'd taken adequate precautions, but what could you have done?"

He turned away, toward the blackness, and let out a slow breath. "Levine warned me. I was there when he was sentenced, and before they took him out he looked over at me and said three words: 'You'll be sorry.' I knew he had colleagues who wouldn't mind extracting some retribution—for the right price. So I watched my back—and Lindsey's. But I didn't watch hers long enough." His voice rasped.

A chair scuffed against the deck floor behind him, and a moment later Moira appeared at his side. She leaned a hip against the railing, facing him.

He didn't want to look at her. Didn't want to risk seeing on her face the condemnation he felt in his heart.

"Cal." Her voice was whisper soft and laced with sympathy as she touched his arm.

Squeezing the railing, he forced himself to turn his head. The light above the door caught the shimmer in her eyes and her soft, compassionate expression.

She didn't blame him for what had happened to Lindsey.

Gratitude and relief poured through him—even if it didn't change his own opinion.

"I don't believe it was your fault." She spoke as if she'd read his mind.

"You haven't heard it all."

She waited.

Cal swiveled around and leaned back against the railing, putting the darkness behind him as he shared the incriminating information he'd never had the courage to tell his partners.

"After Bernie's threat, I told Lindsey I'd like to join her on her early morning walks. That I needed more exercise, and that walking together would give us more couple time. I stuck with it for weeks, but there wasn't so much as a peep from Bernie. I began to believe the danger was past." He closed his eyes. "Bad mistake."

He sucked in a breath and opened his eyes. "A few days before she was killed, I started sleeping in and letting her go alone. I'd been working a case hard, late into the night for weeks, and I convinced myself the danger to her was minimal." He swallowed. "One morning the sound of an ambulance woke me. I knew it was her. All because I put a few extra z's above protecting my wife." He braced himself, waiting for Moira's expression to change.

It didn't.

"What a terrible burden to carry for all these years."

Pressure built behind his eyes at her whispered comment, and he blinked away the sudden sting.

He didn't deserve her kindness, even if it was a balm on his soul.

"I deserve it."

"I don't think so. You couldn't have walked with her every morning forever, not with the demands of your job. And she was probably alone—and vulnerable—at other times during the day. Much as we might want to, we can't protect the people we love every single minute."

There was truth in what she said. Yet it didn't salve his conscience.

"I've told myself that a thousand times. But I could have protected her *that* morning. And maybe if I'd shared the threat with her, she'd have been more on guard for a suspicious car."

"Why didn't you?" Moira's tone was curious, not critical.

"She'd have ended up worrying more about me than herself, and she worried plenty already. She accepted my job, but the danger always freaked her out." He shook his head, his stomach tightening into a familiar clench. "I thought I was doing her a favor by saving her that anxiety. Some favor."

Moira touched his arm again, and the warmth of her fingers seeped into his skin as the evening air cooled around them.

"You did your best. You loved your wife and tried to protect her in every way you could—emotionally and physically—and you continued to pursue justice after the system failed you by striking out on your own to search for answers. There's a lot to admire in that picture."

He wanted to weave his fingers with hers, hold on tight, and believe he deserved her kind words.

Instead, he folded his arms across his chest and faced the truth. "I'm no hero, Moira."

She lifted one shoulder. "Depends on how you define hero, I guess. In my book, a hero doesn't have to be perfect. He just has to do his best." She slid her hand down his arm to his ring finger, leaving a trail of warmth in her wake. "I know from this"—she touched his cross-etched wedding ring—"and from your familiarity with the Bible that you're a man of faith. Have you tried giving this to God? Letting him forgive you for whatever culpability you think you have, even if you can't forgive yourself?"

"I'm still working on that."

"Then it'll come in time."

She removed her hand and settled back against the railing beside him. "You know, I've wondered about the name of your firm. Now I think I understand. It doesn't have anything to do with the city of Phoenix, does it?"

"No." He wasn't surprised she'd figured that out.

"A mythological creature, consumed in flames and reborn from the ashes." She spoke the words softly as she regarded him. "Did you come up with the name, or did the three of you do it together?"

"Dev and I picked it. We both had our reasons for wanting to start over, away from the constraints of official law enforcement. So did Connor, when he joined us." He left it at that. Dev and Connor trusted him with their secrets, just as he trusted them with his. The ones they'd revealed to each other, anyway. "We wanted to help people who fell between the cracks or were involved in cases law enforcement had dismissed."

"Like mine."

"Yeah."

"Well, I'm sorry for the reason you formed Phoenix, but I'm glad you were there when I needed help." She checked her watch and straightened up. "Since you were up late last night collecting trash, I should let you get some sleep. Besides, I don't want to overstay my welcome."

No chance of that. But he left that unsaid as he picked up their empty cans.

"I'll let you out through the front door this time." He crossed to the slider, pulled it open, and followed her in. She snagged her purse off the counter and continued toward the front of the house as he deposited the cans beside the sink. "I'm going to check out a couple of those nursing homes tomorrow."

She paused in the foyer while he unlatched the door. "And I'll be at the Woman's Exchange on Friday. Will you let me know if you learn anything interesting?"

"I'll call you." Either way. Even if the outing was a bust, he'd find some excuse to phone her just to hear her voice. "Thanks for helping sort the trash tonight—and for being such a good sport about it."

She smiled. "All I can say is, you sure know how to impress a girl when you invite her over."

He returned her smile. "That's what Dev said. At least I'll walk you to your car." He was prepared for her to argue, but she didn't.

Was it possible she was as reluctant as he was for the evening to end?

"For the record, I actually had a nice time, despite the agenda. I wonder what that says about me?" They walked down his driveway in silence for a moment, and when she spoke again, her tone had morphed from joking to serious. "I also want you to know I appreciate what you shared with me about what happened to your wife. Trying to get past a tragedy like that has to be a huge challenge."

"It is. And I'm not there yet."

She stopped beside the car and faced him, her eyes warm and caring. "I'll keep you in my prayers."

His throat constricted. It had been a long while

since anyone had looked at him with such kindness and concern. "I appreciate that." He leaned past her and opened the car door. "Maybe yours will get better results than mine have."

She tossed her purse onto the passenger seat. "Could it be you're praying for the wrong things?"

He frowned. "What do you mean?"

A dimple dented her cheek. "When I was a little girl, I used to ask God for very specific things. A new bike, an A on a test, a role in a school play. Sometimes I got what I wanted, sometimes I didn't. It all seemed very haphazard to me. I asked my dad about the whole prayer thing, and he suggested I follow the advice of Socrates."

Intrigued, Cal rested his hand on top of her door. "What did a pre-Christian Greek philosopher have to say on that subject?"

" 'Our prayers should be for blessings in general, for God knows best what is good for us.' " Moira smiled as she quoted the ancient sage, then shrugged. "It made sense to me. After that, I started laying my problems and needs before God and asking for grace and guidance and whatever other virtues he thought I needed."

"That's an interesting approach to prayer."

She smiled and slid into the car. "It's worked for me."

"I'll have to give it some thought, then. Drive safe." With that, he shut the door and backed away.

He waited by the curb, watching the taillights of her car recede down the street. Once they disappeared, he slowly returned to the house, pondering Moira's comments.

Had he been praying for the wrong things?

For years he'd asked God to help him find the evidence to pin Lindsey's death on Bernie Levine so he could make certain the man never enjoyed another moment of freedom. He'd wanted retribution. Justice.

That hadn't happened.

And even though Levine was dead, Cal continued to harbor hate in his heart—maybe too much to allow room for forgiveness to enter.

He pushed through the screen door, set the locks behind him, and wandered back into the kitchen. The two empty cans stood beside each other on the counter. One intact. One smashed.

Frowning, he picked up the one he'd crushed in anger.

Was this what his soul looked liked? Mangled and distorted by anger?

It was possible.

It was also very possible he had, indeed, been praying for the wrong things.

Maybe it was time to ask for blessings in general, as the classical philosopher had advised, and trust that God would give him what he needed to start fresh in his personal life as he had in his professional life. God alone might know what those needs were. After all, he'd sent Moira into his life, hadn't he?

Blessings didn't come any finer than that.

He set the crushed can back on the counter and reread the *Family Circus* plaque. Yesterday *was* the past. No matter how much he grieved, no matter how much he ranted against his fate, Lindsey was gone. He needed to begin living in— and enjoying—today . . . as she had always done.

So as soon as this case wrapped up, he was going to do a whole lot of thinking about how a certain blessing called Moira might fit into his future.

For now, though, he needed to focus on the case.

As he double-checked the locks, flipped off the inside lights, and headed down the hall to turn in, he reviewed their plans for the rest of the week. Tomorrow he'd visit the nursing homes. Friday, Moira would do her surveillance.

And if the evidence continued to align with his growing suspicions, they might be on track to solving the case of the vanishing woman.

Yet anxious as he was to put this one to bed, depending on what they uncovered, things could also get ugly—and dangerous. Fast.

Because desperate people did desperate things.

Meaning another woman he was coming to care for could suddenly find herself at risk.

A possibility that made his blood run cold.

Ken Blaine shrugged into his sport coat, grabbed his phone out of the locker, and exited the surgery unit, scrolling through messages as he maneuvered around gurneys and medical staff. He was an hour behind schedule already, and he had half a dozen hospitalized patients to see before his first office appointment at 1:00.

No lunch today.

No time to return calls, either, unless something significant caught his eye.

His finger stilled at the message with the "urgent" header, sent by Marge Lewis an hour ago. In many ways, she was a perfect secretary for Let the Children Come—handling the paperwork efficiently, maintaining the files, not asking a lot of questions—but she often got in a tizzy over nothing. This could probably wait.

Fifteen seconds later, he stopped again at another message from her, sent earlier in the morning. This one had an "emergency" header.

Maybe it couldn't wait after all.

He opened the message and scanned the text.

Received a call from Dr. Gonzalez. Clinic has been damaged in an earthquake. Funds and supplies urgently needed. Please advise.

Ken's pulse leaped, and he ducked out of the

flow of traffic, turning his back on the bustle in the hall as his mind raced.

He knew almost to the penny how much was in the organization's account, and it was only enough to take care of day-to-day operating expenses until the next infusion of capital—not planned for several months. The small surplus they'd stockpiled for crises had been eaten up two months ago when the clinic's primary X-ray machine breathed its last. There were no funds to cover the kind of emergency expenses an earthquake could entail.

But the children needed the clinic.

Desperately.

They had to find a way to keep the facility operational.

Fingers trembling, Ken scrolled up to Marge's more recent message and opened it.

Can we have an emergency board meeting? I checked our account. There isn't much there. The clinic sustained severe damage and they've had to evacuate. Dr. Gonzalez has set up temporary quarters at the school and needs immediate funds and supplies to treat the many injured. He will email photos of the damage this afternoon.

Ken fought back his panic, his mind racing. In the short term, he could stave off a few of his own creditors for several weeks and float the organization a temporary personal loan. But he'd need to infuse the coffers of Let the Children Come with new contributions quickly so he could replenish his own funds. His annual fifty-thousand-dollar contribution more than maxed out his charitable resources.

"Everything okay, Ken?"

At the question behind him, he forced his stiff lips into a smile, pushed away from the wall with his shoulder, and turned toward the anesthesiologist who'd assisted him all morning. "Have you ever wanted to ditch one of these things?" He held up his phone, praying the man wouldn't notice the slight tremor in his voice.

"All the time. My wife calls it the electronic leash."

"I'm with her." Ken slipped it back on his belt and twisted his wrist on the pretense of checking the time. "I didn't expect that last one to take so long. The necrosis was a lot more advanced than I expected from the imaging. Now I'll have to shift into fast-forward."

"I hear you." The man lifted his hand and moved away. "Good luck playing catch-up."

As the anesthesiologist walked down the hall, Ken pulled his phone off his belt again, reopened Marge's email, and keyed in a response.

Let's meet at 4:30. I'll cut my office hours short.

Then he typed a note to his receptionist. He hated to inconvenience his patients and their parents, but there was no choice.

Emergency at G. clinic. Reschedule all appoint-ments after 4:00.

Slipping the phone back into its holster, Ken continued toward the elevator that would take him to the pediatric floor.

And tried to ignore the trembling in his fingers.

"Mr. Peterson? I'm Nancy Prescott."

Cal rose as the patient-family liaison walked toward him in the lobby of Maryville Extended Care—his second nursing home visit this after-noon. So far, his pretext as a concerned grandson in search of an appropriate long-term care facility for his grandmother was working beautifully—and had generated new information.

He hoped this meeting would be as productive as the first had been.

As the fortysomething woman with short brown hair extended her hand and smiled, he gave her fingers a squeeze.

"Thanks for shoehorning me in on such short notice."

"Responsiveness is a hallmark of our facility. Shall we chat in my office, or would you prefer to take a tour?"

"Why don't we talk as we walk?"

"Excellent choice. I think you'll be impressed with what you see." She led the way toward a set of French doors at the far end of the lobby. "You said on the phone your grandmother may need more assistance than can be provided at home?"

"Yes. We've managed up until now, but at some point . . ." He lifted his shoulders in a what-can-you-do shrug. "Advanced COPD is difficult to deal with."

"I understand. We have a number of residents with chronic lung disease. May I ask how you chose our facility to consider?"

"My grandmother had a friend who lived here. Clara Volk. They chatted on the phone occasionally, and Clara spoke highly of her experience here."

Nancy gave him a surprised look. "I didn't realize Clara had any friends left. She was ninety, you know. A very nice woman. It was such a shame she had no family."

That was the same story he'd heard about Edward Mason—the other major Let the Children Come donor from last year—at the previous nursing home. He had a feeling the donors from prior years would fit that same pattern.

"I didn't know she was so alone. I thought my grandmother mentioned once that a doctor used to visit her on occasion . . . as a friend, not a physician." Cal flashed Nancy a smile as he added that clarification. "I recall Gram saying he sounded like the kind of man she'd like to meet."

"That would be Dr. Blaine. He comes by to see members of his congregation, but he always makes it a point to ask about residents who don't receive many visitors and then takes the time to stop in and chat with one or two. He's the embodiment of Christian charity in action. I'm sure he'd be more than happy to add your grandmother to his list if she comes to live with us. Did you know he just won the state's humanitarian of the year award?"

"Yes. I saw a clip about it on the news."

She paused at the door to a dining room. "Our ambulatory residents eat here. We have a wonderful cook, and we work hard to provide a varied menu."

Cal feigned interest in the space. "Very nice. Gram would enjoy this." He followed Nancy as she continued down the hall. "Was Clara able to eat in the dining room?"

"Not in her last six months. She also suffered from rheumatoid arthritis. A terrible disease. It was almost a blessing when she passed. Of course, we all did our best to keep her spirits up, and Dr. Blaine stepped up his visits with her to twice a week during her last couple of months. One of our aides also took a special liking to her. Clara always seemed perkier after Dr. Blaine visited or when Olivia was on duty."

At the mention of the name Olivia, Cal's antennas went up.

He'd seen or heard that name at the previous nursing home too.

As Nancy showed him a vacant private room

and rattled off some statistics about caregiver/ resident ratios, social programs, and state ratings, he tried without success to put the name in context. It had been a fleeting impression, nothing more. The name had caught his attention because it was a bit out of the ordinary, not because it had any bearing on this case.

"Would you like to see the physical therapy center? It's on the way to my office."

Nancy's question pulled him back to the present. "Yes. Thanks."

As they wound through the maze of generic institutional corridors, Cal maneuvered around wheelchairs and walkers and did his best to ignore the ubiquitous odor that had permeated every nursing home he'd ever visited, only half listening to Nancy's subtle sales pitch as she sang the praises of the facility and showed him the therapy area.

Even though he couldn't place the context of the name, the recurrence bothered him. What were the odds two people who shared the same fairly unusual name would be working at the nursing homes Blaine visited?

Miniscule.

Assuming it was the same woman, could there be a link to Blaine—especially since he was also a common denominator at the two homes?

"Let me get you an information packet to take with you." Nancy led him behind the reception desk in the lobby and down a short corridor.

As he prepared to follow her into her office at the far end, he glanced across the hall at what appeared to be a staff break room, complete with a couple of tables, sink, refrigerator, and bulletin board.

Bulletin board.

That's where he'd seen Olivia's name at the previous place.

She'd been an employee-of-the-month last fall. September, perhaps.

Cal joined Nancy in her office as she retrieved a glossy folder from the bookshelf behind her desk.

Fishing time.

"I'll have to mention to my grandmother that Dr. Blaine is still visiting residents here. She'd enjoy meeting him—and the aide you mentioned, as well. Olivia, I think you said."

The woman handed over the folder. "I'm sure Dr. Blaine would be delighted to call on your grandmother, but I'm afraid Olivia is no longer with us. Such a shame. She was very sweet and caring and reliable, and the residents loved her. Then one day a few weeks ago, she just walked out with no warning. What can you do? The younger generation seems to operate by different rules. In general, though, our staff turnover is very low."

As Nancy went on to reassure him of that by

quoting more statistics, Cal mulled over his next move. He needed to find out if the two Olivias were the same. But he'd use a different pretext to ferret out that information. Asking Nancy any more questions about an AWOL aide he'd never met could raise suspicions.

"Do you know when you might be making a decision?"

Cal smiled at the woman and tucked the folder under his arm. "Soon. I'd like to wrap this up in the next couple of weeks."

"Excellent. Please call if you have any questions."

"I'll do that." He shook her hand and headed out through the lobby.

But he didn't intend to contact the woman again. Because while he had plenty of questions, Nancy Prescott wouldn't have the answers.

He was, however, going to get one of those answers right now.

BlackBerry in hand, he opened his car door, slid behind the wheel, and tapped in the number for the nursing home he'd visited earlier.

The clinic was a wreck.

Numb with shock, Ken stared at the image on the computer screen in the church office conference room.

The 6.9 earthquake had virtually destroyed the adobe structure. The roof was half caved in, one wall had been reduced to rubble, and the main door was hanging by one hinge.

Interior photos showed similar devastation.

"Dear Lord." Reverend Anderson leaned forward, intent on the screen, his hushed words a fervent supplication. "Was anyone killed?"

"No. There were injuries, but none of them life-threatening. Dr. Gonzalez says it was a miracle." Marge pulled up the next photo, which showed a makeshift medical facility. "He's set up temporary quarters in the village school. It fared far better than the clinic. But he's in dire need of supplies, and rebuilding will require significant funds. I emailed him about our meeting, and he said he'd do his best to call in while we were all gathered."

As she finished speaking, the extension in the conference room began to ring.

All of them looked toward the number on the LED display.

"It's him." Marge started to reach for the phone.

Ken beat her to it. He snatched the handset out of its cradle and put it to his ear. "Carlos?"

"Yes. Hello, Kenneth. Marge told me you were meeting this afternoon."

"Were you injured?"

"No. I was spared. But there is much need here . . . did you get the photos I sent?"

"Yes." Ken looked at Marge and the minister, both intently listening to his end of the conversation. "I'm going to put you on speaker. Hold one moment."

Marge pushed the appropriate button on the base unit, and Ken replaced the handset.

"What is your most pressing need?" Ken gestured to Marge to take notes on the tablet in front of her.

"Many of the medications in our supply room survived, thank the Lord, and we salvaged what supplies and furnishings we could from the clinic. But we are very short on sterile goods and equipment. I've been putting together a list."

As a rustling sound came over the line, Ken could hear the background cries of children who were hurt and afraid.

His stomach clenched.

He hated pain and unhappiness. Had devoted his life to alleviating both.

They had to fix this problem as quickly as possible.

Carlos began speaking again, and Marge filled a page before the local physician completed his list.

"The school officials have been kind enough to offer us temporary quarters, but we cannot stay here long," the doctor finished. "We need to begin rebuilding as soon as possible."

Ken ran his fingers through his hair. "We'll discuss this as soon as we hang up, Carlos. I'll call you back within the hour with a plan."

"Thank you, my friend. I know you will find a

way. And now I must return to work. I will pray our next conversation brings good news."

As the line went dead, the minister folded his hands on the table. "How will we manage? If we dip into existing funds to get us past the emergency, we'll have no operating dollars for the next few months."

Silence fell in the room as they all pondered the problem.

"The need is too immediate for any serious fund-raising efforts." Marge finally spoke, frowning as she read over the list Carlos had dictated. "Though in light of your recent award, the media would probably cover this story. I can contact some of the newspeople who called after the announcement went out. Perhaps, with sufficient publicity, some generous donors will come forward. A few medical supply companies might also step up to offer merchandise."

Her reasoning was sound. And it was possible a flurry of donations would get them through the immediate crisis. But based on past experience, Ken knew donations would dry up within days of the media coverage, and the total generated wouldn't be near enough to rebuild.

He rested his elbows on the table and steepled his fingers. "It's worth a try. In the meantime, I can provide a personal short-term loan to get us over the hump. We'll survive this."

"I have every confidence in that," the minister

seconded. "The Lord has smiled on this enterprise from the beginning. Every time our coffers have run low, he's provided. I know the same will be true now. He won't turn his back on such a great need. Shall we pray about that?"

Marge took his hand, and Ken completed the circle, bowing his head as the man asked God to bless them with sufficient resources to continue the noble work of the clinic.

And God would answer.

Ken would see to that.

As he always did.

"I see you finally decided to grace us with your presence."

At Dev's greeting, Cal closed the back door of the Phoenix office behind him, pausing as his partner exited the small kitchenette. "I was here all morning doing an employee background check for our newest client."

"Yeah. Nikki told me. I was just giving you a hard time."

"So what else is new?" Cal sidestepped Dev, who was toting a steaming cup of coffee, and continued toward his office. "How's the surveillance going on the child custody case?"

"Nothing to report to our client yet. I handed it off to Connor at 4:00 and swung by here to catch up on some paperwork. Looks like we have a new protection gig in the offing too. Nikki took the call while we were gone, and I've been following up on it."

"If it's another trip to Bermuda, Connor says count him out." Cal flipped on the light in his office.

Dev followed him in. "Nothing that exotic—but possibly more dangerous. Ever hear of William Santel?"

Cal set his briefcase on his desk as he tried to place the name. "Isn't he president of Santel Enterprises? That electronics corporation head-quartered in Missouri, with manufacturing facilities around the country?"

"Bingo. They also have a plant in Mexico—where he plans to go next week, despite a death threat."

"Not too smart. Mexico is a scary place these days even without a death threat."

"I explained that to him." Dev blew on his coffee and propped a shoulder against the door frame. "He still wants to go—and he wants us to keep him safe while he's there. He's also willing to pay a very nice premium for that service."

When Dev quoted the amount, Cal let out a soft whistle.

"I had the same reaction." Dev took a test sip of the still-steaming java and backed off with a scowl.

"Money's never been our sole criteria for

taking a job, though. And the risk is high. A fat paycheck doesn't matter if you're dead." Cal settled into his chair and waited. All of the Phoenix partners agreed on those points. Meaning there was more to this story—and other reasons Dev thought they should take the job.

"That's true. But there are extenuating circumstances." Balancing his coffee, Dev strolled over to the chair across from Cal's desk, sat, and crossed an ankle over a knee. "Based on my preliminary research, Santel runs a clean, ethical operation that provides an essential service. The company makes high-voltage power supplies for applications like CT scanning, telecommunications, and explosive detection for baggage screening."

"Okay." Interesting but not compelling enough to merit risking life and limb.

"Santel employs five hundred people at his Mexican plant and offers higher wages, better working conditions, and far more benefits than his competitors—which they don't appreciate. He's also assisted authorities in Monterrey, as well as United States Immigration and Customs agents, with drug investigations—which the traffickers in Monterrey don't appreciate."

Cal processed that information. The man treated his employees well and cooperated with law enforcement to bring down drug traffickers, despite the personal risk.

Impressive.

But both of those activities could create enemies.

"Any clue who issued the warning?" Cal laced his fingers over his stomach and leaned back in his chair.

"Nope. It just suggested he stay out of Mexico if he values his health." Dev tried the coffee again and made another face. "I think the heat sensor in the microwave is busted."

"So why doesn't he lay low for a while? Take care of business by phone?"

"There's been some vandalism at the plant, along with some graffiti. The troops are unsettled. He figures if he expects the employees to keep showing up every day, he should set an example by putting in an appearance on occasion too."

Cal picked up his pen and tapped the end against his desk. "When does he want to go?"

"A week from today. Fly down Wednesday afternoon on the corporate jet, hang around the plant on Thursday and part of Friday, fly home Friday afternoon. Short trip, but intense. I peg it as a three-man job, plus a well-armed local security specialist and his crew."

"You have someone in mind?"

"Yeah. He's former law enforcement too. I worked with him on a border case in my ATF days. A good guy to have around if we run into trouble."

"Doesn't matter how good he is. This could still be dicey." Cal pursed his lips. "Santel's got guts, though—not to mention good intentions and admirable principles."

"I checked with one of my former ATF colleagues, who made a few calls to some of his DEA contacts. They confirmed he's cooperated with drug investigations on more than one occasion."

"You've been busy. When did you manage to do all that?"

Dev shrugged. "Surveillance is boring. Making calls helped keep me awake."

As if he'd ever doze off on duty. Dev might kid around at the office, but he was a pro on the job. Serious, focused, intense. The kind of partner you could rely on to watch your back in a dangerous situation.

"Okay. I'm in. Did you check with Connor yet?" His other partner's vote would carry more weight, as they both knew. It always did on protection gigs. He'd also take the lead if they accepted the job, given his Secret Service background. That was one of the things Cal enjoyed most about Phoenix—they recognized each other's strengths, and no egos were allowed when they assigned roles for gigs. The most-qualified man got the job.

"Next on my list." Dev stood. "So how did the trash party go last night?"

"It was productive." Cal gave him a recap of

the items they'd found, his excursion to the nursing homes, and Moira's plans to visit the Woman's Exchange.

While he spoke, twin creases appeared on Dev's brow. "This is sounding less and less favorable to our humanitarian of the year."

"That's my take too. I called the first nursing home from my car after I left the second one, and I managed to get Olivia's last name. It's Lange."

"What ruse did you use?"

"I didn't need one. When I asked for Olivia, the operator asked if I meant Olivia Lange. Then I called the second place and asked for her with her full name. That receptionist told me she no longer worked there."

"So your hunch panned out. It was the same woman." Dev tapped a finger against his mug, his expression speculative. "I wonder why she left?"

"According to my tour guide at the last place, no one knows. She just didn't show up one day. I'm thinking it might be worth paying her a little visit—after I gather some background."

Dev shifted his coffee from one hand to the other. "Funny how things work out, isn't it? That day we took the drive into the country to look over the accident scene, I assumed this case was dead in the water. All we found was a tooth that might not even be human. But this thing is really heating up. Proof that persistence pays off."

"Moira's more than ours."

"I don't know. I think you're as committed now to solving it as she is."

"Let's just say I'm intrigued."

"By the case—or the lady?"

Cal didn't dignify that with a reply.

"I guess that's my answer." Dev smirked at him as he lifted his cup, took a sip—and sputtered out an "ow!"

"Burn your tongue?"

"Yeah." Dev grimaced. "I can't believe this coffee is still scalding. I need some water." He took off down the hall.

Cal watched him leave, not feeling the least sorry for his wisecracking partner.

Yet as Dev disappeared, Cal's mood grew more serious. A burned tongue was one thing.

But in light of the potentially dangerous Mexico assignment and the mystifying case of the vanishing woman, he hoped nothing else got burned.

⇉ 13 ⇇

Ken stared at the syringe in his hand and swiped at the film of sweat beading on his upper lip. "I can't do this."

His father's unyielding gaze locked on him. "Yes, you can. You have to. I can't do it one-handed. The degeneration is too advanced. Look."

Alan Blaine lifted his hand, once strong and steady as it wielded a scalpel with confidence and precision during even the most delicate neurosurgery. Ken had watched his dad plenty of times. The talent and dexterity in his fingers had been awesome.

Now the arm that had guided that scalpel was thin and weak, the muscles atrophied, the fine motor skills in those once-adept fingers deaf to the commands of his brain.

As his father clumsily tried to pick up the fork on the tray of his wheelchair, tears flooded Ken's eyes, blurring his vision.

The utensil clattered to the hardwood floor in his parents' bedroom.

Ken bent to pick it up, choking back a sob as he returned it to the tray.

"If I hadn't fallen two weeks ago, it would be done already." His father's mouth tightened in disgust as he inspected the plaster cast and sling immobilizing his broken left arm. "Now I need your help. I'd ask your mother, but she wouldn't approve—nor have the fortitude for the task. I know you're only sixteen, but you have the inner strength to deal with this—and the courage."

No, he didn't. His insides were quaking just thinking about it.

When he didn't respond, his father groped for his hand. Although his words were slurred these days, his eyes were every bit as alert and decisive as they'd always been.

"Please. Help me." There was a touch of desperation in his voice now.

That was something Ken had never heard before.

His heart began to pound, just like the breast of the terrified robin he'd once rescued after it got trapped in the protective netting around his mother's ornamental peach tree.

"I . . . I can't." He choked out the words, clinging to his father's hand as he pleaded with the man he'd loved, admired, and tried to emulate his entire life. "Please don't ask me to do this terrible thing. It's wrong."

"It isn't a terrible thing. And I wouldn't ask you to do anything wrong." His father struggled with the words, working hard to form them into coherent sounds. "This will be a blessing. I'm not going to get better. You know that. We've talked about it. ALS is merciless. Soon I'll be bedridden. Paralyzed. Unable to speak. I may need a feeding tube to eat and a ventilator to breathe. And in a few months or a year, I'll die anyway. I want to go on my own terms, before I lose any more of my dignity."

"But it's . . . it's murder." Ken barely whispered the word.

"No, it's not." His father's voice steadied, a hint of the old forcefulness and resolve adding weight to his words. "I'm asking you to do this. That makes all the difference."

"It's still against the law."

"No one will ever know what took place in this room except you and me. After you administer the injection, bury the empty vial and the syringe in the woods behind the house. My death will not be unexpected, given the rapid progression of the disease. The truth will remain our secret."

The syringe felt slippery in his sweaty hand, and Ken gripped it tighter. "Medication isn't supposed to be an instrument of death." A quiver ran through his words.

"Not death. Peace. When all hope of recovery is gone, when there is nothing to look forward to except pain and deterioration and dependence, isn't this another way to relieve suffering? The very thing a physician is honor-bound to do?"

Ken furrowed his brow. Was it? He'd never viewed it that way before, but everything his father had ever said had made sense. And despite the ravages of the disease, Alan Blaine remained lucid, his thinking sound and logical.

But it still felt wrong.

"I hear what you're saying, but isn't this like . . . like playing God?" Ken groped for an out, scrambling for an argument his father hadn' considered. "Doesn't it go against the Hippocratic Oath—and our faith?"

"I'm not playing God." His father's voice was growing weary from the exertion of so much talking, but it had lost none of its conviction. "The Lord has already made it clear he intends to call me home. I don't think he'll care if I arrive a little early. I made my peace with this decision long ago." He settled his hands in his lap and looked toward the second-floor balcony that jutted over the steeply sloping rock garden in the back. "If you won't help me, I'll find another way. But this would be easier—and more merciful."

Ken felt as if icy fingers had clamped onto his lungs, squeezing out every last breath of air. He knew that, left with no other options, with few other resources at his disposal, his dad would do whatever was necessary to achieve his goal.

An image of his father's smashed body splayed on the rocks below the balcony strobed across his mind—and knotted his stomach.

"All right." His acquiescence came out in a croak.

Relief flooded his father's eyes. "Thank you. Think of it as the last gift you'll give me. And it is a gift. Never forget that. Now here's what I want you to do."

Despite the unsteadiness in his hands, Ken managed to follow his father's calm, clinical instructions. Once he'd filled the syringe with a lethal dose of morphine, he capped the empty vial, set it on the tray of the wheelchair—and began to shake.

"It's okay." His father touched his arm. "This is what I want. You're doing the compassionate thing by saving me the agony of enduring a life that's no longer productive or worth living. Promise me you'll never have any regrets or remorse about this."

How could he promise that, when his mind was filled with doubts and misgivings, when guilt and grief were already settling into his heart?

"Look at me, son."

Ken lifted his gaze from the syringe in his hand, blinking back tears.

"Someday you'll be a fine doctor. You have the healing touch, and you'll save many lives. Don't agonize over the ones you can't save. Accept that sometimes death is a blessing. Think of mine that way. Now promise me—no remorse and no regrets."

A shudder rippled through him. He tried to speak. Failed. Tried again.

"I promise." He finally managed to squeeze the words past the tightness in his throat.

His father pulled him close, and Ken laid his head on the man's wasted shoulder, as he'd done on occasion as a small child. Except then the shoulder had been strong and broad and capable of bearing the heaviest burden.

A sob escaped his lips.

"No tears." His father extricated himself from the embrace. "It's time. I want this over before your mother comes back from her bridge club."

Ken backed off, and though he tried his best, he couldn't stem the silent tears trailing down his cheeks.

"After you give me the injection, I want you to leave."

He stared at his father. "But I want to stay with you and—"

"No." His father held up his hand, his tone firm. "I'll drift off quickly. You need to take care of the syringe and vial."

"But Mom will . . . she'll be the one who finds you."

"Better that than to let her heart break bit by bit as I wither away. This is kinder in the end. I want your word you'll leave—and not come back until she calls for you."

His father's words were becoming more garbled, the effort to talk wearing him down. But Ken had no problem understanding what his father wanted. What he expected. And all his life, he'd done his best to live up to his father's expectations.

"All right."

"Good." His father shifted sideways and flopped his hand toward his thigh, working to position his index finger. "There. Go through the fabric. Inject it slow and steady." His voice was calm.

Ken went down on one knee. Pulled his father's lightweight pant leg taut. Positioned the needle.

Hesitated.

"Just do it, son. It's an act of compassion and charity. There's a better place waiting for me."

Pulse hammering as hard as if he'd run a five-hundred-yard dash, Ken slowly slid the needle in and pushed the plunger, shooting the deadly liquid into his father's body.

It seemed to take forever in the quiet room, the silence broken only by the muted strains of a Vivaldi CD.

When the syringe was at last empty, he withdrew it and looked up at his father, his vision blurred with tears. "I love you, Dad."

"I know. What you just did demonstrated that better than words ever could. You're a good boy. Honorable and conscientious. I'm proud of you, son." He touched his cheek. "Now go. But open the French doors first so I can see the sky and breathe the fresh air."

Ken lurched to his feet and once more followed his father's instructions.

After he'd repositioned the wheelchair for a view toward the outdoors, he crossed to the hall door and paused on the threshold for one more look at the man who'd been the center of his world for sixteen years. His father managed a crooked smile and a weak lift of his hand in farewell.

The tears started again, and Ken forced himself to turn away. Clutching the syringe and empty morphine vial, he raced down the steps and out the back door, heading for the property line at the edge of the woods. Once there, he stopped and looked back toward the open French doors.

To the room where his father was dying.

"I'm proud of you, son."

As the words echoed in his mind, he tried to stifle his sobs. That's all he'd ever wanted—for his dad, the great neurosurgeon, to be proud of him. Alan Blaine wasn't effusive in his praise, but when he gave it, it meant something. And it was always deserved.

If his father was proud of him, he'd done the right thing.

But that didn't mitigate his feeling of desolation and loss.

He stumbled into the woods. Dropped to his knees. Doubled over. Retched until there was nothing left in his stomach.

For several minutes he lay there, spent. But at last he rose and staggered deeper into the same woods where he'd once played Robin Hood, smiting imaginary villains, pretending to be a hero.

He didn't feel like a hero today.

After collecting a stick and a flat rock, he again dropped to his knees and crawled into a tangle of shrubby growth. With his improvised implements, he stabbed at the loamy soil, damp from the recent rain, thrusting them into the earth over and over and over until he'd created a small, deep hole. Then he dropped the syringe and vial inside and refilled the dark, dank cavity as quickly as possible.

After he finished, his hands felt dirty—and not just from the earth and decayed leaves.

Would they ever feel clean again?

Yet he'd promised his father he wouldn't harbor regrets or remorse, and it was a promise he'd do his best to keep. Whatever it took.

Because he'd never broken a promise to his dad.

Backing out of the scrubby brush, he wove through the undergrowth to the small creek where he used to catch tadpoles. The water was cold, but he plunged his hands in and scrubbed away the dirt as best he could.

Once he'd cleaned up, he returned to the edge of the woods and sat, back against a tree. A cardinal trilled overhead, and he closed his eyes, welcoming the numbness that settled over him. Here, in this quiet place, he could almost pretend everything was normal.

Until his mother's panicked cry an hour or so later shattered his fleeting serenity.

"Ken? Ken!"

He squeezed his eyes tightly shut, trying to block her out, to keep reality at bay.

But her cries grew louder. More insistent.

And then she was shaking him, harder and harder and . . .

Ken's eyes flew open and he gasped, his pulse pounding as he blinked into the darkness.

"I'm sorry to wake you. You were shouting and thrashing. I could hear you down the hall."

That wasn't his mother's voice.

Ken blinked. Shifted his head to the left.

Ellen stood beside the bed, silhouetted from the light in the hall, her face in shadows. He checked the clock on the nightstand: 2:30.

"Sorry to disturb you."

At his shaky apology, she hesitated, as if debating whether to say more. In the end, though, she turned and disappeared into the dark hall.

Slowly he exhaled and released the sheet he'd bunched in his fists. The air-conditioning kicked on, and at the sudden movement of cool air he shivered.

No wonder.

He was soaked with sweat.

As his shivering increased, he groped for the blanket and pulled it up.

Better.

But he couldn't so easily chase away the chill of the familiar nightmare. The one that returned every time he thought about helping a future Let the Children Come donor make his or her contribution a bit sooner than they expected.

Still . . . it was better than the nightmares he'd had before the ordeal with Olivia.

Another chill snaked through him, and he tucked the blanket under his chin, trying to quash the memory of those bad dreams. After all, God had smiled on him that night, intervening to lessen his culpability for the stomach-knotting ethical choice he'd wrestled with day and night. He'd only had to end the drama, not initiate it, and that had been a compassionate deed. Then, to seal the deal, God had erased the evidence with a torrential rain.

What better confirmation could there be that the Almighty's priorities meshed with his?

He needed to put that unfortunate incident behind him and focus on Verna Hafer—the cause of tonight's nightmare. How providential that she'd told him about the alteration she'd made in her will mere days before the earthquake.

Another sign from God.

Still, he preferred to space such generous donations six or eight months apart. But what choice did he have? Children's lives hung in the balance.

Besides, she was confined to bed now, her dignity gone. She had nothing to look forward to except pain and ultimate death. Why prolong that misery? Better to permanently end her uffering, just as he'd ended his father's, even if it vas sooner than planned.

And it would be a double blessing, because in eath she would help hundreds of children live.

His father would be proud.

Moira picked up a necklace handcrafted of beads nd copper, keeping one eye on the front door of le Woman's Exchange. She'd already been here wenty minutes, and unfortunately most of the onsignment part of the shop was in the back, out f sight of the tearoom entrance. She was running ut of merchandise to browse through in the small ront section.

If Ellen Blaine didn't show up soon, the clerks ehind the counter and the hostess for the tea-oom were going to get suspicious.

Draping the necklace back on the stand that held everal others, Moira picked up a cookbook. She ould kill a few minutes paging through that.

And thinking about Cal's call last night.

Her lips curved up. That had been the best part f her day. Not only because he'd discovered ome interesting information during his nursing ome visits that suggested Blaine might, indeed, ave things to hide, but because Cal hadn't been n any hurry to end their call. He'd seemed to njoy their chitchat as much as she had.

Or maybe that was wishful thinking. The man learly still loved his wife, even after five years.

Could be he was just lonely, and their conversation had helped fill up some empty evening hours.

As she mulled over that depressing possibility, movement outside the picture window in front of the store caught her attention.

Ellen had arrived.

Trying to maintain a casual demeanor despite the sudden blip in her pulse, Moira put the cookbook back on the rack and edged closer to the hostess stand, watching as Ellen stepped onto the sidewalk, paused, and waved at someone hidden from view.

Two other groups of women were waiting to be seated, and Moira positioned herself close enough to fall in behind Ellen and the friend she'd greeted outside.

A moment later they came through the door and joined the line. Moira did the same—and tuned in

While they inched forward, the two women discussed the unusual amount of rain, the summerlike temperatures so early in the season, and some lightning damage to a tree in a backyard.

Hopefully they'd talk about more than the weather once they were seated.

When they reached the front of the line, the hostess smiled and greeted them like the regular customers they were. "I saved your usual table, ladies."

She picked up two menus and retraced her

steps into the tearoom, heading for a spot in the far corner, the women following her.

There was an empty table for two beside it, against the wall.

Yes!

The hostess returned and picked up another menu. "How many?"

"Just one." Moira gave her the most winning smile she could manage. "A quiet table would be nice. That one by the wall, perhaps?" She gestured toward the table she had in her sights.

"I'm afraid that one's reserved."

Moira tried to hide her dismay as she surveyed the room. The next best option was behind the two women, with a plant in between. Not as close, and not as ideal for eavesdropping, but what choice did she have?

"How about the one by the plant?"

The woman smiled. "That one I can do."

She led the way, and Moira took the seat nearest to Ellen's table for ease of hearing, though that put her back toward the two women.

"Your waitress will be over to take your order in a moment." The hostess handed her the menu.

"Thank you."

Moira gave the bill of fare a quick scan and made her selection, then focused on the conversation behind her.

"Everything set for the anniversary party on Sunday?" Ellen's voice.

"I think so. Are you certain Ken won't change his mind and join you? I could call the caterer and up the head count."

Moira opened her purse and withdrew a small notebook.

"No. I have a feeling he'll bail on our neighbor's cocktail party tonight too. Not that it matters. To be honest, I'll have more fun by myself."

Interesting. There might be a not-so-pleasant reason the man didn't have any pictures of his wife in his office.

"Is he still acting odd?"

The other woman had lowered her volume, and Moira had to strain to hear her.

"More than ever."

"Hi, ladies. The usual?" A new voice. Must be the waitress.

"Of course. Are we boring, or what?" Ellen's friend laughed.

The waitress responded with a laugh. "I'd say you just know what you like. Nothing wrong with that. I'll have it out in a few minutes."

Silence, broken only by the clink of ice in a glass. They must be waiting for the waitress to move away.

"So what do you mean, more than ever?" Ellen's friend again.

Excellent. They were back on track. If she was lucky, they'd—

"Have you decided what you'd like for lunch?"

Moira jumped as the waitress appeared from behind her.

"Sorry. I didn't mean to startle you."

"No problem. I was lost in thought. I'll have the chicken salad." She handed the menu back without making eye contact. Praying the woman wasn't the chatty type.

"Coming right up."

She disappeared without another word.

Perfect.

Moira cocked an ear toward the table behind her.

". . . civil to each other, but lately he's been short-tempered and distracted."

"Maybe he ought to squeeze in a trip to your neighbor's cabin. Chill out for a few days."

"It couldn't hurt. Ted rarely uses it anymore, and he gave Ken a key years ago. Told him to go anytime." Ice tinkled in a glass. "I have to admit, I've never seen Ken this stressed. He's been having those nightmares again too. Last night, his muttering and thrashing was so loud it woke me. It went on and on, until I finally got up and went to check on him."

"Any clue what it was about?"

"No. Even when things were better between us, he brushed the nightmares aside. Said they were caused by the stress of the job. If you ask me, though, the clinic's to blame. The nightmares started five years ago, when he began expanding from the original modest operation. Since then the thing's taken on a life of its own. I'm sure the earthquake had a lot to do with his bad dreams last night. I don't know what caused the ones a few weeks ago, though."

Earthquake? Recent nightmares? Moira continued to scribble in her tablet.

"How badly was the clinic damaged?"

"He didn't say much, but it must be bad. They've had to move into the local school building."

"Time for some major fund-raising." Ice clinked in a glass again.

"You know he detests asking for help. But if that's what it takes to keep the clinic going, I suppose he'll suck it up and get it done. He'll do anything for those children."

"Here you go, honey. Enjoy." The waitress slid a plate in front of Moira.

"Thanks." She bent back over her notebook, trying to look busy, hoping the woman would disappear.

She did.

". . . long ago, and I've accepted it." Ellen's tone brightened as she changed the subject. "So tell me how that new grandbaby is doing."

Her friend launched into a glowing description of the infant's antics.

Moira dug into her chicken salad and reviewed her notes, keeping one ear on their conversation. But the two women said nothing else during the remainder of their lunch that seemed remotely relevant to her vanishing woman.

Yet as she finished her own meal and watched them exit forty minutes later, she was glad she'd come. Their conversation had yielded quite a bit of interesting information.

Though Blaine and his wife shared a house, they didn't sleep together, nor were they attending an upcoming social event as a couple. Ellen thought her husband was acting oddly, and he'd been short-tempered and distracted. He'd also been plagued with nightmares for the past five years, since he'd expanded the Guatemala facility. Ellen believed he was obsessed with his clinic, which had just been damaged in an earthquake.

And what about that cabin remark her friend had thrown out?

Could said cabin be near Augusta—or better yet, Defiance?

Then there was that outcrop of recent nightmares.

Moira tucked her notebook back into her purse, picked up her bill, and walked over to the cashier, anxious to share the new information with Cal. How it would help them, she wasn't certain.

But she did know one thing.

The more pieces of this puzzle they collected, the better the chance they would find out what had become of the terrified woman on that rainy April night.

Cal parked at the curb in front of the frayed-around-the-edges South County duplex and double-checked the address he'd jotted down for Olivia Lange.

This was the place.

He picked up his clipboard, slid out of the van doing duty today as Sullivan Heating and Cooling, and started toward the front door. Unless Olivia had arrived home in the five minutes since he'd called, no one was going to respond to his ring . . . exactly as he'd planned. He was more interested in nosing around and talking to Olivia's neighbor, who *was* home. She'd answered her phone—and got a hang-up in response.

Thank goodness for his crisscross directory. It paid for itself every single time he needed names or phone numbers for a person's neighbors.

As he pressed his finger to the bell, he assessed the brick housing unit. It needed tuck-pointing, the paint on the trim was peeling, and the windows were the inexpensive single-pane variety. The few scraggly bushes around the foundation were in serious need of some TLC, and bare patches on the ground looked as if they hadn't seen grass for a long while.

Definitely not the high-rent district. More like

the kind of place occupied by people who lived from paycheck to paycheck.

And that fit, based on the background he and Nikki had dug up. Twenty-two, high school dropout at seventeen, product of the foster-care system, Olivia had no tangible assets they could locate. This was the best she could afford.

So assuming her finances were shaky enough to force her to live in a place like this, why would she walk out of a decent-paying job?

And if she'd lined up a better position, why wouldn't she have given the standard notice?

Maybe today would yield some answers to those questions—and perhaps give him a clue about whether there was, in fact, a link between her and Blaine.

When his ring went unanswered, as he'd expected, he knocked loudly on the door. The window in the adjacent unit was open, and if he was lucky, the neighbor would come out to see what all the commotion was about.

If she didn't, he'd try her door next.

Fifteen seconds later, he heard the sound of a bolt sliding back on the other side of the unit. A woman with thinning gray hair in need of combing cracked the door and peered over at him.

"Good afternoon." He gave her a big smile and ramped up the charm. "Do you happen to know if"—he checked his clipboard—"Ms. Lange is home?"

"Not likely. Did Howard send you?"

Cal stepped back from Olivia's unit but didn't approach the other woman. She seemed ready to slam the door if he took so much as one step in her direction, and he needed to keep her talking.

"Howard?"

"Ralph Howard, the landlord."

Lifting the clipboard again, he pretended to study it. "I don't have any information about who placed the call."

She gave a disparaging snort. "I'd be surprised if it was him. Must have been Olivia. I been here six years, and he don't pay no attention to complaints. I've had a leaky faucet for four months, and he ain't done a thing to fix it." She looked him up and down. "You know anything about faucets?"

"Only from working on my own house."

As she started to close the door, he latched on to the first excuse he could think of to keep her talking. "I'm not a plumber, but I'd be happy to take a quick look for you as long as I'm here."

The door stopped moving. She poked her head farther out and scrutinized his van. Gave him another once-over. Opened the door all the way.

"I'd be obliged. If I wait for Howard, it'll never get fixed."

"Let me get a few tools from the van."

Cal went to the back of the vehicle, opened the

door, and grabbed the toolbox. Equipping all the vehicles with a set of basic tools in addition to more standard PI gear had been one of the smartest things they'd ever done. He couldn't count the number of times a screwdriver had come in handy.

Olivia's neighbor was waiting at the door when he returned, and she stepped back to allow him to enter, hacking out a phlegmy cough as he passed.

"Which sink is it?"

"Kitchen." She motioned toward a dim, narrow hallway.

After closing the door, she followed him to the kitchen—a vintage 1970s job, complete with avocado appliances, the air stale with cigarette smoke.

He set his toolbox on the chipped formica counter next to an overflowing ashtray, unwrapped the rag tied around the faucet, and reached to turn it on.

"Be careful or you'll get a faceful."

Cupping one hand over the faucet, he eased it on with the other. Water sprayed everywhere. He shut it off immediately.

"I see what you mean."

"Yeah." She sat at the tiny café table off to one side, her shapeless housedress settling in angular folds over her bony frame, and wrapped her knobby fingers around a half-empty mug rimmed with coffee stains. "The whole place is like that. Toilet don't flush right, either."

No way was he touching that comment. He'd already done a trash cover for this job; he drew the line at toilets.

Instead, he went down on one knee, opened the cabinet door under the faucet, and shut off the water. Then he stood, put the stopper in the sink, and dug around in his toolbox for a flathead screwdriver.

"You think your neighbor might show up if I hang around for a while?"

"Not likely." She hacked again.

The same comment she'd made earlier.

He pulled out the screwdriver and went to work loosening the faucet, keeping his tone conversational. "Why do you say that?"

"Ain't seen her around lately. And I don't think she's paid her rent. Howard was here on the fifteenth to collect, like always, but she wasn't home. He came back yesterday and she wasn't there then, either. I heard him banging on the door."

The woman took a sip of her coffee, and Cal continued to work in silence. Sometimes people said more if you didn't ask questions.

She set the mug back on the table and continued talking, just as he'd hoped. "I suppose she might have gone back to live with that no-good boyfriend of hers. I'd 'a thought she had more ense than that, though. Course, I didn't know her ll that well. Mostly she stayed to herself. Never eard a peep out of her, either. Not like that biker uy who lived there before her and played rap nusic at all hours of the day and night. I'd be orry to lose her as a neighbor."

Cal pulled off the faucet, removed the washer, nd turned to dig through the toolbox. "How do ou know the boyfriend was no good?" He used is shooting-the-breeze voice.

"When she moved here back in November, she ad a doozy of a black eye and a swollen lip. I elt kinda sorry for her, so I bought a coffee cake t the day-old bakery store and took it over. Sort f a gift to welcome her to the neighborhood, uch as it is." She chortled and took another sip f coffee.

The pause lengthened, and Cal restrained his npatience as he waited for her to continue.

"Anyway, she invited me in and we had a nice hat. Sweet little thing. Can't imagine why she ooked herself up with that bad apple. Finally dmitted he beat her, even though I'd figured nat out already. Said it had taken her a long ime to get up enough nerve to leave him, but ome nice doctor she knew from that nursing ome where she worked talked to her about it, elped her see the light."

Cal's pulse spiked.

Was Blaine that doctor?

If so, they had their connection.

But how did Olivia's boyfriend fit into the puzzle?

After fishing a washer out of his toolbox, Cal slid it into place and screwed the faucet back on. "You think she might have gone back to that loser anyway, huh?"

"Don't know where else she would have gone. Didn't have no other family." She hacked again and took another sip of coffee. "You wouldn't catch me getting anywhere close to that guy though, I'll tell you that. He was one mean looking dude. Thought he was going to break the door down, the way he pounded on it a few days after she moved in here. That's when she got the restraining order."

At the woman's casual reference to a restraining order, Cal's pulse kicked up again.

His gratis plumbing job had paid off big time.

As he got down on one knee again to turn the water back on, his BlackBerry began to vibrate. He let it roll to voice mail rather than interrupt the flow of this enlightening conversation. "Did you ever see the guy again?"

"Nope. And I hope I never do. But I plan to remember his name. I ever hear it, I'm heading the other direction."

"Would you mind sharing it? If I have to come back, I'd like to be prepared in case I run into this guy."

"Sure. Wayne Garrison." She gave him a blatant perusal. "Though I expect you'd be able to handle him if he got feisty."

Cal reached for the faucet. "Maybe. But I always avoid trouble if I can." He twisted the faucet, and she rose to join him at the sink. "It's not perfect. You've got a lot of lime buildup on the posts, but it's better than it was."

"A thousand percent. I'm much obliged."

"Happy to do it." Cal closed the toolbox and moved toward the door, Olivia's neighbor trailing behind him. "I wonder if I should even bother stopping by again later in the day. You say you haven't seen the woman next door in a while?"

"Been a month, I bet. Course, like I said, she's quiet as a mouse. During the winter, sometimes two, three weeks went by before I caught a glimpse of her. But with the nice weather, I've had my windows open a lot, and I haven't heard her front door opening. Should have too, because it sticks. Then again, maybe my hearing's going." She snorted. "Everything else is."

When they got to the door, the woman pulled it open. "What are you supposed to fix over there, anyway?"

"I left my clipboard in the van, but I think it had something to do with the thermostat."

"Don't surprise me one bit, knowing Howard. Poor girl probably froze all winter while she waited for him to get it fixed. Serve him right if she up and moved. I'd do it myself, if I could find another place this cheap. Thanks again."

"No problem."

Cal replaced the toolbox in the van, climbed behind the wheel, and pulled a notebook from his pocket. Then he wrote two names: Ralph Howard and Wayne Garrison.

A chat with both of them was high on his priority list.

After tucking the notebook back in his pocket, he pulled out his BlackBerry to check the call he'd ignored. The message was from Moira, left at 3:10.

"Hi, Cal. Moira. Ellen showed at the Woman's Exchange, as we expected, and I learned a few interesting things. Give me a call when you have a minute and I'll fill you in."

He erased the message and weighed the Blackberry in his hand. They did need to compare notes, and a phone call would suffice.

But he was tired of spending his Friday nights at the office working overtime or at home doing chores. Yes, the grass was due to be cut and the driveway needed to be sealed and one of the loose rails on the deck was becoming a hazard. And yes, he needed to put in some time on a couple of background checks for their newest client.

On the other hand, the world wouldn't end if he kicked back for one night and enjoyed some conversation with a lovely woman.

Without laboring over the decision, he scrolled down to Moira's number, pushed dial—and tried to rationalize his decision. This might be a pro bono job, but it was still a case. In a way, this would be a working session.

Yeah, right.

Even he wasn't buying that pretext.

But he hoped Moira would.

Ken tapped in his home security code, pulled the back door shut behind him, and crossed the lawn toward his neighbor's house.

He was *not* in the mood for this cocktail party.

The sound of laughter wafted over the hedge that separated his property from Ted's, and he paused in the shadows to psyche himself up for social pleasantries.

It wasn't easy.

How could he paste on a smile and make small talk when children were suffering in Guatemala because the supplies purchased with his personal loan were barely trickling in through the compromised transportation infrastructure? When he'd just left a distraught mother whose child's life hung in the balance after a bicycle accident? When he was busy formulating plans to deal with Verna Hafer on Sunday?

For an instant, he was tempted to turn around and go home. Ellen would make some excuse for his absence. She'd become an expert at that after his many no-shows these past few years.

But Ted had been a valued and generous friend for twenty years. And he'd taken advantage of the man's hospitality more weekends than he could count over the past two decades, borrowing his cabin in the country whenever he'd needed a mental break. Not so much in the past two or three years, though. There'd been no downtime. But often enough to be forever in the man's debt.

Plus, the place had come in handy recently—for reasons Ted would never know, even if he happened to wander around the property. Ken had seen to that, and the rain had been his ally. Ted hadn't been out there more than a couple of times in the past four years, anyway. Not since he'd hacked himself while cutting wood, then almost bled to death before the paramedics could respond to his 911 call. Ken couldn't blame Rose for extracting a promise from her husband not to go there alone anymore. He was eighty-two, after all.

Sometimes Ken thought the man held on to the place just for him, knowing what a haven it had once been when he'd needed an escape from the stresses of his life-and-death job. And you didn't repay a friendship like that by saying no to an Opera Theatre fund-raiser—or blowing off a party.

Straightening his shoulders, Ken slipped between the arborvitae bushes that separated their properties.

The guests had gathered on the terrace on this balmy night, and the flickering candles, the muted laughter, the fragrance of the roses in their first, profuse bloom of the season should have created a calming ambiance.

But the soft strains of the familiar classical music in the background turned his stomach.

Vivaldi always had that effect on him.

On the other side of the lawn, Ted lifted his hand in greeting and crossed the expanse of lush grass between them.

"Glad you could make it, Ken. I know how busy you are."

"Never too busy for old friends." Ken returned his firm shake.

"I bet you haven't had dinner yet."

Ken lifted one shoulder and managed a smile. "Some days, eating takes second place."

"Well, I'm afraid Rose ordered that namby-pamby finger food, as usual. But I did put my foot down and ask for some heartier fare for the gents." He scanned the crowd, then signaled to one of the tray-bearing waiters who was passing out hors d'oeuvres. "This tidbit should help tide you over for at least a little while."

The man approached them and proffered a tray. The scent of grilled meat from the tenderloin kabobs wafted his way, and though it set off a rumble in his empty stomach, it also made him nauseous.

He tried to tune out the Vivaldi.

"Put a few of those under your belt." Ted handed Ken a napkin and piled several in his palm. "We've got some meatballs floating around somewhere too. I'll round them up for you."

"No!" The rejection was more adamant than he'd intended, and at the man's surprised expression, Ken dredged up a smile to soften his refusal. "This is plenty for now. I'm more tired and thirsty than hungry."

"I understand. I know you've had a long week. Ellen mentioned the earthquake and the problems at the clinic. I was sorry to hear about that. Doesn't seem right, with all the effort you've put into that project. I'll tell you what, you find yourself a seat on the terrace and I'll round up a drink. What would you like?"

"You don't have to wait on me."

"Of course I do. I'm the host. Let's see . . . bourbon and water?" The man shot him a mischievous look.

"You know me better than that."

"Indeed I do. Can't recall the last time I saw you drink hard liquor. How about a glass of cabernet? I do believe I've seen you indulge in that on occasion."

"Sounds perfect. Thank you."

"My pleasure."

As the man took off for the bar, Ken wandered toward a patio table off to the side, away from the clusters of guests congregated closer to the food and drink. He'd force down some food. Sip half a glass of wine. And make his escape as soon as he could politely manage it.

Lowering himself into the chair, he surveyed the crowd. At the far end of the terrace, Ellen was engaged in conversation with the new neighbors across the street, a young couple with whom he'd exchanged no more than a few words since they'd moved in three or four months ago. Fellow was a lawyer, as he recalled. On the fast track, according to Ellen.

God help him.

That kind of commitment and drive could be all-consuming, as he well knew. Not that he harbored any regrets. The work had been worth it. But it was a lonely life. More than anyone could ever understand.

Except maybe his dad.

The Vivaldi once more wormed its way into his consciousness.

Though he met with some success as he tried to tune out the music, thoughts of his father remained.

Alan Blaine, too, had had a deep passion for his work, sometimes to the exclusion of his family. In his younger days, Ken hadn't fully appreciated his father's priorities. Had resented them at times, even. His mom had too, much as she'd loved his dad. He could recall a few occasions when she'd tried to mask her displeasure behind a strained smile after his father canceled out on some important family commitment.

In the end, though, he'd recognized that a gift like his father's had to take precedence over everything. Light was not meant to be hidden. The Bible said as much. It was a gift, and it had to be shared.

No matter the sacrifice.

"Doesn't look like you're making much headway on those kabob things." Ted stopped beside him and handed over a glass of wine.

Ken glanced at the skewers in his hand. The grease was soaking through the napkin, and the meat no longer felt warm. He set them on the table beside him, swallowing past his revulsion.

"I was waiting for the wine."

"Well, have at it." Ted leaned closer. "I'd stay and chat, but Rose gave me firm instructions to mingle."

"Trust me. After the week I've had, I'm more than content to sit and veg for a few minutes."

The man smiled. "I hear you. But if you need anything else, let me know."

As his host disappeared into the deepening dusk, Ken shoved the pile of meat away from him. He'd find somewhere to ditch it before he made his escape.

"Dr. Blaine?"

A sixtysomething woman holding a glass of white wine and a plate piled high with a variety of appetizers approached him. She seemed vaguely familiar, but he couldn't place her.

And he wasn't in the mood for company.

"Yes?" He hoped his polite but cool tone would discourage her from conversation.

No such luck.

She stopped in front of him and smiled. "I thought that was you. Elizabeth Williams. We met at the Opera Theatre gala in April, though I'm not at all surprised you don't remember me. We were at the same table, but we'd hardly said hello when you were called away. Such is the life of a doctor, I suppose."

A vague recollection of the woman stirred in his mind. Very vague. He'd had too many other things to think about that night.

Be polite, Ken. She must be a friend of Rose or Ted.

"I do remember you. I'm sorry we didn't have more of a chance to get acquainted."

"Well, I suppose we can remedy that to some degree tonight. Do you mind if I join you? I love these skinny high heels, but I'm afraid my feet don't. Despite my husband's warning that this would be a stand-up-and-mingle party, I couldn't resist wearing them."

Without giving him a chance to respond, she

settled into the chair beside him and dived into her plate of food.

Stifling a sigh, he eyed the hedge on the other side of the terrace. If he excused himself to top off his drink, he might be able to slip away into the shadows and . . .

". . . ever get hold of you?"

He refocused on the woman beside him, catching only the tail end of her question. "Excuse me?"

She smiled, wagged a finger at him, and took a healthy sip of her wine. "You're as distracted tonight as you were at the gala. But I suppose a doctor always has a lot of serious things on his mind." She tapped the base of his wineglass with her finger. "Have some. It will help you relax. Anyway, I was asking if that nice man who called me about the MontBlanc pen ever got hold of you. I told him I thought it might be yours."

At the non sequitur, he frowned. "What MontBlanc pen?"

"The one that was found near our table at the Opera Theatre benefit. The man who called was hoping to locate the owner."

"I don't have a MontBlanc pen." What on earth was the woman going on about?

"Then I guess it wasn't yours." She giggled and took another sip of wine. "I do hope that nice man found the owner, though. He seemed so anxious to return it. Did he call you?"

"Not that I know of. Unless he left a message at my office."

"Funny. I'm certain he intended to get in touch with you, especially after I told him how you took a call and had to go deal with some emergency. I thought you might have used your pen to jot down a number."

An alarm began to flash in his mind. "You told him I left?"

"Yes. And I praised your dedication. You missed a wonderful evening. The entertainment was—"

"When did this man call you?"

She blinked, apparently thrown by the interruption, a mini quiche suspended halfway to her mouth. "Well, now, let me see." Pursing her lips, she furrowed her brow. "I believe it was last week. Yes . . . yes, it was. Friday. I remember because I was getting ready to meet my aunt. We've been having lunch once a month for years. She's a wonderful woman. When my uncle was alive, they . . ."

Ken tuned her out.

Why had someone from Opera Theatre waited a month to try and track down the owner of a high-end pen?

Unless the man hadn't been from Opera Theatre at all—and he was more interested in the whereabouts of a certain doctor that night.

Or was he being paranoid?

Maybe.

Yet he was getting unsettling vibes about this. Especially in light of his encounter with Moira Harrison only a few days before that.

Had she asked someone to check out the alibi he'd offered her?

But who could she enlist?

If she'd gone to the police, and if they'd listened—both long shots—that wasn't how law enforcement operated. They would have been much more up-front with their questions.

Could she have come up with a ruse and had a friend make the call?

Possibly. She was a reporter, after all.

At this point, though, the whys and hows were irrelevant. The more important fact was that if she had somehow orchestrated that call, she now knew his alibi had a great big hole—and he'd lost his gamble that she'd accept his explanation for that evening at face value.

On the other hand, he could be wrong. This could be as innocent as Elizabeth Williams seemed to think.

But if it wasn't, he'd just been handed a new crisis to deal with.

He rose abruptly, and the woman shot him a startled glance, once again stopping mid-sentence.

"Sorry." He groped for his cell phone and pulled it off his belt. "No rest for the weary."

She sent him a sympathetic look. "My. I don'

envy you being on call at all hours. Are you ever able to enjoy a social event without interruption, or finish a meal?" She gestured to his untouched food and wine.

"On occasion. But not tonight. Excuse me." He jabbed the talk button, put the phone to his ear, and strode toward the hedge as he pretended to carry on a conversation.

Once safely on the other side, the voices and laughter and music muted by the shrubs, he slowly slipped the phone back on his belt and took a deep breath.

It didn't stop the tremble in his fingers.

He balled his hands into fists and shoved them into his pockets as he started toward the house, his mind racing.

It was important not to overreact. People made mistakes when they did that. And he didn't make mistakes. He couldn't afford to. The clinic depended on him, and he refused to put that operation at risk by taking chances. Olivia had been an anomaly, a problem caused by timing, not mistakes. But he'd fixed that problem.

And he didn't intend to let it resurface.

Ken entered the house, deactivated the security system, and headed for his study. The brandy had helped calm him the day Moira Harrison had shown up in his office. Another drink couldn't hurt.

At the bar, he poured himself a scotch. Good

thing Ted couldn't see him now. But he'd never display such atypical behavior in public. That would be a mistake.

The kind he didn't make.

As Ken settled into his chair with his drink and slowly sipped the fiery liquid, he began to distill two clear thoughts from the muddle in his brain.

He had to follow through on his plans for Verna Hafer on Sunday. The situation in Guatemala was getting more urgent by the day, and the clinic required funds ASAP.

But in the meantime, he needed to get a handle on the activities of a certain reporter who was too nosy for her own good.

And if he discovered anything to suggest she was trying to thwart his plans, he'd figure out a way to make certain she didn't succeed.

⇒ 15 ⇐

Steering wheel clasped in her left hand, Moira twisted her wrist to check her watch as she turned onto the Kirkwood street Phoenix Inc. called home. At the same time, she stuffed the last of her fast-food burger into her mouth with her other hand.

It was already 7:30—far later than she'd planned. What a day.

She whipped into a parking spot across th

reet from Cal's office and set the brake. If
ie'd had any idea her last interview was going
⟩ run so long, she'd never have accepted his
ivitation to meet after work to discuss their
eparate reconnaissance missions. She didn't
xpect the man to give up his Friday night for a
onpaying client.

Yet he hadn't backed out when she'd called to
ive him an update on her timing and offered to
eschedule. Nor had she pushed him to. A Friday
ight in Cal's company was far better than one
oent surfing the net, zoning out in front of the
elevision, or even reading the latest bestseller
ie'd picked up at the bookstore last weekend.

She fished her lipstick out of her purse. Too bad
e hadn't suggested they meet at his house
gain instead of at the office. Or offered to host
nother pizza party instead of so readily agreeing
⟩ her proposal that they deal with dinner on their
wn.

With a quick swipe, she outlined her lips,
ecapped the tube, and dropped it back in her
urse. Oh, well. She wasn't going to let that
ninor disappointment ruin her evening.

After stuffing the wrappers from her dinner
ack into the bag, she wadded it into a ball and
lid out of the car.

As she crossed the street toward the Phoenix
ffice, the door opened and Cal smiled at her.

"I saw you pull up." He flicked a glance at the

crumpled bag bearing the familiar golden arche
logo. "Nikki would disapprove."

She slipped past him. "She's not into fas
food?"

"If it's not organic, it's on her cease and desis
list." He closed the door behind her and set th
locks. "I'll get rid of the evidence for you."

She passed it over when he extended his hanc
"Are we meeting in the conference room again?"

"Yes." He held his access card over the pane
beside the door to the private offices, the
pushed it open and stepped aside to let her pass
"I'll grab my notes and join you in a minute."

Moira continued down the hall as he turned le
into his office, chose a seat on the long end of th
rectangular table, and pulled her own notes fror
her lunch at the Woman's Exchange out of he
purse.

He rejoined her sixty seconds later, carryin
two cardboard cups.

"You got ice cream?" She smiled as he set on
of them in front of her.

"I picked it up when I ran out for dinner."

She pried the lid off hers. Mint chocolate chip
He'd remembered.

Some of her disappointment evaporated.

"Thank you."

"Hey, it gave me an excuse to indulge too. S
from what you said on the phone, it sounds lik
you had an interesting lunch."

"Very."

She dug into her ice cream, flipped open her notebook, and filled him in while he jotted a few notes.

When she finished, he leaned back in his seat. "An interesting picture is emerging that doesn't quite jibe with the good doctor's paragon-of-virtue public image. He's short-tempered and distracted at home, estranged from his wife, and has been plagued with recurring nightmares in recent weeks. Plus, we have regular—almost predictable—infusions of capital to Let the Children Come from recently deceased residents of nursing homes he's visited. That's a bit too coincidental for my taste."

As his implications registered, Moira swallowed her mouthful of ice cream and exhaled. "Are you suggesting what I think you're suggesting?"

He lifted one shoulder. "We also have a reference to a neighbor's cabin, which the neighbor rarely uses."

"I wonder if it happens to be near Defiance?"

"I've already made a note to check into that on Monday. The assessor's office in St. Charles is closed until then. But I'm glad they mentioned the man's name. That makes things easier."

"Okay." She swiped at a drip of ice cream on the table with a paper napkin and furrowed her brow. "Here's what I'm not getting. There are easier ways to solicit donations than targeting older people. Plus, none of those deaths apparently raised any red flags."

"No reason they should. The most recent two had chronic, deteriorating conditions. There would have been no autopsy if they died peacefully. And there are ways to make that happen."

The shiver that caused Moira's fingers to tremble had nothing to do with the coldness of the ice cream.

"Now we have an emergency situation at the clinic and an acute need for funds." Cal tipped his head and narrowed his eyes. "That could trigger recurring nightmares for a lot of reasons —including the necessity of accelerating the time-table for a new infusion of dollars. The last donor only died in March."

Moira caught her breath. "You mean . . . someone might be in his sights right now? Assuming the ominous scenario we're constructing is valid?"

"That would be a logical deduction."

"Man, this is getting heavy." She tapped the plastic spoon against the edge of the cardboard cup. "It's also getting complicated. I mean . . . what does all this have to do with my vanishing young woman?"

"I don't know yet. I do, however, have a strong suspicion that Olivia Lange is missing. Let me tell you what I learned today."

As Cal recounted his visit to the aide's duplex

Moira let the last couple of bites of her ice cream melt into a sticky pool in the bottom of her cup.

"So it's probable that Blaine and Olivia did know each other." Moira set her spoon back in the cardboard container as Cal finished.

"Well enough for Blaine to give her advice, it seems—if he's the doctor the neighbor referenced. From what she said, they were on friendly terms."

"But the neighbor hasn't seen her for a month, and the landlord is looking for her. Plus she quit her job for no reason." Moira moistened her lips, not liking where this was going. "Do you think she might be the woman I saw on the road?"

"That possibility occurred to me. But we have to consider the abusive boyfriend angle too. Maybe she did go back to him. I plan to check that out this weekend. In the meantime, though, I spoke with her landlord. He's going back to Olivia's place tomorrow to make another attempt to collect his rent. If no one answers the door this time, he plans to go in. I convinced him to let Dev meet him and do a walk-through. I'd do it myself, but the neighbor whose faucet I fixed would recognize me."

"What pretext did you use to get the landlord to cooperate?"

"None. I told him we were PIs investigating a missing person case. He was happy to assist. I think he figures if we locate her, he might get his back rent."

"What are you hoping your partner finds on this walk-through?"

"A toothbrush, preferably."

Moira frowned. "Why?"

"Because I have a tooth. And I have a feeling the DNA might match."

She wrinkled her brow. "You lost me. You have a tooth?"

"I never mentioned it, because I didn't think it would lead to anything. After you came to the office the first time, Dev and I took a drive out to the accident site and gave it a thorough going-over. I found a tooth. As Dev pointed out, it could have been from a kid who fell off his bike, or an animal. It still might be, but I think it's worth checking to see if we have a DNA match between it and a personal item of Olivia's—assuming we can't locate her in the next twenty-four hours."

She chewed at her lower lip. "This whole thing has gotten a lot more involved than I expected when I first came to you for help—and it's taking you away from your billable clients."

"It's also an intriguing case."

His reassurance was kind, but Moira knew the work he and his colleagues were doing for her was costing the firm money. Maybe she could pitch in, as she'd done today with the doctor's wife.

"Is there anything I can do to help?"

He regarded her in silence as he mulled over

her offer. "I might do a little informal surveillance on the doctor this weekend. Probably on Sunday. If you don't have anything else going on, I wouldn't mind some company."

He wanted to spend more time with her.

That was unexpected.

Moira's spirits took a decided uptick.

"Just church in the morning, but I can be flexible on that. I think the Lord would forgive my absence, given we're working to bring about justice." The pleasure of his company was a bonus.

Or so she told herself, even if God saw through that excuse.

"Why don't I give you a call once I get a better handle on my schedule?"

"Sounds good."

"If you're ready to call it a night, I'll walk you out."

She gathered up her purse and notebook and stood. "You know, one of these days I'll have to meet these partners of yours so I can thank them for all their work on this case too."

"I'll thank them for you." He motioned her out the door, then flipped off the light behind them as they exited into the hall.

"You don't want me to meet them?" She tossed the question over her shoulder as they walked toward the lobby.

"Nope. Especially Dev." He leaned past her to

open the door to the reception area. Giving her another whiff of that toe-tingling aftershave he always wore.

"Why not?"

The security door clicked shut behind them as he followed her toward the entrance.

"He thinks you're hot."

She cast a startled look at him as she reached the entry, uncertain how to respond.

Cal grinned at her and opened the front door. "And for the record, I saw you first."

Was that a backhanded way of letting her know he was interested in more than a business relationship? That as much as he'd loved his wife, he was ready to move on? Or was he just engaging in some lighthearted flirting, the way a lot of guys did?

As he watched her, Cal's lips flattened. "Sorry. That remark came out of nowhere—and it wasn't very professional. I don't usually slip like that. I didn't mean to offend you."

He thought she was offended?

She needed to clear that up. Fast.

"I'm not offended in the least. I'm flattered—and hopeful." If he could be honest, she could too. "The fact is, I've enjoyed our interaction. I that leads to a more . . . personal . . . relationship after this case is finished, I'd be very open to that."

For a long moment he studied her, faint furrow

etching his brow as he gripped the edge of the open door. Then he reached up, rubbed the back of his neck, and shifted his gaze to a large, mounted photo of a stunning sunset on the far wall.

"Did I ever tell you my wife was a photographer?"

Moira scanned the landscapes and still lifes she'd noticed on her first visit. They were similar in style to the ones in Cal's office and his home and all were imbued with a distinct personality. She could almost feel the presence of the woman he'd loved as she examined them.

He obviously felt the same way.

She fought down a flutter of disappointment.

"No. I assume these are hers?"

"Yes. She was very talented—in many ways." He looked back at her. "It's been hard letting her go."

"I can understand that."

"But she also believed in enjoying today and leaving yesterday in the past. I want you to know that since I met you, I've been working on adopting that philosophy. I'm not there yet . . . but I'm finally moving in the right direction."

The warmth and sincerity in his eyes tempered her sudden melancholy—and restored her hope.

"For the record"—she smiled as she borrowed his earlier phrase—"I'm a very patient person. As some sage once said, good things are worth waiting for."

"Now I'm the one who's flattered."

A breeze from the open door behind him wafted that appealing scent her direction again as he looked down at her, and it was all she could do not to reach up and brush her lips over his.

Judging by the sudden darkening of his irises, and the abrupt step he took away from her, the same thought had crossed his mind.

"I'll call you tomorrow morning."

She swallowed and held on tight to the strap of her purse. "Okay. Thanks for staying late tonight to meet with me."

"Not a problem." He touched her arm as she turned away, and she swiveled back toward him. "I think we're making progress . . . on a lot of fronts."

Her pulse accelerated as his fingers warmed her skin. "Me too." The words came out in a slight squeak, and she cleared her throat. "Talk to you tomorrow."

Feeling like a schoolgirl with her first crush, Moira tried to get herself back under control as she crossed the street. She was a grown woman. Thirty-three years old. Way past the infatuation stage. This kind of reaction was ridiculous.

Yet when she paused beside her car and looked back, her heart wasn't listening. In defiance, it did the oddest little skip as Cal raised his hand in farewell and sent her a slow, appreciative smile.

Man, did she have it bad.

With a quick wave of her own, she slipped into the car, shoved the key in the ignition, and started the engine.

At least her feelings weren't one-sided.

She cast one final glance in the rearview mirror before she turned the corner. Cal remained standing by the door, one shoulder propped against the frame, arms folded over his chest. Watching her.

Perhaps wishing the evening hadn't ended quite so early, as she was?

Still, he'd opened the door to tomorrow. That was a plus—and one more incentive to wrap up the case of the vanishing woman with the terrified eyes as soon as possible.

They were close too. She could feel it. Pieces of the puzzle were starting to turn up. Some were fitting together, and despite the gaps, a shocking picture was beginning to emerge. One that sent an icy ripple through her. If their reasoning was sound . . . if Blaine was involved in some sinister, macabre game . . . this could get messy very fast. Maybe even dangerous.

That was scary.

But Cal and his colleagues were up to the challenge. She had no doubt of that. And once they'd compiled sufficient evidence, they'd hand it off to law enforcement for the cleanup.

In the meantime, she had a surveillance gig with Cal to look forward to.

A smile played at the corners of her mouth as

she flipped on her turn signal. Funny. She had a feeling that of all the dates she'd ever gone on, the evening she'd spent sorting through trash with Cal and the hours she'd spend sitting in a car with him on Sunday doing nothing would end up ranking among the most memorable.

And someday, if all went well, she'd tell him that.

⇒ 16 ⇐

As Cal fired the last round in his magazine and lowered his compact Sig Sauer, someone tapped his shoulder.

He turned. Dev, also sporting ear protection and safety glasses, checked out the paper target positioned at fifteen meters, gave a thumbs-up, then inclined his head toward the exit.

After slipping the pistol into the concealed holster on his belt, Cal retrieved his target, picked up the case holding his full-sized Sig, and followed his partner toward the door, dumping the target in a trash bin as he passed. Dev must have found something interesting during his reconnaissance at Olivia's duplex this morning i he'd bothered to track him down at the shooting range.

Once inside the small buffer room that separate the shooting area from the gun shop, Dev glance ver his shoulder to make certain the door had losed behind them, then pushed through the econd door, into the shop.

Cal followed, sliding his ear protection to the ack of his neck as he removed his safety lasses. "What's up?"

Shucking his own safety equipment, Dev estured toward a quieter corner in the store and d the way over to it. "I had an interesting norning. It seems your friend Olivia has, indeed, anished."

A spurt of adrenaline tripped Cal's pulse up a otch. "What did you find?"

"A pile of mail on the floor under the slot in the ont door. Moldy bread in the cupboard. Sour nilk in the refrigerator, dated to expire three veeks ago. The oldest postmark I could find on ne mail was April 14."

"The day before Moira saw the woman on the oad."

"Uh huh. I also got this." Dev fished a kraft-olored evidence envelope out of the inside ocket of his jacket. "The requested toothbrush."

"Any problem with the landlord?"

"Nope. He was very impressed with my PI cense. Not to mention my suave and profes-ional demeanor."

"Let's not get carried away." Cal shot him a wry ook as he set his pistol case on an empty shelf. After pulling a pen out of his pocket, he initialed

271

the envelope, adding date and time. "I'm going t
run this and the tooth by the lab this afternoon."

"I thought that might be your plan." Dev reache
into his pocket and withdrew another envelope
"I swung by the office and picked this up."

"Thanks." Cal took it, dating and initialing tha
envelope as well.

"I've got more for you too. Olivia paid he
first month's rent and deposit with a credit carc
The landlord was kind enough to share th
number and expiration date with me."

"Seriously?" Cal slipped both envelopes int
his pocket. That was an unexpected bonus.

"Hey . . . I told you I was smooth. Anyway,
checked out the number with one of our infor
mation brokers. The last charge was from
Walgreens on April 15."

"I owe you for this."

"I'll add it to your tally." He cocked his hea
back toward the range. "Let's hope you don't nee
to use your stellar shooting skills in Mexico."

"I'm with you. We're discussing strategy for th
trip on Monday, right?"

"That's the plan, as far as I know. Connor's stil
gathering intel and connecting with the Mexica
consulate, but he says he'll have it together b
then. Are you hanging around for a while?"

Cal checked his watch. "Nope. I was wrappin
up when you got here. Thanks for making
special trip."

"No problem. I need to get in a little practice myself before we head south of the border. When you mentioned yesterday you were coming here, I decided to add some practice to my weekend agenda too."

"Are you expecting trouble on the trip?"

"I hope not. But I'd rather be prepared. You need me to do anything else on the vanishing woman case? Maybe talk to your friend Moira? See if my stellar interrogation skills can ferret out any new information she might have forgotten about that rainy night?" Dev grinned and winked.

"Forget it."

"Spoil sport."

"Go practice your shooting."

"I'd rather practice another skill." He waggled his eyebrows.

"That's why Moira is off-limits."

"Getting proprietary, aren't we?"

Cal pulled his ear protection off his neck and ignored that comment. "Listen, I need to borrow the Explorer tomorrow morning. For work reasons."

"You're avoiding the subject."

"So are you. Let's talk about the Explorer."

"You know I hate the van." Dev grimaced and huffed out a breath. "Good thing I don't have any social activities planned for the day. At least I'll have the Explorer tonight. My date thanks you." He gave a mock bow. "So what are you doing tomorrow morning?"

"Surveillance on our humanitarian of th
year. All day, in fact. I'm switching vehicles wit
Connor around noon so Blaine doesn't get sus
picious. If you want the Explorer back befor
Monday, set up a swap with him."

"Nah. I'm just going to finish up some cas
notes tomorrow and veg. Better than surveil
lance, though. You'll be bored out of your mind.

"Maybe not."

Crack investigator that he was, Dev home
right in on that comment. "What aren't yo
telling me?"

"I plan to have some pleasant company."

His partner appraised him. "You're takin
Moira along?"

"Why not? Like you said, it should be quiet—
but it's possible we might discover some worth
while information."

"And if you don't, you'll have spent the Sunda
with a hot chick. I like that angle. It's a win-win.

Cal sent him a watch-your-step look. "It's no
an angle. And she's not a chick."

A few beats of silence ticked by as De
appraised him. "Sorry. I'm sure she's a very nic
woman. She must be, to lure you out of your self
imposed social exile. And all kidding aside, I'n
glad. It's about time you rejoined the land of th
living." He slipped his safety glasses back on, hi
brief serious mood evaporating. "You want t
swing by my place tomorrow morning an

exchange vehicles? It may be a late party night, and I was planning to sleep in."

"Sure. Thanks again for dealing with the landlord today." He picked up his pistol case.

"Piece of cake. The guy was putty in my hands." With a rakish thumbs-up, Dev strolled away and pushed back through the door to the range.

Exiting the building, Cal shook his head. Dev was a piece of work. But one thing you could count on—despite his flippant manner, he was a pro through and through: always prepared, cool under fire, excellent instincts. And in a dicey situation, he could go from Mr. Laidback to the Terminator in a heartbeat. If Cal hadn't witnessed the warp-speed transformation on a number of occasions, he'd never have believed it.

Dev's undercover ATF work, however, had changed him. The difference was subtle, one only close friends and family would notice, but even when he kidded these days his eyes held a hint of sadness.

Cal hit the autolock button on his keychain, tossed his safety gear onto the passenger seat, and climbed in, setting the pistol case beside him. Whatever had happened to his carefree college buddy during his undercover stint had left scars deep enough to make him walk away from the career he'd aspired to for as long as they'd known each other.

Then again, they all had their secrets.

But it had felt good to share his with Moira.

Clicking his seat belt into position, Cal smiled as he backed out of the parking spot.

Dev was right. No matter what information they got tomorrow—or didn't get—the day would still be worthwhile.

An hour later, as Cal double-checked the address for Wayne Garrison against the seedy four-family flat in south city, it was clear that despite the less-than-optimal condition of Olivia's duplex, she'd moved up in the world when she'd left this place. Tape was holding the broken glass in place on a second floor window, the front door hung open, and the edges of two of the concrete steps that led to the sagging porch had crumbled.

Places like this were one of the reasons he'd never stopped carrying a gun.

He slipped it out of the concealed holster and into his pocket. Then he slid out of the van, locked it, and started toward the front door, skirting pieces of broken pavement in the sidewalk.

A set of wooden stairs inside led him up to 2-A, past one unit emitting rock music and another in which voices were raised in argument. A crumpled fast-food bag had been tossed in a far corner, and the distinctive skunky scent of marijuana hung in the air.

At Garrison's apartment, he stopped outside the door and listened.

Music was playing in there too—tuned to a more reasonable level—but he could also distinguish male and female voices.

Excellent. Garrison was home.

After one more sweep of the hall, he knocked.

The voices inside went silent.

A few seconds later the door cracked open, and Cal gave the man who answered a swift scan. Early twenties, sporting several days' growth of stubble and unkempt longish hair, he wore worn jeans and a dirty T-shirt with a picture of Mickey Mouse on the front. His feet were bare.

On the plus side, his eyes were clear—if suspicious. It was a lot easier to get answers from people who weren't high.

"Yeah? Whaddya want?"

Not the most cordial greeting he'd ever received.

"Wayne Garrison?"

"What's it to you?"

"I'm trying to locate Olivia Lange."

"She ain't here." He started to shut the door.

Cal stuck his foot in the jamb. "Do you have any idea where she might be?"

The man eyed his foot. "No."

"When did you last see her?"

"Why do you want to know?"

"Was it the time you pounded on her door and she got the restraining order?"

Garrison glared at him. "Are you a cop?"

"Not anymore." Cal pulled out his credentials and flashed them at the man. "I'm a private investigator."

"Yeah?" Olivia's former boyfriend squinted at the license. "Why are you looking for her?"

"Because she seems to be missing."

"So who's payin' your bill? PIs don't come cheap." The man's features hardened. "That doctor put you up to this?"

Cal maintained his placid expression despite the sudden surge in his pulse. "I'm not at liberty to disclose the name of my client."

"I'll bet it was him. Liv didn't have any other friends."

"Why would he pay us to find her?"

Garrison shrugged. "Maybe they had a thing going. She liked him okay, I guess. I didn't. Wasn't for him, we'd still be together." His grip tightened on the door, whitening his knuckles. "Serve him right if she walked out, like she did on me."

"Any idea where she'd go?"

"Don't know, don't care." He started to shut the door again.

"You do realize, given your history with her, you might be a person of interest to the police if we don't find her." Cal removed his foot and played his ace, hoping it would win him a little cooperation.

The door stopped moving.

"I had nothing to do with her going missing."

"You weren't mad when she walked out? Revenge can be a strong motive."

"Sure, I was mad at the beginning. That's why I went over to her new place once. But I never went back again. Found me a new woman." He leaned away from the door and looked back into the room. "Get over here, Roz."

Cal waited, and a few seconds later a blonde moved into sight, cowering behind Garrison. He couldn't see much, just a glimpse of a low-cut halter top, short-shorts—and what appeared to be the fading yellow of a bruise on the jaw of a girl too young to be involved with some deadbeat who got his kicks abusing women.

He swallowed past his revulsion. Reminded himself he wasn't here to bust Garrison, just to get information.

"See. I don't need Olivia no more." The man jerked his head toward the girl. "Why don't you check out that doctor dude who hired you? She might've liked him, but he also made her nervous."

That could be a significant piece of news.

"Why was that?"

"Beats me. Had something to do with an old guy who died at the place she worked. She was real upset about it for weeks. I didn't ask a lot of questions."

"You know this doctor's name?"

The man sneered. "As if you don't."

"I'd still like you to tell me."

"Yeah? What's it worth to you?"

Cal had seen that calculating, this-may-be-a-way-to-make-a-buck look before. And he wasn't above paying off sources when necessary. In this case, though, it wasn't.

Looking past the man, he spoke to the girl in the background. "How old are you, Roz?"

"Don't answer that," Garrison barked out.

"My guess is fifteen, sixteen. Underage." Cal locked gazes with him. "Cops would be interested in that. I have a lot of buddies on the force."

As the man considered him, a bead of sweat popped out on his temple. "Okay. Fine. His name started with a B. Bland, Blame . . . something like that."

Close enough.

"Thanks." Cal shifted sideways so he could see the hovering girl again. "You want my advice? Ditch this guy before he hurts more than your jaw."

Garrison cursed and slammed the door in his face.

Watching his back all the way, Cal retreated to his van, grateful Garrison's apartment wasn't in the front of the building. If one of his windows faced the street, he wouldn't put it past the guy to draw a bead on him.

Once behind the wheel, he wasted no time

putting some miles between him and Olivia's former boyfriend—and calling Roz's situation in to one of his contacts at the Division of Family Services. If the girl turned out to be as young as he expected, Garrison was in big trouble—an unexpected bonus of his visit.

But there were many others. The brief interchange had confirmed Olivia hadn't reconciled with Garrison, sealed the connection between Blaine and Olivia, and suggested that an incident with Blaine and a nursing home resident had made Olivia nervous.

Coupled with the evidence Dev had found at her duplex, it was apparent Olivia had not only disappeared but vanished under suspicious circumstances.

And Cal was becoming more and more certain that only Blaine knew where she was.

Ken tapped a finger on his steering wheel and glanced around the grocery store parking lot. Between the fishing hat he used to wear at Ted's cabin and his dark sunglasses, he doubted anyone would recognize him. He'd also left the Claddagh ring that had caused all the trouble in the top drawer of his dresser. But he didn't like his clandestine stuff. It reeked of skullduggery. Nor had it been fruitful. Moira Harrison had done nothing with her Saturday morning to suggest she harbored the slightest suspicion about him.

He was probably overreacting to that whole pen incident Elizabeth Williams had referenced at last night's cocktail party.

Still, he couldn't shake the feeling it wasn't as innocent as it seemed—and his instincts had rarely let him down.

The nosy reporter came out of the store, pushing her groceries, and he slunk lower in his seat, keeping an eye on her. She loaded her bags into the trunk, returned the cart to the designated area, and backed out of her parking space.

He turned on his own engine, determined to keep her in sight for the next few hours.

By 1:00 in the afternoon, however—after following her to a dry cleaner, a shoe repair shop, and finally home—he'd discovered a big fat zero.

But his uneasiness hadn't dissipated . . . fueled, perhaps, by his plans for tomorrow.

At least he wouldn't have to worry about Olivia this time.

A twinge of regret pricked his conscience, and he let out a slow breath. It was a shame about her. She'd been a nice girl, and she'd had a tough life. How sad, too, that there was no one to miss her—no family, no friends, and certainly not that scumbag of a boyfriend she'd ditched, with his encouragement.

In a way, though, it was lucky—or providential—that of all the people who might have caused him problems, it had been someone like her. Someone who could disappear without causing waves or creating a void in another life. Someone whose absence would prompt no grief—nor an investigation.

Ken watched Moira haul in the last of her groceries and close the front door. After all the errands she'd already run, it was reasonable to assume she'd be home for a while, and he had rounds to do this afternoon. The Ravitch procedure he'd used yesterday to surgically correct the Davis boy's pectus excavatum had gone well, but he wanted to make sure no fluid was collecting under the skin and check for any signs of infection. The parents could use some hand-holding too.

That would be a far better use of his time than sitting outside Moira Harrison's condo.

But he'd give it another fifteen minutes.

Just in case.

Now that was very interesting.

From behind the tinted windows of the van, Cal scrutinized the black Lexus parked a few doors down from Moira's condo. Lucky thing she'd warned him about dripping sap from the pine trees when he'd called en route. If she hadn't suggested he park on the other side of the street, he might have pulled in right next to the guy in the odd hat and dark glasses whose attention was fixed on her front door.

Cal retrieved his pen and notebook from his pocket, jotted down the license number, then pulled his BlackBerry off his belt and hit speed dial.

Moira answered on the second ring, her greeting telling him she'd recognized his caller ID. "Didn't we just talk? Are you lost?" Her tone was teasing.

"I'm in front. But there's been a new development. Do you have a back door?"

"Sure. It leads to the patio where I sit and listen to the neighbor play country music. Why?"

"I'm going to park around the block and come in that way. Can you wait out there for me? I'm not sure I'll recognize your unit from the back." He put the van in gear.

"Why don't you come in the front?" Her playful inflection had given way to puzzlement.

"Someone's watching your condo."

Silence.

He hated to scare her, but facts were facts—and forewarned was forearmed.

"Hang tight, okay? I'll be there shortly. And boot up your laptop, if it's not on." He tapped the end button, slid the BlackBerry back into its holder, and headed for the corner—glad now he'd given in to the impulse to swing by her place and fill her in in person rather than on the phone.

But he was also concerned.

What slip had he or his colleagues made to alert someone to their investigation?

The answer eluded him. Nor did it matter, as long as they got this situation resolved before the risk to Moira accelerated.

Because he'd put another woman he cared about at risk once upon a time, and he didn't have the stomach for another tragic ending.

Moira wrapped her arms around her body and scanned the perimeter of the common ground behind her patio, doing her best to suppress the shiver that rippled through her despite the warmth of the late-May day.

Someone was watching her.

It was surreal.

And since she wasn't doing any serious investigative work at the moment, that someone had to be connected to the private investigation she'd initiated. But no one knew about that except Linda, and her friend would have kept such sensitive information under wraps.

"Moira . . . I'm here."

Despite Cal's calm, quiet tone she jumped as he materialized from around the bushes that gave her some modicum of privacy from the patio next door.

He put a finger to his lips and motioned her back inside.

She went without a word but turned toward him as soon as he entered and rolled the door closed behind him.

"What's going on?"

"I'm about to find out." He started toward he laptop, which was sitting on the dinette table.

She followed in silence as he sat and logge into REJIS.

"I thought only police had access to that." Sh leaned over his shoulder as the home page fo the Regional Justice Information Services wel site opened.

"Licensed PIs do too—except for arrest infor mation. We can only get convictions. The trut is, for a price, we have legal entrée to almos everything law enforcement does, except NCIC The FBI guards its national crime databas closely." After entering his security codes, Ca typed in a series of numbers and letters.

As a car registration appeared on the screer her lungs stalled.

Kenneth Blaine.

Staring at the name, Moira sank into the cha beside him. "I don't believe this."

"I suspected it might be him as soon as I sav the high-end car." He blew out a breath. "I wonde how long he's been keeping an eye on you?"

"I'm guessing long enough to realize I'm tryin to get to the bottom of that rainy night. He mus have followed me to your office or your house. couple of those were evening visits when h might have been free."

"That's possible—but if so, you'd think he'd b

concerned that we're tailing *him* and not so blatantly follow *you*. Because his presence here confirms he has something to hide and he's worried we might discover his secret. Rightly so, by the way. Evidence of wrongdoing keeps piling up, especially now that we've confirmed Olivia is missing."

She listened as he filled her in on Dev's visit to the duplex, as well as his stop at the lab to drop off samples and his conversation with Garrison.

"But do we have enough to prove anything?" She folded her hands into a tight knot on the table.

"No. At this point, it's all circumstantial. A scratched shoe. A verified connection between Blaine and Olivia. An alibi that has holes. Regular infusions of capital from deceased seniors to Let the Children Come. None of those mean much in themselves, but the individual pieces are beginning to pile up. If the DNA samples match, that might warrant getting law enforcement involved and launching an official investigation."

"When will you have the results?"

"Best case, Tuesday. Wednesday afternoon at the latest. Unfortunately, the three of us will be gone to Mexico on a personal security gig from Wednesday until Friday night." He frowned and rested his forearm on the table as he shifted toward her. "I wouldn't be too concerned about the timing if Blaine hadn't shown up here today.

The fact he's taking that kind of chance suggests he may be getting nervous. And fear is a powerful motivator—especially if you have secrets that could destroy your life."

Blaine wasn't the only one who was nervous. A coil of anxiety tightened in the pit of Moira's stomach. It wasn't a new sensation—she'd had it on occasion while doing investigative pieces for the newspaper—but for some reason this situation had an even more menacing feel.

And she wasn't thrilled to learn Cal would be out of the country. Somehow, knowing he was a phone call away had made her uneasiness manageable.

As if sensing her anxiety, Cal covered her clasped hands with one of his. "I think this is a lot bigger than either of us suspected that first day in my office."

"No kidding."

"I'd turn this over to law enforcement if I thought it would speed things up, but considering their caseload, the lack of hard evidence, and Blaine's reputation, I think we're better to pursue it ourselves for now. We'll give it a higher priority than they would. But since we'll be on our own, we also need to proceed with much more caution."

"I agree."

"Are you still up for some surveillance tomorrow?"

"Sure." Better than sitting around alone, worrying.

"Okay. Here's how we'll play it, in light of this new development. I'm going to have Connor stake out Blaine's house in the early morning hours. I'll have him follow Blaine to his first destination, which I assume will be Sunday services. The church secretary told me he never misses. Once we have that confirmed, I'll swing by to pick you up and we'll take over for Connor. Can you be ready to go at a few minutes' notice?"

"Yes."

With a nod, he rose and moved to the front of the condo. Stepping to one side of the large window in the living room, he checked out the street through the slanted mini blinds. "Looks like he's gone. I'll head out too, the same way I came—in case he's skulking around somewhere."

He detoured to the front door and paused to examine the keypad beside it. "Do you use your security system?"

"Yes. I arm it whenever I leave and at night."

"Good."

She followed him as he crossed back to the patio door, and when he turned toward her, the faint parallel grooves etched on his brow told her more eloquently than words that he was worried about her. While that warmed her heart, it also increased her own anxiety level. Strong, capable professionals like Cal didn't spook without reason. If he thought there was risk . . . there was.

"Do you have any other plans for today?"

"I was going to meet my friend for a walk, but I can cancel that."

"I think that would be wise. Let's not take any unnecessary chances for the next few days, until we sort this thing out."

"Okay." She did her best to smile. "I'll keep Euripides's advice in mind."

His lips twitched, softening the taut planes of his face. "And what did the ancient sage have to say on this subject?"

" 'Chance fights ever on the side of the prudent.' "

"Courtesy of your philosopher father again, I presume?"

"Of course." Her smile relaxed into the real thing. "I can't believe how many of those philosophy quotes stuck with me. Along with a few from Shakespeare, since he's also a great fan of the bard."

"I'd like to meet your dad someday."

"I'd like that too."

As his gaze caught and held hers, her heart skipped a beat.

"We're going to nail this, you know. Soon."

"I hope so."

He reached for the door. Hesitated. A muscle clenched in his jaw.

Then he turned back to her, lifted his hand, and touched her cheek.

Her lungs stopped working.

As every instinct in her body screamed at her to step forward—into his arms—she shoved her hands into her pockets. It was too soon. He'd admitted to her that he hadn't yet managed to let go of his wife. She had to be patient.

Even if it killed her.

"I'll call you tomorrow."

"Okay." Her voice cracked.

Throwing her yet another curve, he leaned close and brushed his lips across her forehead. "Lock up after me."

Before she could respond, he pulled the door open, moved outside, and closed it behind him. Prompting her with a twisting motion of his hand, he gestured to the lock.

Somehow she managed to flip the catch in spite of the tremble in her fingers.

With a final wave, he melted into the bushes at the side of the patio.

She remained where she was, staring at the spot where he'd disappeared, giving her pulse a chance to slow.

In all the months she'd dated Jack, despite the seriousness of their relationship—on her part, anyway—she'd never, ever felt this nerve-tingling excitement.

Giving her one more reason to be thankful for

the discovery of his betrayal, which had been devastating at the time but a blessing in the long run.

After flipping the lock, she closed the vertical blinds, blocking out the sun—and any prying eyes that might be about. Gloom settled over the room, and another shudder replaced the warmth of moments ago. There were so many unanswered questions.

But one thing for sure.

Until she was certain no one was watching her—perhaps with evil intent—she had a feeling she was going to spend her nights waging a mighty battle with insomnia.

⇒ 17 ⇐

"How are you feeling today, Verna?" Ken sat in the chair beside her bed and gave the elderly woman a quick assessment, the question no more than a polite formality. The nasal cannula feeding her oxygen was new since his last visit a week ago, yet her breathing remained labored. In addition, the bottom half of the bed was elevated, meaning her legs and ankles were swollen. Edema wasn't unusual with congestive heart failure, but hers was getting worse.

Blinking, she turned her head slightly and

squinted at him out of the sides of her eyes as she tried to focus. Not an easy thing to do with advanced macular degeneration. Especially in a dim room made dimmer because he'd closed the door most of the way when he'd entered.

"It's Ken Blaine, Verna."

Her brow smoothed. "Ah. Dr. Blaine. I didn't hear you come in. I guess I dozed off. It's nice of you to stop by."

"I always enjoy our chats."

"I'm afraid I'm not in a very talkative mood tonight. It's been a rough day." She sighed. "Maybe tomorrow will be better."

He slipped his hand into the inside pocket of his jacket. Fingered the syringe.

"I'm sure it will be. Why don't I just sit here for a while and keep you company? No need to talk."

A smile touched her lips. "My Henry used to do that when I was sick. Come in and sit by me. Hold my hand. I miss him so much."

He caught the glint of moisture in her eyes from the sliver of light spilling into the room through the crack in the door.

"But you'll see him again."

"I know. In a better place."

"There's a better place waiting for me."

His father's words from forty years ago echoed in his mind.

"To be honest, I'm looking forward to it."

293

Verna's fingers worked the edge of the blanket that covered her. "This isn't much of a life I'm leading, is it?"

Ken touched the syringe again.

"When all hope of recovery is gone, when there is nothing to look forward to except pain and deterioration and dependence, isn't this another way to relieve suffering?"

"I agree that quality of life is important, Verna."

Her eyelids drifted closed. "I wish I could still do all the things that used to give my life meaning. I was an excellent teacher in my day. Even after I retired, I tutored. And I always had a volunteer activity or two. I think people should contribute to society. Now I feel so useless." Her voice broke. "It's a hard thing to bear, Doctor."

"You're doing the compassionate thing by saving me the agony of enduring a life that's no longer productive or worth living."

"I'm sure it is. We all like to feel we're making a difference."

"The only thing I do these days is take up space. And I'm tired all the time."

"Why don't you let yourself drift off? I'll just sit here with you for a few minutes until you're asleep."

"You must have better things to do with Sunday evening than waste it on an old lady. Her words were faint, already slurring as sleep overtook her. "What time is it?"

"Close to 9:00. And I don't consider spending a few minutes with a friend a waste of time."

Especially when that friend also happened to be a Let the Children Come benefactor.

"You're a good man, Doctor."

Silence fell, broken only by the sound of Verna's breathing.

Keeping one eye on the door to the private room, Ken withdrew the syringe from his pocket, lowered it to his lap, and removed the plastic cap from the needle.

"Accept that sometimes death is a blessing."

In Verna's case, death was, indeed, a blessing. She had nothing to look forward to. No family living. No hope of improved health. No opportunity to lead a meaningful life. This was an act of compassion and charity, as it had been with his father forty years ago—and every time since. Plus, in death Verna would get her wish. Her life would matter again, thanks to the legacy she was leaving to Let the Children Come.

It was a no-brainer.

When her respiration evened out, he edged closer to the bed and folded back the covers. Her body was wasted beneath the shapeless, institutional hospital gown with the open back that was convenient for medical personnel but demeaning to patients, robbing them of their individuality. Here, Verna was simply Room 610—an old lady whose history was irrelevant because she had no future. Because she was playing a waiting game.

A game that was about to end.

Ken eased the edge of the hospital gown out from beneath her until he had a view of her upper leg. After positioning the needle, he slowly pushed it in.

She moaned and her eyelids flickered open.

Holding her leg in place with one hand, Ken leaned close as he kept a steady pressure on the plunger with the other.

"I'm still here, Verna. Dr. Blaine."

She blinked and grimaced at him in the dim light.

"My leg hurts."

"Let me have a look for you."

He withdrew the syringe, recapped it, and slipped it back in his pocket as he stood. "Where does it hurt?"

"On my thigh." She gestured to her leg.

He pretended to examine it. "I don't see any thing. Would you like me to turn on the light so can get a better look?"

"No." She let out a soft breath. "It's not as ba now."

"Good." He tucked her gown back under he resettled the covers. "Just relax. I'll stay unt you fall back asleep." He retook his seat.

The minutes ticked by in the silent room. On Two. Three. As her breathing slowed, Ke bowed his head.

Please welcome her home, Lord. Reunite her with her husband. Let her know that in death her life once more had meaning.

Reaching over, he touched her hand.

"Good-bye, Verna. Safe journey. And for all the children who need the clinic, thank you."

He rose and moved around the bed toward the door, checking his watch in the crack of light. 9:15. Perfect timing. The aide assigned to this room would be on break. He'd visited Verna often enough to learn staff patterns.

Still, he scoped out the corridor. He wanted no witnesses to his time of departure. That's what had gotten him in trouble with Olivia. Had he known she sometimes spent her breaks visiting with residents who had no friends or family, he'd have picked a different shift to end Edward Mason's suffering.

Instead, when he'd exited Ed's room that night he'd been headed his way. Panic had gripped him; it was dangerous to link the man's death too closely to his visit.

Thanks to the quick, clear-thinking genes he'd inherited from his father, however, he'd handled the crisis masterfully.

Blocking the door, he'd engaged her in conversation. Asked about the bruise on her cheek that he'd tried to cover up with makeup, one of many he'd noticed during the months he'd been visiting the facility. Subtly reminded her he'd

once found her sitting in a patient's room, hal
asleep, when she was supposed to be on duty.

That had drained the color from her face.

But he'd oozed sympathy, pretended to care,
he assured her he understood how stress at hon
could lead to sleepless nights and fatigue on tl
job, and wasn't it lucky he'd been the one to fir
her rather than one of her supervisors? Becau
they wouldn't take kindly to such a thing, wou
they? It might even be grounds for dismissal. F
was on her side, though, and if she had any issu
at home she'd like to talk about, he'd be happy
chat with her on his next visit. In fact, he'd bui
in some time for that, just in case. Would she lil
that?

A smile tugging at the corners of his mouth, Ke
slipped out the door of Verna's room without
backward glance and strode down the hall towar
the exit.

Olivia had fallen for his I-care-about-you-an
want-to-help spiel hook, line, and sinker. They
chatted often during his visits after that, and he
assumed the role of counselor, advising her
leave her abusive boyfriend. With his encourag
ment, she'd taken that positive step. All had bee
well, the incident in Edward's room forgotten.

Until it happened a second time.

Ken's smile faded as he once more consulte
his watch, then recorded an earlier departure tin
in the visitor registry at the front desk. Since l

was such a fixture at the place, no one paid much attention to his comings and goings, especially at this hour on a Sunday night. All part of his well-thought-out plan.

Planning was everything.

But he hadn't planned on Olivia.

He should have stayed in touch with her after he stopped visiting the nursing home where she worked. If he had, he'd have known she'd taken a new job at Maryville. But he hadn't seen any reason to continue their relationship. The incident with Edward had been history at that point.

And then she'd shown up at the door of Clara Volk's room just as he was slipping the syringe back into his pocket.

Talk about bad luck.

Ken stepped outside and drew in a lungful of the fresh air. Willed the knot in his stomach to loosen. That had been a terrible night. He'd done as much damage control as possible on site, certain she'd seen nothing specific in the dim room—but also certain she'd be suspicious when Clara turned up dead. That's why he'd invited her to meet him for a chat on Friday evening, ostensibly to catch up. But in the two days between their encounter in Clara's room and their get-together, as he'd wrestled with his dilemma, he'd decided on the only plan that would guarantee him the freedom to continue helping children here and in Guatemala.

A fine mist began to fall, prompting him to

retrieve his keys from his pocket and continu
toward his car.

Too bad he now had a reporter to worry abou
Still, he'd covered his tracks. And how muc
could she know? He'd been careful. He wa
always careful.

Lives depended on it.

The mist intensified, and he picked up his pac
Just one more task to take care of tonigl
before he headed home.

Once behind the wheel, he pulled the syring
out of his pocket, cleaned it with a wet wip
and dried it with a tissue. Probably overkill,
light of where he planned to dispose of it, bu
better safe than sorry. It was important to tak
care of all the details. Leave nothing to chanc
His father had taught him that, and he'd taken
to heart. In fact, if his dad were here right now
he knew exactly what the man would say.

Again, a smile touched his lips.

"I'm proud of you, son."

"Can you see what he's doing?" Moira leane
toward the dash in the Taurus.

Cal aimed the binoculars through the tinte
windshield at Ken Blaine, who was sitting behir
the wheel of his Lexus across the nursing hom
parking lot.

"No. It's too dark. He might be checking phor
messages."

300

Moira sank back, sighed, and extracted another celery stick from the plastic bag on the seat beside them. "You know, after spending the past ten hours with you doing surveillance that hasn't produced a thing, I can see that the glamour bestowed on the PI profession by Hollywood and novelists is highly overstated." She dipped the celery in a jar of peanut butter and chomped on it.

"We do have exciting moments now and then."

"Yeah?"

He kept the binoculars fixed to his eyes, lips bowing at her skeptical tone. "There's another bottle of water in the cooler behind you."

"No, thanks. After that last high-speed emergency trip to the ladies room, I'll hold off."

Cal's smile broadened as he thought about her fidgeting on the seat beside him, then muttering "Finally!" and racing for a fast-food restroom while he circled the building and Blaine filled his tank at the gas station across the street.

As the doctor's car began to move, Cal set the binoculars beside him, recorded the time in his surveillance log, and started his own engine. "For the record, this has been one of my more enjoyable surveillance jobs. I don't usually have company. And you've been a great sport, considering the less-than-gourmet food I supplied and the Chinese fire drill bathroom stop."

"It's been an experience, that's for sure. But

truthfully? I enjoyed it too. Almost as much [as] sorting through trash in your garage."

He chuckled and began to follow Blair[e], keeping two cars between them. "I'll try to [do] better once this is over."

A beat of silence passed.

"Is that a promise?"

Her tone was still lighthearted, but he al[so] heard the hopeful note in her voice.

Was he making a promise? Implying he intend[ed] to ask Moira on a real date down the road?

Yeah. He was. Finally. After a lot of so[ul]-searching . . . and saying good-bye . . . he w[as] ready to see where this chemistry between the[m] might lead.

"That's a promise."

She didn't respond, but when he flicked [a] quick glance her direction, he could see the hi[nt] of a smile on her face despite the shadows [in] the car.

They drove in comfortable silence for a fe[w] minutes until Blaine's route became clear.

"I think he's going home." Cal groped for [a] celery stick. If it wasn't so late, he'd sugge[st] stopping for some real food once this was over. [It] was a shame they hadn't gotten more out [of] the day than some pleasant conversation and . . .

"I wouldn't have pegged Blaine for a Taco B[ell] man."

At Moira's comment, Cal jerked his attenti[on]

om the bag of veggies back to the road. The
octor was turning into the parking lot of the
st-food eatery.

He wasn't a Taco Bell man himself, but even
fried beans sounded appealing about now.

Slowing, he approached the entrance at a crawl.
laine passed up the parking spots near the door
nd continued toward the back, where he stopped.

"Grab the binoculars. Let's see what he's up to."
al killed his headlights and swung into the lot.

Moira fitted them against her eyes and aimed
em at Blaine.

Cal stopped halfway down the lot and pulled
to a parking spot that gave Moira a view out
er side window to the back of the building.

Blaine got out of his car, looked around as if
verify no one was watching, then strode toward
dumpster.

"Can you see what he's holding?" Cal leaned in
loser to Moira's shoulder.

"I think it's his Panera bag from when he
topped there this afternoon. But why would he
itch it here? Why not wait till he got home?"

The man lifted the lid on the dumpster, tossed
e bag inside, and returned to his car, still
canning the parking lot.

Moira lowered the binoculars as Blaine
acked up and circled around the other side of
e building, moving toward the exit. "What do
ou make of that?"

"Highly suspicious." Cal tapped a finger on t[he] wheel and furrowed his brow. "Okay. I want [to] check out the dumpster, but I also don't want [to] lose Blaine in case he's not going home y[et]. We'll come back here as soon as we verify h[is] destination. I doubt there's a dumpster pickup [on] Sunday night, and a Panera bag will be easy [to] find at a Taco Bell."

On the opposite side of the building, Blai[ne] pulled back into traffic. Cal exited the wa[y] they'd entered and fell in behind him.

Six minutes later, after Blaine pulled into h[is] driveway, Cal retraced their route to Taco Bell.

As he backed close to the industrial-sized dum[p]ster, Moira gave it a skeptical perusal over h[er] shoulder. "How are you going to get the bag out[?]"

"Oh, I have a few tricks up my sleeve." Cal s[et] the brake, retrieved a pair of latex gloves fro[m] the glove compartment, and popped the trun[k]. "Want to watch?"

"Anything to stretch my legs." She was out t[he] door in two seconds.

He followed more slowly, hoping whatever w[as] in that bag would give them the solid lead th[at] had eluded them up until now.

Because he wanted this case solved—soon[er] rather than later.

Moira waited for him by the trunk, watching [as] he sorted through his equipment and pull[ed] ut some sort of reaching device and a flashlight.

"See?" He held up the gadget that had a claw at ne end and a pistol grip at the other. "These ren't just for senior citizens or people with isabilities."

"I'm impressed."

"Hang on to this and stick close while I take a uick look."

He handed her the device, stepped up onto the ar bumper, and swiveled toward the dumpster. After lifting the lid, he aimed the flashlight inside nd clicked it on.

"Got it. Four feet down. Let's switch." He xchanged the flashlight for the reacher, leaned ver, lifted out the bag, and dropped back to the avement. The whole maneuver took less than a ninute.

"Pretty ingenious." Moira leaned against the ide of the car as he stowed the equipment back n the trunk.

"PIs have to be." He gestured to her door. "Let's et back in before we check out what we have. 3ased on the weight, it's not much."

Once behind the wheel again, Cal uncrimped he top of the bag. As he looked inside, his xpression went from curious to grim.

In silence, he tipped the bag toward her.

Bracing herself, she peeked in.

A syringe lay in the bottom.

Her stomach clenched as she met his gaze

again. "I'm getting really bad vibes from this."

"So am I. I don't think whatever was in ther was intended to make someone better."

"Should we call the nursing home?"

He turned his head and frowned into th darkness. "Yeah. But we can't accuse Blaine anything or even hint at criminal intent unt we know what was in the syringe and if ther are any repercussions. My main concern is have them check on the people he visited, mak sure they're okay." He looked back at her. "A you up for a little pretext?"

With a life possibly hanging in the balance, sh was seeing the use of pretext in a whole differen light.

"Yes."

"Okay. My thought is a phone call from Elle Blaine saying her husband may have left h cell phone there tonight and she's trying to trac it down for him. You could say he was calle away on an emergency, so you aren't sure wh he visited, but wondered if someone there migh know, and could they check those resident rooms while you wait? Sunday nights should b slow enough to make that feasible, and Blaine well known enough to merit a little extra effo from the staff. Still with me?"

Her palms started to sweat. A lot hinged on ho well she pulled this off—and she wasn't used t lying. But she'd bluffed her way through som dicey situations in her investigative work. She could do this.

"Yes." She fished her phone out of her purse.

"We might turn you into a PI yet." He shot her a teasing look, took her phone, and keyed in several numbers. As he said the name of the nursing home for the automated directory assistance operator, he pulled a notebook and pen out of his pocket. A few seconds later, he jotted on the pad, ended the call, and tapped in another series of numbers before handing her the BlackBerry. "I've coded it to block caller ID. Good luck."

She took a deep breath, put the phone to her ear, and focused on the Taco Bell sign.

By the time she worked her way through the automated menu and got a live person, her pulse had slowed and she was ready to turn on the charm.

"Good evening. I'm so sorry to bother you with this, but my husband was in earlier tonight. You might know him. Dr. Ken Blaine? He comes regularly to visit members of his congregation and others who might need some companionship."

"Yes, I've seen him here. How can I help you?" The woman sounded cordial—and receptive. A positive sign.

"Well, if it's not too much trouble, I wondered if you could check the rooms he visited. He seems to have misplaced his cell phone, which is also his pager. As you can imagine, that's a disaster for a doctor. I'm afraid I don't know who he stopped in to see tonight, and I can't reach him to ask. An emergency came up."

"I'll be happy to ask around. Would you like to leave a number and I can call you back?"

"Actually, I don't mind waiting. It's very important that he find this ASAP."

"It may be a few minutes."

"That's not a problem. I'm always looking for an excuse to do some reading." She gave a little laugh.

"All right. I'm going to put you on hold."

Recorded music came over the line.

Moira moved the phone away from her mouth and shifted toward Cal. "They're checking."

He gave her a thumbs-up. "You did great. You almost had me believing you were a concerned wife."

"What's scary is that it was almost too easy."

"Only because there's a greater good at stake."

"I hope that's the reason. I'd hate to think have a natural propensity toward lying." She glanced into the backseat. "Since there's a ladies room close at hand"—she nodded toward the Taco Bell building—"I think I'll have the last bottle of water. Unless you want it."

"Nope." He reached between the seats, flipped open the cooler, and pulled out the solitary bottle. After twisting off the cap, he handed it over.

Moira took the bottle and guzzled half of

before stopping to catch her breath. "Better."

With a half-hitch grin, he leaned over, opened the glove compartment, and withdrew a folded brown envelope and a small plastic bag. As she watched, he signed the envelope, dated it, and wrote a description. Still wearing his latex gloves, he carefully retrieved the syringe, deposited it in the plastic bag, then put both the plastic bag and the Panera bag into the envelope and sealed it.

"What are you going to do with that?"

"No matter what we find out from the nursing home, I want a fingerprint check on the syringe. There's probably not enough trace liquid left to test, since it's been plunged, but it's worth a check. If everything's quiet at the home, I'll drop this at the lab in the morning." He set the envelope on the backseat. "Do you mind if I check my voice mail and return a few calls while you're on hold? My BlackBerry has vibrated a couple of times in the past twenty minutes."

"No. Go ahead."

As Moira waited, she couldn't help overhearing Cal's side of the conversation with one of his partners about their upcoming Mexico trip. He was tossing around terms like ambush, fake roadblock, gunmen, and drug traffickers. Then the discussion moved on to weaponry and vests. Bulletproof, she assumed.

So not all the cases Phoenix took involved

safe, low-key activities like today's surveillance. Some put them in the line of fire.

That was more than a little unsettling.

"Mrs. Blaine?"

As the woman from the nursing home came back on the line, she forced herself to refocus.

"Yes. I'm still here."

Cal cast a look her direction, spoke softly, and ended his call.

"Sorry for the delay. We checked with Sarah Kincaid, the member of Dr. Blaine's congregation who he visits regularly. She told us he'd also planned to stop in and see another resident before he left. I'm sorry to say when we went to check her room for your husband's phone, we discovered she'd passed away. That's why this took a bit longer than I expected."

Shock rippled through Moira as her gaze connected with Cal's. "I'm so sorry."

"It wasn't unexpected. She's been very ill for months. But we didn't have a chance to do a thorough search for your husband's phone."

"Of course. I understand. If you do come across it, would you call his exchange?"

"We'll be happy to. If you could let him know about Verna Hafer's passing, we'd appreciate it. He's been visiting her for some time."

"I'm sure he'll want to know. Thank you for your help."

As Moira ended the call, Cal spoke, hi

expression solemn. "The woman he visited died."

"Yes."

"We need to get an autopsy done." He tapped the keypad of his phone. "Time to call in the big guns."

≫ 18 ≪

Moira stifled a yawn and blinked at her computer screen, trying to focus on the text in front of her.

No dice.

Between the hustle in the newsroom, fatigue from her late night, and the questions pinging around her brain about a certain humanitarian of the year, no way could an article on the controversy over a new wastewater facility hold her attention.

The trill of her cell phone gave her legitimate grounds to put the story aside for a moment, and she grabbed at the excuse. Especially when she checked caller ID and saw it was Cal.

"Good morning." She swiveled away from her desk. "What time did you get home last night?"

"About 1:00."

She wrinkled her nose. "Ouch."

"I had a feeling it would run long. That's why I asked if one of the patrol officers could run you home. Suffice it to say, St. Louis County PD was very interested in our theory."

"Interested enough to act?" She hoped so. It had been clear in last night's session with the police that Cal's former colleagues respected him—enough to take the off-the-wall story they'd listened to far more seriously than if it had come from most run-of-the-mill PIs.

"On Verna Hafer, anyway. The nursing home has been notified an autopsy is going to be performed by the medical examiner, and the body is being retrieved as we speak. County is also going to have the prosecuting attorney authorize lab analysis on the syringe. Plus, they're planning to call her attorney today and see if Let the Children Come is mentioned in her will."

"How long will all that take?"

"Too long, for the most part." His voice was taut with frustration. "Typical red tape stuff and an overworked staff. The medical examiner's report could take six weeks. The analysis of the syringe, about a week since they're going to make it a priority. On the positive side, we might have an answer on the will a lot faster, depending on how cooperative Verna's attorney is."

"What happens with Blaine in the meantime?"

"Nothing. There aren't sufficient grounds yet to bring any sort of formal charges. But there's no much chance he'll disappear. Prominent figure don't vanish easily."

"Only people like Olivia." She sighed. "Isn't i sad that someone could fall off the face of th earth and not even be missed, let alone have anyone who cared?"

"Yeah." A beat of silence ticked by, followed by an answering sigh. "The best we can do for her at this point is get some answers, and I'm working on that. I have a meeting this morning, but I did get a full name from my crisscross directory to go with the neighbor's cabin Ellen Blaine mentioned. Ted Lauer. I placed a call to St. Charles to see if I could sweet-talk the assessor's office into checking property deeds in the area, and they promised to have something by tomorrow."

"So it's a waiting game."

"Yes. But at least the pieces finally seem to be falling into place."

"They're not creating a pretty picture, though." Moira stared out the window on the far wall, where dark clouds were beginning to mass on the distant horizon. "The problem is, even if we get a DNA match between the tooth and tooth-brush —and despite the fact my so-called Good Samaritan wore a Claddagh ring—we can't directly connect Blaine to Olivia on that rainy night or prove any kind of foul play."

"Yet. Key word. Trust me, I've seen much tougher cases solved. This is going to shake out sooner or later."

"I hope so. I started this whole thing because a woman's terrified eyes sucked me in and pleaded with me to help. No matter what else we find out about Blaine, I want answers for Olivia's sake."

"That's still a top priority for me too."

She heard an indistinguishable voice in the background, then Cal spoke again.

"I've got to run. I'll let you know what I find out about the neighbor's property before I leave on Wednesday for Mexico. If you need me while we're gone, don't hesitate to call. I'll have my BlackBerry with me at all times."

"Thanks." She fiddled with a paper clip on her desk. How much could she ask about the trip without breaching client confidentiality issues? "Listen . . . I don't want to pry, but I couldn't help overhearing your side of the phone conversation last night while I was on hold with the nursing home. This Mexico job sounds dangerous."

There was a brief pause, as if he was debating how much to tell her.

When he responded, his words were measured. "It's a situation that has more potential for danger than most, but all three of us are going and we'll be watching each other's backs. Plus we'll be fully equipped and well briefed."

"I didn't think most PIs carried guns."

"Most don't. But we're all ex–law enforcement so carrying is part of our DNA."

"Even in Mexico? Isn't that illegal there?"

Another pause. "It is. But because of Dev and Connor's backgrounds, we have . . . connections

Most of the heavy firepower will be handled by the local guys we subcontract, though—all of whom are experts. We'll be fine. Listen, gotta run. I'll give you a call before I leave."

The line went dead, and she pushed the end button, set the phone on her desk, and turned back to the computer.

But despite the encroaching deadline, her focus wasn't on the words about raw sewage that were running across the screen.

She wasn't buying Cal's reassurance about the Mexico trip, but what could she say? This was his job, and she had to trust the Phoenix crew had crossed all the t's and dotted all the i's. Nothing she'd observed so far led her to believe they wouldn't be thorough and buttoned-up. It was a professional operation, and Cal and his colleagues had plenty of experience.

Nevertheless, she knew that for the next few days, she was going to worry.

A lot.

And say far more prayers than usual.

The medical examiner was doing an autopsy on Verna Hafer.

As the bottom fell out of Ken's stomach, he angled away from his colleagues and let Sarah Kincaid's voice mail wind down.

There could be only one reason for an autopsy, considering Verna's age and health problems.

The police suspected foul play.

Why?

Pulse pounding, Ken replayed the message that had come in on his cell while he was in his regular Tuesday morning surgery. The older woman from his congregation was always talkative during his visits, but he tuned out most of her gossip. A few nods and uh-huhs seemed to satisfy her.

This, however, was big news.

"Dr. Blaine, I do apologize for calling on your personal line, even though you so thoughtfully gave me the number. But my goodness, we've had some excitement here! Since you and Verna Hafer were acquainted, I thought you'd want to know she passed away Sunday night. Now here's the odd thing—the police took her body. They're going to do an *autopsy*. Can you imagine? As if the poor woman hasn't suffered enough these past few months." Her tut-tut came over the line. "Anyway, I did think you'd appreciate being informed. I'll look forward to your next visit, as always."

Ken jabbed the end button, shoved the phone back onto his belt, and ducked into the surgical unit's men's room before any of his colleagues could initiate a conversation.

Once inside the stall, he leaned against the wall, closed his eyes, and forced himself to keep breathing.

Don't panic. Think this through logically. What could they know?

He ran through the events of Sunday evening in his mind. There had been no slipups. No witnesses. No evidence left behind. There was nothing to tie him to Verna except his weekly visits.

Was there?

Had he, by chance, missed something?

Beads of sweat broke out on his brow, and he grabbed some tissue off the roll. Swiped at his forehead.

Even if he'd made some minor mistake, though, he'd disposed of the syringe. And no one had seen him administer the morphine.

But the medical examiner would find it in Verna's body.

Still, they couldn't link him to it. Besides . . . why would they try?

Unless that reporter had somehow pieced things together.

He crumpled the tissue in his fist, his stomach clenching. Perhaps he'd underestimated her. She'd been nominated for a Pulitzer prize for investigative reporting, after all, according to the info he'd uncovered on his Google search. Meaning she was dogged and determined and fearless.

Plus, she'd noticed the stupid ring.

It wouldn't cause any more trouble, though. He'd left it in the top drawer of his dresser after he'd removed it on Saturday, before tailing her, as safety precaution. That's where it would stay too It made him sick to look at it.

But the damage had been done.

He tossed the wadded-up tissue in the toilet an flushed it away. Wishing he could do the sam with whatever evidence Moira Harrison ha stumbled across that had been powerful enoug to convince the police to demand an autopsy o Verna.

The question was, how much did she know?

Had she also, somehow, identified Olivia?

If so, could she have figured out his destination on that rainy night?

A surge of panic froze his lungs.

No. Not possible. If she had, the police woul be searching Ted's place with cadaver dogs b now.

They soon might be, though—unless he coul come up with some way to stop this thing befor it went any further.

His hands started to shake as he tried to thin through his options. There weren't many. Any thing he did could raise suspicion.

So what *could* he do?

Make sure there's nothing to find.

As the obvious solution echoed in his mind, h swallowed past the bile that rose in this throa at the prospect of that grim task.

Yet it had to be done. Tonight, if possible

Because if they found Olivia, they might find other incriminating evidence. A stray hair on her body, perhaps, despite the hood he'd worn. Or the stud from his tux shirt that had gone missing.

He should have gone with the river alternative he'd considered originally, instead of opting for land disposal.

But it was too late for second thoughts.

Twisting his wrist, he checked the time. He was done with surgery for the day, but he had a full schedule of appointments that would keep him at the office until late afternoon.

That was okay, though. He couldn't risk going out to the cabin in broad daylight, anyway. He needed the cover of darkness. Besides, he had preparations to make. Things to buy. Nylon rope and concrete blocks and . . .

His cell phone began to vibrate, and he yanked it off his belt to check caller ID. Marge. As he put it to his ear, someone else walked into the men's room.

Pushing through the stall door, he acknowledged his anesthesiologist.

"No rest for the weary." The man mouthed the words.

Somehow Ken managed the ghost of a smile as he nodded to the man and continued toward the door.

"What's up, Marge?" He exited and moved toward his locker.

"Sorry to bother you during surgery hours, but Dr. Gonzalez called again with a request for additional funds. We're operating on fumes right now, but I wanted to talk to you before I gave him the bad news."

Ken yanked his jacket out of his locker. After all the work he'd put into establishing the clinic, after all he'd done to keep it alive and growing, he was not going to let his dream crumble.

"Wire him everything that's left except for five hundred dollars. Tell him I'll supplement with some additional personal funds." He could manage another short-term loan. That should hold them until Verna's bequest came through. She'd told him her assets were in a trust, meaning no probate delays.

"All right. We've been getting some donations as a result of the follow-up media coverage of the earthquake too. They're only trickling in, but I'm praying God will provide."

"I'm confident he will. Tell Carlos I'll touch base with him later today or tomorrow. I have to run."

He ended the call, shoved the phone back onto his belt, and slammed the locker shut.

Those children needed Verna's money, and he was going to make sure they got it. No one—*no one*—was going to derail his operation. He clenched his fists at his sides, restraining the urge to kick the locker.

Turning, he found that his colleague had emerged from the men's room and was watching him with a surprised expression.

Not good.

Kenneth Blaine was always calm, cool, and in control. In public, anyway. He couldn't afford to let that image slip. That, too, would raise questions—and he was dealing with enough of those already.

"Problems with the clinic?" The man walked over to his own locker.

"The fund-raising is slow going." He kept his tone conversational, shading it with a touch of frustration, and relaxed his fingers. "And the need is great."

"Those kids down there are lucky to have you. Good luck."

"Thanks."

But as Ken walked away, his mouth settled into a grim line. Luck was overrated. As far as he was concerned, people created their own luck through planning, perseverance, and hard work. By taking on the hard jobs and doing what had to be done. No matter the cost.

Just as he had done in the past.

Just as he would do again tonight.

Double bingo." Cal set his phone back in the cradle on his desk as Dev passed his office, paused, and backed up.

"Good news?"

"News, anyway. That was one of my buddies from County. Verna Hafer's attorney was more than happy to confirm she left a very sizeable chunk of her very sizeable estate to Let the Children Come. And get this—she made that change in her bequests less than a month ago."

Dev gave a soft whistle and dropped into one of the chairs across from his desk. "I think you've latched on to a big one this time."

"I have more. I also talked—"

"Is this a party?" Connor stuck his head in the door.

"Sort of." Dev motioned him in. "Cal's closing in on our humanitarian of the year."

"Yeah?" Connor settled into the chair beside Dev. "What's the latest?"

Cal repeated what he'd told Dev. "Here's the other piece of news. St. Charles called five minutes ago with an address for the neighbor's property. It's closer to Defiance than Augusta. On a spur off the same road where Moira had the accident, a half mile farther down toward Highway 94."

"It would be interesting to take a look around that place." Connor crossed an ankle over knee. "Especially if you get a DNA match on the tooth."

"I had the same thought." Cal rolled his pen between his fingers. "I might have to come u

322

ith a pretext for the neighbor to get me legally
n the property this weekend."

"And if you don't get permission, you could
lways be checking out real estate in that area
nd find yourself lost," Connor offered.

"That did occur to me."

"You might want to take Moira with you
gain," Dev added. "A couple is always less sus-
icious. And if anyone does give you trouble,
ust tell her to smile. They'll be putty in your
ands."

"Thank you both for all the advice. I'll take it
nder advisement." Ignoring their grins, Cal
estured to a file in front of him. "You guys want
) run through our ops plan for Mexico one last
me? I spotted a few potential glitches we
hould discuss."

Connor rose and stretched. "You're reading my
nind. I've made a few modifications since my
hone conversation with our client earlier this
norning that I need to pass on anyway."

"I'll grab my coffee." Dev stood too. "But I
ave a call to return first. Give me ten. You want
) meet in the conference room?"

"Works for me." Cal reached for his phone
gain. "I've got a call to make too."

Dev exchanged a look with Connor. "I bet it's
Moira."

"I don't bet against sure things." Connor
isappeared out the door.

"Good point." Dev strolled off, whistling "Some Enchanted Evening."

Cal sent a dark look toward the doorway. He was hooked up with a bunch of comics. Shaking his head, he tapped in Moira's number.

Too bad they were right.

Except he had more than a phone call in mind.

⇒ 19 ⇐

Moira pulled into the parking lot next to Cunetto's, her pulse ticking up as she caught sight of a white van.

Cal was already here.

Pausing to check her lipstick in the rearview mirror, she tamped down the little flutter that cropped up every time she thought about the impromptu lunch invitation he'd extended three and-a-half hours ago. So what if it was premised on business? It might be true he had some updates to pass on before he left for Mexico but he could have done that by phone.

This was a semi-date.

At a real restaurant.

And there was no trash sorting or surveillance involved.

She'd take it.

Three minutes later, as she entered the front door, Cal removed his sunglasses, gave her slow, appreciative perusal, and smiled at her across the room.

She reciprocated, which did nothing to smooth out the sudden erratic beat of her heart. In his knife-crease gray slacks, white shirt, navy blue blazer, and rep tie, he was one very appealing man. A fact the woman behind the bar had also observed, based on the not-so-discreet glances she was sending his way.

Not that Cal had noticed. His focus was on her.

It had been *so* worth juggling a few commitments and deadlines to fit this lunch into her schedule.

As she crossed the room and joined him at the hostess desk, his smile broadened and those deep brown eyes warmed. "Hungry?"

Oh yeah.

She blinked. Wait. He meant food.

A flush crept up her neck, and she did her best to keep it below the collar of her mock turtleneck. "Starved. Your idea to come to The Hill was inspired. They have the best Italian food this side of Italy. And this place has killer cannelloni."

"No arguments from me. Besides, I owe you after the veggie sticks and peanut butter routine last weekend."

He took her arm as they followed the hostess to a table, the gesture merely polite—but that didn't stop her from savoring the proprietary touch of his fingers on her bare arm.

Once they were seated and had ordered, Cal leaned forward. "I have news."

She draped her napkin across her lap and rested her forearms on the table. "And I've been waiting with bated breath to hear it. You have my full attention."

As he passed on the latest information, all of which reinforced their conclusion that Blaine was playing a deadly game, some of her upbeat mood evaporated.

When he finished, she caught her lower lip between her teeth. "So now that we know Verna Hafer left a large bequest to Let the Children Come, and we also know Blaine needs funds for the clinic, can we assume he decided to step in and claim it sooner than God intended?"

"I think that would be a safe bet. Her drug screen will tell us a lot."

"Weeks down the road." She tapped a finger on the white tablecloth. "Did the lab have any luck with the syringe?"

"No. There were no prints, which didn't surprise me. I think we're dealing with a very thorough, careful subject. And as I suspected, there wasn't enough liquid left inside to test."

"Did you hear from your lab about the DNA on the tooth?"

"Not yet. I'm hoping to get the results tomorrow."

"So what do we do now?"

The waiter delivered their salads, and Cal dived in. "Nothing at the moment. Except hope Blaine stumbles. We know he's nervous, or he wouldn't have been watching you. He'll be more nervous when he finds out about Verna's autopsy. Since his *wife*"—he shot her a quick smile—"didn't pass on the news that she died, he'll stop in as usual to visit her next week. It would look odd if he didn't, given she's on his regular circuit. And nervous people make mistakes."

She suppressed a shudder and forked up some of her own salad. "I still can't believe a man like that would be involved in such a nefarious scheme. Why would he do it? He has position, prestige, power. He's been lauded for his charitable efforts by the governor, by the media, by other organizations. And he does commendable work in Guatemala. It doesn't compute."

"It does to him."

Moira tipped her head. "What do you mean?"

Shrugging, Cal continued to chase lettuce and cheese around his plate. "In his own mind, whatever he's done or is doing makes sense. It always does to the killer."

Killer.

Her bite of salad jammed halfway down her throat, and Moira picked up her glass of water to wash it down. "Hearing that actually put into words is jolting."

"I think it's accurate, though." He waited while

the server set their dishes of cannelloni on the table, then fixed her with an intent look. "I want you to promise you'll be careful while I'm gone."

Her heart skipped a beat—and this time the stumble wasn't due to chemistry. "You don't really think he'd come after me, do you?"

"Desperation can send people over the edge. He can't know how much you know, and that has to be driving him crazy. Correction: crazier. It would be foolish for him to target you, and he's been smart up till now. I don't think there's any real danger, but killers aren't always predictable." He sighed and raked his fingers through his hair "I wish we had enough to justify a full-blown official investigation, but we're not there yet."

"I'm beginning to wonder if we ever will be." Moira gathered what was left of her salad into a small, neat pile in the center of her plate. "He' covered his tracks well. We might never find connection that's more than circumstantial."

"Maybe not. But we're rapidly approaching preponderance of evidence that's both clear an convincing. And if we exhume a few bodies, tha will add even more weight to the case."

"Finding out what happened to Olivia woul help too."

"I agree—and I have a feeling the neighbor property may hold the key to that, given i proximity to your accident site. I'm going to se if I can get permission from the owner to do

alk-through this weekend, using some sort of
retext."

"If you want some company, I'm available."

Amusement softening his lips, he set aside his
ılad plate and moved the cannelloni front and
enter. "Dev suggested that."

"The one who thinks I'm hot?" She shot him
n answering smile and batted her eyelashes.

"That's the one. Rather than asking permission,
e suggested we pose as a lost couple looking for
roperty to buy—who happened to wander onto
ed's land."

"I could play that role."

He broke off a piece of cannelloni with the
dge of his fork. "You're really getting into this
retext thing, aren't you?"

More the couple thing than the pretext thing . . .
ut she left that unsaid.

She started on her own entrée. "I just want this
ver as soon as possible. If there's anything I can
o to help, count me in."

"I'll hold you to that this weekend. Plan on a
rive to the country. Now why don't we enjoy the
est of our lunch without discussing mayhem
nd murder?"

"I'll drink to that." She lifted her water glass,
nd he clinked his against it.

True to his word, he kept the conversation
ght during the remainder of the meal, even
ianaging to elicit some laughs with stories

about a few of Phoenix's tamer investigation:
She got a good chuckle out of the one about a
insurance fraud case in which they videotape
the subject, who'd claimed to have a disablin
back injury, competing in a bowling tournamer
and skydiving.

By the time they parted, she felt more relaxed.

Until he mentioned Mexico again as he walke
her to her car.

"Remember, call anytime if you need me. Ou
BlackBerries are calibrated to work outside th
United States, so you can reach me with n
problem."

"Okay." She pressed the auto button on her ke
chain, and her locks clicked open. "But you'll b
a long way away."

Faint furrows appeared on his brow as h
stopped beside her car. "If for any reason yo
sense danger, don't hesitate to call 911. That'
why they're there."

"To be honest, I'm more worried about you
It sounds like you could meet up with some roug
characters down there."

He smiled, and the furrows disappeared. "W
can handle it. Don't worry, okay? Although
must admit I'm flattered by your concern."

She did her best to match his lighter tone. "Yo
should be. I don't give my concern to every ma
I meet, you know."

"I know." His eyes softened, turning his iris€

velvet brown, and he lifted his hand to finger her hair.

She stopped breathing.

Then he bent down and oh-so-gently brushed his lips over hers.

Her eyelids flickered closed. The rest of the world faded away. The ground beneath her shifted.

Had she stepped into a romance novel, or what?

When he backed off, she groped for the car behind her. She needed something steady—and solid—to hang on to.

Once more the corners of his mouth flexed up. As if he'd discerned the dramatic effect his kiss had had on her—and was pleased. "I'll call you as soon as I get back, okay?"

"Okay." The word came out shaky, and she cleared her throat.

He pulled her door open, and she slid in. After two tries, she got her key in the ignition, started the engine, and backed out.

Right before she lost sight of him in her rearview mirror, he raised his hand in farewell. As if he'd expected her to be watching him until the last minute.

And that was okay. She wanted him to know he was interested. Very interested. That was why she wasn't crazy about this Mexico trip. But he'd be back soon—and she had the weekend reconnaissance outing with him to look forward to.

In the interim, she'd just have to put up with a few boring days on her end.

Because despite Cal's warning to be careful, she seriously doubted Ken Blaine would be foolish enough to put her in his sights.

There was a light on in the cabin.

Ken peered through the woods at Ted's modest weekend retreat and killed his headlights.

Who could be there? Ted had told him once he'd never offered its use to anyone else. Only his longtime friend and trusted neighbor. And the older man hadn't been out here in a long while.

But someone was in there.

Now what?

He wiped a hand down his face. Clenched his fingers around the steering wheel. Could he do what had to be done without alerting the occupant to his presence?

No.

He might be able to dig quietly, but he needed to drive to the back of the property to deal with the rest of the task, and the crunch of gravel would give him away—because if the cabin was occupied, the windows would be open. There wasn't any air-conditioning. What was the use of going to the country if you were going to breath recycled air, Ted always said. You could do that at home. So if you were in the cabin in nic weather, you opened the windows or it got too stuffy. Ken knew that from personal experience.

Tonight's trip was a bust.

But who was in the cabin? And how long would they be there?

Maybe he should poke around, as long as he'd made the drive out here.

He flipped off the dome light but left the motor running. It would make too much noise if he had to restart it. Then he opened the door and stepped out. Hesitated. Should he change into the work boots he'd bought, or leave on his dress shoes? He scoped out the ground. Dress shoes. He wasn't going far, and the earth was dry.

Ken scanned the road behind him as he clicked the door shut. He'd pulled far enough into the drive that his car shouldn't attract attention. There was minimal traffic on this narrow two-lane stretch, anyway, especially late at night, and he wouldn't be here long.

Braving the poison ivy, he hugged the edge of the overgrown drive, avoiding the gravel as much as possible as he kept one eye on the house. The light was still on, but there was no other sign of activity.

When he reached the back of the cabin, a late-model Acura came into view.

His neighbor's car.

Ken stared at it through the darkness. Ted had come out here . . . how often? Two, three times in the past four years? And he'd picked tonight to pay a visit? How odd was that?

His neighbor wouldn't stay long, though. He never did, these days. A night or two, max. Ellen might know his plans. She talked to Rose a lot. He'd have to see what he could ferret out tomorrow.

For now, he might as well call it a night. There was nothing he could do here without risking discovery. He'd have to psyche himself up all over again in a few days and try again.

Living with the delay, however, would be difficult—and worrisome.

But he had no choice. He'd have to suck it up and cope.

Turning, he started back toward his car, once more staying off the gravel as much as possible, doing his best to reassure himself and mitigate his gnawing anxiety. There couldn't be much chance that reporter knew about his connection to this place. How would she have found out? He hadn't been here since that night, and there was almost no chance she'd ever met Ted.

Then again, how had she known about Verna?

Despite the balmy air, a ripple of unease shuddered through him as he slid behind the wheel, put the car in reverse, and slowly backed toward the road in the darkness. The gravel crunched beneath his tires, and he cringed, holding his breath until he was safely back on the asphalt and pointed toward St. Louis.

As the car accelerated, he exhaled.

He hadn't accomplished his mission tonight.

But he'd be back soon to finish the job.

"Ted. Ted!"

At the prod in his side, Ted blinked himself back to consciousness and turned toward Rose. She stood beside the bed, backlit by the light from the hall, her face in shadows, hugging her robe around her.

"What's wrong, honey? What are you doing up?"

"I was thirsty. But I heard a noise when I was in the kitchen."

He stifled a sigh. No doubt she had. The country was full of noises, and she was a city girl through and through. Every tiny unfamiliar sound scared her. Squirrels scampering through the leaves. Acorns falling on the roof. The hoot of an owl.

Still, she'd offered to come. And he wanted her to come again. It was the only way he got out here these days, thanks to the promise she'd extracted from him after that stupid move he'd pulled with the ax four years ago. Best to humor her.

"What did you hear?"

"It sounded like somebody pulled into the drive. heard gravel crunching."

"Could have been a car turning around."

"At 11:30 at night?" She cast a furtive glance over her shoulder. "It might be someone who's up to no good. There are a lot of hoodlums running around these days."

"Maybe it was a deer."

"Deer don't make gravel crunch as loud as a tire."

He couldn't argue with her logic.

Resigning himself to a midnight foray, he flung back the covers and stood, pausing for a moment to give his eighty-two-year-old body a chance to adjust to the shift from horizontal to vertical. Time was, he could bound out of bed and take off at a gallop. Hard to believe he had eight decades behind him. Sure didn't feel that old most days.

"What are you going to do?"

At Rose's question, he grabbed his own robe, pushed his arms in the sleeves, and shoved his feet into the boots he wore for tromping around the place. "I'll take a look around."

"Outside?"

At the alarm in her voice, he circled the bed and drew her close. "Now, Rosie, don't you worry. I've been coming here for almost half my life and I've never had a bit of trouble, except for those hunters I caught trespassing once twenty years ago."

"The world is a different place now. And there aren't any neighbors close. If someone wanted to do bad things, this would be a perfect place for it. It's very isolated here." She clung to him.

He preferred to think of it as private and peaceful, but he let her comment pass.

"Tell you what. I'll take my trusty sidearm, okay?"

She backed off a bit, a frown deepening the permanent wrinkles on her brow. "I don't like guns."

"They serve a purpose, though. Like providing protection—and peace of mind." He touched her cheek, then crossed the room and retrieved his classic Smith & Wesson .38 from the hidden drawer in the antique chiffarobe he and Rose had picked up at an estate sale years ago. This whole thing was overkill, but if it made her feel better . . .

"Is it loaded?" Her words were laced with trepidation.

"Of course it's loaded. Doesn't do a person any good if it's not." He walked toward the hall. "I'll be back in a few minutes."

She followed close behind. "Maybe we should call 911 instead."

As if the police didn't have anything better to do than investigate a wayward deer or some kids out for a joyride.

"Let me take a quick look first." He hoped that would placate her.

"All right. But be careful."

Mission accomplished.

Gun in hand, feeling like an idiot, Ted exited through the front door. The moon was full, giving him excellent visibility despite his old eyes. The only sounds he heard were the typical stirrings of a country night. The rustle of wind in the trees. The muted buzz of cicadas. The scurrying sound of some rodents when his trek disturbed their nocturnal wanderings. But he circled the house. Checked the drive. Walked back far enough to survey the perimeter of the lake.

Nothing.

Stifling a yawn, he trudged back inside and smiled at Rose. "All secure. The only mean critter I saw was a raccoon that hissed at me after I interrupted his canoodling." He put his arm around her shoulders and guided her back toward the bedroom. "What do you say we snuggle up and do a little canoodling ourselves?"

She leaned into him, and he felt her relax against his weight. "You always were a sweet talker."

"Is it working?"

She gave him a playful nudge. "We're in our eighties. We're getting too old to canoodle."

"Says who? There's a lot of life left in these old bones. And I still think you're pretty as the day you stole my heart at that long-ago church picnic. The day your father told you to watch out for me because I had a roguish eye."

A soft flush spread over her cheeks. "Then you need to get your vision checked. I'm an old lady with white hair and wrinkles and baggy boobs."

"And feisty as ever." He gave her a squeeze before growing more serious. "But I don't need to get my vision checked. When I look at you, I see with my heart—and you're beautiful."

She smiled and touched his cheek. "I love you, Ted Lauer. Happy birthday."

He checked his watch. "So it is. Just. And I appreciate you coming out here to help me celebrate, even though I know you'd rather be at the Ritz. I'll also call the sheriff's department in the morning and ask them to do a few more night drive-bys here, if that makes you feel more comfortable. In the meantime"—he grabbed her hand, planted a kiss on her cheek, and tugged her toward the bedroom—"I'm all ready for my birthday present."

⇒ 20 ⇐

"Dr. Blaine?"

Blinking, Ken slanted a glance at the nurse on the other side of the draped patient. The surgical mask and cap hid most of her face, but the emotions in her eyes were easy to read—surprise, concern, puzzlement.

Had she asked him something?

He checked out the rest of his team. They were all watching him too—until one of them looked down.

Dropping his own gaze, he discovered his fingers were trembling.

Shock rippled through him.

That had never, ever happened to him in surgery.

Then again, he'd never before allowed himself to be distracted, even during a routine procedure like this laparoscopic appendectomy.

Until today.

Quickly reorienting himself—they were done, and all that remained was the cleanup—he kept his tone neutral as he spoke. "Did you have a question?"

"No. You just . . . stopped. I wondered if anything was wrong."

Plenty. But he couldn't let his off-the-job problems interfere with his work. The patients had to come first. This was *not* going to happen again.

"I'm fine. Let's remove the bougie and come to the outside. A single monocryl suture in each spot should be sufficient."

Everyone went back to their tasks in the silence typical of his procedures. He'd worked with most of the team members long enough to minimize the need for instruction. In general they anticipated his directions—and they didn' need him to hang around while they finished up.

He was out of here—before he made another mistake.

Stepping back, he tossed one final comment over his shoulder as he strode toward the exit. "Good work."

He didn't wait for an acknowledgment.

Once outside the door he paused, his gut churning. He'd done that entire procedure on autopilot. That was unprofessional—and wrong. Every single patient deserved his full and undivided attention.

His father would not approve of his lapse.

Fingers fumbling, he pulled his mask down. Inhaled, slow and steady. Tonight, he'd find out what Ellen knew about Ted's plans. Until then, however, his patients had to come first. He had to compartmentalize and give his full attention to the job at hand.

Because he couldn't afford any more slips—or suspicions.

"Thanks. I appreciate the fast turnaround." Cal pressed the end button on his BlackBerry and watched through the passenger-side window of the Taurus as a plane took off from Spirit airport.

"Was that the lab?" Connor looked over at him as he swung into the hangar area.

"Yeah. It's a match. The tooth belonged to Olivia Lange."

"That moves Blaine closer to the hot seat."

"Close isn't good enough." Cal expelled a frustrated breath. "Everything we have is circumstantial."

"You need to find Olivia."

"High on my priority list when we get back. And I know just where to start."

Connor pulled into a parking spot, and he reached for the door handle as the other man set the brake.

"Cal."

At his partner's serious tone, he stopped and glanced back. Connor was wearing his don't-mess-with-me-I-want-the-truth expression.

"Are you gonna be with us on this protection gig?"

His buddy's query was like the proverbial bucket of cold water over the head. Based on the intel Connor had gathered, the trip to Mexico was rife with risk. Far more than they'd initially anticipated. Last week, another executive had been ambushed and wounded while traveling in the very area they were headed. Hopefully their own trip would be hassle-free, but they all needed to be at the top of their game and on full alert in case things went south. None of them could afford to be distracted.

Cal exhaled. He had to put the situation with Blaine—and his worry about Moira—out of his mind and focus on the job at hand until he got back. His partners trusted him to carry his weight, and he had no intention of letting them down.

"Yes." He met Connor's gaze steadily. "Once we get on that plane, my head will be in Mexico."

Silence for a moment as Connor appraised him. Then he gave a curt nod. "Okay." Pulling the keys out of the ignition with one hand, he gestured behind Cal with the other. "Dev's here. Let's roll."

Cal opened his door, grabbed his duffel bag off the backseat, and followed Connor toward the hangar. He'd keep his promise and switch gears as soon as they boarded the waiting corporate jet. He'd become an expert at that sort of mind-shift after Lindsey was killed. It had been a matter of survival.

But before he transitioned fully into Mexico mode, he intended to keep his promise to Moira and pass on the lab results.

As well as one last warning to be careful.

"I thought Friday would never get here." Linda settled a hip on the corner of Moira's desk. "Any big plans for the weekend?"

"Nope." She shut down her computer. "Unlike someone I know, who's planning to spend the next two days in Chicago."

Linda wrinkled her nose. "I'm not all that excited about the trip, to be honest. From everything I've heard, attending a spouse's high

343

school reunion is about as exciting as peeling hardboiled eggs."

Sniggering, Moira slung her purse over her shoulder, shoved her laptop into its case, and stood. "I have to admit, relaxing with a book on my patio does sound like a better option. Unless my neighbor is in a country music mood."

"If you hear it often enough, you might become a fan."

"Don't hold your breath."

"Maybe Cal will get back in time to rescue you. He's coming home tonight, isn't he?"

"Yes. Too late to get together, though."

Linda pushed herself to her feet. "Did you hear from him at all while he was gone?"

"No. I didn't expect to. It was an intense trip."

"Maybe he'll make up for that lack of communication tomorrow or Sunday." Linda nudged her and stretched. "If so, be sure to take advantage of whatever he might offer."

"I'll keep that in mind. And during our walk on Monday, I want a blow-by-blow of the reunion."

"Okay, but prepare to be bored out of your mind. Oh, well . . . the food might be enjoyable, at least. The dinner's at some gourmet restaurant." With a wave, Linda sauntered back toward her cube.

Hefting her computer, Moira headed for the elevator in the opposite direction. A night of reading, possibly serenaded by country music, was sounding less appealing by the minute.

She pushed the button, and the elevator door opened almost at once. That was a nice change of pace—except it was packed. Taking a firm grip on her computer, she wedged herself in with the anxious-to-start-the-weekend crowd, most of whom no doubt had more exciting things to do with their Friday night than she did.

As the elevator began its descent, she chewed on her lower lip. Surely there had to be a more interesting—and productive—way to spend her evening than reading and listening to twangy music. Like advancing their case against Blaine, perhaps?

But what could she do? As Cal had pointed out, they were in a waiting mode. Verna Hafer's autopsy was key to the next steps.

The door opened, and the surging crowd thrust her into the lobby. Sheesh. You'd think there was a prize for the first person who made it to the exit.

Resettling her purse on her shoulder, she followed at a more sedate pace. Once outside, she joined the throng moving toward the parking lot, keeping a lookout for a certain black Lexus. Not that there was much chance Blaine would be following her at this hour of the afternoon. Based on his schedule the day she'd shadowed him, he'd still be at his office.

But speaking of following . . .

As an idea began to percolate, she fished her keys out of her purse. She didn't have anything better to do, and an evening of surveillance might be more stimulating than the book she was reading. Even if she didn't learn anything new, at least she'd be making an effort to contribute to the case. After all the gratis hours Cal and the other Phoenix PIs had invested in the effort, it was the least she could do.

Moira settled behind the wheel, started the engine, and put the car in gear. Cal had warned her to be careful, but how dangerous could this be? Most likely Blaine would pull into his driveway and stay put for the night. She'd end up spending the evening listening to music of her choice— rather than her neighbor's—while she sat down the street and watched his house.

And if he did happen to go anywhere, she'd stay far enough back to keep from being spotted. She'd also pull her hair back with the scrunchy she kept in her purse and wear her sunglasses. Her windshields were tinted too, though not as dark as the vehicles in the Phoenix fleet. But sufficient to give her some privacy. And she'd keep her doors locked.

She released the brake. As far as she could see, there was no downside to her plan—and it was far better use of her evening.

Angling her wrist, she checked her watch. Blaine was following his usual routine, b wouldn't leave his office until 6:00. That gave her time to grab some food and a beverage. A small one. She'd learned her lesson on that score the hard way. She could also swing by the condo and rummage through the closet for the binoculars her dad had given her years ago for their occasional outings to the bleachers to see the Cards play or to take in an outdoor show at the Muny from the nosebleed section. They might come in handy, as they had the night she and Cal had followed Blaine to the Taco Bell dumpster.

As she joined the going-home traffic headed toward the I-64 westbound ramp from downtown, she toyed with the idea of calling Cal and filling him in on her plans. But he was busy. Besides, she could imagine his reaction: *Leave this to the experts.*

And maybe that was sound advice.

Still, what could it hurt to follow Blaine from a safe distance, if he in fact went anywhere? Besides, if he did, his destination might provide clue of some kind. *Someone* needed to follow him more diligently. Cal and his cohorts were doing as much as they could in between paying jobs, but who knew what Blaine was up to when no one was watching? And the police weren't yet interested enough to devote a lot of resources to this investigation. Who did that leave?

Her.

She switched lanes and pressed on the

accelerator as she began to merge into the I-64 traffic. Okay. It was settled. She'd observe Blaine. Follow him, if necessary. Keep her distance.

And she'd also do her best to keep her promise to Cal and not take any unnecessary chances.

This was the night.

Ken put the phone back into the cradle on his desk, his fingers quivering with nerves and anticipation. Ellen's information had been correct, as Ted had just confirmed. Rose had surprised him with a trip to the cabin for his birthday, and they'd returned this afternoon after a wonderful three days. Ted had also brushed aside Ken's apology for the belated birthday call, saying he'd gotten their card—Ellen's doing, of course; she was good about remembering those sorts of social niceties—and with Ken's busy life, he'd understood how it would be easy for yet another birthday from a neighbor who'd had so many to slip his mind.

He'd also suggested that Ken carve out some time for a visit to the cabin. It might be exactly what he needed to help him unwind and lower his stress level.

An excellent suggestion.

One he intended to follow this very day.

And if all went well, in a few short hours one very large stressor would be disposed of for ever.

•••

Stifling a yawn, Moira adjusted the buds in her ears as she listened to Sarah Brightman from the original London cast recording of *Phantom of the Opera*. The soaring, dramatic music was the perfect thing to keep her awake as the digital clock on the dash slowly clicked, minute by minute, toward 9:30.

Phantom was better than listening to someone sing about a redneck woman, but surveillance had been a lot more fun when Cal had been in the car with her. And three-and-a-half hours of restricted sitting behind her wheel was beginning to take a toll.

Ten o'clock, she decided, as she rotated her neck to dispel the kinks. Blaine had been home for three hours, and if he didn't venture out by then, there wasn't much chance he had any plans for the evening that would take him away from the house.

Two minutes ticked by. Four. Six. Eight.

She was gaining a greater and greater respect for the kind of patience required to endure long-term surveillance.

At the ten-minute mark, just as the chorus began to sing "Masquerade," Blaine's garage door opened four houses down, as if on cue to the music.

Straightening up in her seat, Moira grabbed her binoculars.

It was his Lexus pulling out, all right. And though she couldn't make out the figure behind the wheel, she'd lay odds it was the doctor, not the wife.

Where would he be going at this hour?

Setting the binoculars back on the seat, she turned the key in the ignition but, following Cal's example, left her headlights off. Too bad she didn't have one of those nifty buttons he'd shown her on his car. The one that disengaged the backup and brake lights.

Blaine backed out of the driveway and drove toward the entrance to the subdivision. She waited until his taillights receded, then pressed on the gas pedal. There could be a perfectly logical explanation for his excursion, of course. A late night run for Chinese food. An emergency at the hospital. A sudden craving for a frozen custard from Ted Drewes. She'd been guilty of the latter herself on more than one occasion.

But he drove by two Chinese restaurants. Ted Drewes got knocked out of the running when he turned west on I-64 instead of east. And the hospital emergency theory deflated after he passed up the exit for Mercy.

He continued west. Toward Chesterfield. Toward the Missouri River bridge.

Toward Defiance?

Moira kept a steady pressure on the gas pedal, debating her next move. If Cal was here, it would be a no-brainer: call him and turn this tail over. Pronto. It was rapidly moving out of her league.

But he wasn't available—and she didn't have his police contacts. A call out of the blue from her to law enforcement wasn't likely to produce much action, and someone needed to follow Blaine or significant information might be lost.

Keeping one hand on the wheel and one eye on Blaine, she opened her purse and fished out her distance glasses. Thank goodness she'd brought them tonight. She also snagged her cell phone. Cal had said to call him if she needed to, and her quiet-surveillance-turned-daunting-tail qualified. With his connections, it was possible he could muster the troops via phone. Get an unmarked cop car to fall in behind Blaine, based on her description of his location. It was worth a try. He should be close to landing, anyway. Maybe she'd get lucky.

With one finger, she pressed Cal's speed dial number.

Three rings later, the phone rolled to voice mail. So much for luck.

She waited for the beep. "Cal, it's Moira. Since I didn't have anything better to do tonight, I thought I'd skulk around Blaine's house and watch to see if he did anything interesting. Much to my surprise, he did. I have him in sight now, and he's heading west on I-64. He just passed the Chesterfield Mall exit. I'm thinking this is pretty suspicious, and I wondered if you might be able to get some law enforcement involvement through one of your former detective buddies at County. I figured you'd have a lot better chance of finagling some support than I would. So when you get this, will you call me back ASAP?"

She pressed the end button and set the phone on the seat beside her. Hoping it would ring soon and she'd find Cal on the other end of the line.

But if it didn't, she'd stay the course.

Because after all the effort they'd put into solving this case, she wasn't about to let what could turn out to be the break they needed slip through her fingers.

Even if that meant she had to hedge on her promise to Cal and take a few more risks than she'd planned.

≫· 21 ·≪

Flexing his hands on the wheel, Ken at last let himself switch gears and think about the mess task ahead. He'd maintained excellent mental discipline over the past few days, putting aside his worry as he focused on his professional duties. There had been no more slips, no more short-changing his patients. He'd mastered his anxiety, stayed the course, and done his job.

His father would be pleased.

But now it was time to focus on a different job.

He flicked a glance in the rearview mirror as he approached the turnoff from Highway 94. With the curvy road, it was impossible to see very far back. To tell if he was being followed. Not that there was much chance of that. No matter what Moira Harrison had told the police to get them to do an autopsy on Verna, there was no solid evidence against him. And the police were stretched too thin to assign anyone to watch him round the clock based on mere speculation.

Most of the traffic he'd encountered had been going the other way, anyway, back toward St. Louis. People who'd attended one of those weekend dinners on the deck at Montelle Winery, perhaps. After this was all over, maybe he'd invite Ted and Rose there one evening. They'd like that, and the man had been kind to him through the years. Some of his happiest hours had been spent sitting by the lake near Ted's cabin.

Unfortunately, the place could never again hold the same allure.

It didn't matter, though. He had no time for such indulgences anymore.

As he prepared to turn onto the small side road that led to his destination, he took one final glance in the rearview mirror. There were some headlights in the distance, but too far away to cause much concern. Still, why take a chance?

Slowing, he twisted off his lights and swung

onto the road without applying his brakes or flipping on his turn signal.

And at that very instant, as if God was smiling on his mission, one of the dark clouds that had been gathering all day drifted over the almost-full moon, blocking the light.

If someone did happen to be following him, he'd just disappeared.

Where had Blaine gone?

Moira squinted into the darkness ahead, blacker than ever now that the moon's glow had been snuffed out. His taillights had been there a moment ago. Now they'd vanished—kind of like the man himself had done on the rainy night she'd first encountered him . . . along with a nameless woman she'd since learned was Olivia Lange.

Pressing harder on the accelerator, she kept her gaze fixed on the spot where she'd last seen him.

People didn't just disappear.

He'd gone *somewhere*.

And this time she intended to find out where.

It was unfortunate she hadn't asked Cal to be more specific about the location of the cabin Blaine's neighbor owned. All he'd told her was that it was on a spur off the road where she'd caught Olivia in her headlights, a half mile closer to 94 than the accident site.

Close to the area she was in right now.

She slowed as she neared the spot where she thought Blaine had disappeared. To her left were farm fields. To her right were woods.

Continuing to creep along on the deserted road, she swung her head from one side to the other. There was nowhere to go, nowhere to . . .

Wait.

She jammed on the brake.

A narrow, two-lane ribbon of asphalt forked off on the right, like the one where she'd seen Olivia on that rainy night. Mendelson Road, according to the police report.

She blinked at the weathered sign on the pole, trying to bring it into focus, but even with her glasses on it was impossible to read in the dark. If she took the time to get out and examine it up close, though, she'd lose Blaine—assuming he'd detoured here. And that was a safe assumption; as far as she could tell, there was nowhere else to turn close to this spot.

So why had his taillights disappeared? The road wasn't enveloped by trees for the first dozen yards.

Unless . . .

He must have switched off his lights, the same way Cal had done at Taco Bell, to avoid detection.

Why?

Did he suspect he was being followed?

Had he learned about Verna Hafer's autopsy?

Was that why he'd come back to this spot?

A solitary drop of rain splattered against her windshield as she put the car in reverse, turned off her own lights, and drove up the road. If only Cal had returned her call. He might have been able to get her some backup. A summons from her to the authorities, on the other hand, was unlikely to produce any quick results. She had nothing illegal to report, just suspicion. By the time she got to the right person and tried to convince him or her to help, Blaine could be finished with whatever task he'd come here to do.

And there was no doubt in her mind he was here on a mission, not a weekend visit to the country to relax. Extinguishing his car lights was a dead giveaway.

She cringed at the unintended—but perhaps accurate—pun.

All at once, taillights flicked on in the distance through the trees. As if they'd been flipped back on.

Her guess had been correct. Blaine had turned here.

Following more slowly in the dark, she watched as his brake lights flickered. Then the car swung to the right.

She accelerated slightly, stopping at the one-lane gravel track where he'd turned. His tail lights were still visible through the trees, but the foliage would obscure them within seconds.

This had to be the spur that led to his neighbor's cabin.

Once more, Moira plucked her cell off the passenger seat and tapped in Cal's number. She was certain he'd have returned her call if he'd gotten her first message, but it wouldn't hurt to try once more. Worst case, she'd leave him an update.

Three rings later, his voice mail kicked in again.

Her stomach bottomed out, but she did her best to adopt a calm tone.

"Cal, it's Moira again. I followed Blaine, and my hunch was right. He headed straight for his neighbor's place. I'm going to see if I can get a closer look at what he's up to, because I doubt he came out here to commune with nature. I'll stay undercover in the trees and call you back as soon as I have anything to report."

After slipping the phone into her pocket, she maneuvered the car as far off the road as she could, shoved her purse under the seat, and grabbed her binoculars. She couldn't drive down the narrow lane. If she had to exit fast, there might not be anywhere to turn around.

This job had to be done on foot.

Lucky she'd worn rubber-soled flats today. And her black slacks and black knit top would help her blend into the darkness. It was as if she'd dressed for the part.

But she'd have handed the role off to some-one—anyone—else in a heartbeat.

Not an option, unfortunately.

As she slid out of the car—away from the safety of locks that could help protect her and wheels that could whisk her away—a wave of fear tightened her throat. After encountering her share of hairy situations and bad actors in her investigative work, she didn't scare easily. But there was something especially spooky about this situation. Maybe it was the forsaken country road. Or the cloud-shrouded moon. Or the wind rustling through the dark woods.

Whatever it was, a caution sign began to strobe in her brain, along with a warning.

Back off. This is risky. Go home.

Yet on the heels of that warning, an image of Olivia's terrified eyes flashed through her mind. The woman who'd disappeared unnoticed on this very road. Who'd had no one to miss her. Whose silent plea that night, in the instant she'd been caught in the headlights, had gone straight to Moira's heart.

She had to do this for Olivia—because some instinct told her that whatever was happening tonight held the key to her disappearance . . . and might be their last chance to prove the link between a missing woman and a lauded doctor.

Binoculars gripped in her fingers, pulse pounding, Moira started down the foliage shrouded drive, hugging the edge, staying close to the brushy woods as possible. All the while praying she wasn't making a mistake that would jeopardize their investigation.

Or her life.

"We're about to land. Buckle up."

At the prod to his shoulder, Cal pulled himself back from the edge of exhaustion and blinked across the aisle at Connor—who looked disgustingly alert.

"What time is it?" His words came out half slurred.

"10:45. You've been out cold for two hours."

He looked toward the front of the private plane, where their client was also wide awake and intent on his computer screen.

Of course, William Santel had slept while he and Connor tag-teamed night duty then doubled up coverage during the day as the man maintained a grueling pace and ventured into places that kept both of them on high alert. Despite the local security backup, this job had definitely merited the full contingent of Phoenix PIs.

Too bad Dev had been sidelined the first night.

Fumbling with his belt, he checked out his her partner over his shoulder. His complexion was still pasty, and he hadn't uttered a wisecrack almost forty-eight hours. Funny. For all their concern about dodging bullets and dealing with drug traffickers, they'd never factored in the possibility one of them could be felled by a nasty case of Montezuma's revenge.

Go figure.

"Feeling any better?"

Dev made a face at him. "If I never see another Immodium tablet, it will be too soon."

"Just be glad I had some on hand." Connor tossed him a pack of saltine crackers. "Eat these. And keep drinking juice."

"Why were you so prepared, anyway?" Dev ripped the cellophane off the crackers.

"Ask me sometime about my trip with the vice president to Kuwait."

"I thought all the stuff you handled was classified."

"Not diarrhea."

Stifling a grin, Cal watched out the window as the plane descended toward Spirit airport. He was looking forward to a soft bed, a cold drink —and perhaps an ice cream excursion with Moira tomorrow.

He checked his watch. If a weather delay hadn't pushed their departure back, he'd have called her tonight. Given the hour, though, there was a strong possibility she was already in bed—and late-night calls could be alarming. He'd had more than his share of those, and the adrenaline surge could keep you awake for hours.

Better to wait until tomorrow and let her enjoy a peaceful night's rest.

• • •

The shovel did not give her a warm and fuzzy feeling.

From the spot where she'd wedged herself between two cedar trees after encountering a faceful of cobwebs, Moira watched through the binoculars as Blaine removed the implement from the trunk of his car. He'd pulled back onto the property as far as possible, past the small cabin nestled among the trees, his black car blending into the night.

He was also dressed in far more casual attire than he'd sported on the other occasions she'd encountered him—jeans, a long-sleeved shirt, a pair of heavy work gloves, sturdy boots. The kind of clothing people wore if they were planning to do serious physical labor.

Only the glow from the trunk light broke the dense darkness, giving his face an otherworldly aura as he bent forward to move a . . . concrete block?

Before she could verify what she thought she'd seen, he shut the trunk and struck off for the woods, shovel in hand.

In moments he was out of view.

Great.

Lowering the binoculars, she debated her options. She could sit tight and wait for him to come back—but it appeared the action was going to take place elsewhere.

She had to follow him.

At a distance.

As she crept forward, the clouds shifted, bathing the night in moonlight, and she hesitated. This was trickier. She'd have to be very careful to stay in the shadows to avoid being spotted. On the plus side, though, she might be better able to see what Blaine was doing without getting too close.

The sound of a shovel hitting dirt guided her, and when she spotted him through the trees she found another spot to wedge herself into. Training the binoculars on him, she watched him pause to brush aside some debris, then continue excavating.

Within minutes, it became clear he was digging a hole.

A very big, rectangular hole.

Big enough to hold a body.

Her stomach clenched.

Okay. Time to call in the big guns, as Cal had once said. This was getting hairier by the minute. She'd use some pretext to get the cops out here. Say she'd stumbled across someone who was hurt. That should produce a fast response.

And if, by some slim chance, Blaine had come to the woods late at night to dig holes for jollies she'd pay the consequences for the false alarm. No way was she going to hang around for absolute proof of her suspicions. She didn't have the stomach for that.

Besides, she'd taken too many risks for one night anyway.

Because if Blaine had killed Olivia and buried her in the woods, he'd kill again if he was discovered.

Sucking in a deep breath, Moira lowered the binoculars.

She was out of here.

Tactical bag in hand, Cal straightened his jacket with a shrug of his shoulders. At least this job hadn't required ties. Then he followed Connor down the aisle of the private jet, Dev bringing up the rear.

It was good to be home.

William Santel was waiting for them at the bottom of the gangway and shook each of their hands in turn as the co-pilot unloaded their luggage from the compartment on the side of the plane.

"Thank you, gentlemen. I appreciate your professionalism and thoroughness. Once I put myself in your hands, I never worried about my safety for a minute."

"That's why we were there." *And why you paid us the big bucks.* But Cal left the latter unsaid as he took the man's hand.

"I hope you're feeling better soon. I had a similar bout on one of my first visits to Mexico and I never forgot it." Santel gave Dev a sympathetic smile. "I appreciate your efforts in spite of that impediment."

"My colleagues picked up the slack and did the bulk of the work. Let's hope this doesn't convince them I'm expendable."

Cal studied him. He must be feeling better if he was starting to joke again.

"I doubt that. I'll say my good-byes here. And I'll keep you in mind for future trips." With a lift of his hand, Santel climbed into the car that had pulled onto the tarmac to greet him.

As the vehicle drove away, the pilot emerged from the plane, holding a BlackBerry. "Did one of you leave this behind? I found it stuck between two seats."

Cal checked his belt in unison with his colleagues.

The holster was empty.

"Mine's missing." Cal retraced his steps to the top of the gangway and took it from the man. "Thanks."

"No problem." The pilot disappeared back into the plane.

Cal rejoined his partners, and after collecting their duffel bags they headed toward the small terminal.

"Lucky he spotted that or you'd spend half the day tomorrow tracking it down." Connor gestured to the device on Cal's belt.

"Yeah. I guess it fell off when I was trying

find a comfortable position before I zoned out."

"Wouldn't surprise me, the way you were sprawled on the seat with your mouth hanging open."

Cal shot him a dark look. "Why are you so perky, anyway? You didn't get any more sleep than I did."

"Secret Service training."

"How come I'm not buying that?" Cal didn't attempt to hide his skepticism.

Connor chuckled and pulled open the door to the terminal. "Okay. Try this. I've learned to do with less sleep thanks to my on-the-job experience of trying to keep up with the vice president."

"Better." Cal followed him into the building and slid the BlackBerry off his belt while Dev made a beeline for the men's room. "Give me a minute to check messages, since I was obviously out of touch for a couple of hours."

"No problem. I need to return an email, anyway. And I want to make sure our friend is up to driving before we take off too." He gestured toward the door where Dev had disappeared after dumping his duffel bag on a chair in the waiting area.

As Connor moved off a few feet, Cal crossed to an upholstered chair and sank down into the lush softness. Nice. Day and night difference from the attached chairs in the main commercial terminal at Lambert, his usual departure point

365

when he travelled. Those were designed for utility and durability, not comfort.

Tapping in his access code, he stifled a yawn and leaned back against the cushions. Wishing he had a little more of Connor's fortitude.

"You have three messages."

As the automated voice intoned, he pressed the button to listen to the first voice mail. His sister. Sounded like she just wanted to chat. He pushed the skip button, making a mental note to give her a call tomorrow.

At the message from Moira, however—left an hour ago—he straightened up.

She was tailing Blaine? A probable killer?

What was she thinking!

Stomach clenching, he stood and jabbed at the button to play the third message that had been left twenty minutes ago, pacing as he listened.

She'd followed Blaine to his neighbor's property by car, then continued the surveillance on foot. Leaving her exposed. Vulnerable.

And she'd never called back with the promised update.

"What's up?" Connor slipped his own Black Berry on his belt as he walked closer. Across the room, Dev pushed through the door and joined the group.

Cal gave them both a fast download, dialing Moira's number as he spoke. It rang once. Twice. Three times. Rolled to voice mail.

His gut twisted.

"She's not answering." He shoved the Black-Berry onto his belt. "I need to get out there. I'm halfway to the property already from here. Dev, if you drop Connor at home, I can take the Taurus."

"If there's any trouble, it's not a one-man job. I'm in." Connor snagged his bag and strode toward the parking lot.

"Me too." Dev grimaced as he picked up his own duffel, clearly still experiencing the after-effects of his bout with Montezuma's revenge. "But if you want to drive, I won't argue."

Without waiting for a response, he, too, started for the exit.

Cal's throat tightened as he fell in behind them. This kind of unified front was one of the reasons he was glad the three of them had hooked up to form Phoenix—not to mention the skill set each of them brought to the table.

But he hoped the strong tactical expertise in their tool bag wouldn't be needed tonight.

⇒ 22 ⇐

Balancing a shovelful of dirt, Ken froze as the mechanical strains of "Für Elise" shattered the stillness of the dark woods.

A phone was ringing—and it wasn't his.

Someone was nearby.

Watching him.

Tossing the shovel aside, he ducked into the shadows of the dense woods and took off at a run toward the Beethoven melody as it came to an abrupt halt.

But he didn't need the music anymore. The crashing sound of the interloper scrambling to escape through the brush guided his steps.

He increased his speed, pulse pounding, fear clawing at his throat. That phone didn't belong to a couple of underage kids seeking a secluded spot to drink beer or smoke pot. Not with a classical ring tone. Besides, kids would have been more interested in socializing than in stealth.

Someone was spying on him.

Someone who'd already seen too much.

Someone he had to stop.

Up ahead, he caught sight of a shadowy wraith weaving in and out of the trees, heading back toward the road. Moving more quickly than him.

Panic swelling, he pushed himself harder.

And then, out of the blue, the heavens smiled on him.

The figure stumbled. Went down on one knee. Lurched upright.

It was only a brief falter. But those precious seconds gave him the advantage he needed.

Yet as he closed the gap between them,

sickening realization seared itself across his brain.

Tonight's mission had just gotten a lot more complicated.

Stupid! Stupid! Stupid!

The rebuke drumming in her mind, Moira scrambled to her feet, adrenaline surging. How could she have forgotten to turn off her cell? And why hadn't she paid more attention to her footing instead of trying to snag the phone from her pocket? The damage had already been done the instant it rang. Now she'd lost her lead.

And Blaine was hot on her heels.

A sob caught in her throat as she stumbled toward the gravel road. It would offer fewer impediments to her progress than the thicket, and she didn't have to worry about the crunch of gravel underfoot giving her away anymore. If she could get to her car and lock the doors, she might be able to drive away before he could smash a window and stop her.

But her throbbing ankle was protesting with every step. Slowing her down. Giving him an advantage.

She could hear him gaining on her.

Pushing herself forward as fast as she could, she caught a glimpse of her car. Almost there. In another fifteen seconds she'd—

Something slammed into her legs.

She went down in a hard belly flop, her hands skidding on the gravel, her cheek burning as it slid over the loose stones.

Gasping, she tried to force her lungs to kick back in.

They refused to cooperate.

And then Blaine's weight was on her. Fingers closed over her neck, squeezing hard. Harder.

Her vision blurred.

No! She fought against the waves of blackness. *I'm not going to let him win!*

Mustering every ounce of her energy, she writhed beneath him. Trying to throw him off.

But he didn't budge. Didn't say a word. All he did was breathe. She could hear the harsh intake of air. She knew it was his; her own supply of oxygen had been shut off.

The world began to fade, and blackness pulled her down again, deeper and deeper as she clawed at the relentless hands that had an iron grip on her throat.

This wasn't how she'd expected her simple little surveillance gig to end.

But as her consciousness ebbed, as her limb stopped cooperating, she had one consoling thought.

This time, Blaine wouldn't get away with it.

Because unlike Olivia Lange, she had people i her life who cared—and who'd make certai justice was done.

You're killing her.

As the warning echoed in Ken's mind, he loosened his grip on the reporter's throat. He hadn't seen her face, but he knew it was her—the woman who was bent on destroying everything he'd worked so hard to build.

But choking someone to death . . . he couldn't do that. Morphine was a far better alternative. Gentler and more humane.

Except he hadn't brought any with him.

So what was he supposed to do with her?

Resting one hand on the ground, Blaine leveraged himself to his feet and looked down at her crumpled form, forcing the left side of his brain to engage. If the cops were on her side, if they believed her story, they'd be here, not her. Maybe she was working an investigative angle. Hoping to break a story that would earn her another Pulitzer prize nomination.

Not going to happen.

A few feet ahead of her, on the drive, her silver cell glinted in the moonlight. Thank goodness it had rung and alerted him to her presence. But if it was equipped with GPS, as most were these days, it could also lead the authorities to her when someone reported her missing—as someone would. Her father, at the very least. She'd told him they had a good relationship. Like the one he'd had with his own father.

It was wrong to cause a father worry—but he couldn't have the police swarming all over the place.

With one more glance at her motionless body, he strode over to the phone and smashed the heel of his work boot onto it. Once. Twice. Three times. After a final grinding motion, he picked up the mangled piece of equipment and tucked it in his pocket. Later, he'd lob it into the lake.

Behind him, the reporter moaned and stirred slightly, and he moved back beside her. Who should he deal with first, Olivia or Moira? The hole was half dug out back. Olivia could wait, however; she wasn't going anywhere. Moira, on the other hand, could cause trouble. But what was he going to do with her?

His hands started to shake as his brain shut down.

One thing at a time, Ken. Concentration is the key to success. Always remember that.

His father's voice from long ago echoed in his mind, and he took a deep breath. Another. His racing pulse slowed. His mind began to clear.

Better.

Okay. It made more sense to focus on this new complication first. Think through his options. The cabin would be the perfect place to do that. He'd always liked sitting in the rustic kitchen where life seemed simpler and more straight-forward. Yes. A few quiet minutes there would help him put his thoughts in order, make some plans.

Dropping down to one knee, he turned Moira Harrison over, hefted her up, and staggered back to his feet.

Funny. She felt a lot like Olivia had in his arms.

And even though he intended to think this through, he was pretty certain she was going to have to meet a similar end—even if nightmares plagued him for the rest of his days.

Because the welfare of God's children had to come first.

She was being carried.

The jostling, plus the grunt of exertion, clued Moira in to her situation as consciousness seeped back.

Ignoring the burning sensation on her cheek, the pain in her throat, and the ache in her ankle, she peeked out from under her eyelashes.

Blaine was carrying her—and they weren't outside anymore. She could see walls.

Were they in the neighbor's cabin?

And how long had she been out?

Not long, most likely. She doubted he'd have let her lay out there while he finished his other task. He must have scooped her up at once and was now bringing her inside.

A door banged shut, as if he'd kicked it closed behind him. Then he laid her on the floor, turned away, and disappeared into the adjacent room.

She felt for the car keys in her pocket. Still there.

Thank you, God!

She worked them out and gripped the autolock device in her fingers. With him in the other room, this could be her best chance to escape.

Perhaps her only one.

Sitting up as quietly as she could, she waited for a wave of dizziness to pass. Rose. Crept toward the door. Eased it open.

It squeaked.

Loudly.

At the muttered oath behind her, she yanked the handle back and took off, praying the adrenaline spurt would give her the speed she needed to beat him to the car, despite her injured ankle.

But she didn't make it past the porch.

As she started down the two wooden steps fingers gripped her arm and yanked her back.

So she did the next best thing.

She screamed.

An instant later, a hand was clamped over her mouth.

She bit it.

Another oath sounded behind her—but Blaine didn't loosen his grip. Instead, he towed her back inside, her heels dragging across the wooden floor of the porch.

Although she fought him as best she could, th

374

man was far stronger than she was, his grip around her midsection like a vise.

After he kicked the door shut behind them again, he let her squirm and struggle as he sucked in air. And the more she thrashed about, the more he tightened his grip—like a choke collar on a dog, except this pressure was aimed at her rib cage.

"You might as well stop trying to get away." He wheezed out the words. "It's not going to happen." To prove that point, he squeezed harder.

Moaning against the fingers covering her mouth, she quieted. Trying to squirm free wasn't working. She'd have to come up with another plan.

Slowly he loosened his grip around her middle, allowing her rib cage to expand enough to let her breathe as he muttered, "Why couldn't you have minded your own business? All you've done is cause problems."

He propelled her forward, and she stumbled toward the back of the cabin. Toward the kitchen, as it turned out.

Flipping on the light switch with one hand, he kept a firm grip on her arm with the other. After shoving her toward a chair, he pushed her down.

"I need to think."

He stared down at her for several moments, then began to pace.

She eyed the back door. It appeared to be

secured with a simple slider bolt. If she could push it back and yank open the knob in one smooth motion, maybe he wouldn't . . .

"Don't even consider it."

She jerked her head back to him. He was watching her from across the room. As far as she could tell, he wasn't armed. A well-placed kick might slow him down enough—

As if reading her mind, he yanked open a drawer beside the sink and pulled out a roll of hemp twine.

When she realized his intent, she stood and prepared to bolt.

He was beside her in two long strides. "Sit down."

Instead, she kneed him in the groin and took off for the back door as he doubled over.

She shoved the bolt back. Twisted the knob Pulled.

Nothing.

The door had a dead bolt.

Her hopes crashed.

But there was still the front door.

She swung back toward the room. Blaine hadn' yet straightened up. She darted past him.

Not fast enough.

He grabbed her arm, whipped her around, an sent a hard right straight to her jaw.

Bright colors exploded behind her eyes, an she staggered back. Tasted blood. Lost he alance. Before she could recover her senses and quilibrium, he shoved her into the chair. The ext thing she knew, he was binding her hands ehind her. When he finished with that, he ropped to one knee and began to secure her nkles to the legs of the chair.

Things were going downhill fast.

But as the disorienting effect of the blow waned nd her brain began to process again, she noticed omething interesting.

His hands were shaking.

Did that telltale sign suggest he had no stomach or what he was doing? That he wasn't just a old-blooded killer with no conscience?

His next comment seemed to confirm that onjecture.

"I'm sorry. I never wanted to hurt you." He ooked up at her as he tightened the knot on the ope.

The contrition in his eyes was real.

How weird.

But could she use it to her advantage? Play on is apology and what appeared to be genuine emorse to buy some time?

Because that's what she had to do. Cal must ave received her phone messages by now. The ll-timed call on her cell had probably been him rying to reach her. And since she hadn't nswered . . . since he'd found no promised ollow-up call from her in his voice mail . . .

she'd be willing to bet he was already all ove
this situation.

Best of all, he knew exactly where she was.

A fact she did not intend to share with Blaine.

She watched as the doctor crossed to the sin
dug a dishcloth out of a drawer, and dampened
with water, her mind racing as she tried to formu
late a plan.

When he rejoined her and lifted his hand, sh
tensed. What was he up to?

But he simply dabbed at the scrape on he
cheek and wiped away the blood trickling dow
her chin, his touch gentle.

"I'm sorry. A doctor is supposed to help, no
hurt."

She tried to read his face as he continued t
clean her injuries. Was he sorry he'd hit her—c
sorry for what he was going to do later?

Perhaps both, since he couldn't let her wal
away.

Yet his regret appeared to be genuine.

The man was a study in contradictions.

*Talk to him, Moira. Engage him in conversa
tion. Distract him from making plans for ho
he's going to deal with you.*

Right. She wasn't here to figure out what mad
him tick. She just needed to use up some time—
and keep trying to loosen the cord that boun
her wrists.

"Were you sorry about Olivia too?"

At her soft question, his hand stilled and twin creases appeared on his brow. "That wasn't my fault."

"But you killed her, didn't you?" She tried for a conversational tone. She wanted to divert his attention, not rile him.

He shook his head and moved a few feet away, gripping the bloody cloth in his fist. "No. You killed her."

She blinked at his unexpected comeback. "What do you mean?"

"You hit her with your car. She suffered critical injuries. No one could have saved her."

"Did you try?"

He regarded the red-stained cloth, threw it onto the kitchen table, and sank into a straight-backed chair, shoulders slumped, head bowed. "She couldn't live."

"Why not?"

"She suspected too much. Just like you do."

Moira did her best to ignore the obvious implication. Letting panic get the upper hand wasn't an indulgence she could afford.

Focus on loosening the rope. Keep him talking.

"She knew about the people at the nursing homes, didn't she? The ones you gave injections to—like Verna Hafer."

His head jerked up, denial in his eyes. "They were all dying, anyway. I merely smoothed out the process. Made it easier for them with a little

morphine. They're all in a better place now.
was the compassionate thing to do. They slippe
away easily, without pain. And all my childre
benefited."

It took her a second to grasp his meaning.

"You mean the children at the clinic i
Guatemala?"

"Yes. Verna and all the others—their deatl
were a blessing in many ways. I gave their live
meaning. It's what they all wanted, you know. T
be useful again. To matter. They told me that.
only fulfilled their wish, like I did for Dad. Bi
Olivia wouldn't have understood." He sighed.

What did his father have to do with the peopl
he'd killed?

This was getting creepier by the minute.

"She saw me with Ed, you see," Blaine cor
tinued, his attention fixed on the bloody rag. "An
then again with Clara. It was just bad timing."

When he fell silent, she gave him a quie
prompt. "So you decided to take care of her th
night of the Opera Theatre benefit."

Suddenly he rose and began to pace, the tau
lines of his body spelling agitation in capital letter:

Moira's pulse spiked.

Uh-oh.

With such volatile mood swings, this situatio
could degenerate quickly. The rope was cuttin
into her wrists worse now, but she worked
harder anyway.

"What happened that night, Doctor?"

His gaze darted around the room, focused on
othing—except perhaps an image in his mind.
We met in the parking lot at McDonald's. I
 old her we'd drive around for a while and talk
while she drank the strawberry milkshake I'd
ought for her. Catch up. And I promised to
xplain what she'd seen at the nursing homes. But
he got nervous when I headed out here—and
he drank too slowly. The midazolam didn't kick
n as fast as I hoped."

Midazolam. Moira frowned. That was a seda-
ive of some kind, wasn't it?

He stopped beside the window that offered a
iew to the back, toward the hole he'd been
igging. Not that he could see out. All the
hades in the cabin were drawn. Nevertheless, he
vatched the blank white surface as if it was a
novie screen.

"So what did she do?"

He clenched his fists at his sides. "She
emanded that I stop and let her out. She was
voozy by then, but when I kept driving she
tarted grabbing at the wheel. I realized I'd have
o give her the morphine sooner than I planned, so
pulled over—but the second the car slowed, she
pened the door and bolted out into the rain."

3laine turned toward her with an expression
lmost of wonder. "Funny thing how she ran
ight in front of your car. Let you finish the job I

381

began. It's strange how God works, isn't it? Th[at] was a message of vindication, don't you think?"

Hardly. But she remained silent.

He continued without waiting for a respons[e], as if he hadn't expected an answer.

"All I had to do was end her suffering. An[d] there was plenty of morphine left in the syring[e] for that after I put you out of commission."

Moira stared at him. The nonexistent broken glas[s] in her car . . . the bruise on her thigh . . . the loss [of] consciousness Cal had always thought suspect—all the pieces fell into place with a sickening thu[d].

She swallowed past the fear tightening he[r] throat. "And you buried her here."

"Yes. That was part of my plan. I dug the hol[e] a few days before, then covered it with pin[e] branches. I've always been a meticulous planne[r]. Like Dad. It would have worked flawlessly to[o] if you'd minded your own business. I neve[r] intended to move Olivia until you came along . . . and now you know even more than she did. But [I] don't have any morphine with me."

He resumed pacing, his movements stiff. Jerk[y]. Panic rippled through his eyes, and his fac[e] contorted. Finally he stopped and looked up, as [if] toward the heavens, and anguish splintered th[e] words he uttered. "What should I do, Dad?"

As she watched the man in front of he[r] crumble, Moira began to tremble. Blaine was fa[st] losing whatever tenuous hold he had on hi[s] sanity—as well as whatever diminished ability he still had to distinguish between right and wrong. Soon, his survival instinct would take over—and she would be history. Letting her live would destroy the foundation of lies on which his life was built.

All at once he walked to the counter, yanked open a drawer, and removed a dish towel. He ripped it in half lengthwise, tied the ends together, and approached her. Aiming for her neck.

"No!" She twisted away, trying to evade the length of cloth, and opened her mouth to scream.

But he slipped the cloth between her teeth and tied it tight behind her head before she could utter a sound.

Then he moved to the back door. Extracted a key from his pocket. Unlocked the dead bolt. And exited without a word or a backward glance.

Chest heaving, Moira renewed her struggle with the cording on her wrists. She had to free herself. Cal might not arrive in time, and it was clear Blaine was done talking. Even in the unlikely event she had the opportunity to try and convince him he'd never get away with yet another murder . . . that people were already aware she was in danger . . . that they knew where she was . . . she had a sinking feeling the eminent surgeon and humanitarian of the year had already lost his grip on reality.

This time for good.

⇒ 23 ⇐

"You holding up okay?" Cal shot Dev a quick look as he barreled down I-94, taking the curves at speeds far faster than the posted limit. The rocking motion must be playing havoc with his buddy's stomach.

"I'm fine."

The gritted-teeth delivery said otherwise, but it couldn't be helped. Moira came first.

"In five hundred yards, exit right."

Following the mechanical voice instructions of his TomTom, Cal slowed and flipped on his blinker, checking in his rearview mirror to verify Connor was in sync. The Taurus followed him onto the secondary road.

Cal killed his lights.

Connor followed suit.

Half a mile up the road, as they approached the spur that led to the cabin owned by Blaine's neighbor, a dark shape became visible off to the side of the road.

"Is that a car?" Dev squinted and leaned forward.

"Yeah." They were too far away to make out color or model, but Cal would lay odds it was Moira's Camry.

He pulled onto the miniscule shoulder. Connor

did likewise. "I'm going to take a look. Get Connor on the phone. Fill him in. I'll be back in two minutes. Keep him on the line."

Without waiting for a response, he killed the dome light, opened his door, and pulled out his Sig—the regular duty model he'd carried on the Mexico assignment. It had gone unused there.

He hoped it didn't see service tonight, either.

In a half crouch, he covered the distance to the car in less than thirty seconds.

It was Moira's.

And it was empty.

He retraced his route to the Explorer and slid back in. "Connor, you with us?"

"Yeah." The other man's voice came over the speaker phone.

"It's Moira's. There's no sign of her. You have your earpiece handy?"

"Already out."

Leave it to Connor to anticipate tactical moves.

"We need to get in close and check this out." He grabbed his bag off the backseat and rooted round for his own earpiece, then fitted it into place as Dev did the same. "Dev can come in from the front." The man next to him was in no shape to be crawling around in the woods, but at least a front approach would require him to cover the least amount of terrain. "I'll circle to the back from the right. You take the left."

"Got it. You want to notify the sheriff's department?"

Cal hesitated. So far, they had no hard evidence of wrongdoing. And if Moira had been discovered and was in danger, he'd rather not have a bunch of local deputies muddling things up. The three of them probably had more tactical training and experience than the whole sheriff's department combined.

"I want to wait until we see what we have."

"Agreed."

"Okay. Let's do this."

Dev ditched his jacket, tossing it in the backseat before exiting on his side of the Explorer, night-vision binoculars in hand. Cal dispensed with his jacket as well, then grabbed his own binoculars and melted into the woods that rimmed the road.

After half a minute of picking his way through the dense undergrowth, he spotted a cabin through the leafy branches. A dim light shone behind shades that hid the interior from view.

"I have the cabin in sight."

"Copy. I do too," Dev confirmed.

"So do I." Connor's voice was calm and cool, as always—no matter the danger.

"I'm circling around to the back." Cal did his best to minimize noise as he approached—not easy in the heavy brush. The last thing they wanted to do was alert Blaine to their presence by crashing through the foliage like a startled deer.

"There's a dark-colored Lexus parked in the back." Connor's voice again.

"That's Blaine's car." As Cal reached the rear of the cabin, he spotted the car as well. The trunk was open, and he trained his night-vision binoculars on it—then paused. Listened. "I hear some noise at ten o'clock, behind the cabin."

"I'll check it out. I'm moving that direction anyway," Connor said.

Cal adjusted the binoculars and refocused on the trunk. Frowned. Concrete blocks? Coils of rope?

Odd cargo for a pediatric surgeon.

"I have Blaine in view. He's digging. A rather large, grave-sized hole."

As Connor reported that news, the unusual items in Blaine's car suddenly made perfect sense—if the man was hoping to dispose of a body in water.

But where was Moira?

In the cabin, perhaps?

If so, they could get her out before Blaine even noticed she was missing—assuming she was okay . . . and they were in time.

And he was holding fast to those assumptions. No other option was acceptable.

"I'm going to work my way closer to the cabin and—"

The distinctive crunch of tires on gravel, back near the main road, echoed in the night.

What the . . . ?

"Dev . . . what have we got?" As Cal snapped out the question, his pulse took a leap.

"I'm changing position to take a look."

"Our subject's on the move." This from Connor

Even as he spoke, a shadowy figure emerged from the trees on the far side of the cabin and darted toward the back door.

Though Cal couldn't get a clear view of him, i had to be Blaine.

And despite some serious jockeying, the leaf branches foiled his efforts to get an unobstructed line of sight with his Sig before the man shove through the door and slammed it behind him.

Their best chance of getting inside easily had jus evaporated.

Deputy Sheila Orr spoke into the microphone a she drove slowly down the gravel lane to chec out the reported scream heard by an adjacer landowner.

"I'm not seeing any activity on site, but there a light in the window, and there are three ca parked near the entrance on Mendelson Road."

"Copy. You want some backup?"

"Could be just a family gathering. And th reported scream could have been the loser in coon fight." The city slickers who owned a lot these spreads were notorious for reporting t sounds of nature as danger signs. She shook h head.

Her radio crackled back to life. "We did have a request from the owner to keep an eye on the property. He said he's rarely there. A Ted Lauer."

"Okay." She stopped the car a hundred feet away from the cabin. "Someone's here, that's for sure. Maybe Lauer's making one of his rare visits. Let me check it out. I'll let you know if there's any suspicious activity."

"Copy."

Sheila pushed the door open, secured her radio on her belt, and put her hand on her sidearm as she started toward the cabin. She'd never had to use her weapon in the line of duty, but there was always a first time.

She hoped this wasn't it.

Something was going on.

Adrenaline surging, Moira looked with trepidation toward the hall Blaine had charged down moments ago after securing the sliding bolt in the back door and locking the dead bolt. Now frenetic noise was coming from the adjacent room.

It sounded as if he was ripping the place apart.

Then the noise stopped.

Ten seconds later, Blaine reappeared in the doorway—holding a revolver.

Her heart stuttered, but he spared her no more than a quick glance as he raced to the front of the house.

What was happening?

Was Cal here?

Had Blaine spotted him?

She worked harder at the rope securing he
wrists, ignoring the burning protest of her rav
skin. Whatever was going on had spooked Blain
badly. And that could mean only one thing.

Time was running out.

Slouching down as far as she could in the chai
she tipped her head back and tried to use one o
the upright spindles to shove the gag higher an
loosen it, all the while continuing to twist he
wrists. If she could get her hands free or regai
the use of her voice, she'd be able to . . .

A knock sounded at the front door.

Moira froze.

That wasn't Cal.

He wouldn't knock.

She heard Blaine twist the lock on the doc
When it creaked open, she strained to hear tl
conversation.

"Can I help you?"

"Good evening, sir." A woman's voice. Muffle
"I'm Deputy Orr from St. Charles County. A
you Mr. Lauer?"

"No. I'm a neighbor of his from St. Louis. I
often lets me use this place for weekend getaway:

"May I see an ID."

A slight hesitation. "Sure."

Fifteen seconds of silence.

"Thank you, sir. And you brought guests?"

Two more beats of silence ticked by.

"What do you mean?"

"There are three cars on the road."

Three cars? Moira's spirits took a decided uptick. ...e of them had to belong to Cal—and perhaps ...v or Connor had come with him.

"Yes. A few friends joined me."

Moira heard the quiver in Blaine's voice. The ...ws about three cars had to have him worried. ...t she doubted the deputy would pick up on his ...btle tremor. Considering how frenzied he'd ...en when he'd torn through the kitchen in ...arch of the gun minutes ago, he was doing a ...narkable job holding it together.

Remarkable enough to convince that deputy all ...s copasetic.

Adrenaline spiking, she went back to work on ... gag, focusing all of her efforts on loosening it ... she could call for help before he shut the ...or and muffled the sounds from within.

"All right. I just wanted to make sure there ...re no problems."

"I know Ted will appreciate your diligence. I'll ...l him you stopped by."

"Have a good evening, sir."

Moira rubbed the back of her head against the ...indle, pushing the gag even harder. All at once ... shifted higher, the taut fabric between her ...th loosening.

391

Yes!

She spat out as much of it as she could and tri
to call for help.

Only a hoarse croak emerged from her parch
mouth.

She switched to a scream. It wasn't loud, but
did the job.

The front door slammed. A gun was fired. Gla
broke.

The pretense was over.

Blaine was in the hot seat.

That was the good news.

But on the flip side, he no longer had anythi
to lose.

Nor any reason to delay silencing her voi
forever.

Blaine had a gun.

And he had Moira.

Heart pounding, Cal low-crawled toward t
deputy who'd dived for the brush when the sh
rang out. Never had he been so grateful they
shelled out the extra bucks for earpieces wi
voice-activated mikes.

"I'm closing in on the deputy. Where are y
both?" He grunted out the words, using h
elbows for leverage.

"Also on my way to her." Dev's words came c
in a pant, reminding Cal how far his partner w
from being at the top of his game. Even a fiv

mile run didn't typically cause much of a blip in the man's respiration.

"I'm covering the back in case he tries to make a fast exit from the rear." As usual, Connor sounded cool, steady, and in control.

"I need backup ASAP." The deputy was speaking into her radio, her gaze still on the cabin, her pistol at the ready. "I have an armed subject with a hostage."

The radio crackled to life. "Copy. I'm dispatching as we speak."

As the deputy set the radio beside her, Cal spoke from several yards away, keeping his voice low enough to be heard but loud enough to carry. Sneaking up on a gun-toting law officer wasn't smart.

"You already have some backup."

As it was, she whipped toward him, gun aimed his direction. "Identify yourself."

Pretty gutsy tactic, since she couldn't see him in the concealing undergrowth and he was armed too. Lucky thing he was on her side.

"I'm a PI, deputy. There are three of us on-site. All former law enforcement—ATF agent, police detective, Secret Service. The former ATF agent behind you is extending his credentials."

With a gasp, she spun around. Dev was holding out his creds, a small flashlight focused on the tense and shielded from Blaine's view with a cupped hand.

The woman examined the document, and her taut posture relaxed a fraction.

"What are you people doing here?"

"Working a case that just became the purview of law enforcement, now that our subject has fired shots. And according to my colleague behind the cabin, there's plenty of incriminating evidence back there too. Until your reinforcements arrive, I'm going to try and get a look inside. We have a dangerous subject who's losing patience and a hostage who's at high risk."

"We need to wait."

"If we wait, the hostage could die." He rose to crouch.

"And if you make a mistake, she could also die."

His stomach bottomed out. "Thanks for reminding me."

"We need to hold until official reinforcements get here."

"Sorry. You can arrest me later for refusing follow instructions. In the meantime, I'd suggest you have an ambulance dispatched as well."

Without waiting for a reply, Cal began to weave through the woods, speaking into his earpiece he approached the structure.

"I'm moving to the cabin. If there's a way in I plan to find it."

"I can see a shadow behind the shades in the back." Connor's voice was subdued. "I'll try

t close and check for a crack somewhere that
ght give me a view inside."

"That would help."

So would a whole lot of luck.

Because when you were dealing with someone
e Blaine who had obviously cracked, things
uld go south very, very fast.

And Moira was directly in the line of fire if
ey did.

's over, Dr. Blaine." Moira did her best to speak
a soft, understanding, empathetic tone—and to
nore the gun Blaine was juggling as he paced
ck and forth in the small kitchen. "Too many
ople know you've killed multiple times. All
ose deaths at the extended care facilities of Let
e Children Come donors will be investigated.
e best thing to do is give yourself up."

f he heard her, he gave no indication. When he
oke, it was more to himself than to her.

"Everything will turn out fine. I didn't do
ything wrong. I just helped those people so they
uld help my children, and helping people is
at doctors do. Dad said what I did wasn't
ong, that it was a blessing, and he never lied to
e. Ever. He'd still be proud of me too, like he
as that day I did what he asked. When he told
e I was strong and courageous." He paused and
oked up again. "You *are* still proud of me,
en't you, Dad?"

Moira stared at him.

The man was in total meltdown.

Heart thumping, she moistened her lips. D Blaine even remember she was there? Possib not. Maybe if she stayed motionless and ve quiet, he'd retreat further into whatever wor he'd entered and forget she existed—at lea long enough for Cal or that deputy to get insi and take the gun away from him.

He started to pace again. To mutter. To grip t revolver. He rambled on about his mother cryin About burying something in the woods—a thin not a person. About honoring the Hippocra Oath.

At this point, she was only half listening to l rant. Her focus was on the gun he was kneadi between his fingers.

The loaded gun.

The one that was pointed at her whenever turned to his left.

Two minutes ticked by. Three. Four. He stopp muttering and dropped into a chair to stare at t floor. Quiet descended.

Until the distant wail of a siren shattered t stillness.

Blaine froze. Cocked his head. Listened.

Then he started to shake.

"No!" The agonized word came out in whisper, and the color seeped from his face.

He swiveled toward her.

She stopped breathing. His eyes were haunted. Hollow. Desperate. But lucid now rather than glazed.

"I never thought it would come to this." His words were choked.

He looked down at the gun in his hands—and slowly the panic in his demeanor melted into resignation. The taut lines in his face slackened, and a profound sadness settled in his eyes as he lifted his chin and turned her direction again.

"I don't have any choice, you know. I messed things up, and it's too late to fix them."

"No." Terror clutched at her throat. "It's not too late. If you tell people your story, they'll understand. They'll help you." Not necessarily true, but she prayed he'd buy it.

He didn't.

With a shake of his head, he swallowed. Ran his fingers over the gun. Took a deep breath. "I'm sorry, Dad." The broken words came out on a half sob.

Then he lifted the gun. Aimed it. Hooked his finger in the ready position.

And as Moira screamed, he closed his eyes and pulled the trigger.

⇻ 24 ⇺

Moira's scream, followed by the sound of a single gunshot, ripped through the night as Cal was checking a window on the side of the cabin, hoping to find one unlatched that would allow a stealth access.

His heart stumbled.

But his feet didn't.

Rounding the cabin, he vaulted onto the rough-hewn planks of the porch and sent his partners a terse message. "I'm going in."

"I'll take the rear." Connor's voice crackled back.

"I'm coming in from the other side in front," Dev chimed in.

Assessing the wooden front door as he sprinted toward it, Cal angled sideways and smashed his right heel below the lock. The door splintered.

After a second kick sent it flying, he tucked himself beside the frame. Dev took up a position on the other side, pistol poised.

There wasn't a sound from inside.

Bad sign.

With a quick dip of his head, Cal communicated his intent to Dev. The other man nodded.

Ducking, he entered the living room.

Empty.

He stayed low as he crossed the living room, pausing next to the door that led to the back room. Dev positioned himself on the opposite side.

With a silent plea to God that Moira had somehow been spared, he steeled himself and stole a look around the edge of the frame at the same instant Connor kicked in the back door.

His stomach lurched.

The kitchen was a war zone.

The white refrigerator, along with the tile and counter beside it, were covered with bright red spatters that gravity was already turning into long streaks. A chair had been overturned. Blaine lay sprawled on the floor a few feet from Moira, a large pool of blood forming below his head.

Cal sized up the situation in one quick sweep, came to the obvious conclusion, and turned his attention to Moira.

She was bound hand and foot to a straight chair, face bruised and bloody and white with shock, shaking as if the tectonic plate of the New Madrid fault had just undergone a massive shift.

But she was alive.

Thank you, God!

Blinking to clear the sudden moisture from his eyes, he holstered his Sig and crossed the room, dropping down on one knee behind her to free her chaffed, bleeding wrists while Dev went to work on her ankles.

"You're okay, sweetheart. Take some deep breaths. It's over." His fingers fumbled the bloodied hemp twine, and he didn't argue when Connor handed him a glass of water, nudged him aside, and slipped a pocketknife under the knots to cut her free.

He circled around to the front of the chair blocking the grisly view from her sight. Not that it mattered. Her eyes were squeezed shut and her breath was coming in quick, shallow gasps. If she kept that up, she'd hyperventilate. Fast.

The liquid in the glass he was holding sloshed and he realized he was trembling almost as much as she was.

"You're safe now. It's okay to open your eyes." He leaned down and rested his fingers against the uninjured part of her face with a whisper touch.

She flinched. Sucked in a sharp breath. Slowly opened her eyes.

"Cal?" The word was no more than a rasp as she reached for him.

He grasped her cold fingers. "I'm right here. Drink a little of this, okay?" He pressed the glass to her lips, cupping his own fingers around hers to help steady them as she took several long, greedy swallows.

That's when he noticed the strip of cloth caught in her hair and hanging near her cheek. A gag. It must have sucked her mouth dry.

"The paramedics are here."

At the female voice over his shoulder, Cal shifted sideways. Deputy Orr stood in the doorway, slightly green around the gills as she surveyed the carnage. Obviously not a seasoned veteran.

He freed the strip of cloth from Moira's hair. "We'll meet them outside, in front."

The deputy bobbed her head, as if glad to have an excuse to leave the bloody scene for a moment.

Moira clutched at his arm, her pallor still alarming. "He . . . he put the g-gun in his mouth." Her broken whisper was fraught with horror.

"I know." The man's technique had been obvious the instant he'd seen Blaine. That was the most effective way to accomplish his goal, as any physician would know. "But it's over." He straightened up, then reached down and drew her to her feet, using his body to shield her from the gory sight. "Let's get out of here so the paramedics can check you out."

She wavered as she rose, and he tightened his grip. Keeping one arm around her shoulders, he bent and slid the other under her knees, nestling her against his chest, close to his heart.

"I can walk."

"Later."

She didn't argue.

He bypassed Dev, who'd commandeered one of the kitchen chairs and settled in it as far from Blaine as possible, his back to the scene, and

shouldered past one of the many deputie
swarming the place. He heard Connor's measured
voice in the background as his partner took
charge. Good man.

That left him free to deal with more important
things.

The paramedics were waiting at the base of the
porch, a deputy standing by with a high-powered
flashlight to give them illumination, and Ca
carefully lowered Moira to the stretcher.

"I don't need to go to a hospital." She clung to
his hand, her voice stronger, color seeping back
into her cheeks as she tried to rise.

He restrained her with a hand against her
shoulder. "I hope that's true, but do me a favor
and let these guys check you out, okay? It will
give me more peace of mind."

Positioning it as a favor to him did the trick.
She stopped resisting, then sank back. But she
didn't relinquish her grip on his hand—and he
was in no hurry to let her go.

"Can you work around me?" He directed the
question to the paramedic across from him.

"We'll try."

He moved down the gurney as far as possible
give both technicians access to Moira. H
medical knowledge was rudimentary, but he
been around enough accident scenes to be able
interpret some of the terms they tossed back an
forth as they examined her. All of her vitals we

good, and based on her own description of her injuries, there didn't seem to be much chance she'd suffered any internal damage.

Their biggest concern appeared to be the bruise on her jaw and her swollen ankle.

"Nothing's broken." Her tone was more forceful now. "The bruise will fade, and my ankle's just sprained. An elastic bandage and an ice pack will take care of it."

"There's no harm in getting an X-ray, though." The paramedic on the other side of the gurney continued to clean her raw wrists and apply antiseptic.

"I'll get an X-ray if it still hurts in a few days." She was exhibiting more and more of her usual spunk with each passing minute.

That, too, was a blessing.

But it wasn't going to protect her from the nightmares he suspected would disrupt her sleep for weeks—perhaps months—to come.

"You want to try and convince her to let us take her in?" The lead paramedic beside him directed the question his way.

"I just want to go home." She locked gazes with him. "I need TLC, not an IV."

After studying her, Cal gave the paramedic an apologetic shrug. "I have to side with the lady."

"Okay. We'll finish cleaning you up and have you sign a release form . . . whoa. Wait a minute." He eased down the collar of her mock

turtleneck and let out a low whistle. "You didn'
mention this."

Cal leaned closer. Angry purple bruises marred
her neck. The kind he'd seen on strangling
victims in his previous life.

A simmering anger erupted in his gut. If Blaine
wasn't dead already, he'd do his best to make
sure the man suffered for what he'd done to
Moira and all his other victims.

"Did you lose consciousness?" The para
medic leaned forward to check out the bruises.

"Very briefly."

"I'd feel a lot better if you'd let the ER doc
check you out. There could be damage to the
larynx, trachea, or other bones in the neck."

"No." She swallowed with obvious difficult
as the man gently probed her throat. "I'
breathing fine. My throat's just bruised. Cal?" She
looked to him for support.

He wavered. "They might be right, Moira."

"I want to go home." Her words quavered, as
she was on the verge of tears, and the plea in her
eyes went straight to his heart.

"Will someone be there with you for the ne
thirty-six to forty-eight hours?" The paramedic
stowed his stethoscope in his kit.

"Yes." Cal answered the man's question, but h
focus never wavered from Moira.

"That's too much of an imposition." Her prote
came out halfhearted at best.

"Never."

The paramedic glanced between the two of them. "Okay. If you have any difficulty breathing, or excessive hoarseness, or reddening in the whites of your eyes, get to an ER fast. We're done here, but the sheriff's department will want a statement." He nodded over his shoulder.

Cal twisted around. A deputy was hovering in the background. The last thing Moira needed to do was tax her throat with a lot of talking. Fortunately, he'd conducted enough victim interviews to know how to expedite the process.

And once they were all free to leave, he'd toss the keys to the Explorer to Dev, drive Moira home, and spend the night on her couch as she slept mere footsteps away.

Because until he was convinced she was ready to be left alone, he wasn't straying far from her side.

Moira fingered one of the velvet petals on the long-stemmed yellow rose, adjusted the fern behind it, straightened the bow. Though the flower in her lap was proof the nightmare had been real—as were her many lingering aches and pains—in the intervening two weeks the whole experience had taken on a surreal quality.

If only her memory of the terror would fade as quickly as the bruises on her body.

As she sighed, Cal sent her a concerned glance

from the driver's seat of the Explorer. "Everythi
okay?"

She managed to summon up a small smile. "Y
Thanks in large part to you."

He dismissed her praise with a self-deprecati
shrug. "I didn't do much."

Not true. All week, he'd hovered as much
his and her jobs had allowed. He'd slept on h
couch for three nights, despite her protests, clo
at hand to comfort her when she'd awakened
the middle of the night, shaking and cryir
He'd also cooked for her, made her laug
taken her out for ice cream. And when she'd to
him her plans for today, he'd volunteered n
only to accompany her but to participate.

"Sorry. I disagree." She braced as he swur
between the two gates flanking the entrance
their destination. "I think I'll be in your de
forever."

"Consider the debt repaid with this." He tapp
the newspaper tucked beside his seat. "Tl
phone's been ringing off the hook since the fir
part of your series ran. I'm sure we'll have mo
calls after today's wrap-up piece, with all tho
quotes you used from me. Business at Phoenix
booming."

"I'm glad, after all the pro bono hours you gu
put in on the case."

"That's not why we took it." His gaze connect
with hers.

"I know. Justice First." Phoenix truly lived that motto, as she'd learned over the past weeks.

"Always." He transferred his attention back to the road in front of him. "You said you got directions?"

"Yes." She snagged a slip of paper from the pocket of her shoulder purse. "Make the first left, then the third right. He said we'd spot it without any problem. It's the only one in that area."

In silence, Cal navigated the narrow road. As he swung into the last turn, she leaned forward. "There it is."

"Yeah. I see it." As he approached the site, he pulled onto the edge of the road. "Sit tight while I come around." He lifted the lid on the storage compartment between their seats, grabbed a small black book, and slid from the car.

By the time he joined her, she had the door open.

"Watch your step. The ground isn't level and you don't need another sprain." He took her arm as she carefully put weight on her elastic-wrapped ankle.

Once she was steady, he closed the door. The grassy knoll was, indeed, on the uneven side, and he was grateful he kept a firm grip on her arm as they crossed the lawn.

They walked in silence until they reached the mound of freshly turned earth—Olivia Lange's final resting place, paid for by contributions from readers who'd been touched by Moira's story

about the woman who'd had no one to miss h
when she'd disappeared.

There would be a marker too. Evidence that
death, if not in life, someone had cared about he
Moira would shoulder the cost herself if the
weren't enough contributions to cover it.

As they stood in the stillness, rays of ear
morning sun announcing the start of a new day,
cardinal trilled from the branch of a nearby tre
Farther afield, muted sounds filtered through tl
summer air. A lawn mower hummed. A do
barked. A radio played. Someone laughed.

Life went on.

For some.

Moira blinked back a tear.

An instant later, strong, lean fingers twine
with hers.

"Olivia had someone to cry for her after all."

At Cal's soft comment, she looked over at hir
The tenderness in his eyes was a balm on her hear

"Even though I never met her, I almost feel as
I knew her. Far better than I knew Blaine, who
did meet."

"He's a tough nut to crack."

"Tell me about it." She'd dug deep this week a
she'd written her articles, searching for answer
about what made the man tick, but she'd con
up blank. Blaine's colleagues and friends alik
had been dumbstruck by the news. His wife ha
had no comment.

"I think the experience he referred to with his father, when he was talking to you in the cabin, may be the key." Cal put his arm around her shoulders.

She tightened her grip on the rose, avoiding the thorns. "But do you really think a father would ask a sixteen-year-old son to administer a lethal dose of morphine?" They'd debated that possibility, but she was having a hard time believing any parent would lay such a burden on a child.

"It fits, based on the things he said to you. And if Blaine did that, despite the fact he may have been honoring a request . . ." He shook his head. "Man, that could mess with a kid's mind. Imagine living with the guilt of killing a father you loved, even if you did it with his blessing."

"I can't. Nor can I imagine a loving parent making such a request."

"Their relationship may have been a lot more complicated than Blaine let on." He hefted the black book in his hand. "Are you ready for this?"

"Yes. I have no idea what faith Olivia practiced, if she practiced any at all. But I think someone needs to commend her to the Lord."

He lifted the book, spine in palm, and she noticed it opened naturally to the passage he'd selected. As if he'd turned to it many times.

When he began to read, his choice of Scripture didn't surprise her.

While he recited the words of the twenty-third

psalm in his resonant baritone voice, she closed her eyes and said a silent prayer of her own that the Lord would welcome Olivia home with the kind of love, compassion, and mercy she'd never known during her earthly life.

After Cal finished, he steadied her elbow as she bent down and laid the single rose on the earth.

Then, with one final scan of the new grave, she stood, took his hand, and turned back toward the Explorer.

They didn't talk again until they passed through the gates of the cemetery.

"Do you have any other plans for the rest of the day?" Cal sent her a quick look as he maneuvered through the traffic.

"No. Why?"

"I know a great lunch spot with a garden near Ste. Genevieve. It's a nice day for a drive, and we could both use some time to unwind and decompress."

"Amen to that."

"Is that a yes?"

She smiled at him, doing her best to vanquish her lingering sadness over Olivia's sad end and to embrace the joy of this new beginning. "It' most definitely a yes."

His lips quirked up, and he changed lanes "Okay. That takes care of today. Do you have any plans for tomorrow, other than church?"

"Dad phoned this morning. He wants to drive ver from Columbia for a visit. Even though I've alled him every day since the story broke, I don't link he'll believe I'm really okay until he sees le in person."

"Perfect. I've been wanting to meet him. Why on't I join you for church, then treat you both to runch? Later, we can take a picnic to Forest Park or the Shakespeare Festival. It's *Taming of the hrew* this year. I bet your dad would enjoy that."

Warmth filled her heart, and the last trace of rain in her smile evaporated. "Are you trying to utter up my father and monopolize my time?"

"Guilty on both counts." He turned his head nd winked at her. "And I plan to do a lot more f both in the future . . . if the lady's willing."

Chuckling, Moira settled back in her seat. More than. But there is one little complication."

Twin furrows dented his brow. "What?"

"When I stopped by your office last week to rop off that thank-you cheesecake for the guys nd a whole-grain coffeecake for Nikki, Dev ook me aside and warned me to be careful. He aid you're a smooth talker."

A scowl replaced Cal's frown. "I am going to ave a long talk with that boy first thing Monday norning."

She burst out laughing. "That's exactly what he aid you'd say. I guess I owe him another cheese-ake." Reaching over, she touched his shoulder,

411

exchanging levity for sincerity. "For the record, he also said I couldn't find a better guy."

His glower faded. "Okay, then he's off the hook. As long as you agree with him."

"To plagiarize the bard, 'I would not wish any companion in the world but you.' Good enough?"

He flashed her a grin, folded her hand in his, and gave her fingers a squeeze. "Good enough."

⇒ Epilogue ⇐

Five Months Later

Cal pressed the end button on his BlackBerry slipped it back on his belt, and checked hi watch. The call with the new client had taken fa longer than he'd anticipated, and he did *not* wan to be late picking up Moira.

Especially today.

Patting the pocket of his leather jacket to verif the presence of the small box he'd placed ther earlier, he strode down the hall from his bedroom No time to brew coffee, but he could at leas grab a quick glass of juice. Breakfast would hav to wait until later too—but that was okay. H was too nervous to eat, anyway.

Proposing could do that to a man.

It was time, though—even if he'd never quit banished his feelings of guilt about falling i love again. All he could do was hope that down the road, the niggling sense that he was being disloyal to Lindsey would fade.

But if it didn't, he'd live with it—because he didn't want to live without Moira.

He crossed the kitchen, pulled the container of juice from the fridge, and poured himself a short glass. After replacing the bottle, he downed his quotient of vitamin C for the day in several long gulps. Then he turned to the sink to rinse the glass—and froze.

A single fuchsia-colored flower was blooming on the barren cactus Lindsey had rescued long ago, the vibrant blossom justifying her optimism. While the ugly plant might have looked dead on the outside, it had harbored life within. Life that had been waiting to burst forth at the appointed hour.

It will bloom when the time is right.

His wife's words echoed in his mind as if she'd said them yesterday.

He gripped the edge of the counter and stared at the colorful flower. It had taken six years for her prediction to come true—why today, of all days?

It couldn't be anything more than a weird coincidence, though. He didn't believe in signs.

Yet as he touched the fragile petal, as the brilliant color seeped into his soul and brightened the corners darkened by guilt, he suddenly felt lighter of heart than he had in years.

And more ready than ever to leave the past behind and treasure the gift of today.

"How come you won't tell me where we're going?" Moira shifted sideways in the passenger seat to look at Cal. There was something different about him today—but she couldn't quite figure out what it was, though she'd been trying diligently since he'd picked her up twenty minutes ago.

"It's a surprise."

"I don't like surprises."

"You'll like this one. I hope."

She gave him a disgruntled look. "You aren't going to budge, are you?"

"Nope."

"Fine. I can be patient." She settled back in her seat.

"Since when?"

"Ha-ha."

Determined to hold her tongue, she managed to rein in her questions—until he turned into a tree-filled subdivision in West County.

"Are we visiting someone?"

"Nope." He swung into the driveway of a contemporary-style house, parking behind a Corolla. The home wasn't overly large, but it was well-designed, with clean lines and lots of glass and skylights. Just the kind of architecture that appealed to her.

"Nice."

"I thought you might like it."

A fortyish woman climbed out of the car in front f them, and Moira arched an eyebrow at him.

"Stacey Holloway. Hang on a sec."

That was all he offered before he slid from ehind the wheel.

Like that name was supposed to mean some-hing to her?

He paused to exchange a few words with the voman. A handoff appeared to take place. Then he woman got back in her car while Cal circled round to her door.

The minute he pulled it open, she began eppering him with questions again. "What's oing on? Who's Stacey Holloway? Why are we ere?"

"All questions will be answered in less than en minutes. I promise."

Ten minutes.

Okay, she could hang on that long.

He took her arm and guided her to the entrance. 3ut instead of knocking, he slipped a key in the ock, twisted it, and pushed the door open. "After ou."

She stepped past him into a great room with a oaring ceiling, glassed-in fireplace, impressive eams—and no furniture.

"Like it?"

At his question, she swiveled toward him.

"What's not to like? Especially if the rest of th house is as spectacular as this room."

"It is. I'll give you a tour in a minute."

"But it's empty."

"That's because it's for sale. Or it will b tomorrow unless someone grabs it first. Stacey been watching the market for me, and when sh showed this to me yesterday, I was pretty sure was the one."

She blinked at him. These past five month their relationship had progressed steadily. She' assumed they were headed for the altar, soone or later—though sooner was her preference. Y he'd been looking for a house and was thinkin of moving without even consulting her? Sh scanned the appealing contemporary space agaii Had she misread his signals?

"It just needs your seal of approval."

Her gaze snapped back to his face.

"Because I'm hoping you'll share it with me Till death do us part."

As his words registered, her heart stoppec Stumbled on. "Is that a . . . are you proposing?"

He lifted a hand. Reached inside his jacke Pulled out a square jeweler's box.

"Oh, wow." She stared at his fingers.

Fingers that weren't quite steady.

Double wow.

Nothing ever rattled Cal. He was the steadies guy she knew.

As she watched, he flipped up the lid to reveal a dazzling square-cut diamond.

"According to Plato, everyone becomes a poet when they're in love, but somehow that didn't happen with me." The corners of his lips crept up, and he gave a self-deprecating shrug. "However, with your father pointing the way to some excellent sources, I found the exact words I needed. So here goes."

He took her hand and captured her gaze with his. "From Plato again: 'Every heart sings a song, incomplete, until another heart whispers back.' Your heart whispered to mine and made it whole.

"From Aristotle: 'Love is composed of a single soul inhabiting two bodies.' That's how I feel about us.

"From Euripides: 'It is a good thing to be rich and strong, but it is a better thing to be loved.' I'm not rich or a world-class weight lifter, but if I was, I'd trade both in a heartbeat for your love.

"And finally, from the bard himself: 'For where thou art, there is the world itself, and where thou art not, desolation.' "

His voice hoarsened, and he cleared his throat.

"The truth is, I never expected to love again. Then I met you—and the rest, as they say, is history. You stole my heart almost from the moment you walked into my office. Now I can't imagine my life without you. So . . . Moira . . . will you marry me?"

417

In answer, she extended her left hand and somehow managed to squeeze a reply past the pressure in her throat. "In keeping with the spirit of your proposal, I'll respond with another quote: 'I'll be yours through all the years till the end of time.'"

"Shakespeare?"

"Elvis Presley." She grinned and wiggled the fourth finger on her left hand. "But don't tell Dad."

Smiling, he plucked out the ring, tucked the box back in his pocket, and slipped the thin gold band over her finger. "Why do I think life with you will be a grand adventure?"

She stepped closer, wrapped her arms around his neck, and tipped her head back. "Because I'm bold, brave, exciting, daring, enthusiastic, energetic, dynamic, vivacious . . . and modest?"

A chuckle rumbled in his chest as he rested his hands on her waist. "Don't forget funny. You have a great sense of humor."

"That too." She beamed up at him, loving the killer dimple that appeared in his cheek whenever he smiled at her. "So yes, our life may very well hold adventures—but no more like the recent one, I hope. However, I'm open to other, more pleasant suggestions. Got anything in mind?" She ran a fingertip along the strong line of his jaw and snuggled closer.

His irises darkened, his grip tightened—and she stopped breathing.

"I can think of a few." At his husky words, her heart faltered, then tripped into double time. "Let me demonstrate."

He leaned down. She rose on tiptoe to meet him halfway.

And in the instant before their lips joined, in the moment before they sealed an engagement that would open the door to a bright new future for both of them, one final quote from Plato flashed through her mind.

He who love touches walks not in darkness.

Her philosophy professor father was right.

The wisdom of the ancient sages was timeless —just like love.

⇝ Acknowledgments ⇜

Writing suspense books involves huge amount of research. But even though I spend hours on th net, I could never achieve optimal authenticit without the input of experts. I'm very grateful t my valued sources, whose generous assistanc allows me to add the final, subtle touches c realism to my stories.

For their help with this book, my heartfe thanks goes to:

Tim Flora, president of Mid-West Protectiv Service, Inc. (one of the most respected PI firm in the Midwest), who stood ready to assist m whenever I had a PI-related question. Like m hero, Cal, Tim had a long career in la enforcement before striking out on his own. He a certified polygraph examiner and has als received training from the FBI, U.S. Dru Enforcement Administration, U.S. Secret Servic and the ATF—making him the perfect PI sourc not only for this story but for my entire Priva Justice series.

Lieutenant Tom Larkin, Commander of the S Louis County Police Department's Bureau Crimes Against Persons, who gracious answered my questions on police procedure.

D.P. Lyle, MD, Edgar-nominated novelist, author of *Forensics for Dummies* and consultant for writers of many popular TV shows—including *Law and Order*, *Cold Case*, and *House*—who reviewed the medical sections of this book.

Second Lieutenant Steve McCreary of the United States Army, who gave me a tutorial on weaponry and guided me through my very first visit to a shooting range.

Captain Ed Nestor from the Chesterfield, Missouri, Police Department, who continues to refer me to amazing sources.

The incredible team at Revell—editorial, marketing, sales, cover design, promotion. It's a joy to work with you.

And finally, my deepest love and gratitude to my husband, Tom, and my parents, James and Dorothy Hannon, who add such joy to my life.

✐ About the Author ✐

Irene Hannon is a bestselling, award-winnin
author who took the publishing world by storm a
the tender age of ten with a sparkling piece o
fiction that received national attention.

Okay . . . maybe that's a slight exaggeration. Bu
she *was* one of the honorees in a complete-the
story contest conducted by a national children'
magazine. And she likes to think of that as he
"official" fiction-writing debut!

Since then, she has written more than fort
contemporary romance and romantic suspens
novels. Irene has twice won the RITA award–
the "Oscar" of romantic fiction—from Romanc
Writers of America, and her books have also bee
honored with a National Readers Choice awarc
a HOLT medallion, a Daphne du Maurier awarc
a Retailers Choice award, and two Reviewer
Choice awards from *RT Book Reviews* magazine
In 2011, *Booklist* named *Deadly Pursuit* one c
the Top 10 Inspirational Fiction titles of th
year.

Irene, who holds a BA in psychology and an M
in journalism, juggled two careers for mar
years until she gave up her executive corpora
communications position with a Fortune 5(

mpany to write full time. She is happy to say
e has no regrets. As she points out, leaving
hind the rush-hour commute, corporate politics,
d a relentless BlackBerry that never slept was
sacrifice.

A trained vocalist, Irene has sung the leading
le in numerous community theater productions
d is also a soloist at her church.

When not otherwise occupied, she loves to
ok, garden, and take long walks. She and her
sband also enjoy traveling, Saturday mornings
their favorite coffee shop, and spending time
ith family. They make their home in Missouri.

To learn more about Irene and her books, visit
ww.irenehannon.com.

Center Point Large Print
600 Brooks Road / PO Box 1
Thorndike ME 04986-0001 USA

(207) 568-3717

US & Canada:
1 800 929-9108
www.centerpointlargeprint.com